HIGHWAYMAN

A NOVEL

M.J. PRESTON

WILD BLUE PRESS

WildBluePress.com

HIGHWAYMAN published by:
WILDBLUE PRESS
P.O. Box 102440
Denver, Colorado 80250

Publisher Disclaimer: Any opinions, statements of fact or fiction, descriptions, dialogue, and citations found in this book were provided by the author, and are solely those of the author. The publisher makes no claim as to their veracity or accuracy, and assumes no liability for the content.

Copyright 2019 by M.J. Preston

All rights reserved. No part of this book may be reproduced in any form or by any means without the prior written consent of the Publisher, excepting brief quotes used in reviews.

WILDBLUE PRESS is registered at the U.S. Patent and Trademark Offices.
ISBN 978-1-948239-09-7 Trade Paperback
ISBN 978-1-948239-08-0 eBook

Interior Formatting by Elijah Toten
www.totencreative.com

AUTHOR'S NOTE

This novel is a work of fiction, any resemblance to persons living or dead is purely coincidental; however, the author has taken the liberty of using historical characters, references and places to enhance the reader experience.

References to known and convicted criminals, along with political figures and places have been added to enhance the story and lend realism to the fictional tale contained in this story.

References to police departments or bureaus of investigation, including local, state and federal are a fictional account. This story does not reflect in any way on the organizations mentioned or their level of professionalism. This is a fictional tale as are the characters and events, any resemblance is again purely coincidental.

Any omission or error rests solely with the author.

In Memory of Duane Hillaby
This book was always for you, brother.

TABLE OF CONTENTS

PART I

FLEDGLING KILL

"I always had a desire to inflict pain on others and to have others inflict pain on me. I always seemed to enjoy everything that hurt."
— **Albert Fish,** *The Gray Man*

BOOK I

The following crimes occurred between
7 May, 2000 - 8 September, 2007

PROLOGUE – THE REPORTER

17 May 2008

Louisville, KY

He'd been waiting for over two and a half hours. His back hurt, his pants were too tight, and his ass itched without mercy. It was hot, he needed a shower and, he reminded himself, he also needed to dump about eighty pounds.

You're getting way too old for this shit, Ace, he thought. That was what he called himself in his private thoughts. Thoughts that were usually advisory. Like, *Take it easy, Ace. Don't let him bait you, Ace.* And of course, the repetitious, *You're getting way too old for this shit, Ace.*

Publicly, he never called himself Ace, too cliche for a reporter. It sounded like something out of a comic book. So he told people who might be uncomfortable with his real name to call him Harry. His real name was an old name, hardly used these days, but it was that real name that would be attached to his byline and emblazoned on his business card, and, he hoped, by the end of the year, on the cover of the book he was writing.

His real name was Horace Montillo.

How many police waiting rooms had he sat in? It had to be in the thousands by now. His start came as a crime beat reporter back in the late '70s working for the *Atlanta Journal*. His first big break had been covering the Atlanta Child Murders. That would be the beginning of his love affair with crime reporting. He didn't want anything else, so he worked the crime beat his entire career. He'd been at all the majors: *The Times, The Tribune,* and even *Huffington Post.* He covered the underground police massacre at the famed *Run-off-31* in Chicago, Illinois. He reported on Milwaukee Cannibal Jeffrey Dahmer, and even wrote an award-winning piece for *Time Magazine* called "Serial Murder in American Society."

He didn't have to be here. Technically, he wasn't in the newspaper business anymore. He wasn't even a reporter. Horace Montillo was the senior editor at *Crime Scene Examiner,* a throwback to the true crime magazines his mom used to leave lying around their apartment in Gary, Indiana. Sure, it wasn't *The Tribune* or *The Times,* but it was crime beat, and best of all he was a quarter partner in the magazine. He didn't have to be here for the piece he intended on writing, could have sent one of the twenty reporters they had on contract, but he didn't. Because Horace missed the stink of a police station, and he longed to be away from his desk chasing down a story. And this story deserved chasing because it made his strained heart run like a twenty-something. It was also going to be the focus of that book he intended to finish.

So, he ignored the button of his pants—which dug into his belly—cutting the circulation in his hips and making his backache. He did his best to overlook the beads of sweat that trickled down between his butt cheeks and inflamed an itch that demanded to be scratched.

You gotta get your ass into a gym, Ace, and work off the lard before old man heart attack comes calling, he thought, but it would always be the day after tomorrow.

At least I quit the smokes.

True and he could always lose the eighty pounds he'd accumulated since giving up the darts. Cancer was the boogeyman; the big casino had killed seven people he'd known. Cancer couldn't be run off on a treadmill or beat in a CrossFit competition. But he remembered what Doc

Acheson told him. How he'd rather have cancer than a heart attack, because if you survived cancer, you carried on living, while a heart attack left you in fear for your remaining years.

Tomorrow I get my ass to the gym.

"Horace Montillo?"

He looked up and saw a tall, thin man standing over him. He had a mustache that had been trimmed in such a way that it almost looked as though it had been drawn with a pencil. He was holding the business card Montillo had given his lieutenant, shifting his gaze between the name and face.

"Yes." He stood up to meet this tall drink of water and was still forced to look up to meet his eyes.

"Man, your parents must have hated you." The detective grinned.

Montillo laughed. "Most folks call me Harry. Horace is my pen name." He put out his hand.

"I'm Detective Perkins; my boss said you were looking for a bit of my time." The man wore an earnest look; like he had better places to be. "I'm going out for a smoke, you can join me if you like, but I'm working a double that I have to get back to."

Montillo glanced through the glass doors and out into the sweltering inertia. The daytime high was going to be 93 degrees, high even for Kentucky in mid-May. He guessed it was around 90 right now. It would have been so much nicer to sit down at a table, in an air-conditioned room, but that was the exception, not the rule.

What the hell did people have against air conditioning?

"You coming?" Perkins asked.

He smiled thinly and said, "Sure."

"Okay then." Perkins pulled a cigarette pack from his breast pocket and carried it between his index and middle finger as they marched to the entrance. "We'll have to cross the street. The new chief of police is a reformed smoker, and that pretty much makes him a born-again motherfucker."

"Okay, Detective." He had to stretch out his pace just to keep up. Perkins was all legs. "You mind if I record our talk?"

Perkins stopped dead and turned back to face him. "Look, I'm not all that good with the press. If you know anything about me, you might have heard that. The only reason I agreed to talk to you is because my boss says he knows you and that you aren't the typical garden-variety reporter."

"Thanks, I think."

"You're welcome." But Perkins didn't look all that charitable. In fact, he looked like he might regret agreeing to meet with the reporter. Montillo could see the regret in his face and knew he'd have to do a bit of reassuring.

"I'm not run of the mill. I've been working with cops for over thirty years. You talk to me, and I won't write anything that you don't want public."

Perkins bit his lower lip and sighed. "Let's go, then."

They pushed through the main entrance and onto the street. The sun beating down on them as they crossed the road to a small park. Trees towered overhead, offering some comfort of shade, but it was still plenty hot. Perkins stopped underneath the canopy of an oak tree and lit his cigarette. "Which one you here about? Highwayman or Norris?"

"Both."

"Get out your recorder, Harry." He took a draw on the cigarette and exhaled. Even five years off the damn things, Horace felt a craving tug at him. "You got until I finish this smoke."

Montillo pulled out the voice-activated recorder and pressed the record button. "Okay, I'm all set."

"Ask your questions."

***

CHAPTER 1 – INFAMOUS

1

7 May 2000

Syracuse, NY

The time was 1:00 a.m., Wednesday night, and the bar was dead. Wendy Birrell had been tending bar at Murphy's for three years. Her wage was eight bucks an hour, plus tips. That was on weekends; on weeknights, the place was a tomb except for the odd barfly, so tips were scarce. Tonight, like most, she wore tight, low rider jeans that hugged her slim figure, and a plaid button-down shirt that draped neatly across her ample breasts. Her hair flowed in straight, dirty blonde cascades over her shoulders and onto the swell of her breasts. This was done purposely to arouse the male patrons. Aside from her figure, it was Wendy's eyes that turned a man's head. They were deep glacial blue, a color found in arctic waters lapping against icebergs.

Wendy Birrell was twenty-eight, she had a high school education and only one motivation in life. His name was Patrick. He was four, had his mother's eyes, and curly, corn silk hair. Patrick's father, also blond, had been a marine. Had, because he'd been killed in Iraq when Patrick was only four months old. He and Wendy were never a couple. He had been a fling, nothing more, but had he lived, she would have included him in her son's life; had he known. He hadn't and Wendy didn't have a lot of options, so she tended bar, lived paycheck to paycheck and, for now, that was enough.

Most of the regulars were gone at this hour. Shuffling out after a few too many, slurring their words as they put on a coat or slung a purse like awkward preschoolers dressing to go outside and play. All gone. Except for one young man sitting at the corner of the bar sipping a Rolling Rock and stealing glances at her. He couldn't have been more than twenty-one. He'd been in a couple of times this week, sitting unremarkably on the corner stool. She would have carded him, but then that would have chewed up any chance at a tip, and he'd left her a ten spot every time he was in. No one at Murphy's left a ten spot. She figured him for a college kid, or maybe he'd been working at one of the vineyards during the spring plant. Tonight, just like every night he'd been in, he sat alone, glancing her way and checking her out. When she looked over, he would avert his contemplation to the beer bottle he held. No doubt perusing the alcohol content or maybe the origin of the brewery. Men were such predictable animals. She was checking him out as well, but it wasn't as obvious. Eventually, she worked her way to that corner of the bar, and he began to chat her up.

"You from around here?" He was looking directly at her.

"I live in Westvale." She polished the bar with the rag as she spoke.

"You go to SU when you're not working?" he asked.

She laughed, shook her head. "No, I'm not exactly what you would call university material."

Silence then, hanging between them uncomfortably.

"I just thought..."

"What? That I was working my way through college." She smiled scathingly. "Isn't that what half the strippers say over at The Chub?" The Chub, aka Chubby's, was what some might call a gentleman's club. "Why aren't you there?"

"Sorry, I guess I was mistaken."

She stopped then, furrowed her brow and the cynical smile fell away. Why had she spoken to this guy like that? He wasn't anything but nice, and he had slipped her a ten every night he's been in. "Aw, shit. That didn't come out right. I'm sorry, I didn't mean that."

"It's okay. I shouldn't have been nosy."

"No, I shouldn't have been a bitch. Let's start over."

"Okay."

"My name's Wendy. What's yours?"

He looked up from the beer and grinned. "Devon."

She dropped the cloth on the bar, stuck out her hand and said, "It's nice to meet you, Devon. Are you from around here?"

He took her hand, his skin warm, smooth, and without callous. "I'm going to the university."

She pulled her hand back, placed it over her mouth, giggled and then broke into laughter. He shook his head and smiled. When the laughter subsided, she grabbed him another beer. He reached for his wallet, and she said, "This is on the house."

It was an hour before closing, and at that moment, she really didn't think that she would end up sleeping with him. She hadn't been with anyone for some months. But when she got home that evening and squared Patrick away, well... The idea of a warm body next to hers seemed appealing. This idea hadn't begun to brew in the beginning, but as he sipped his beer, talked a bit about what he was taking at Syracuse University, the word "maybe" began to echo in the back of her subconscious.

Fifteen minutes later, she set another Rolling Rock on the bar at his request, and she said, "You're not driving are you, Devon?"

"No, I walked. I'll probably grab a cab back to the university."

And then she decided. "I'm off in half hour. I can drive you to the university if you like."

"Aw, that's okay. I don't wanna be any trouble."

"No trouble. Besides, you'll never get a cab at this hour. I can drive you back to the university if you like, or maybe we can go somewhere for coffee." His eyes brightened at this, became charmingly boyish. She imagined a lean, young man beneath those clothes. Virile young man too. He would probably only last thirty seconds after getting into bed, but he'd be quick on the rebound.

"I don't have any classes until tomorrow afternoon."

"That settles it then," Wendy said, and as he finished his beer, she went about the business of closing down. She moved around the bar collecting glasses, wiping things down, and eventually squaring up the cash. He sipped the last of his beer, watching her every move.

This was going to be easy.

She had him step out and wait on the front walk while she put away the evening deposit and set the alarm. Devon was the consummate young gentleman. He'd only had three beers, and if she made an offer to bring him back to her place, she guessed it wouldn't affect his performance in the least. When she slid the deadbolt over and removed her key, she made her final decision. He was cute.

"Let's go." She led him to her car, a beat-up Chrysler Cirrus sitting curbside. She unlocked the car. They climbed in. She turned the key in the ignition, and the engine came alive. She reached over, placed a hand on his, and said, "You want me to take you back to the university, or would you rather come home with me?"

He smiled. "What do you think?"

She slid her hand up his leg and held it there, a finger teasing his manhood. "I think you want to come home with me." Then she kissed him. Wendy was not promiscuous—this was definitely out of the norm for her—but she was a single mom, and that was a lonely business. She pulled back from the kiss, put the gearshift into drive, and pulled away from the curb.

The ride to her house consisted of touching and feeling, but very few words. There was no need for discussion. It had been established: they were going to have sex. As she steered the car with her left hand, the right reached down between his legs, rubbing and massaging. He answered by caressing her breasts, causing her nipples to harden and stirring something inside her. This anticipation was almost too much and Wendy considered pulling the Cirrus over and jumping into the back seat with him.

No, she couldn't do that. Patrick was at home, and... oh shit, she'd almost forgotten about her mother. She pushed him off gently. "Devon, I need you to do something when we get to my house."

"Okay. What?"

"My mom, she's watching my son. You'll have to stay outside until she leaves."

Devon laughed, "You want me to hide in the bushes or something?"

She turned left up another street and said, "How about you just duck down in the car until I give you a signal."

"I could do that, but what if she catches me and..."

He was going to say *calls the cops*. But Wendy cut him off.

"I park my car in the front of the house, on the street. There's only one parking spot out front, so my mom parks in the back alley. She won't be coming out the front. She won't catch you if you duck down low. I'm sorry about all the cloak and dagger stuff, but I just don't feel like explaining to my mother that I'm bringing a stranger home for the night."

"How long will I have to wait?"

"Probably not too long, my mom sometimes falls asleep in front of the TV. So I may have to wake her up. I don't know, five maybe ten minutes."

"Alright. I don't generally do this on first dates, so I hope you'll appreciate all the effort."

She grinned. "I do, and it'll be worth your while."

They rolled up to the curb five minutes later. About a hundred feet before coming to a stop, she told him to get down and lay his head on her lap. And with that, she parked and cut the engine. He could feel the heat coming off of her. It was a subterranean heat. Brought on by the petting and groping.

She shut off the ignition and whispered, "Ten minutes and I'll come get you."

"Okay, ten minutes," he agreed.

She slid out from underneath him, leaving his head to rest on the cloth seat. She closed the car door, and he heard her footsteps as she made her way up the walk. He heard the clicking of steps as she climbed the porch, then the screen door creaked, a door handle clicked over, or maybe it was a deadbolt. He couldn't be sure. He couldn't see anything above the orange bleaching of the dashboard from the arc sodium street lamps.

Ten minutes, he thought.

He wondered if the mother would come out and catch him hiding in the car. Or maybe a local patrol notified by a nosy neighbor. What if she were to deny his presence? "Oh no, officer, I don't know him. I have no idea why he was hiding in my car." The game would have ended right there. He'd be carted off to jail. He was sure shit like that happened from time to time. What would his father say to that? The old man would be royally pissed.

This made him grin.

3

None of those things happened. As promised, in less than ten minutes, she came down the steps to the car and whispered,

"Come on, the coast is clear." He sat upright, and she opened the car door.

"You're sure it's safe?"

She smiled, took his hand, and led him up the path.

When she closed the front door behind them and turned the bolt, she reached over, pulled him in and gave him a long kiss, running her tongue over his. Then she drew back and said, "I have some beer in the fridge."

She kissed him again.

He said, "Maybe later" and began touching her all over. She ran her hands down to his nether regions, feeling his hardness. He did the same, feeling her heat. They kissed, an intertwining mess of fumbled gropes that were desperate and blurry with sexual need. All the while, they worked their way toward the bedroom, once almost tripping and falling down. She laughed and pulled off his shirt. He tugged off hers. She stroked his chest, barren of even a single hair. He unsnapped her bra. By the time they were at the bedroom door, she was in her panties, he in his briefs. Behind them a debris trail of clothing. She dropped her undies and tugged at his briefs. When they dropped, she cupped him, and suddenly stopped and looked down. Then she looked up at him.

"My last girl didn't like hair."

She looked down again. She held onto him. Not even a single hair. "Why?" she asked. "What was her problem with hair?" She brought her eyes up to his, still holding his manhood tightly.

"She said, 'It ruined the mood if you had to lick the pillow.'" He started to grin.

Wendy giggled and worked her hand.

They fell onto the bed side by side. No more talk, just touching.

But then...

"I gotta get something out of my jeans," he said.

"I have condoms in the nightstand," she whispered, and she reached over with one hand and pulled the drawer clumsily open. She brought a strip of condoms up and held it before him. He bit down on the corner with his teeth, and she removed it and went to work. It rolled on with ease, she supposed the smoothness of his clean-shaven skin helped in that regard.

Then they got busy.

He lasted longer than she initially thought. Over two minutes. Then she went to work on him and got him back into the game in under four. Young men bounced back so quickly. With the old condom tied off and discarded, she rolled a second one on and they found their rhythm. This time, he lasted almost twenty-five minutes. When it was over, she was spent.

"Thank you," she said.

He didn't say anything, he just lay there watching her, a thin smile on his face.

"I gotta check on my son. Do you want that beer now?"

"I'd love one," he said.

He sat up against the headboard, watching her naked form disappear through the doorway, fading in the dim light of the hall. She was wraith-like, melting in and out of reality. A little while later, she returned with a can of Budweiser and handed it to him. It was ice cold.

"Thank you," he said and sipped. Then added, "That was fun."

"More fun than a college girl?"

He turned his head and said, "Way more fun than a college girl."

"And no pillow licking." She giggled.

"Yeah."

She wrapped herself around him. Using his bare chest as a headrest and he listened to her breathing. In no time, she was falling asleep. He counted down the space between each inhalation and exhalation, the gap was widening. He'd been afraid he wouldn't be able to perform, but he'd come through. She was, and he meant it, way better than any college girl. Most of the girls at SU were fucking airheads, but moreover, they were dead fucks. Not her. She wrapped her legs around him, then literally squeezed from inside as he thrust. That was talent. Definitely a sign of experience. He hadn't expected this to happen: he was planning on a couple beers and fully intended on heading back to the dorm.

He grinned. Fate was a strange thing.

Half an hour later, cossetted in sleep, she rolled off him, turning her back and pressing her buttocks against his leg. He lay still, fully alert, considering the situation as he ran a hand over her shoulder and into the hourglass of her waist. She had a nice body for a woman who had a child. He guessed you made it your business to look good, especially when you were raising a kid alone. He wondered where the father might be. Guessed that he wouldn't be too happy if he were to walk in now.

Somehow, he doubted this scenario was likely. Daddy was long gone. He looked at the two spent condoms sitting on the nightstand.

Then slid quietly from the bed.

There was much to do.

4

She hadn't known what woke her. Dream or premonition, but she had come up out of the sleep into a sitting position even before her senses were roused. Her mind pricked, pins and needles, her eyesight still unfocused. She had heard her name. Not urgent, but calling in a whisper.

"Wendy, wake up. Wendy, wake up."

Slowly, she pulled focus adjusting to the dark of the room. She saw a naked silhouette standing in the bedroom doorway. It was him. Devon.

"What are you doing?" she asked.

"Are you awake now?"

"Come back to bed."

He said nothing, stepping through the doorway, moving closer. He was holding something in his right hand. She couldn't quite see.

He took another step.

It didn't register at first. Or wouldn't register.

Something in his hand, something in his right hand. What was it?

He took yet another step.

"Wendy?"

"What are you holding?"

He took another step.

Then it began to register.

No. Oh dear God, no. No! Oh my...

"It's okay. He never felt a thing."

Never felt a thing? No!

She felt the scream building, expanding inside her, a hard, jagged ball in her throat, cutting her oxygen. It wanted to escape, but she couldn't find her voice.

Or wouldn't.

To do so was to acknowledge the unthinkable.

He took another step.

The small, round object hung from his right hand. Like the head of a doll.

No, not a doll: bigger.

It was...

She knew then.

Oh my god!

"Patrick," she moaned and then the scream began to rise like a whistling tea kettle.

Why?

He closed in then, his pace quick and deliberate. His other hand rising—moonlight gleaming off steel—before she could scream, he severed her windpipe. She felt an initial sting, and then there was a pop, but no actual pain. He hovered, watching intently as the darkness turned the black to blue, light to gray. Her life was spilling out, like a river running into the sea, swallowed by the abyss.

Her eyes closed.

Opened.

It was better this way. At least she would be with him.

Then nothing.

5

He showered. Massaging the water over his skin, pushing into the contour of each muscle and rubbing away the blood. There had been a lot of blood. Some had already congealed on his naked form, and when he touched it, it flecked away. He worked his way to the shower, using a towel to pull back the curtain and stepped in. The water had been cold at first, causing his limp penis to contract even further. At his feet, the water puddled in swirls of diluted crimson before being pulled to the drain in tendrils. He followed the drops as they fell into the pool.

Plop... Plop... Plop...

It was a lot of blood.

A lot of DNA, he told himself.

He shouldn't have had sex with her. But then, he hadn't planned on killing her. No, that wasn't quite right. He was thinking about killing her. She was the one who had initiated the sex. He had been thinking about killing her from the first time he saw her, but he thought about killing people all the time. It wasn't unique to her. He could have easily taken the ride back to the dorm and continued his fantasy.

He rubbed the back of his neck, the hot water beating away even more blood.

How did that get back there?

Correction. He hadn't planned on killing them. Yes, them, but he needed to be thinking about other things. "DNA," he said aloud. How much DNA had he dropped here? "A lot of DNA." He rubbed the back of his neck and considered his penis. He'd used a condom, but there would be drops left on the bed. And what of his skin? The bump and grind they'd performed would have rubbed off dead skin. He'd shaved down there for that reason, but there was still the short, cropped cut on his head. His eyebrows.

"Fucking DNA."

He wasn't in a database anywhere. He had no record.

But your DNA will be now and if you're ever picked up?

"Fucking DNA!" He smashed a fist against the tiling.

He inventoried his body. Every nook visible to the naked eye and thought he was clean. He then took a cloth and used the shower head to rinse the tub in swirling gyrations. Why? He wasn't sure. He'd probably left enough fiber and DNA lying around for an easy conviction. He needed to get dressed, clean up, and consider his options.

He climbed from the shower onto the bath mat and toweled off. Once dry, he dressed and stared into the small vanity. Was it how he thought it would be? This being his first. No, but then was it ever going to be? The act had been deliberate and mechanical. He didn't think it was the act that he sought for gratification anyway. No, the act was just a means to an end. He thought of all the others he read about. The killers who'd risen through the ranks to stardom. Ted Bundy, John Wayne Gacy, whose names were as household in modern culture as Van Gogh or da Vinci. Perhaps even more.

He wiped the tub with the towel.

"Notoriety," he said. That's what they had in common. But that wasn't exactly right either. Then the word came to him. He wandered back to the bedroom. Looked in on them. The clock on the nightstand read 3:34 a.m.

"Fucking DNA." He glanced out the window into the back yard. There was a small aluminum gardening shed back there. On either side of the yard, tall hedges offered relative privacy.

Better get to it, he thought.

He went out the back door as quietly as possible and found the shed unlocked. He slid the door over, the aluminum scraping against the track in weak protest. He had rubber gloves on now. The yellow ones used for washing dishes. Condoms for the hands. Glancing around he saw a tricycle, presumably Patrick's, lying on its side. There was an old lawnmower. Beside that, a five-gallon jerry can, much too big for the likes of a lawnmower. He could see Wendy struggling with that jerry can, splashing gas all over the lawn mower.

Not anymore, he thought and smiled.

Neither she nor Patrick would be visiting this shed again.

He lifted the jerry can; it was half full.

It'll have to do.

Inside the house, he retraced his path, as best he could remember, splashing the gas in places where he thought he might have left evidence. He doused the bodies, the condoms, the towels he'd used. He gave the bed where they'd had sex a good soaking. The kid's crib also got a good soaking. When he emptied it, he placed the can at the foot of her bed.

He then went back to the kitchen and opened the stove. It was an electric job. He turned the oven on and watched the burners. They immediately began to glow. He switched it off and searched the cupboards. He needed more accelerant. This place had to burn. The DNA had to be destroyed.

"Fucking DNA," he grunted again and pulled out a bottle of vegetable oil. He unscrewed the cap and soaked the counter. That wouldn't burn as fast, but it would still burn. Then he grabbed a bag of sugar and spread the granules into the oil. He'd seen sugar burn, had tossed it into a fire once, it flared and left a sweet scent in the air. He wandered into the living room, careful not to step on the trail of gas he'd left on the carpet. The vapors that hung in the air were intoxicating, and he was getting the beginnings of a headache. He'd been very careful not to get any on him, but he would probably still smell of it. He'd have to get his clothes into the wash as soon as he got back to SU.

He found a stack of newspapers and magazines by the couch and brought them back to the kitchen. He arranged them on the oven rack and considered. It looked plausible. Stove ignites papers, papers ignite the gas and soon enough the house would be on fire and...

"No more fucking DNA," he said.

How long would it take? Five minutes? Ten?

He wasn't sure. Arson wasn't his strength.

He'd have to move fast.

He gazed at the body of the woman and that of her decapitated son, burning the images into his mind.

This is like painting a masterpiece and setting it on fire, he thought.

He took one last glance around the house. Then the word came to him. He turned on the oven and tossed the rubber gloves onto the counter. Tore off a roll of paper towel and used it to wipe the doorknob as he exited the house. *Infamous,* he thought. *That was the word I was looking for. Infamous, and I just did something that would be remembered for a long time.*

"And I just burned it all up," he muttered in a low, angry grunt.

Lighting fire to a masterpiece.

Not yet; it was only art at this point. He had to hone his craft. Polish his work, and if he didn't get caught for this, he would be well on his way. He made it four blocks and disappeared around the corner when the paper flared up.

By the time he was a mile away, fire snaked down the halls into the adjacent room to the main sources of gasoline. The smoke detectors in Patrick and Wendy's room cried out, but only briefly, falling victim to the intense heat.

He walked all the way back to SU, drawing the attention of a slumbering homeless man, but only for a second and it rose no alarm.

When he reached the dorm, he stripped and put his clothes in the wash. An hour had elapsed, and miles away, the little, post-war bungalow was burning savagely. He was stepping into the shower when the fire department arrived. They turned on the water, sprayed it on all sides, but it was already too far gone, burning out of control. The volunteer fire captain had no illusions; there wouldn't be anyone in the furnace left alive to save. The chief was on his way. All they could do was try and protect the neighboring houses.

Showered, Lance, not Devon, dressed in sweat pants and a Syracuse University tee. "Infamous," he said and lay back on the bed. He hoped that he'd gotten everything. He'd heard the sirens calling in the night, at first far off. Then, another set of sirens awoke, and he knew they were on their way to help. He considered going online, to see if there was something about it on one of the local media sites, then thought better of it. Too dangerous. The Internet was like a strand of DNA, maybe even worse; he didn't want to leave a trail. But that would all change, because he was learning about the Web, and soon he'd be learning about the Deep Web, and in those murky waters, a predator could hide in plain sight.

"Next time," he said. "Next time, I will be prepared." He thought about Bundy, about Gacy, as if he were aspiring to their greatness, their infamy. No, he would be better. He had no intention of being caged, electrocuted or injected. His achievements would be greater, would shock and horrify. He shut his mind down then, falling off to sleep, sliding in the shade of dreamlessness.

***

CHAPTER 2 – OUT OF THE ASHES

1

8 May 2000

Westvale, NY — Crime Scene

A morose collectiveness hung over the scene, infecting all involved, painted on the faces of rescue workers, the uniformed cops. With it, a pungent aroma of septic water, slag, and cooked flesh hung in the air. The house was gone except for the framework of charred wall studs that looked like black toothpicks spiking out of the floor plan. The scene smoldered beneath the thousands of gallons of water that had been poured upon it. Crime scene tape surrounded the property, twisting in the morning breeze. The tape had been put up by a uniformed cop after the fire chief told him to do it. The chief called the Syracuse PD asking for a homicide detective.

Hayward had caught the case and was waiting on the fire chief to fill him in. The lawn below his feet had been scorched by the intense blaze. Blades of grass, now coarse straw, crunched beneath his shoes as he drifted just outside the perimeter.

What am I looking at? he wondered.

"I'll be right with you, Detective." The man calling to him was Westvale Fire Chief Ronny Bush. Hayward knew

Bush; they were related through marriage. Bush's daughter had married Hayward's nephew. Though they didn't fish or drink together, they had eaten an occasional meal at an outdoor barbeque or three. He thought Bush was a decent guy.

Hayward raised his hand, acknowledging the fire chief, running over the unknowns in his head. Even the uniformed cop, he'd shown his shield upon arrival, had been tight-lipped about the victims. Hayward didn't push the kid, figured he probably didn't have much anyway. As he waited, he considered the scene. He'd been to plenty of fires and those that involved homicide were usually murder-suicide. Some mutt, who's on the cusp of divorce, decides to off his family, then kill himself. It wasn't always a man, women could be equally selfish. Maybe that's what this was, individual kills lover or perhaps kid, then lights the place up and checks out.

Makes sense, he thought, *but after an inferno like this, how would first responders know? The bodies or body would be burned beyond recognition, and the body snatchers weren't even here to transport the victims back to the morgue. So how does everyone know it's a crime scene?*

Hayward knew he was going to find out. In fact, it was down to minutes—but he was a creature of inquisition—not all that good at waiting. Speculation was the mental game he played at crime scenes in anticipation of the facts. It was his way of staving off impatience and prepping to compartmentalize emotion. For him, emotion was the enemy when investigating a murder. Not that he was a heartless bastard, he wasn't. Becoming attached to a victim, no matter what the mystery novels said, was never what led to closing a case. He'd seen his share of fellow detectives become attached, usually as a case grew colder and solving it became less likely. He had a case that he was close to, that had never been solved, probably never would be, but he knew if he were going to continue to be a homicide detective, he had to jettison his emotions. Not completely, but as much as possible.

Bush was at his left, drawing him out of the mental game. He'd finished with his own detail and giving out orders to his own people. "We have two victims. One adult and one child."

"Okay, Ron, and I am here because?"

"You're here because the victims didn't start the fire. They were murdered before the fire was started."

Hayward turned towards the chief, an intrusive smile tugging at the edges of his mouth. "You say this fire was started by someone else, okay. What makes you think it was a murder?"

Bush's face transformed then, his complexion graying, his demeanor softening, even empathetic. Ronny Bush looked Hayward straight in the eyes and said, "Because we found a skull in the adult victim's bedroom. It was a child's skull, and it should've been attached to the body, which we found in another bedroom."

"Fuck." Hayward heard himself say, then, "Go on."

"I don't know what could be left for evidence. The place is a mess. We really soaked it down. It'll be really muddy in there. Shit, some of it is still smoldering, and my guys have tromped all over it. We found a molten gas can, we think that's the accelerant. Right next to it, we found the skull at the foot of what used to be the adult victim's bed. When we found the kid's skull, we backed off." Bush took a deep breath. "I've seen a lot of horrible shit as a firefighter, but this takes the fucking cake. It's not just horrible. It's fucking abominable. The worst part, Brad. Worst fucking part is we might have assisted this animal in destroying whatever evidence you might need to catch him." Bush sat down on the hood of Hayward's car. He was knocked over by this.

"Take it easy, Ron." Hayward patted him on the shoulder, then he was on the phone. Calling for more backup and crime scene techs, more uniforms to canvas for witnesses.

As he did this, he was assessing. The street would have to be cordoned off better than this. Sooner or later, there'd be a lot more press.

He looked past Bush and waved over the uniform who had let him on to the scene. When the kid came up, he told him to gather everyone who worked the scene and have them meet at his car.

"Ron, we need to keep a lid on this."

"Keep a lid on it?"

"The murder will get out, but the details... The kid's head being cut off. Can you get your people to dummy up on the details? It's important. I need to hold stuff back. There'll be wackos confessing to this."

"Yeah, I think so."

"Good, let's gather 'em up and have us a chat." His cell rang and he answered. "Hayward." This was followed by "Yeah." And "ETA?" and "Whatever you can give me."

Bush was listening, rubbing his pug nose and collecting himself at the same time. He felt weak, ashamed, and he wondered if his own people had seen that weakness. He stiffened, let out a brooding sigh, one of a man who is waiting for an unpleasant situation to end.

2

9 May 2000

Syracuse University

The police showed a full twenty-four hours after the murders. Almost to the exact time. The call came on his cell. The ringtone, an Animals' tune, "House of the Rising Sun," woke him. When he picked it up, the caller ID read Unknown Caller. He pushed the answer button and said, "Hello?"

"Hello, is this Lance Belanger?" said a man's voice.

He sat up, wiped his eyes. "Yes."

"Lance, my name is Detective Brad Hayward. I need to speak to you. I am parked outside your dormitory. Can I confirm your room number and come up?"

Panic cut through him. He gave his head a shake, trying to jar the sleepiness. "I was sleeping."

"Yes, I understand and I apologize, but I need to talk to you."

"Um, okay? But what is this about?"

"Son, I would prefer to come up and speak to a person."

"Okay, I'm in room 341."

"You have a roommate, Lance?"

His stomach churned.

He's here to arrest me! They know about the killings, something I left behind. Something I missed! He swallowed—his throat clicked—he needed water. He croaked, "No... I have my own room."

Did that sound desperate, afraid?

He thought so.

"Alright, I'll be up in a minute." The detective's voice had the sound of regret. Or maybe it was disappointment. Yes, disappointment at having to arrest a young man with his whole future in front of him. Lance began to panic. What was he going to do?

Calm down, he thought. *There's no way the cops would call me if they were coming to arrest me. It has to be something else.*

Maybe, but why take a chance?

He stood, the blood in his veins diluted with adrenaline, and went over to his desk. He yanked the drawer open, rummaged through it until he found the pocket knife. *If he's here to arrest me, I'll have to kill him and run. They will freeze everything within hours. I'll need to empty my bank account.* Which wasn't much, maybe nine hundred dollars. He didn't want to go to jail. He'd do whatever he had to. That included killing a cop. He pulled on his sweats, opened the blade and carefully placed it into the pocket.

Then he waited.

There was a knock. A courtesy, he supposed, extended to the other students in the dorm. No point in ruining everyone's night. He took in a breath, wrapped his hand around the knife and opened the door. The man on the other side was an inch shorter than him, roughly fifty years old, and balding. The crown of his head shone under the hall fluorescents. His face was pudgy, much like his stomach. He held an expression of deep concern. "Lance?"

"Yes."

"Can I please come in?"

There was no SWAT team behind him.

"Sure." Lance stepped back and opened the door wider with his left hand, while his right was gently touching the blade in his pocket. He wondered if the anxiety he felt showed on his face. "What's this all about?"

The detective stepped inside, looked around, pulled out the computer chair and said, "I think you better sit down, son."

Lance placed both hands into his pockets, his right tightening around the handle of the knife. "I don't want to sit down, I want to know what this is about."

The second he says anything about the murders I'll cut his throat.

"There's been a fire," Hayward said and sighed.

Lance tightened his grip, readying himself.

"I don't know how to tell you this, son, so I'm just gonna come right out and say it." He stared directly into Lance's eyes and his voice seemed far off. "There was a fire..."

I knew it! I don't have a choice.

"I am afraid I have some really bad news for you."

"Bad news?"

"There was a fire, son. Your parents, they died in a house fire." The detective studied him, waiting for a reaction. They were still investigating the fire, but he doubted this kid had anything to do with it, but still, he waited. He'd seen a few rich kids murder their parents. But he didn't think that was the case here. Then again, he was getting a weird vibe off this kid.

"A fire?" Lance was computing what he'd said. *My parents? I never killed my parents? Was this some sort of cop ruse? Some misdirect?*

Hayward reached out and placed a hand on Lance's shoulder. He stared directly at him, trying to get a bead on what the kid was thinking.

Lance thought that if he knew, Hayward would be reaching for his gun.

Hayward didn't think the kid was guilty. He'd been waiting for a sign, and thus far, there had been none. "I am very sorry, Lance."

Lance lowered his head, unknown to Detective Hayward, he was suppressing a smile.

They're dead, he thought. *A fire.* He wanted to laugh out loud, but he couldn't. There was the knife to think about. He had to say something. "They're dead? Both of them?"

"I'm afraid so."

Safe, he thought. But his reaction. *Was it authentic?*

He sat down on the edge of his bed, and in turn, Detective Hayward took a seat in the computer chair. It creaked under his girth. Hayward was eyeing him, and Lance suddenly realized he was going to be free.

Not if you smile and spook this fat, pig detective. But a smile was coming, completely involuntary, and he wasn't sure if he would be able to stop it. He took evasive action. "I'm sorry, but I think I'm going to vomit." He popped up and pushed passed the detective, opening the door and running down the hall.

Hayward was completely caught off guard. Lance was out the door and halfway to the shared bathroom before Hayward thought of following. The return spring on the door closed behind him, and that was enough time to pull out the knife and dump it into the garbage can as he ran by.

When he reached the bathroom, the detective was opening the door and following.

I have to do this fast, he thought. Then he pushed into the toilet stall open and dropped to his knees. Simultaneously, he thrust two fingers, the middle and index, into his throat—accidentally scraping the nail of his index against his uvula. He did not hold back and a second later, the contents of his stomach came up, splashing down over his hand and into the waiting bowl. By the time Hayward got to the stall, he was unspooling the toilet paper to wipe his mouth.

Lance stared into the bowl. A slick of yellow bile, peppered with half-digested food, floated in the center of the toilet water. Like an acidic iceberg, it held its molecular form. A sour stench permeated from the stall. Tears welled up in his eyes, not from remorse, but from the forced discharge of stomach content. *This is good,* he thought and was pulling a large wad of the roll just as the detective entered the stall. He did not wipe the tears, he instead let them track down his face.

"They're dead," he moaned. "I'm... I'm sorry."

"It's okay, son," Hayward said running his hand between his shoulder blades. "This is a perfectly natural reaction."

"I'm alright," Lance said. "Shit, it stinks in here."

"I understand completely." Hayward removed his hand and stepped back as Lance stood up and wiped his mouth.

"I'm not gonna throw up again, Detective," Lance said. "We can go back to my room." He tossed the toilet paper into the bowl but didn't bother to flush. Then he led the detective back to his room.

When they got there, Hayward filled Lance in on what he could. He still didn't know what had caused the fire. The detective was sympathetic and compassionate considering what he'd seen that day. Lance had no idea that Hayward had been on the scene of two fires. The first being set by Lance and the second being coincidence. Hayward only attended the second fire thinking there might be a connection.

Normally, a uniformed officer would have been dispatched to deliver the news. Hayward was doing this as a courtesy; he was pretty sure the second fire had nothing to do with the individual he sought. Or with this young man who sat across from him.

"For now, it has been deemed a fire of unknown origin. It's under investigation. Once the fire investigator is done, we'll know more." He patted Lance on the knee. "I'm sorry, Lance. There is no easy way to deliver news like this. Is there someone who can come down and stay with you? A relative maybe?"

Lance nodded. "I have a few friends here. And an uncle in Clarence."

"Would you like me to contact them?"

"No, Detective. I can do that."

Hayward felt guilty relief. As much as he felt sorry for this kid, he was on the hunt. There was a killer out there. A monster that had taken the life of a young woman and her child. He wasn't up for babysitting the bereaved. That might sound insensitive, but he had to get back to his case.

3

In the weeks that followed, there was progress on the fire that killed the Belangers, but little movement on the fire that killed Wendy and her son, Patrick.

Bernie Koch. That would be the name that came up when the investigators traced the cause of the fire that killed Lance's parents. Poor workmanship was what had caused the fire. Death by a contractor who had absolutely no idea what he was doing when it came to installing electrical wiring. His father, for all his money, was a cheap fuck because he refused to hire a proper contractor. Lance's father, Wallace Belanger, would say, "I'm hiring local. Propping up the economy." Local, yes, but he paid about a quarter what you gave the average tradesman.

The fire had started in the rec room, which was a multilayered code violation if anything else. His father brought in a framer, if you could call him that. The guy was essentially a drifter. Some mope down on his luck. He had some ability when it came to carpentry, but his skills were definitely distracted by the need of drink or maybe drugs. That's what Lance thought anyway. Dear old Dad, cheap fucking bastard that he was. He hired local, paid shit, and as an added bonus, avoided the taxes.

To get the job right would have been at least ten grand if he'd hired some decent people to do the work. But why do it right and get real contractors when the peasants can do it for you? So the first week, the framer came, banged in the studs, not to perfection but close enough. And bitching about poor workmanship was a bartering chip if you wanted to chip a little off the job. The second week, an electrician, if you could call him that, arrived to install the wiring, and then came the drywall to seal the deal. Seal the poorly spliced wiring.

The culprit wound up being a drywall screw piercing the insulation surrounding the house wire and arcing against the aluminum wall stud. This wouldn't happen overnight—in fact, the electrical job would be almost four months old when the fire was sparked—but it was traced back, and Bernie Koch would be arrested and charged for operating without an electrician's license and performing unauthorized work causing death. Lance thought it sort of unfair; good old Bernie had done him a favor, but he had to keep up appearances.

4

In the months that would follow, nothing would be posted in the media about the horrific circumstance surrounding the murder of single mom Wendy Birrell and her four-year-old son, Patrick. They ruled out the possibility that Wendy had killed Patrick and took her own life. The fire would be the factor that would rule her out, based on its source in the kitchen. Hayward knew in his gut that the killer had started the fire to cover his tracks. Had, in fact, timed the fire to make a clean getaway. There could have been a number of factors that initiated the murders—drugs, a lover scorned—but the beheading of the child told a more sinister tale. Hayward speculated that the killer had done so with the intent of spreading terror. It was the only way to explain the brutality. But who was the intended victim of this macabre act? Hayward thought it was the woman, Wendy. The investigators managed to keep Patrick's beheading out of the news. That would thwart any of the crazies apt to confess away.

And many did.

Hayward had no idea that he had been in the company of the killer he sought. He had all but forgotten about Lance Belanger. He'd considered the Belanger fire an unfortunate coincidence and focused on a murder investigation that was leading nowhere. The fire had destroyed any evidence, Wendy's Chrysler was impounded and a thread was found on the seat, but no hair or skin that could yield a DNA sample.

5

For Lance, two things happened on that fateful night. The first was that Lance had been freed from the clutches of his father and mother. He was no longer tethered to their faux morality, and he would not have to carry on with the double life he had been cultivating.

The second thing that happened was that he was soon to be a very rich man. Wallace Belanger's estate had a net worth of over eight million dollars. And that didn't include the generous accidental death insurance payout of one million for his father; and eight hundred thousand for his mother. If Lance was smart, and he was, he would never have to work another day in his life. Once they'd determined the fire was the result of shoddy workmanship (*thank you very much, Bernie Koch),* the insurance adjusters signed off and the money was forthcoming.

Lance decided that he would need to take a year before he could disappear. He kept up appearances, had dinners with his Uncle Rob in Clarence. He continued his schooling and received a degree in computer programming and web design. He was going to need that. He also played the grieving son well, kept to himself, and was quiet and thoughtful.

That first year was key, and Lance knew that if his destiny was to be realized, he would have to show restraint and patience. He read a bit about the murders in Westvale, but only through the local paper. He did not peruse the Web; he didn't want to leave any sort of a trail. He wondered why they didn't reveal the details of the crime. Thought that either the fire had covered it up or maybe the police were withholding information?

A week before Lance graduated, Bernie Koch went to jail for two years, pled down from five, when it was discovered that his unlicensed wiring led to the fatal fire that killed both of Lance's parents. Tough break for Bernie.

After graduation, he sat before his father's lawyer, Bob Hawkins. Lance had never considered his last name. His father had called him "Lawyer Bob" and that was how Lance thought of him. Between them, in neat stacks, were the settlement documents laid out on his big oak desk.

"You have no idea how sad this makes me," Hawkins remarked. "Your parents were very good people."

Lance looked down at the stacks of paper, his face expressionless. Inside, he was thinking, *Any second he will start groveling about how to manage my money.* "Where do I sign, Bob?"

Bob pushed the first stack across the table. "Are you going back to school next year?"

"I don't think so. I'm going to take a year off. Do a little traveling."

Lawyer Bob frowned. "Lance, on the surface this might look like a lot of money, but if you don't plan carefully, you'll burn through this pretty fast."

"I'm not stupid." Lance's face darkened.

"I never said that you were, but you're a young man."

"What did you think, Bob? That I'd run a few million up my nose." Lance grinned, reveling in the sudden surprise he had raised on the lawyer's face. The mask hiding the contempt had slipped, but Lance couldn't care less and continued. "You think that maybe I'd start buying cars for strippers and whores? Bankrupt myself in a year or two?"

The lawyer opened his mouth to defend the accusations Lance was making, but he was cut off.

"I finished school, even after burying my parents. I managed to graduate with honors. I'm going to take a year off, not that it's any of your business, then I'll probably figure out if I want to pursue a degree."

Lawyer Bob's face also changed, hardening. He said, "I never thought that at all." But that was exactly what he was thinking, along with *Go fuck yourself, Lance.*

Lance spoke up again. "Do your job, spare me the fake concern, and show me where to sign."

The lawyer frowned, pushed the documents across the table, and indicated where to sign. When he was done, Lance left without another word.

He had just inherited over nine million dollars, two properties: one in Syracuse, NY, and a cabin down in Pennsylvania. He also had four vehicles at his disposal. He was rich and could do whatever he wanted, but most of all, he was free. Free to pursue the lifestyle he had fantasized about.

From the ashes of two fires, a phoenix would rise. His path clear. The fledgling murder of Wendy and the kid was only the beginning. He was already thinking about the next one. How it would be different.

Better, uglier, and soon, infamous.

***

CHAPTER 3 – HOMELESS STEVE

1

07 July 2001

Cleveland, OH

The second killing was the next step in the learning process and would change Lance Belanger's status from killer to serial killer. From everything he'd read, three kills seemed to be the threshold. Although the police would not make the connection between the murder of Wendy Birrell, her son, Patrick, and his next victim, Lance wanted that status, craved it almost as much as he desired to kill. This might be his third, but would be treated as a single killing, thus robbing him, albeit temporarily, the status of recognition. Irrationality insisted he should send something, either to the media or the police, but Lance pushed that away. He would have to wait. There was a bigger picture to consider. In the eyes of the law, this would be a single, random murder. With that in mind, he decided that this killing would be the signature of all killings to follow.

On that July morning, he landed at Cleveland Hopkins International Airport and rented a car. After renting the car, he proceeded to a local hardware store called Mossman's Hardware and purchased the items he believed he would need. He avoided bigger box stores, like Home Depot or

Lowe's, thinking the closed circuit security cameras posed a heavy risk. Mossman's had a single camera, but they were small and had a sizeable section dedicated to camping. Under this guise, Lance purchased a pup tent, forty feet of nylon rope, a propane stove, a cooler, a hatchet, tent spikes, a ten-piece cook set, a sharpening stone, and a machete.

"No fishing rod?" the male clerk asked and pointed behind him.

Lance turned and saw a carousel of fishing rods. A sign invited *On Sale! $14.99*. He turned back to face the clerk. "I'm not much of a fisherman."

"Me either," the clerk said and punched in the order.

Lance also visited a Wegman's, where he purchased canned goods, water, a six-pack of soda, and a bag of ice. He packed these things into the cooler and set out to find a suitable site to camp. He drove out of Cleveland, following Interstate 90 north/east toward Erie, Pennsylvania. The day was sunny, the traffic heavy, and it was warm. He was looking for just the right place. Because it was summer, there would be lots of campers, and he intended on using a known campsite, but that was only going to act as a home base.

He set up in a KOA campsite west of Painesville, OH. There, he pitched a tent, assembled his stove and melted in with the other campers enjoying the sunny weather. There were a lot of people milling about the grounds, most friendly, but Lance guessed the volume of people was considerably lower than the previous 4th of July weekend. He doubted he would have found a campsite at all and that the celebrations would have hindered his plans.

He'd purchased a map when he gassed the rental, and he studied it. He cooked a meal on the stove, baked beans, and sipped a Coke while looking over the terrain. To the east, sitting on the shore of Lake Erie, was a nuclear power plant. The town of North Perry, for which the plant was named, stood as a barrier between the plant and Interstate 90. The area was heavily forested but wouldn't be suitable for his needs. He needed complete seclusion, and if he ventured into that area, he'd probably find himself coming face to face with a roving security guard. After dinner, and waiting for the sun to go down, he read. Lance carried two books with him on that day: *The Stranger Beside Me* by Ann Rule and *Ted Bundy: Conversations with a Killer* by Stephen G. Michaud and Hugh Aynesworth. He had read the Ann Rule book on the plane, and now thumbed through the second book with interest. He admired Ted Bundy, although he didn't think the killer would have been nearly as successful if he had started down the path of serial murder at the turn of the century, as Lance was. Bundy had left his DNA at almost every murder scene, but DNA did not play a role in his capture because the science of DNA profiling was non-existent in the '70s. Ted had it easier; police jurisdictions didn't communicate, so he was able to hop over all over the county and state lines without detection, murdering to his heart's content. He also didn't have to contend with the FBI, who at the time was still under an umbrella of secrecy when it came to sharing information with other police departments.

Lance had read a dozen books on serial killers and an equal number about the men who hunted them. He also admired FBI agents John Douglas and Robert Ressler, considered the fathers of profiling and crime scene classification.

He thumbed through the Bundy book and waited for the darkness. With the sky darkening, Lance finished the second book before dusk took hold, so he studied his map and found a road to the southwest. It was not part of the KOA grid, but presented a great possibility, as it was not more than three miles out and would be accessible by vehicle. He was filled with anticipation, waiting for the cloak of darkness.

When it came, he set out on foot to find the kill site.

2

Lance returned to Cleveland the next day. He had found a suitable spot and was on the hunt. He drove into the seedier part of the city where he found a smorgasbord of possible victims. All of them were unfortunates. Drug addicted, and most were prostituting themselves. He trolled the area three times. In the second pass, he spotted a scruffy guy. Lance estimated him to be somewhere in his mid-thirties, but it was hard to tell for sure. He looked well beyond his years, his face a landscape of sores and a roadmap of deeply etched lines. He was tall and lanky, hunched over, and an addict. Probably a crack user or a meth head. He was fidgety, like an animal overcome by constant hunger. In the morning, Lance had watched him get into a car with an older man. The two drove away. Forty-five minutes later they returned. The homeless guy got out of the car and set off on foot. Lance rounded the block and caught sight of him passing off money to a kid. Presumably his drug dealer. The kid nodded to another guy who was standing out in front of a liquor store and sent the homeless guy to retrieve his purchase. After that, he disappeared down an alley. Lance decided to leave the area and grab a bite of lunch. He decided that if the homeless guy was there when he returned, he'd take him.

The homeless guy did not return until almost 3:30 that afternoon. He was back on the same corner, hustling for more cash. That's when Lance decided to make his move. Lance scanned the area for police cars and saw none.

This was it.

He passed the homeless guy, made eye contact and parked a little way up the street. There, he waited. The homeless guy watched him, but also scanned the area. Making sure it was safe to approach. From the passenger side mirror of the rental, Lance watched his prey approach, taking long, bounding steps up the sidewalk. He took another look around, paranoid that someone might be watching.

There was a knock on the glass.

Here we go, Lance thought and lowered the window.

"Hi," the homeless guy said.

Lance turned and faced him. "Hey."

"Nice day out. How are you doing?" The guy smelled, an intermingling aroma of bad breath, perspiration, and piss. Closer now, he looked even worse. His shoulder-length hair was a snarl of knots, clothes dirty with stains and worn out. He was still high, but coming down, and the hunger for his drug of choice was not sated. "You looking for something, man?"

Lance took a breath. "Maybe."

"Good, I might be able to help you out."

"Yeah?"

"Sure. You got a nice ride here."

Lance ignored the question and asked, "What's your name?"

"Steve."

Lance nodded.

"What's yours?"

Lance thought about this and said, "I'd rather not say."

Steve, who Lance now thought of as Homeless Steve, nodded. "No prob. What can I help you with, man?"

Lance didn't ask for anything specific. He just pulled out a wad of bills, peeled off a twenty and passed it over. "I'm looking for some company." Lance didn't get any more specific than that, but Homeless Steve did.

"You want me to suck you off, man? I could do that. But you got to wear a condom. I don't want any mouth disease or HIV. You know," he said.

Lance looked at him incredulously, almost laughed aloud. He was astounded that Homeless Steve would be in the business of practicing safe sex while performing fellatio on guys for drug money. Considering his oral hygiene, which consisted of yellow, gunk covered tombstone teeth, Lance would have also insisted on the use of a condom, maybe double bagged. Not that it would ever get that far.

"We can talk about that later," Lance said and peeled off another bill and held it. Homeless Steve's eyes grew. He was eyeing the wad of bills Lance held, like a dog at dinner time. *I bet you're thinking about robbing me right now, aren't you?* Lance mused, and he was right in that assumption. Steve was thinking about getting that wad of cash, wondering how much glass he could buy with such a bankroll. Lance saw this, purposely dangling the bait and thought to himself that he needed to hook this guy up with some product just to slow him down. He might look well beyond his years, but he was still a brute of a man. He needed to subdue him, getting him higher would make that easier. The problem was he was a drug addict, and addicts couldn't keep secrets. So how did he get this guy some drugs without him telling half his pals?

"Man, I'd really like to get some glass before I go party with you." Steve seemed to be reading his mind. The non-murderous part anyway. He rubbed his arms and shivered, glancing back over his shoulder.

"I gotta tell you something right now, Steve. That sort of concerns me. I gave you a twenty, and now you're talking about booking. Maybe you're going to leave me here like an idiot, score some glass and find two or three friends to laugh off how you scored on me. Or maybe you sell me out to the cops, and I get picked up. I'm married, Steve. You could fuck up my marriage."

"No. No way, man! I would never do that. There's a code. No ratting. Steve don't rat to Five-O..."

"You say that, but I need discretion. I might even slide you another twenty to exercise that discretion. My old lady finds out, she'd divorce me. She doesn't understand my needs."

"Fucking bitches," he said, then wondering if he'd misspoke. "I mean... No disrespect to your woman. I get it, man. I was married once." He seemed to zone out, as if remembering that time or imagining the lie he might be telling.

"So, if I give you another twenty, you'll find yourself some glass and keep it low profile? Maybe when you come back, I'll give you another. You got to be on the up and up, Steve. No hanging me out to dry with the law." Lance seemed to think about it. "Shit, maybe this isn't such a good idea. I'm getting nervous." Lance reached for the gear lever, ready to pull away.

"No! No, man, I won't tell anybody. I'll score and come right back. I'll come back, we'll get high, and we'll party." Steve made a cross over his chest. "God's honor."

"Okay, Steve, I'm going to trust you. If you take off with that forty bucks, I guess I'm the fool; that's peanuts compared to what you'll get if you do right by me. Think of me as the golden goose. You can eat me all at once or cash in the eggs. I got a lot of eggs, Steve. Don't disrespect me." Lance gazed into the drug addict's eyes. They were pools of confusion. "Deal?"

"Yeah, yeah, man. We got a deal. I won't fuck you up. You want to follow me, just to make sure, no problem, man."

"I just might do that. From a distance."

Lance took the gamble, letting Steve go out and score his meth. He didn't split, and he didn't talk, even though Lance was sure he would. He didn't want to follow. It was a remote possibility, but Steve might be working with vice.

How fucking bad would that be?

If he were to be arrested, his name, his photo and his fingerprints would go on file. He doubted they'd take DNA, but there'd be a record. It was too late to turn back now. He had to take this one chance, let Steve get his crystal meth and then get the hell out of Cleveland.

3

To his credit, Steve did what he said he would do. He went to the dealer, bought some glass, and made his way back. He never disclosed who Lance was, not that he knew his name. He was hungry, his golden goose laid golden eggs. There were a lot more bills on that roll, and the guy was insecure about his woman. Steve was sure that this guy would give him more money. He returned a half hour later, climbed into the car, and they drove out of the city.

As they drove, Lance stole glances over at the jittering man beside him. He needed a fix. The sun was low on the skyline when they pulled into a rest area along Interstate 90.

"We're stopping here?" Homeless Steve asked.

"You look like you need another hit. The car's a rental, so you can't light up in here. I'd have to get it detailed. So go outside. Okay?"

Steve didn't complain. He stepped out, pulled out his works, and he gave Lance a look. "You want some?" He wasn't offering, but he was asking. When Lance shook his head, Steve's face lit up. He didn't want to share, but said, "Okay, man, just thought I'd offer. Seeing how you're the one that bought the product."

"Knock yourself out. Drugs aren't my thing anyway." Lance's smile inferred that his interests were elsewhere and to further suggestion, he gazed down into Steve's groin area.

Steve grinned and said, "We'll get to that, man. I promise."

Once Steve was done, he got back in the car, and they carried on down the road.

Forty-five minutes later, under a canopy of stars, they found themselves parked on a gravel road. They were in a park, not a campground, but on an abandoned service road. There was a smell in the air—water close by—they were on the shore of Lake Erie.

Immediately upon exiting the car, Steve lit up again, the smell of the stuff was chemical-like. Ammonia intermingled with lighter fluid. Lance moved away from it, turned off by the aroma. He was making his way around to the trunk when

Steve cut him off, his free hand touching Lance's thigh, moving upward.

Lance pushed his hand off and said, "No. Not yet. Have another hit. I gotta get ready for this."

Steve frowned and backed away. "Alright, man, I'm just trying to oblige. You've been good to me, so I want to make it worth your while."

Then he went back to his pipe.

Lance kicked off his shoes, removed his shirt, then his pants, folding each article of clothing methodically. He stripped naked, folded his underwear and placed them on top of the neat pile in the trunk, then removed the item he had placed there. He did not close the lid but came back around the car, machete dangling from his right hand.

At first, Steve laughed. "You're naked? Hey, what are you doing with that?"

Lance smiled. "I thought maybe I'd chop you up."

Much to Lance's surprise, Steve never hesitated. He just turned and ran. Lance was sure there would have been at least another question in there somewhere. That would have given him a chance to strike, but no. Steve, the homeless drug addict, knew right away that this was no joke.

"Oh boy." Lance laughed with giddy surprise. The bastard was running. He might get away and then the game would end even before it started. In the instant before he gave chase, a scenario played out in his mind. What would happen if this drugged-out derelict got away? Maybe he would say nothing. Homeless types, especially drug addicted ones, avoided the cops. But then, Steve might appear down the road and finger him. *"He was a crazy, naked dude with a machete!"* How far was it to the interstate? A mile and a half? Maybe two? If he didn't bring him down by then, he'd have to get the hell out of here.

His paralysis broken, Lance tightened his grip on the machete and set out after him. Still giddy, laughter spilled out of him as he called out, "Hey, Steve, I'm just kidding."

Steve wasn't buying it and kept running.

Instead of panic, Lance found this both funny and exciting. The peril of losing the prey was almost as exciting as the looming kill. Beneath his bare feet, the rocky earth bit into his soles, and he was aware that his manhood was swinging left and right, up and down, bouncing with each piston of his widening stride.

Lance felt alive, more alive than he had in his entire life. And he had to give some of that credit to Homeless Steve. He was no marathon runner. But shit, for a junkie he still knew how to beat his feet. They ran approximately four hundred yards, Lance gaining ground, tightening his grip on the blade. When he was close enough, he swung the machete in a sideways motion and caught Steve right below the elbow. There was a wet thud, and part of Steve fell onto the road. His right arm. Lance almost tripped over it. And still, Steve kept going, ropes of blood now spirting from the severed stump.

Then, he simply collapsed.

Lance jumped on top of him, raised the blade and suddenly felt a red-hot sting below his chin. Homeless Steve lashed out with his good arm, digging his nails into his Lance's neck, raking away at the flesh. Lance pulled down his arm—turned the machete—brought it down. There was another sound, one he had never heard before. A gurgling sound. Steve's assaulting left arm went stiff, clawed the air and fell away. He was still for a moment. Lance took a breath, thinking it was over, then Steve bucked under him, splashing in the expanding pond of his blood. He fought with the last of his strength. Lance finally pushed down on the blade, and after piercing a lung, it broke through the flesh and into the dirt below.

He held him there. Waited for him to bleed out.

In labored breaths, Steve asked, "Why are you doing this?"

No reply from Lance.

"I would have serviced you, man."

Again, no reply.

Steve coughed up blood, trying to say something. Then his eyes went motionless, pupils contracting. His life force was gone.

Lance deliberated over the body. Much in the same way he had with the girl and her kid. He felt something spiritual in this act. He caressed the dead man's cheek with the back of his hand.

"Where have you gone?" he asked. "To heaven? To hell?" A single drop of blood plopped down onto Lance's hand. He reached up, touched the wound below his chin. A single scrape, dewdrops of blood pinched through the scratch and smeared beneath his probing finger.

"Fuck!"

Nothing went as planned. The initial drama was exhilarating, but it could have easily gone the wrong way. He considered the blood, the mess and most of all the offending hand. Next time, he'd have to be better prepared. When the blood from Steve's wounds stopped pumping, he went to work.

He severed Homeless Steve's head, legs, and the remaining arm. He left the torso in place and moved the amputated body parts proximately a foot away from each severed joint. Homeless Steve looked like a macabre puzzle. Before he wrapped up, Lance looked down at that troublesome hand, the one that had come up and taken a strip of his skin.

"Fuck," he said again and cut off the offending hand.

He had wanted to arrange the body with all appendages complete and severed from the torso, but this one had run and screwed that up. He looked at his arms; there was blood on them. Steve's blood. He gazed down at himself and realized he had an erection.

He laughed.

When had that happened?

After cleaning up, he wrapped the hand in a plastic bag
and took it with him. An hour later, he ventured out into
a treed area and buried the hand. He buried it deep. He
disposed of the machete in a pond and left the camping gear
on a picnic table in another rest area along I-90. He took
the rental to a carwash and had them do an interior cleaning
on it. There was no evidence of violence in the car, but he
wanted to be sure it got a thorough wipe down.

4

The following day, as the state cops were taping off the
grisly scene, Lance was on a plane bound for Williamsport,
Pennsylvania. The rental car he dropped off was already on
the road with a new customer.

***

CHAPTER 4 –THE EXPERIMENTS

1

Phase I

04 September 2001

Lawrenceville, PA

If Homeless Steve had been anything, he'd been an education. Lance had underestimated the drug addict's survival instinct and had spent the rest of the summer working on a remedy to the problem. He did not want to deal with the drama of fighting with his victims; it was far too risky. Steve might have gotten away, but worse, if Steve had used his head and turned on him, he might have overpowered him and gained control of the machete. That was a very real possibility as Lance was not a big man, standing only five feet nine inches. The other issue was the struggle itself. Steve had caught a swatch of skin from under Lance's chin, and that meant that the hand could not be left.

Lance had done a great deal of reading on the subject of true crime and paid interest to forensics. According to a pathologist out of Houston, the human body drops DNA everywhere it goes. Hair and skin mostly. When you wrestle with someone, the possibility of your skin cells ending up in a fold of the other's clothing is higher than average. In fact, one killer's DNA was found within the ligatures he used to strangle his victims, and it was this evidence that would lead to his undoing. The story alarmed Lance because he had struggled with Steve before killing him, and that fight had included wrestling. They might have his DNA right now, and Lance concluded that it was probably 50/50.

What he thought might help his case was the three days of summer thunderstorms that followed the killing. He hoped that the rains would wash away any dropped DNA. Hoped, but still, if he were that lucky, shaving and stripping down before the ritual would not be enough. He'd need to incapacitate the next one, but he'd also needed to encapsulate himself. Stop the shedding, so to say.

The first order of business was disabling his subjects. He'd thought about using drugs, but that came with a whole list of issues, so he abandoned that idea right off. He began studying human anatomy, thought he needed a sleeper pinch of sorts. Then as he examined the skeletal makeup of the human body, it came to him. The spinal cord. It was the pathway from the brain that carried messages to all appendages. If he could block that, it would make his job all the easier.

He'd need test subjects.

2

The guinea pigs came in the form of a wayward dog and a feral cat that roamed the woods behind the cottage. The dog, owned by the couple who ran the gas station in Tioga, was an affable mutt, allowed to roam free and came willingly into his vehicle after he held out an offering. Happy, tongue hanging from its mouth and inquisitive, the dog was oblivious to the danger. It was a mutt to be sure, a black lab mixed with something from the sheep herding family. Lance wasn't sure of the breed, nor did he care; he just wanted to test his theory.

He got back to the cabin and led the dog out of the vehicle. He set up a bowl of water, and it drank as he got out a few more treats to entice its trust. He led the dog to the grounds behind the cabin, telling it what a good boy it was and dropping another dog treat.

The mutt was wagging its tail, crunching away on the Milk-Bone he'd provided, completely unaware that the man was producing an instrument of pain.

The dog only heard his praise.

"You're a good boy. So very hungry and so very smart."

The dog finished the Milk-Bone, enjoying a final pat on the head. Then came betrayal, agonizing pain, and fear.

When Lance stabbed it with the pick, there was a crunch of breaking cartilage, but once that gave way, the pick disappeared three inches into the dog's back. What came next was pain, not for the dog, but for Lance. The mutt turned its head lightning fast—probably without its volition—biting him on the hand. It was a reaction to the attack, the last defense against an aggressor, pure instinct.

Lance pulled his hand away, leaving the pick embedded between the dog's shoulder blades, curling it up defensively against his breastbone. It had hurt him, but it hadn't broken the skin. Ignoring the pain, he studied the dog with morbid fascination.

It whined a whistling sound that conveyed confusion, pain, fear, and then it tried to take a step and stumbled. Lance did not approach; he simply watched as it tried to will itself up and flee the bad man who had betrayed it.

"Eureka!" he cried, happy with his experiment.

Then the dog let out a long, unnerving yelp of agony, calling for rescue. It began to howl, again and again, seemingly louder with each cry, and echoing out across the forest to God knew where. He thought it might relent, but the shrieks only grew louder, more desperate and accusatory.

Lance panicked. What if a neighbor were to hear? He tried to quiet the dog, stupidly telling it to hush but it ignored his attempts to calm and carried on with its harangue. "Quiet," he said. "Quiet, someone will hear!" He reached out with a hand, and then pulled it back when it bared its teeth at him. What was he thinking? The mutt had already bit him, and now with an ice pick embedded in its back, it wouldn't accept his comfort. The dog let out another long, agonizing call. It was a call for help, to anyone who could save it. And it was echoing out into the valley.

Someone will hear this! It's too loud!

The dog, although immobilized from running away, did not let up continuing its call.

Fuck fuck fuck!

He had lost control of the experiment. There was a risk of being discovered from the howling dog. The neighbors up the road... *if they were home*... might hear this. He got to his feet, darted for the back of the cottage, the cries going out into the day.

Shut up! Shut up! Shut up!

He grabbed the axe handle, heaved up, prying the blade from its resting stump.

The dog let out another high, anguished howl.

He bounded back in great strides, lifting the axe overhead.

It readied itself for another, and the axe came down.

The cries had been stifled.

Lance was electric with terror, but the exhilaration was dominant. He felt that same rush of sexual excitement he had when he killed Homeless Steve. He was hard, and thought he might ejaculate. So he left the dead dog, went to the edge of the woods, and finished what had involuntarily started. When he reached climax, the release was pinnacle, and he fell to his knees. Letting out great gasps, he smiled, then laughed giddily. "That was close!" He zipped up. "Oh fuck, that was close!"

He walked back, put a tarp on the dog and axe, and made his way around the cottage to the driveway where he stood perfectly still. He listened.

A minute passed, then two, then three.

Nothing.

A grin crept across his face. A snicker of triumphant laughter escaped him.

"Fuck, that was close," he said and turned to walk back up the short drive.

Then he heard a vehicle, and his heart began drumming.

"Shit." He turned back around, saw a truck coming up the road. It was Donny Williams' GMC Pickup. Williams owned a summer place about a mile up the road. He and Lance's father had never gotten along, but the man was always nice to Lance.

Lance stood erect, watching the truck as it approached and slowed. "Great," he said through gritted teeth. The only plus was that Williams was coming back from town, instead of going the other way. So it was unlikely he had heard the yelping mutt.

The truck stopped, and the electric window on the passenger side rolled down.

Lance walked down to meet him. In the back of his mind, he thought he should open the door, and drag the old guy out of the pickup, and try out the ice pick on him. It wasn't like Donny Williams had a lot to live for. He was into his seventies, and his wife, Sandy, had died the previous summer. Now he was just a lonely old man, who stopped to say hi all the time. He even showed sympathy when Lance's father and mother died. Told him how sorry he was. But Donny Williams was a native Pennsylvanian, and he considered Lance's dead father a New York blowhard.

"Afternoon, Lance."

Lance hunched over to look in the window. "Hi, Mr. Williams."

"You back from school?"

Lance paused before responding, noting the bottle of Jim Beam laying on the seat. It was half empty, and the fragrance wafted from the passenger window. Apparently, Donny

Williams was drowning his sorrows in a bottle, drinking and driving to boot. "I finished school last year. I might go back for a while to reinforce a few courses, but I'm done."

"Ah, okay. Listen, if you want to chat or come up for a drink..."

Lance nodded, thinking. *Miserable old man, I should take you back, use the ice pick on you.* But he said, "Thanks, Mr. Williams. I'm not much of drinker. I appreciate the offer."

Williams smiled, then his brow furrowed. "What are you doing out here all by yourself, Lance? Seems to me a boy your age should be chasing down young ladies. Ain't it kinda lonely without your parents there?" Williams had slurred slightly between the last three words of his question.

"Yes," Lance lied. "I miss my mom's cooking and going hunting with Dad." While thinking, *I should open the door to this truck and drag you out. I could poke you repeatedly with the ice pick and watch you bleed out like a spaghetti strainer.*

Williams nodded, albeit faux sympathy. "How long are you hanging around?"

None of your fucking business, Lance thought, and said, "Probably into November, I'm going to do some renovations on the place. Fix it up a bit."

"Ah, okay. Are you getting Tony Pride to do the reno?" Tony Pride was a local contractor.

My oh my, Donny, aren't we nosy? Lance kept up the grin. Ignored the urge to drag the old coot from the truck and said, "Actually, no. I'm going to do them myself. Mostly just replacing old wood with new and changing up some old electrical."

"Good idea, don't need no fire..." Williams' face fell, realizing what he said. "I'm sorry, Lance. That just slipped out, no disrespect to your mom and dad."

Lance stared at him, his eyes stabbing into him. The remark hadn't offended him, and if Donny Williams hadn't said anything, it would have been ignored. But Lance saw an opportunity to intimidate the old guy and latched onto it. "It's tough, Mr. Williams. I still have nightmares about it."

"I'm sorry. I misspoke." Williams looked sincere.

"It's okay, I guess you feel the same way what with Mrs. Williams withering away from cancer. My mom always said, 'She was such a nice lady,'" he said, and failed to add that his mother also included that "She was much too nice for the likes of that old coot Donny."

Williams' mouth twisted into a tangle. He was overcome by grief.

Lance pushed it a little further. "We all have ways of dealing with grief. I choose to build and create. You choose..." Lance reached in and flicked the JB bottle with his index finger, and it gave out a *tink.* "I'm not judging you, Mr. Williams. I'm guessing it's tougher for you than me. I've got time on my side and a future."

Williams was frozen in disbelief.

"You shouldn't drink and drive, Donny. Someone might get hurt. Maybe you."

"That's from yesterday. I... haven't had a drink today."

"Yes, you have, and I believe that you are well over the legal limit. Someone might call the police. You could get in trouble. There are kids around here, Donny. What if you ran one of them down? Losing a wife or a parent is terrible, but a child?" Lance flicked the bottle with his middle finger again, and then there was another audible *tink.*

Williams looked down at the bottle then brought his guilty eyes up to meet Lance.

Lance decided that was enough. "We're neighbors, Mr. Williams, and that means we look out for each other while minding our business. Do you understand what I mean?"

Williams hadn't the foggiest, but nodded anyway.

Lance withdrew from the window and smiled pleasantly. "Have a nice day, Mr. Williams."

Williams' response was clunky, mechanical, alarmed. "You too, Lance."

The pickup crept away, its driver stealing frightened glances in the rearview mirror.

Lance waved, but the farewell was not returned.

When the truck rounded the bend and disappeared, Lance turned and went back up the drive. Listening again and satisfied that he would not be bothered, he removed the tarp from the dead animal.

Sitting beside the lifeless carcass, he considered the outcome of the experiment. It had, except for a minor dog bite and the unnerving cries, been a success. The pick had done its job. He reached over and extracted it. A thin sheen of ruby droplets coated the metal spike.

Puncturing the vertebrae would incapacitate a victim, but it would not quiet them. The dog had shown him that. A man or a woman would likely beg and scream until they shredded their vocal cords.

So a remote location was a must, not that it hadn't been before. He decided he would need one more test subject, and this time he had one in mind who wouldn't be missed or find their picture tacked to a telephone post or taped to a store window.

3

Phase II

09 September 2001

Lawrenceville, PA

The cat had been trickier. Lance used an old animal trap he found stored in the shed to capture the cat. The trap had been around for at least ten years and was still in fair shape, but needed to be oiled and cleaned up. His father had bought it to capture and kill raccoons, possums, and any other animal he deemed a nuisance. The steel trap had become a regular death row for nocturnal critters until a skunk came along and infected the thing. His father couldn't be bothered to clean it up, so he abandoned it, along with the notion that he couldn't completely cleanse the property of critters.

Lance discovered the trap at the edge of the property on an evening when his father and mother had left him home to go for drinks in town with friends. It smelled horrible but invited possibilities. He went into the cabin, raided his father's bar fridge, and brought back two large cans of tomato juice. After giving it a good soaking, he let it sit for a few hours, and then dragged it back toward the house where he used the garden hose to clean it off. It still smelled, so he repeated the process, methodically wiping the mesh cage with a tomato juice-soaked rag. After a few more hours, the trap didn't smell of skunk, but the tomato juice residue on the ground was a disaster. It didn't soak in, floating atop the grass in congealing clumps, and Lance had to spend more time with the hose and the garden rake to make it disappear.

Even then, at the tender age of nine, he was aware that his actions were wrong, that a boy trapping animals to torture and kill would not be acceptable to adults. He knew it was not the normal thing to do. But the need outweighed the norm, and so he went to great lengths to cover his tracks. The repeated torture and killing of small creatures commenced with a ground squirrel and evolved to rabbits, raccoons, possums, but no skunks.

When Lance retrieved the trap from the shed, he wondered how it had gotten there. The last thing he remembered was leaving it at the edge of the property, where his killing ground was. Perhaps his father had found and retrieved it? Maybe. It didn't really matter; his father was dead.

The trap had been cleaned up, set out in the back forty and a tin of open tuna had been set as bait. Sometime during the night, the feral cat had been trapped.

That had been the easy part; the hard part was getting it out of the cage. He had to get on a bunch of protective gear, including a thick jacket, two pairs of leather gloves and a towel in which to wrap the razor claws, which would undoubtedly tear him to pieces.

He could control the cat before spiking it, but he was quite sure the beast would have come back and killed him out of spite had it gotten away. It fought hard, hissing, growling and twisting like an insane mongoose. He opened the top of the cage and put a towel over the animal. It struggled, knocking the towel away. With no other choice, he raised the ice pick, aiming the spike into its vertebrae. The animal lifted from the trap floor, let out a short cry, then fell still.

Lance slowly removed the towel from the cage. The feline lay still, all four of its legs hung limp. It did not howl like the dog, but let out whispery growls. "Fuck with me and I'll take something very precious from you," those growls warned.

He unlatched the trap's door and half-expected the cat to make a bolt out the opening. He kept his eyes on the beast as he wrapped the towel around his gloved hand. He couldn't accomplish what he wanted within the confines of the cage, so he reached in, placing the towel over its head, and pulled it out. It hissed and snapped beneath the towel, one of its needle incisors piercing terry cloth, but not the leather work glove.

Once he had it out, they locked eyes as it snarled and spat at him. Lance admired the cat, thinking how steadfast it was in standing its ground. Even without the ability to pounce or claw, it kept up the provocation. He reached out with one gloved hand checking each limb of the animal, tugging it for a reaction and there was none. After confirming the creature was paralyzed, he sighed.

One thing left to do, he thought and went for the cleaver.

He buried the cat next to the dog. Another deposit into a large field of animal bones, although the bones of those dead were almost a decade old now. The earth had all but eaten the frames of the animals he had hunted here in his childhood.

Phase III

11 September 2001

Lawrenceville, PA

He'd thought shaving everything would have eliminated a chance of DNA shedding at a kill, but he had learned that was not the case. He was now aware that if he had just taken the condoms after making his first two kills, his DNA would have been harvested by crime scene people.

He'd made the mistake of having sex with her, rubbing his skin against hers. This gave him a visual of the flaking skin caught between their rubbing bodies. Exploding into the air and then onto the bed sheets along with his droplets of perspiration, her pubic hairs, all carrying within their fiber the building blocks of life. The floating spiral staircase that told the world everything about you.

Lucky to have burned the house, but was he lucky with Homeless Steve? It had started raining when he left Steve's body in the road. Raining hard. Had the rains washed it all away? How would one go about finding out such a thing? Certainly, the authorities would not make such information public unless they had a suspect.

He agonized over Steve for quite a while.

Then he let it go.

I can't change that.

He couldn't, but he could avoid dropping further DNA at future kill sites, and make sure that even if they had his, they wouldn't be getting any future specimens. The question was...

How?

The answer came to him in a deep state of meditation on the morning of 9/11. On his father's fifty-five-inch big screen, the World Trade Center burned after being hit by two commercial aircraft. Then the Pentagon was hit. Then, in the very state in which he spent torturing and killing two animals, a plane nosedived into a field near Shanksville, Pennsylvania.

He watched the towers crumble live on his television; thousands being murdered before his eyes, and all he could think was the architect of this masterpiece had stolen his thunder. Then he thought he'd better get back to the next phase of his experiment.

5

First, he tried lotions, walking to the back of the property like a loner nudist. The scent of Jergens skin lotion attracted mosquitoes better than any dinner bell. He had to run back to the cabin with a swarm of bloodsuckers in tow. By the time he got inside and under the shower, he had at least forty fresh bites.

He did a bit of research about mosquitoes and was surprised to discover that perfumes of any sort attracted them in droves. The four bottles of lotion he'd purchased from CVS in Lawrenceville went right into the garbage.

That was when he settled on Vaseline.

It had next to no scent and did not absorb into the skin as fast as a lotion. Absorption was a big deal—he wanted to contain—if it absorbed, the building blocks of life would again fall where they may.

Using clippers, Lance shaved his head and looking in the mirror, he began to apply the Vaseline oil. Finished he went back out into the property under the milky glow of the moon. As he trudged naked, he thought about real-life cannibal Edward Gein.

Gein, who had only killed two people, inspired the likes of Norman Bates and the *Texas Chainsaw Massacre*. Gein liked dancing under the cover of darkness in a suit fashioned from the skin of the dead. He was just a crazy grave robber who liked to use body parts in the pursuit of arts and crafts. Two victims, maybe three if you included his brother, but that was never proven. But still, Ed Gein had become a household name. It was all about presentation. That house, the soup bowls made out of skulls, chairs upholstered in skin... so what if he'd only killed two or three people, Ed Gein was a master presenter.

He felt something fly into the small of his back and stick. It flapped violently. He kept moving across the property, catching glimpses of his naked form as the moon's rays cut through the gaps in the trees. Something else hit his leg just below the buttock. He hardly noticed; he was thinking about the dog and cat, mostly the cat, and when a ray of full moonlight caught his groin area, he saw the erection he hadn't felt.

He stopped, looked down at himself. Another flying creature banged against the nape of his neck but managed to break free. He stepped out of the shadows into the direct light of the moon, glimmering in its milky white light. More insects beat against him, sticking to the Vaseline. Lance ignored the creatures, instead staring up at the moon and began masturbating like crazy old Eddy Gein.

Later, when he entered the cabin, his grip left the front doorknob greasy. He pushed into the bathroom. Considering himself in the mirror, he saw that he was coated with hundreds of them. Most of the moths were flapping their death throes as they succumbed to the greasy substance which held them and stole the powder from their wings. Anyone else would be nauseated, but Lance just smiled.

His legs were weak, the session of self-gratification had been long and purposely drawn out. He turned on the shower and stepped in. The insects fell away as the water pulsed against his body, but they did not fall intact. The Vaseline held onto broken limbs and wings until he applied the shaving cream to dilute the Vaseline. He smoothed off the outer skin, the war paint he would use in his next killing. Under the wash of water and shaving cream, the remaining bugs became a muck that rolled off him. At his feet, gray bits of insect swirled toward the open drain and were eventually gone.

Drying off, he considered the difficulty of removing the greasy substance from his entire body, but more so the space on his back where he couldn't reach. The Vaseline was not a total failure, but he would have to find a better way to encapsulate the rest of his body.

6

13 September 2001

Lawrenceville, PA

Two days after the Twin Towers disappeared from the Manhattan skyline, Lance had an epiphany. The third came when he was thumbing through a Lowe's flyer and saw the neoprene painter's suit. They came in all sizes, were throwaway, and he began to think about his next kill, and how this one had to be perfect. The presentation was almost as good as the meal. This next one would be methodical, and set to send a message.

Sitting before his laptop, he brought up a map of the United States, gazing over the landscape while zeroing in on major cities. Those cities would be his hubs, ones with large airports and car rentals. As he scanned, his eyes caught on a strange name. Missoula. Was that Native?

***

CHAPTER 5 – THE ONE-EYED MAN

1

12 October 2001

Old US Route 10, east of Riverbend, MT

Barber didn't consider himself homeless, or what some would call a bum. He had money, he worked odd jobs, and he was always on the move. Drifter seemed unfitting as well; the stigma attached to the name always rubbed him wrong. Drifters usually meant trouble, like thievery, and were usually represented as so in the movies. Barber considered himself honest, and other than an arrest or two for vagrancy, he kept his nose clean. When interacting with law enforcement, he was sure to be respectful, using "Yes, sir" and "No, sir" when addressing even the most arrogant cop.

On his back, he carried a jump ruck, something from his days in the airborne. It was an olive drab piece of canvas fitted over a tube-steel frame that sat high on his shoulders. It was comfortable and carried all the provisions he needed to set up a camp.

Barber had been a sergeant in the 82nd Airborne and served the country in three campaigns, but after losing his left eye in 1999, he was released back into the civilian world. The loss of his eye came not from enemy fire, but a poorly maintained .50-caliber machine gun that exploded during range practice. The year after was spent in a VA hospital, which resulted in rebuilding his eye socket and fitting a glass eye. That had been the year of pain, he recalled. A year of oxy, constipation, and eventual withdrawal. It had also been the year he realized that, like most veterans, he was a throwaway.

In 2000, with a newly-fitted eye and no fixed address, he hit the road. He had little time for people. Even less time for a wife who bedded men while he was laid up on his back in the VA hospital. He took his meager pension, packed up his gear, and set out to walk the highways of America. He'd been walking ever since, wearing the soles from numerous pairs of shoes. He also hitchhiked and was not afraid to take the kindness of strangers, but his closest confidant was God, whom he spoke with regularly. Although God didn't answer, Barber was confident that He was always listening.

2

Montana: state of rolling hills, winding rivers, and dense forest. Not only a haven for campers and anglers, but provided many secluded sites in which to carry out heinous acts. As Barber walked towards a road where he thought he might explore and set up camp, a vehicle exited out that same road and passed him coming west.

The car seemed insignificant at the time. It was a mid-size sedan, but he could no more remember the make than the physical attributes of the driver. Had he known what he would find, he would have paid closer attention, but he had seen so many cars come and go along the routes he walked, and this one was no different.

Except it was.

When it passed, he raised a friendly wave, which was not returned. No big deal, plenty of folks regarded travelers like him with a suspicious eye. Barber walked on toward the side road as the car continued its westerly jaunt. What caught Barber's one good eye was that the car slowed as it rounded the bend. Only moments later, he was sure he could feel himself being watched.

He stopped, gazing back over his shoulder, trying to catch a glimpse of the voyeur, but saw nothing. His vision was only half that of the normal man, with poor depth perception and lousy far sight. But he still had a sixth sense about being watched, a harkening back to his days as a military man.

"What's that all about?" he asked God.

He had a feeling something wasn't right, that the driver of that car was watching him, to see what he'd do. He moved off the shoulder and unclipped his hunting knife. As he did, he took in the side road the car had come out of and was now sure that the driver was waiting to see if he ventured down it.

"He's back there. Isn't he?"

God's silence was answer enough.

3

Lance was still riding on a high of murder when he spotted the drifter coming down the road. Up until this point, everything had gone perfectly. He'd picked up the female hitchhiker outside the state capital and incapacitated her when they pulled over for a pee stop on the shoulder. The pick had worked perfectly, and so he drove to the spot he'd chosen earlier and went to work.

The entire ritual lasted two hours. He greased his face with Vaseline and got into the white neoprene painter's suit. Then he stripped her of all her clothing, placed the garments into a bag, and washed her body with rubbing alcohol. She had begged and cried, offered him sex, offered him anything to spare her. Lance ignored the begging, sponging her skin with the cool alcohol, wiping away any evidence. He did not engage her even in the slightest; *she* had become *it*. It had been his third since Homeless Steve.

"Please let me go. I won't tell."

He removed the machete from its sheath.

"No. Please, please, please." It was crying.

He raised the blade and said, "It will all be over shortly," then brought it down. It screamed as he knew it would, but the screams weakened after that first cut, diminishing with each beat of its heart. Its complexion turned alabaster as its lifeforce bled out. He proceeded with the dismemberment, the other arm, the legs, and finally the head.

He hunkered over the body, his face gleaming in the afternoon light and listening to the sounds of the forest. He positioned each limb a foot away from the point of severance. Once finished, he proceeded to the river and cleaned himself and his tools up.

Two hours and fifteen minutes later, he turned back onto the highway, intent on melding into the world of anonymity. In his trunk, the woman's belongings, encapsulated in a black garbage bag along with the painter's suit. He would dispose of those in a dumpster far from here. They would probably end up in a landfill somewhere, burned or buried before anyone would be the wiser.

That's when he saw the drifter coming up the road. A lanky man a little over six foot, carrying a pack and using a walking stick. He pulled out onto the highway, drove toward the man, thinking about what to do. He considered just stepping on the gas and running him down, but that would leave damage on the car and questions when he returned it to the airport. He also considered pulling over, sticking the big man with the pick, and maybe getting a two-for-one deal. This fellow looked like he might be as dangerous as the feral cat, possibly more. No, better to just drive on by. Maybe keep an eye on him. So that's what Lance did. He drove by, the man waved, Lance kept his eyes to the front, and he waited until he rounded the bend before stopping the car and putting on the four-way flashers.

He got out of the vehicle and moved up a hill into the trees beside the highway. If anyone asked, he was pulling over for a piss, nothing more. He climbed the bank and moved along until he got a glimpse of the drifter. He wished he had a set of binoculars, but he could see the old guy was looking back over his shoulder.

"Can you see me, old man?"

As if called, the old guy turned toward him.

He pulled back defensively, then snuck another peek. The old guy was looking his way, then looking at the road Lance had come out. "Come on, do something."

Something, Lance hoped, was walk on down the highway and forget about that road. If he went down that road, Lance would be forced to follow and kill the old guy.

4

Barber sensed danger, was sure if he walked back, he'd find that car idling on the side of the road with the driver watching him. He sensed it the very same way he sensed the enemy on the battlefield. But why? Why would the guy in the car care about a loner like him?

"Maybe he's a drug dealer?"

God remained quiet.

He gazed out the road once more and pondered. *If I go down that road, he might just double back and follow me. If I pass by it, he'll likely carry on and forget about me.*

But Barber wanted to know what was down that road; it was bothering him. He wanted to know. Being inquisitive was Ray Barber's Achilles' heel. Even though he knew going down that road might bring to his world unforeseen troubles, he knew he just couldn't walk away and forget it.

The immediate issue was whether to see if the onlooker was real or imagined.

"Should I stay? Or should I go?"

Barber decided to make a game of it. He was about one hundred yards from the turnout. The rules of the game were simple. He would walk to the turn. If his left foot touched the ground upon reaching the corner, he'd carry on; if he dropped his right, he would turn right and take his chances.

5

He was in his own world of debate. One which would decide the life of the indecisive man standing on the highway.

If the guy turns right, I go back down that road and chop his head off, he thought. *No rituals. Just get in, kill him, and carry on.*

He'd already seen the car, so there was no point in taking chances. But there was a chance to be had in killing this man, so if he carried on, Lance would let him go. Yes, carry on is what Lance wanted him to do because after two or three cars passed this drifter on the highway, the rental would begin to fade from the old guy's head.

The man began to walk, and Lance bit his lower lip as he watched. He didn't want to kill the older bugger, not because he had sated the bloodlust with the hitchhiker, he just knew the risk of doing something uncalculated might lead to his undoing.

The man walked with purpose, his stick bobbing along beside him as he strode out a hundred yards to the side road. Lance also considered the man might prove a dangerous adversary who might have something up his sleeve. The knapsack looked military, the walking stick looked daunting, and the character himself looked formidable.

You really want to try and knock that down?

He didn't. He wanted that man to keep on walking and forget about what might be up that road. Keep walking and do them both a favor, because he felt he'd already hung around too long. What if a cop came meandering along, or a game warden looking for poachers? The drifter was almost two-thirds the distance now. Thirty plus yards from the road.

Keep walking, old timer. Don't stop.

Fifteen yards and Lance could actually feel his pulse elevating. He should just go down to the car and drive away. This was insane, the risk was too high. He didn't want to get caught.

Hurry up, damn it!

Five yards now, and the old guy was slowing down.

Lance had the car keys in his right hand, squeezing them tight, the metal had become slick with sweat and biting into the skin of his palm. "Keep going!"

6

When Barber reached the corner, his right foot lifted off and his left touched down. That decided it, and he kept walking, never bothering to look down that road, nor turning to catch a glimpse of the voyeur he was sure had been watching. He marched on, and before he knew it, the road was a hundred yards behind him, then two. He had no idea how close his brush with death had been. Or the relief exhibited by the watcher who was now making his way back to the car.

He pushed on down the highway, tapping his walking stick against the asphalt, shifting the pack, and thinking about the side road he'd left behind. Before long, the sun slipped away in the west, and the sky was speckled by a million pinpricks of blue light. The night air was cool against his face, and he figured he'd walked at least three miles since abandoning the desire to investigate the side road.

He stopped.

It had been long enough; he could go back for a look now without the intrusive eye of the stranger. A three-mile walk would take at least forty-five minutes if he made it a brisk pace. He could do that, he was in good shape, the muscles in his legs were solid, hardened by the thousands of miles he'd already marched. Some other traveler might fret about backtracking three miles they had already covered, but not Barber. He had no place to be, no real destination, and up until that defining moment when he realized he was being watched, he had planned on setting down for the night.

He started back.

It actually only took thirty-five minutes, his pace had been strong and steady, reminiscent of the forced marches he did when he was in the airborne. Standing on the side road, he gazed down Old US Route 10, listening for approaching traffic. He even considered walking to the bend where he was sure the stranger had been parked and watching, but that was half a mile, and he deemed it unnecessary. The guy had to be long gone. For all he knew, the feeling might have been nothing more than paranoia.

Bullshit, he was watching.

"Okay, but he's gone now," Barber muttered to himself before walking down the road. The pavement lasted for about two hundred yards, then it broke up, turning first to gravel and eventually hard packed sand. He could smell the water from the river, which led him to the thought this might lead to a boat launch, a fishing hole, or even an old campground. Fishing hole and campground sounded fine to him. Maybe the guy was down there smoking a bit of pot, doing a little illegal fishing?

Maybe.

The road narrowed, leaving barely enough room for a single vehicle. There were wheel ruts on either side of a center crown that certainly posed a risk to a car's oil pan. Overhead, the trees clasped branches, making Barber feel as though he were walking inside a tunnel of foliage. The wind picked up ever so slightly, sending ghostly whispers through the canopy and a shiver up his spine.

He was nearing the river, could hear the water lapping against the bank, and saw the road widening out enough for a vehicle to turn around. He also could see something else at the end of the road on the ground about fifty yards up. As he closed in, it became more apparent what it was. Twenty yards away, he stopped, his heart palpitating in his chest, and listened. He turned his head to look back, half expecting the stranger to be standing there in front of the car that crept in under stealth. He could hear the stranger saying, "You should have kept walking, pal."

But there was nobody.

Just the same, Ray Barber unsheathed his hunting knife and hung it by his side, then he ambled toward the body. His temples were pulsing—sweat beading on his brow—as he reluctantly closed in on the horrific find.

Jesus. Jesus. Jesus.

Barber had seen some very grotesque things during his time as a soldier. He had born witness to the worst kind of atrocities, seeing women and children murdered at the hands of extremists, and though one would think that his nerve would be unshakable, nothing could be further from the truth.

"Who would do such a thing?"

He was standing over the body of a woman who had been cut into five pieces. Head, arms, legs all removed and placed neatly at the point of severance. Even in the dark, Barber could see the stain where the first cut was made. There the blood was a thick, dark syrup under the night sky and floated above the dusty road like motor oil. The other cuts did not have puddles with the same circumference, which left him to presume that the heart was winding down by the second, third, fourth, and fifth cuts.

He could have identified each in succession by the amount of blood spilled, but Barber wasn't feeling particularly analytical. He was thinking about what would have happened if he had dropped his right foot to the ground instead of the left. What if he had come down here while being watched by the man who did this?

The monster who did this.

He was backing away, bringing the knife up in front of him and turning to make sure no one was watching, waiting, feeling so exposed. He stepped off the road and into the wood line where he tripped and fell down. He went face first; turning the knife sideways, he caught himself before taking out his good eye on a protruding branch. The thought of being completely blind was even more terrifying than what he had found. He got on all fours, then carefully raised himself up.

Slowly he moved into the tree line away from the side road, while his brain countered every scenario like, what if this was just the first body? What if he's bringing back more victims? What if this is a dumping ground? What if he's cruising around now looking for the one man who saw him and his vehicle?

I never really saw him.

Nor had he really seen the car. It was a sedan, but he wasn't even sure of the color. What was it? Tan? Green? He wasn't sure. Barber hadn't felt a need to zero in on the stranger. As far he was concerned, the man was just one among thousands, who posed zero threat, he'd seen in his travels.

He doesn't know that!

Barber worked his way through the woods, tapping into his past and becoming the soldier he once was. He listened with the same heightened attentiveness he had when patrolling in hostile territory. He was afraid, there was no doubt about that. This wasn't a "Johnny Rambo Movie," this was real life, and the guy who had cut up that body was as deadly as any crazy Rwandan or self-righteous Croat. He moved slowly, pushing branches carefully aside, stepping lightly. Listening to the night.

Twenty minutes later, Barber stood at the edge of the wood line on Old US Route 10, approximately a mile east of the access road. He looked in both directions, reassuring himself that the coast was clear. It had been at least two hours since the encounter and Barber reasoned that hanging around would have posed a risk of being caught. Only killers in horror movies came back. This monster had to be long gone. This made sense, but his nerves were still humming electrically, and he shook in the upshot of an adrenaline rush.

What do I do now?

The obvious answer was going to the police. What would he tell them? Maybe they would think he did it. After all, he was a war vet, a drifter, and a one-eyed man. Wasn't the freeway killer Henry Lee Lucas a drifter, and hell, he even had one eye.

"Maybe they'll try and pin it on me," he mumbled.

God was silent.

Barber knew he'd have to report it, and he'd have to come back with them and show them the body's location. The person on that road needed him to do the right thing. If that meant enduring unwarranted accusations or suspicious minds, so be it. He was east of Riverbend; he thought they would probably have trooper detachment there or at least some local cops. Even if they had neither, they would have a phone.

Ray Barber got moving. He walked for almost an hour when an approaching car began to slow. Unable to identify what type of vehicle that loomed behind the headlights, he felt his anxiety rise. He reached down and unclasped the metal button which locked his hunting knife into its sheath.

Just in case, he thought.

The car pulled onto the shoulder, gravel crunching beneath its tires until it came to a complete stop. Barber also stopped and faced the vehicle, looking for an out if things went sideways.

The fan on the car kicked in, and the sound made Barber jump. He expected the driver's door would swing open and the man behind the wheel would get out. Two things happened next.

A female voice on the loudspeaker called, "Please stand there and don't move." Next, the light bar on the Montana State Trooper car came alive and painted the night red and blue.

Ray Barber let out a bewildered sigh and got his hands out where the police officer could see them. Under his breath, he said, "Thank you, Lord."

***

CHAPTER 6 – CONNECTING THE DOTS

1

18 October 2001

FBI Headquarters - Quantico, VA

FBI Agent Lewis Ash was waiting to see the deputy director. He had been contacted by a cop out of Sistersville, WV, who had connected the dots on three murders of similar circumstance after entering data about a stranger killing into the Violent Criminal Apprehension Program, ViCAP for short. The investigator, Corporal Fred Riordan, was assigned the case by the Sistersville Police Department after a body of an unidentified male victim was found in a wooded area off State Route 7.

Initially, Riordan had drawn a similarity between his murder and that of a murder committed up in North Perry, Ohio. The similarities were the locales of the bodies. Both had been in dense forest, located off a highway, and with a river nearby. But the way the murders had been committed was what caught Riordan's eye. Both victims had had their head, arms, and legs amputated from the torso. The only significant difference was that his victim had been naked while the male victim in Ohio had been clothed. Also, for some reason, the North Perry victim was missing a hand.

Riordan was a tenacious police officer, and even though there was not much in the way of physical evidence, he was convinced that the Ohio killer and his killer were one and the same. He also thought it was only a matter of time before the perpetrator would strike again.

It took a week and a half.

An investigator out of Riverbend, MT, entered data on a killing that had occurred off Old US Route 10. The similarities between Riverbend and Sistersville were uncanny. Riordan contacted the investigators from North Perry and Riverbend and had lengthy conversations, comparing notes. Once he was sure, he took it to his boss, Sheriff Greg Keagle, who agreed that the murders were connected and authorized him to contact the FBI.

Lewis Ash was the one who read the email request sent to the director of the National Center for the Analysis of Violent Crime (NCAVC). Normally, the request would have gone to a regional department of the FBI, but Riordan had sent it directly to Quantico. A lucky mistake on his part because the FBI was in the throes of a post-9/11 world. Terrorism had taken priority over everything. If the request had gone to the regional department, it would have slowly worked its way through the bureaucracy, and by the time it was assigned a liaison agent, it could have been months.

Ash intercepted the email, and after looking at the ViCAP entries for all three crimes, he got on the telephone to Riordan, and they had a conversation. Riordan confided to Ash that they had very little in the way of physical evidence. A tire impression in the mud, but nothing else. "Our medical examiner said, 'The victim was wiped down with rubbing alcohol pre-mortem.' The victim also had a puncture wound just below the neck, and this individual severed every appendage from the torso."

"Do the other two victims have puncture wounds?" Ash asked.

"The one in North Perry didn't, but then he was clothed and missing a hand. So maybe he's not connected," Riordan said but figured the victim was. It had been his first connection after all.

"Possible. It could be coincidence, but I wouldn't knock him off the list just yet. Could be your boy was just starting out and now he's refining his technique," Ash said.

"You think it's a guy?"

"Yeah, unless we're talking about a real Amazonian lady with an axe to grind, but you've got both male and female victims, and that points to a male perpetrator. Also, your victim was over six feet tall. I'm doubtful your killer is female. But then, I've been called a dinosaur who is insensitive to the gains the feminist movement has made in the last decade," Ash said dryly.

Riordan laughed. "Who calls you that?"

"A female agent in Behavioral Science." Ash paused. "I trained her, and she is one of the best."

There was a moment of awkward silence, Riordan didn't really get the joke, so he reverted to his issue. "I'm not sure how to proceed here, Agent Ash. If this guy is killing in multiple states, we don't have the jurisdiction or the budget to mount an investigation. That's why I contacted you folks."

Ash was quiet. That was why local law enforcement always contacted the FBI. But in this case, Riordan was right. The killings were occurring across state lines, and this made it a federal concern.

He finished up with Riordan.

"Okay, send me the phone numbers for the other two investigators. If you could send me your case file, I'll take it home with me and follow up with the other two investigators. If I can make a case that they are all connected, I'll see if I can get in to see my boss on Monday and see how we can proceed."

"I'll email everything I got," Riordan said.

Ash gave him his bureau email address and said, "Corporal Riordan, nice police work. I'll be in touch after the weekend."

After making the calls to the same people Riordan had called, going over the case files he requested from Riordan and the other departments, Ash was convinced they had a serial killer on their hands. One who may have committed more murders than the three they had open cases on.

He met with Deputy Director Charles Wilkins that morning and got authorization to open an investigation. He also requested that an agent named Michelle Leigh coordinate from Quantico and that FBI Pathologist Wilbur Simons be assigned to the case.

"Ash, as much as I hate to say this, we are under a lot of pressure from Washington on the terror issue," Wilkins said. He wasn't kidding either; the Ten Most Wanted fugitives had been wiped clean and names like 9/11 architect Khalid Sheikh Mohammed had found their way into the top ten. Wilkins continued a song and dance about manpower shortages. How everything was taking a back seat to terrorism.

Ash, a thirty-year veteran of the bureau, finally said, "Charlie," the deputy director's first name, "this killer is just getting warmed up. If we don't get moving on this, there will be a lot more victims."

Wilkins sighed. "Okay, Lewis. You can use Leigh and Simons, but you're the field agent. If you are going to go hopping all over the country, I better not get expense reports for BMW rentals or high-end hotels."

"What about Mercedes?" Ash smiled and stood up.

"Not funny." Wilkins shook his hand.

"Thank you, sir."

"Yeah." Wilkins smiled, but he looked exhausted. The attacks on 9/11 had taken a toll on the FBI, and they were under extreme pressure to redirect their focus.

The FBI investigation was authorized.

Special Agent Lewis Ash had been right in his prediction.

2

2 November 2001

Central Falls, RI

Victim four turned up three weeks after the Montana discovery. Investigators identified her as a homeless person who resided in Providence, RI. Like the others, her body was dismembered. Head, arms, and legs all removed. The first victim, Steve Quinn, had been killed outside of Cleveland, Ohio. Upon being killed, his right hand had been removed in what the Ohio investigators thought to be trophy collection. They were wrong, and Ash thought it was obvious why the hand was removed.

In police circles, the killer was referred to as Highwayman for obvious reasons. Highwayman, right from his initial kill, had dismembered every victim, but after that first kill, he began undressing his victims before dissecting them. All the amputations had been done by the same weapon. FBI Pathologist Wilbur Simons said, The clean cuts pointed to a machete. They were similar to comparisons he'd seen before. When Ash asked him how many machete murders he'd been privy to Simons said, "Thousands." When Ash pushed him, thinking the number to be a joke. Simons explained he had been a part of a United Nations inspection team after the Rwandan genocide in 1994. "You don't get clean cuts like these with anything but a machete, Lewis. An ax will dull, and it splinters the bone. A sharp machete cuts clean."

Also, in every case, the victim had been driven to the scene and surprisingly not one tire casting matched. Some were BFGoodrich, some Goodyear, a lot were aftermarket tires. So Ash knew that their man came to the scene with a new vehicle every time. Investigators believed the perpetrator of these crimes might be stealing vehicles. But they weren't sure. "He sure as hell isn't carrying around three different sets of tires." Aside from that ridiculous notion, the wheelbase on each vehicle was different. Ash had local law enforcement going through all the car thefts in the area.

Back in Quantico, Special Agent Leigh was working up a profile based on what they had so far. The profile put Highwayman somewhere between the age of twenty-seven and thirty-five, Caucasian male. He was meticulous, likely educated, and sadistic as well as narcissistic. Profiling wasn't the psychic magic portrayed by Hollywood. Investigators don't know every detail of a suspect based off a profile. Profiling itself was still under heavy scrutiny by police departments.

Ash knew it for what it was. A framework of facts married to comparable crime data. They only figured Highwayman for a white guy because most serial killers murder within their own race. There were no crystal balls when they came to this sort of thing. Leigh's report identified him as a narcissist, sociopathic, and planned. The Highwayman was an organized killer, he left little trace evidence and brought his own tools. The cuts on the bodies were becoming more precise. Stephen Quinn had been cut up chaotically, but Ash thought this was all a part of the killer's evolution. He was honing his craft, improving with every kill.

He gazed down at the body, scratched his chin, thought about it for a second. Thought about the others. *He wants us to see this. It's probably driving him crazy at the thought this has not made it onto the national news.*

Lewis felt a sudden vibration against his breastbone, it was a cell phone. He stood back up, removed the phone, glanced at the screen; it was Leigh. He answered the call. "Ash."

"How's it going there, Lewis?" Michelle Leigh asked.

"Female victim. Same MO, except there aren't any tire tracks to cast this time. Too much snow." He gazed down at the body. The exposed muscle was bubblegum pink, the torso and severed appendages had puddles of frozen blood between them, dusted over by snow. The victim's skin had a hue of pale blue.

"Does she have the same puncture wound?"

"Can't tell right now, Michelle. The body is literally frozen to the ground. We are going to have to warm it up before transport."

The puncture wound Leigh spoke of was a puncture between the victim's second and third cervical vertebrae. The puncture was likely done by a sharpened pick. Wilbur had referenced an ice pick, but Ash wasn't even sure if ice picks were used anymore. Whatever the weapon of choice, it was sharp and effective. They were sure that he used the puncture as a way of immobilizing his victims. Once the spinal cord was breached, the victim would lose all motor action. And then, this was where the sadist part came in. With his victims still alive, he would amputate. Ash thought the severed cord would alleviate the pain, but Wilbur doubted it. He told Ash that even quadriplegics sometimes felt pain in their invalid extremities.

"Holy shit," Ash had responded.

"Holy shit indeed. We need to catch this guy, Lewis. He's a torturing sadist."

"Yeah, you're probably the hundredth person to tell me that, Wilbur."

"Lewis?" Leigh snapped him back from the thought.

"Yeah, Michelle. If I were a betting man, I'd say this is definitely Highwayman. Where is Wilbur right now?"

"He'll be landing in Providence in two hours."

Wilbur Simons was the best forensics man the FBI had. A former New York City coroner, he had overseen thousands of autopsies involving murder victims. He was a stout little man, standing just shy of five foot four, but what he lacked in height he made up in knowledge. Wilbur was highly respected within the law enforcement community. He had worked on some of the highest profile cases in the United States. He had written the textbook on crime scene gathering. He preached that every crime scene was an evidence field that had to be treated with the utmost respect. If Wilbur had his way, he would dig the soil out around a body to preserve the evidence. He insisted that everything from snow to water to mud be brought to the coroner's office to be examined. Some considered Wilbur Simons as arrogant, anti-social, or even just a plain SOB. And that might well have been true, but he was the best, and that was why Ash asked for him directly.

The Highwayman was ramping up. He would be increasing his portfolio of victims exponentially. The problem with that was the fear that after fulfilling his fantasies, he might go dormant. The latter concerned Lewis a great deal. He did not want to be at the head of an investigation that went dormant.

Lewis walked out of the crime scene leaving the body behind. Outside of the cordoned off area, Rhode Island State Troopers were gathered in a group. Among them were two troopers, a sergeant, and a lieutenant. Lewis liked the Rhode Island State Troopers, they were keeping everything locked down. Very professional. They were also very accommodating in a situation when tensions could get high. Nobody appreciated some government guy coming in and taking over their case.

With the Ohio cops, it got territorial, but these guys were accommodating. Ash had spoken with the colonel over the phone. That was another thing he got a kick out of. Rhode Island cops used military rank structure. Well, actually most state police did, but the Rhode Island cops went right up to full bird colonel.

"Agent Ash," the lieutenant, named Bart, said. "When can we remove the deceased?"

"I'm waiting for our lead pathologist. He'll want a look before she's moved. Also, I don't want anybody walking over this crime scene until he's had a chance to go through and get the body out."

"Is this him?" Bart said. "The Highwayman?"

"Yeah, looks to be," Ash replied.

"So this is the Highwayman for sure?" The lieutenant sounded excited, like maybe he was getting the media bug.

Ash bristled and turned his eyes up to meet Lieutenant Bart. "I want you to listen to me right now. You saw what happened in there. This bastard is chopping his victims into six pieces. He's crying for attention. If he gets it, he might just double down. I don't want to hear the word *Highwayman* mumbled anywhere around the media. You guys want to talk amongst yourselves, that's fine, but understand me. If you give this fucking ghoul a platform, he will up the body count. I've seen it before. Make sure you rein in your troops, no leaks. Not about Highwayman, not about the crime scene details. Do we understand each other?"

Bart nodded. "Completely."

Lewis studied him for a second. He could feel this man's dislike at being ordered around, and Ash couldn't blame him. Nobody likes getting their case walked on by an outsider. He tried to be empathetic, but he had little time for that sort of thing.

Highwayman. Jesus Christ. That's exactly what this guy wants.

He wanted a handle because with that came notoriety. This one was leaving bodies a certain way because he's an attention whore. Lewis was surprised they had not received a letter or a manifesto from the freak. "Look, we both want the same thing. To get this fucking creep off the street. I've been doing this a long time, I know what I'm talking about." Ash managed a smile.

Bart seemed to relax a little. "I understand."

"I'm going to need a rundown of any stolen vehicles you have in the last twenty-four hours. That might be helpful."

"You think he stole a vehicle?"

"Here's a little off the record for you. Every crime scene we've been to, we've collected the tire tracks and not two vehicles are the same. This guy is bringing a different vehicle to every crime scene. The way I figure it, unless this guy is Jay Leno and has a huge car collection, he is stealing a vehicle before he commits each crime to throw us off. We're not a hundred percent on this, but that's the way we're leaning. Best to run down the stolen vehicles, maybe we'll get a hit."

"Maybe we already have him in custody," Bart said.

"Maybe," Lewis said, but he didn't believe it. This guy was just too smart for that sort of thing. He wasn't completely sold on a stolen car theory. But that's all they had right now. Lewis looked up. The sky was pallid gray threatening more snow. "We're going to need to get a tent over this body before my man arrives."

3

An hour and a half later, Wilbur Simons arrived at the scene and was led down by Ash. He was pleased by what he had found. "Well, Lewis, maybe this time we'll catch a break," Wilbur said.

"What makes you think that?"

Wilbur smiled. "What would you say the temperature is?"

"I don't know twenty-nine or thirty degrees," Lewis glanced at his phone, it was thirty-one degrees. "You think he left something behind?"

"I absolutely think he left something behind."

"Yeah, why do you think that?"

"A hunch."

"It's getting late, Wilbur. My feet are cold. Please get to the point."

"He hasn't left a thread or a button behind. You'd think we would've found something: a thread, a pubic hair maybe, but nothing. I believe we're going to find something this time."

Ash jammed his hands in his pockets and stamped his feet. "You already said that. Why?"

"The cold. It holds onto things. Judging by the state of the body, I'd say that it began to freeze not long after the heart stopped beating. If our friend dropped even a single fiber, it's somewhere in this mess that used to be a woman."

"I hope you're right."

Wilbur Simons said, "Me too. Tell the ME he can come down, and to bring a couple of men with shovels. I want everything gathered up, snow, ground debris, *everything*, and brought back to the morgue."

4

4 November 2001

Quantico, VA

An autopsy was performed in Providence under the direction of Simon and Chief Coroner Billy Keen. Keen had found the fibers caught in the frozen coagulant lifted from the ground. There were thirteen samples recovered, and they were sent priority to the ontology department in Quantico.

The fibers were matched to throw away neoprene coveralls. The type that could be bought at almost any hardware store, mostly used for painting or cleanup. Wilbur had been right, and if they could find those coveralls, they could match them exactly to this crime scene.

Leigh contacted Ash via cell to tell him the good news, and he had flown back to Quantico for a meet. They were sitting at a conference table, the case files spread out uniformly, the crime scene photos punctuating each file.

"Looks like our boy messed up," Lewis said and smiled.

"You don't think this guy was stupid enough to buy the coveralls locally?" Leigh asked.

"No, I don't, not in Central Falls, but maybe in an adjacent town in Mass or Connecticut."

"That's a lot of real estate," Leigh said.

"I know." He sighed. "The fucking guy's killing me. What have we got to lose? Let's get local law enforcement to canvas hardware stores from Central Falls to Providence. Who knows, maybe we'll get a hit? Not too many painters work in the winter. Maybe we'll shake something loose."

"Okay, I'll get the word out."

***

CHAPTER 7 – ROGUE MESSIAH

1

19 April 2002

Portland Police Bureau - Shift Briefing

"Moving to the last item on our list," the staff sergeant said to the room of police officers, "I have received a ViCAP update from the Federal Bureau of Investigation."

There were heckling "boos" from a couple of officers.

"Alright, knock it off!" He set his steely gaze upon the room, and that silenced them. "Right now, there is an unknown subject hopping from state to state and killing. The killer has taken at least nine lives. All have been procured from a separate state, usually from a major city, and all have been taken to a remote location and murdered. The MO of the perpetrator is as follows. He trolls areas of each city where drug use and homelessness are high. Modes of transportation have varied, but the murders are definitely connected." The sergeant cleared his throat and continued. "The deputy director of the FBI has asked all major metropolitan police departments to be on the lookout for any suspicious characters trolling areas of high prostitution and drug use. The chief has authorized extra patrol cars in assigned areas. Check the roster to see if you have been assigned."

More groans—papers shuffling—then whispers.

"Pay attention," the sergeant commanded. "The man they are looking for has struck at least nine times. We need to keep our eyes open, folks, this guy hasn't struck in Portland, but he might. Questions?"

"Do they have a description of the suspect?" a female detective from Vice asked.

"No. At this time, there are no witness descriptions of the suspect. They don't have anything."

"That's a tall order, Sarge," an older uniformed cop said.

"I know." The sergeant lifted a single sheet of paper from his podium and held it before his audience. "I have copies of the ViCAP alert outlining the crimes already committed. I know we don't have a lot to go on, but make your presence known. Question anyone who is driving a car and propositioning the locals. Do a search, but make sure you have cause. If you should snag an individual who feels strange, use extreme caution, call for backup. This guy is probably carrying a murder bag. Any other questions?"

There were none.

"Alright, that's it for the main shift. Be sure to pick up a copy of the ViCAP alert on your way out and check the roster. I need the following people from Major Crimes to stay behind for a more in-depth brief: Jorgens, Walters, Pinelli, Helmand..."

2

20 April 2002

Portland, OR

It was morning; the rain fell from the sky, beating against his windshield and obscuring the view. The wipers were on full, barely keeping up with the sheets of rain. They gave a steady *Whump! Whump! Whump!* as they swept back and forth. The rain was not making it easy.

He was on the hunt, cruising for a suitable subject. But the streets were quiet, and the pickings slim. He'd checked the weather network, and they had predicted sunshine.

"Bunch of fucking liars," he seethed. That was when the police siren squawked and his back windshield came alive with red and blue light. "Fuck."

He pulled the car onto the shoulder. His stomach became a knot of worms, twisting and writhing. He glanced into the rearview, could barely make out the shape of a police cruiser, and began to go over his rehearsed story.

"I'm down to do some camping. Just flew in and thought I'd check out Portland, maybe have some breakfast."

The police car door opened.

Lance reached into the center console, got the rental agreement. Pulled out his driver's license. "I got lost, don't know the area very well. Shit, that sounds like bullshit."

From his driver's side mirror, a single police officer was getting out. It was a man.

Calm down, it's just a routine stop. Maybe you have a taillight out.

Then the passenger door opened, and another cop was getting out. Female.

"Oh fuck," he said and wiped his hands on his pants. He took a couple of deep breaths and let the last out slowly. He put both hands on the steering wheel where they could be seen and tried to relax. *It's all good, you got lost on the way from the airport. You're going to spend the week camping and fishing in Longview.*

They were coming. One up the right. The other up the left.

He reached over and pushed the buttons, lowering both the driver and passenger windows. Then he placed his hands back on the wheel and waited.

"Good morning," the male officer said.

"Hi," Lance said, out of his peripheral he could see the female cop looking in the back of the car.

The male cop smiled. "Can I have your license and registration?"

Lance reached onto the seat and lifted the prepped items. "Did I do something wrong?" He handed them to the male cop.

The male cop didn't answer his question. Instead, he studied the license. "New York? What brings you to Portland, Lance?"

Lance, not Mr. Belanger, he thought. *Condescending fuck!* Then. "I'm taking a week to go fishing up in Longview. Spring break." He gave a weak smile, trying not to gaze in the direction of the female officer, who was inventorying the items on the back seat that she could see: fishing rod, sleeping bag, army duffle, an electric lantern.

Simultaneously, Lance was thinking about the things she couldn't see: machete, white neoprene painter's suit, ice pick, garbage bags, a bottle of rubbing alcohol.

He asked again, "Did I do something wrong?"

The male officer said, "You're going the wrong way for Longview. You've come south, you should be headed north."

"I had to buy camping supplies," Lance said and then regretted it. *What if they asked for a receipt? The machete is on the receipt. They might conduct a search.*

If they did, he was screwed.

The male cop said, "Hang tough, Lance. I'll be right back."

The cop walked back to the cruiser while the female cop hung out at his passenger window. She was looking down at the passenger seat. "That your map?"

Lance was still looking out the side view mirror watching the male cop. "Huh?" He turned toward her, trying not to show how worried he was.

"Your map." She pointed.

"Oh yeah." He locked eyes with her. She was only a year or two older than him. Not bad looking, a little flat chested, but fit. She had brown hair pulled back in a bun and tucked neatly beneath the brim of her cap. Her name tag read Rollo. He figured that Officer Rollo was probably a rookie.

"Mind if I look at it?" She smiled reassuringly.

"Sure." Lance picked the map up off the seat and passed it to her. He forced himself to relax. *They don't know anything,* he thought. *If they did, I'd be in the back of their cruiser. And they'd be tossing this car.* He stole a glance in the rearview. The male cop was on the radio.

Officer Rollo checked the Oregon road map and saw that Longview was circled. "How come you aren't spring breaking in Florida?"

Lance grinned. "I'm not much of a party hound. I'd rather go fishing than spend a week nursing a hangover."

The male cop was getting out of his car, coming back.

Lance braced himself.

The male cop, Lavers according to his nametag, hunkered down so that he and Lance were eye level. "You know why I pulled you over, Lance?"

"Honestly, no." Lance shook his head.

"This part of Portland is a high crime area, lots of prostitution, drugs, the occasional murder. We've got gang activity around here. When we see a car out of place, like yours, it raises a red flag. A lot of people who wouldn't normally be found here usually come for one reason or another. Do you know what that is?"

Lance said, "To buy drugs?"

"Yeah. Drugs or even sex. You're not here for either of those things. Right?"

Lance laughed. "No. I honestly got lost. I just want to get out of the city and up to Longview."

Officer Lavers smiled. "Okay. I ran your license and you've got no priors. I'm going to give you the benefit of the doubt and send you on your way." He handed the license and rental agreement back.

Lance took them. "Thanks."

"You're welcome. You need some directions to get out of here?" Lavers grinned.

"I'd really appreciate some," Lance said. He did his best to look embarrassed.

As Officer Lavers gave him directions, Lance jotted them down on his map. When he was done, he gave him a final warning. "I don't want to see you down here again, Lance."

"Don't worry, I have no interest in coming down here. Especially after what you told me." Lance smiled and said, "Thanks for your help."

"Have a nice day," Lavers said.

"Good luck with the fishing," Rollo added and when Lance pulled away, the two officers made their way back to the cruiser. Rollo turned to her partner and asked, "What do you think?"

"Probably telling the truth, he came back clean."

"He had Longview circled on the map. He also had fishing and camping gear in the back seat. And he was young. I doubt he's a serial killer, more likely a nerdy kid who can't read a map."

"Or get laid," Lavers joked. "But just to be safe, I'll put his name to the list."

The rain stopped.

3

20 April 2002

Interstate 5 - 26 Miles East of Grants Pass, OR

It was dark. Sheila was stumbling along the paved shoulder of Interstate 5, focused on the thin pencil line of light ahead. She had to get to Rogue Valley. Her head was a soup of nonsense and voices, feet bare and raw from the sandpaper friction of the blacktop, but she had to get there. To passerbys, not that there were any, she would have looked drunk or stoned, but Sheila was neither. She was following the voice of the Gray Man—he was leading her to the one who held her baby. The Gray knew what they had done with her baby, he was calling to her through a remote viewer.

"You have to come, Sheila," the Gray urged. "Come to Rogue Valley. By whatever means necessary." Whatever means had been her feet, because she wasn't allowed to drive. They'd taken her license after the accident. The car hauled away on a tow truck never to be seen again. She missed her car, but they saw to taking that away, saw to taking her baby as well. It was a machination because they knew that he was the second coming. "Move your feet, girl. The dogs of Satan are all around us, and they want to sacrifice your baby." She picked them up, placed one in front of the other, ignoring the sting of broken blisters.

"I'm coming," she said and continued on. She'd come back to life, waking from the drug-induced dream her mother and father had placed her in. The Messiah's children were being slaughtered all over the world, by fundamentalists, by the governments, and the legions of Satan's Army were doing this for one purpose. To stop the second coming. To prevent her child from freeing the world.

That was why they took her car. Why her parents shut off the Internet, and took away her home computer. It was why they insisted she was sick. Why they took her child, who was born of the immaculate conception night last month.

"Take these pills, Sheila," her mother said. "You aren't well. They will help you feel better."

"I want my baby!"

"There is no baby. You're sick, Sheila."

"No! You bring my baby back right now!" She struck her. Some would be aghast that she would hit a woman in her sixties, but the wrinkled skin was just a cloak, she was much younger. The Devil's children wore the skins of old people.

Strong hands fell upon her, her father's, Satan's advocate, the man who had handed her child over to the worshippers of Hell. He restrained her, and soon people showed up, wearing uniforms, disguised as paramedics, but she saw the black gloss in their eyes. More sycophants of the Antichrist, looking to quiet her about the child's birth, the savior she had sacrificed her femininity to bring forth, the salvation of the world.

They took her away, poked her with needles and restrained her for all to see in her neighborhood. She screamed out for help, begged for God to come, but she had to bear this burden alone. Soon, the drugs her mother said would clarify her world muddied it. She was silenced about the Messiah, his dark other and the unfolding of the rapture. Soon, she was swimming in the purgatorial murk, away from the judges and lawyers, while her son, the chosen one, would be hidden from the world that needed saving.

That was when the voice began speaking to her, telling her that she had to comply with their wishes at least until they let down their guard, and she could do something to find him.

"I am with you," the voice said. "I will be with you until you find him."

"Why can't I see you?"

"Because I am the Gray. Take the treatments and the pills, Sheila. If you resist, they will lock you in Purgatory indefinitely until they find a way to kill the chosen one."

"No, they can't!"

Overhead, the air conditioning duct blew cold air down upon her, the restraints on her wrists and legs biting into the skin as she struggled with the terrible news.

Why? Why would they kill the child of light? Her child. God's child!

"Stop resisting," the Gray said, "You must lull them into believing that you are going back to sleep, forgetting all that you know. You have to stop fighting, Sheila."

So she did.

It took three months.

Reprogramming, medication, and doing everything they told her. She cried when it seemed applicable, agreed when they told her she'd been sick. Gave them every reason to believe she was getting better. She took the pills that silenced the voices. She sat with Mom and Dad, listened to their fabrications and lies and agreed that she had been the source of the misery. That there was no child, no worldwide conspiracy, even though Christians were being beheaded and children were being murdered. Satisfied, Doctor Roland, if there ever was a phonier name, signed her release and she went home.

During the first days of freedom, she continued the pills, conforming, hugging her emotional mother. That was so hard, like embracing a tree of serpents. Her mom frequently cried, often asking, "How are we today, Sheila?"

To which she would respond, "Getting better every day, Mom."

And she was, but not how they thought. She took the pills. At first, she swallowed them when it was clear that both her mother and father were watching closely. Then she stored them under her tongue, sometimes until they almost dissolved and were near impossible to spit out or wash from her mouth with a glass of water that could be poured down the drain. Eventually, they began to trust her, or maybe they just became exhausted with the process altogether and gave up. Either way, the clarity returned. The Gray, who was always there, told her what to do and say.

"They are already lost, Sheila," he told her. "You have to leave and find your son before the Devil takes his heart."

"His heart," she whispered.

"Yes, the Devil will feast on his innocence. Then he will cast his darkness forth upon the land. He has already gotten to those you loved. You have to leave and find your son. Let no one stop you!"

4

The lights of Rogue Valley loomed just ahead—a mere two miles. From behind, headlights pushed her shadow diagonally across the blacktop.

"Oh no," she whispered. "Is it them?"

The Gray said nothing.

There was a flicker of high beam, on then off. An engine growled, geared down and slowed on approach. Sheila widened her stride, didn't dare look back, afraid the vehicle was going to bear down on her. But it rolled past and slowed, brake lights polluting the night with crimson radiance.

Then it stopped on the shoulder, only twenty feet ahead.

Sheila froze in her tracks, wishing the car would drive off, hoping the driver would change their mind, but after a few seconds, the driver's door swung open.

Out stepped a silhouette. It was a man, she knew this much, but she couldn't make him out. He said nothing at first, standing against a backwash of the car's headlights, barely illuminated in the glow of the tail. He was waiting for her to come forward, sizing her up.

She mustered her courage. Then called to the silhouette, "I'm okay." He didn't move, only stood there watching. So, she added, "You can go. I need to walk."

More silence, but the apparition standing next to the car held firm. He was a ghostly figure. Gray against the night. Sheila wondered if this might be the Gray Man?

"You need a ride," he said, not a question, a statement.

"No, I'm only going to Rogue Valley." Why had she told him this? He could be...

"I'll take you. That's why I'm here."

She felt a sudden hope. "Are you..."

"Yes," he said cutting her off.

It was him, the Gray Man had come. She took a step and stopped. She wanted to ask but didn't dare. *Talk to me*, she thought. *If this isn't you, please give me a warning.*

"Your feet are all bloody. You can't keep walking," he said.

"I don't know what to do." She felt the sting of hot tears.

"There isn't much time."

It was him. He was the Gray Man; he was here to help her. He moved around the back of the car to the passenger's side and opened the door. For an instant, he was caught in the glow of the car's interior light. He was thin and young, his hair slicked back, tight against his scalp. He returned to the driver's side.

"Rogue Valley awaits."

She hesitated, but only for a second, then moved forward right along the back of the car and up into the waiting passenger seat. She left the door open, and he climbed in beside her, closing his door. "I don't want you to fall out, can you please shut the door?"

"Okay," she said and pulled it shut.

He put the car in gear and got moving.

Sheila watched the lights, and he put on his signal. A sign indicated that they were approaching Highway 99. They passed the lights of the town and she said, "I'm going to Rogue Valley, you told me you'd take me there."

"I am, that's Gold Hill, not Rogue Valley." He wheeled the car up over the interstate, the town lights she'd been following washed across the interior of the car, lighting his face. He was young and thin, in his twenties.

He said, "Do you really know where you're going?"

"To Rogue Valley," she said but sounded unsure. "Do you?"

"Yes." He turned and smiled. "To the River, the Rogue River."

"Is that the place where they have him?"

He smiled. "Yes."

"You're taking me to him?"

"Yes." He turned his attention back to the road, they were now traveling along Highway 99 following the contour of the Rogue River. He drove in silence, focused on the lines, and Sheila faded in and out. She was tired and afraid, but she did not ask him the question that seemed so appropriate.

Not yet.

The bottoms of her feet burned horribly against the rubber floor mat. On the dashboard, she saw a sticker that said Thank you for not smoking. All Avis rentals are smoke-free.

"This isn't your car?"

"No, it's a rental. I don't own a car."

"How long until we're there?"

"Maybe five minutes. I'll have to kill the lights and park a ways out. We'll have to walk in. Don't want anyone seeing us." He turned to her, willing a reaction.

"It is you," she said.

"Yes." He smiled reassuringly.

5

Five minutes turned into ten when they rolled off the main road and onto a path that paralleled Interstate 5. Gravel crunched beneath the wheels as they slowed to a stop. Sheila watched the man, who seemed steadfast and determined.

"How far will we walk?"

"Not far."

"And that is where he is?"

"Yeah."

He got out of the car, came around, and opened her door, then helped her from the vehicle. She felt the pain the minute her feet touched the cool, hard ground. "It hurts."

"Shhh," he soothed and placed a finger across her lips. "We don't want anyone hearing us."

She bit into her cheek as they walked down a path to the clearing ahead; she was suddenly unsure. She could hear no voices, no indication that this was the place the Gray had spoken of. Only the river lapping against the bank and the wind tickling the tree branches. She stopped again, and he did as well.

"Come on," he said and approached her.

Then she asked, "Are you the Gray Man?"

"No." He was only feet away, reaching out and suddenly he grabbed her, pulling her into an embrace.

She tried to cry out, but all that came was a shrill squeak. She tried to pull away, saw his free arm rise as she was spun around. She pulled out of his grasp, thinking she might be able to run away on her bloodied feet, but then...

There was a burning, just below the nape of her neck. He had stabbed her with something, in the spine, just over the shoulder blades. Hot, liquid pain bowled down her spine, across her shoulders, scalding agony. She could not cry out.

Then he twisted it, and she heard the cartilage snap, vertebrae crunch, felt the fluid leaking, and she knew that it was not just blood. Her legs buckled, they along with her arms had become clay-like. In them, a faint static electricity tingled. Gravity took her then, she could not bring her arms up, and she fell to the ground striking her cheekbone against a jutting stone.

She lost consciousness.

He dragged her to the clearing, undressed her, and prepared for the ritual. He squeezed the tube of Vaseline, burnished his face, got into the coveralls. His skin glistened under the night sky, he looked almost alien. She was still unconscious when he removed her clothes, positioned her, and sponged her body with rubbing alcohol. She hadn't been planned, not like the others, and there was an element of risk, but that risk excited him.

They were on an outcropping, hidden from the interstate by a collection of trees, the Rogue River was at least a quarter mile out. He would use that to clean up when he was done.

6

When she regained consciousness, he was leaning over her, watching. Her cheek had swollen, flecks of grit from the rock embedded beneath her skin. She could not feel her arms or legs but knew that she was naked. She could not even turn her head, her neck a jumble of bound, cramping muscle. She traversed her eyes left and right, caught sight of his naked form glistening under the stars.

Demon, she thought. *He's going to rape me.*

"Where were you really going?" he asked.

"To get my child." Her voice was a whimper.

"In Rogue Valley?"

"Yes," she moaned.

Why was he asking? Surely this demon knew that?

I am going to die.

"Why were you walking, barefoot?"

I must confess my sins before Satan infects me with his seed!

"Holy God, Lord most gracious! Rebuke me not in your anger, nor chasten me in your wrath," she prayed.

"Answer my question."

"I confess to you that my heart was not pure. That I did deeds of murder. I feel unworthy, for I have failed you again and again." Her voice was a chant.

"Murder?" He was reaching for something.

"Have mercy on me, O God."

"Who is the Gray Man?"

"Oh Lord, Heavenly Father. Have mercy!"

He brought the machete up for her to see. Her eyes caught sight of the long blade. "I'm going to ask you again. Who is the Gray Man?"

He was lifting it, preparing to strike.

"Accept me into your heart, oh Lord."

"Enough," he said and brought the blade down. There was no pain, a chunking sound of separating meat and bone, a ropy glut sprayed upward, then rained across her bare breasts. His voice became hard, irate. "Who is the Gray Man?"

He pulled the severed arm away from the milking shoulder, positioning it as he had with the others. It suddenly felt cold. Then he, demon above, circled, and she thought he might yet rape her.

"It's okay, Sheila. You can tell him," the Gray whispered.

She barely managed. "I thought you were the Gray Man."

He held the blade up, ready to strike again and held there for a moment. "No, I am not the Gray Man."

"Who are you?" she moaned, slipping.

"I am the Highwayman," he said and chopped off her leg.

His words became far off.

Then he was gone.

7

Finished, Lance stood over the dismembered body, marveling at his handiwork, thinking how odd this one had been. Had she been lying? Or had she actually killed her parents? He wished he'd waited a little longer; this one had been different from the others, he might have learned something more, and his curiosity was on fire.

"Gray Man," he said to her. He still didn't know. Maybe the Gray Man was a cop. "Did you actually kill someone?"

Mute, lifeless eyes stared up into the night sky.

She had probably escaped from an asylum. A delusion, nothing more. But was it? What if this woman had killed somebody? If she had... If she'd killed someone, that would make her a hot commodity.

He stood, gathered his tools and walked down to the river to clean up. He was shielded from the interstate when a car drove by, and for some reason, that stirred a pool of anxiety in his heart. He cleansed himself in the water, using soap to wash away the Vaseline. The skin on his face was pocked from acne brought on by plugged pores.

Another car passed as he dressed.

The need to leave this place became paramount.

They might be looking for her already.

8

21 April 2002

Portland International Airport

Already through security, Lance leafed through the newspaper and found nothing to confirm a murder in Grants Pass or anywhere in and around the Rogue Valley. She was obviously insane, but by the time he was called for pre-boarding, he got his answer.

CNN's Oregon affiliate was reporting a double murder in Grants Pass. An elderly couple, William and Mandy Carbone, had been brutally murdered in their home.

"Officials from the Josephine Sheriff's Department are working in conjunction with the Grants Public Safety in relation to a double homicide. At present, both departments are looking for a third person of interest."

A picture flashed of the woman.

Lance was making his way forward, his identification ready to show the attendant.

"Sheila Carbone is the daughter of the two victims and has been missing since sometime yesterday. Grants Pass Deputy Sheriff Sheryl Landis has given the following statement. 'We are now searching for Sheila and are concerned for her well-being as she suffers from mental illness.'"

The spokesperson, presumably Landis, appeared on the screen. She was bookended by local and state police on either side. Cameras clicked and whirred as questions were asked.

"Is the daughter a suspect in the killings?" an unseen reporter asked.

"I cannot comment except to say that we are searching for her and that the public is not to approach her. As I said, she is mentally ill, and that makes her actions unpredictable. We do not know if she is a participant or a victim in this homicide."

She really did it, Lance thought. *She killed her parents.*

He almost laughed.

"Sir?"

He turned away from the television monitor and faced the attendant at the podium. She had her hand out. "Sorry," he said and gave her his ticket and identification.

"Quite alright, Lance." She said reading from his identification. "You are in 4C, on the aisle."

"Thank you," he said as she handed it back.

He passed through the archway and down to the waiting aircraft. As he walked, he thought that it was time to stop for a while. They would be hunting for this woman, and when they found her, they would believe that Highwayman had killed those people and killed her as well.

Was that such a bad thing? It would up his number by two. Thing was, he didn't want to be credited with something hadn't done. It felt like cheating.

It was time to go home. Recharge his batteries and start thinking about the next stage. He doubted the woman had covered her tracks. He was pretty sure that she'd left enough evidence behind to implicate herself in the murders, but what of this Gray Man she spoke of? He should have kept her alive a little longer. Asked her more questions about the Gray Man.

Was he real? Imagined?

Once in the air, he thought about his options. Portland had been close. Too close and he thought that being pulled over was no coincidence. It might be time to go dark for a while and change things up.

No more rentals. Rentals could be tracked. There would be records, there was also GPS and EZ Pass. It was time to change his hunting ground. He could feel them watching for him now.

You're just being paranoid, he told himself.

No, not paranoid. They were actively looking for him now. It was what he wanted, but now he had to be cautious. The crazy woman had been a stroke of luck, but he would have to think long and hard about how to proceed from here.

***

CHAPTER 8 - STARFISHED

1

3 May 2002

Off US 12 - Mayfield Lake

Near Mossyrock, WA

The day almost was done, the sun sinking into the Pacific. It was cool, the air hygienic from the cleansing April showers. A mild breeze whispered through the park's trees. If not for the circumstances, Ash thought that this might be one of the most beautiful places he'd ever seen. There were four police cars stacked up on the hard pack in single file. Except for the state police car blocking the main gate to the park, none of the car lights were flashing. He pulled his car in behind the last vehicle, a sheriff's car, and parked.

Highwayman had struck five more times since the body was found in Central Falls, RI, upping his kills to nine, and that wasn't including this latest discovery. As with the other killings, all had occurred in different states. Maine, Michigan, Wisconsin, Minnesota, and North Dakota were now added to the list of states visited by the Highwayman.

As with the other crime scenes, Ash found himself in the awkward introduction stage as he set out to meet the female detective in charge of the scene. Female cops were sometimes harder to work with than males, especially when it came to jurisdiction issues. "Hopefully, she's not a man-hating lesbian," Ash had said when Michelle gave him the contact info.

"Jesus Christ, Ash. You're a fucking dinosaur," Michelle Leigh had said on more than one occasion. "A misogynistic dinosaur at that."

"That might be, but I'm still right."

Michelle fell silent. He wondered if it was because she agreed with him. Or she'd given up?

He had his identification out and was making his way up to the uniform standing outside the crime scene tape. The young cop was sporting a thin, blond cookie duster above his lip. "FBI," Ash said. The cop, kid, didn't look old enough to drive, let alone carry a gun.

They all look like kids, he told himself. *I'm just getting old.*

"Agent Ash," said a woman behind the cookie duster. It was a black woman coming up the path. Obviously, the lead detective. She wore charcoal slacks and an open-collared, white button-up shirt. Her detective shield clipped to her belt and strangely, she wasn't carrying a gun. "Let him through, Ben."

The young cop looked back at the detective, nodded, and lifted the tape. "Go ahead, Agent."

"Thanks," Ash said and put away his ID. He stepped under the yellow tape as she came up to meet him.

"Detective Ann Gordon," She reached out a hand and he took it. Her grip was light, her skin soft and she smiled.

That was a good start.

"Lewis Ash." He shook. "Nice to meet you. What do you have?"

Gordon looked at him, tilted her head like a confused dog, and her smile widened. "I'd say your boy has come to Mossyrock."

"My boy?"

"The Highwayman."

Ash was ready to protest but decided against it. He was tired of lecturing cops, and besides, thus far Detective Ann Gordon seemed accommodating. No jurisdictional crap. No need for him to give a speech about it being an FBI case. Why mess with a good thing? He softened. Even grinned, and said, "Okay, I'll bite."

Her smile widened. "Same MO, the victim was starfished."

Starfished was a relatively new axiom. It had rolled through the police ranks and was destined to find its place among other veteran slangs like House Mouse, or Skell, or Keister-Bunny. Starfished meant chopped into six pieces, head, arms, legs and torso. Ash wasn't sure if it was specific to Highwayman, but he'd never heard it before. That was usually how these slangs got started. Someone sits down over a beer with another cop, and he recounts the scene and says, "The guy was all chopped up, like a starfish." Before long, every cop is using it or a variance thereof. Sooner or later, a victim who is decapitated or cut in half might earn a partial or half starfish.

"Can you fill me in?" Ash said.

"Sure, that lady over there," Gordon pointed at a blonde woman in her mid to late 30s sitting down on a picnic table unattended. Next to her was a dog and bicycle, "was out for a ride with her dog. As I understand it, the dog took off down the trail and into one of the camping spots. Thinking the dog might be after a wild animal, like a skunk, she stopped her bike and followed on foot."

"You got a lot of skunks around here?"

"A few, enough to concern the average dog owner. Coyotes are worse they'll set up a dog and kill it in a heartbeat."

"They were walking toward the crime scene."

"That's a big dog, what is he, a Great Dane? He looks like he'd make a meal out of a coyote."

"Bullmastiff," Gordon said. "And it's a she." She paused for effect.

"A she?" Ash stopped, gave her a quizzical look. "You'll have to excuse me, Detective Gordon, I'm genderblind."

There was a moment of uncertain silence between them. Then she smiled, and even let out a small laugh. "Coyotes don't fight fair. Even a dog that big could be taken down by a nasty pack of coyotes."

Ash stopped again. "Really?"

"Yeah, really." Gordon gazed up at him, Ash found her sort of charming. "Anyway, the lady follows the dog through the campground into the clearing behind, and on the other side of the bushes, she finds her dog gnawing on the victim's left arm."

"Oh, that's bad."

"Be happy the pooch didn't make off with it."

They turned into the camping spot. Beyond it, Ash saw a tent set up over the scene. It was a bright, mustard yellow modular. That was encouraging. "The dog gets props for not leaving the scene." He could smell the decay as they closed in. He studied the ground beyond the tent, looking for anything that might have been missed. "The arm inside the tent?"

"Yeah, along with our victim."

"The victim is male?"

"Yes, somewhere between twenty and forty. We can't determine the age on sight; he's undergone some pretty serious decomposition."

Ash moved around the tent, careful to not catch a peg corner with his foot. There was nothing worse than falling on your face at a crime scene, except maybe tossing your cookies. He seen both happen, he did not want to join those ranks or be remembered as a piece of slapstick. With this in mind, he pulled out a tube of menthol and dabbed below each nostril. The vapor overloaded his nostrils, but didn't completely wipe out the smell. You never blocked it all.

"Your people have already started collecting?" The question was moot; he knew they were already collecting, he was just making small talk as they entered the tent.

"Yeah."

He reached into his pocket, put on a set of gloves and looked down at the victim and said, "Starfished."

The body was in far worse shape than the others and he wondered why. Highwayman wanted his victims found, was making a statement by leaving them where they'd be easily located. Why was this one different?

"Any guesses on how long he's been here?"

"He was probably killed in the winter."

"Why?"

"The decomposition. We had a late winter this year. The snow just started to disappear a week ago. Most of the blood has soaked into the ground or been washed away, and if he'd been killed a few weeks ago, he would have been dragged off by other animals." She reached down and pointed at the torso. "The skin discoloration indicates freezing. If he'd been baking under the sun, we'd be looking at a mummy instead of the decaying specimen you see here."

Ash considered the victim, glanced around on the ground for other signs. "Did your people pick up any fibers?"

"They did, they are in the trunk of my car. White fibers. And there was a clear gelatin substance on two of the tree branches. I don't think its semen."

"It's Vaseline and the fibers will be from a coverall, but I'd like to send both to our lab in Quantico for testing."

"Vaseline?"

"Yeah, we've found it at two of the sites. We thought he might be using it for lube, but there is no trace of semen or DNA in it. No sexual interference with the other bodies."

He used his index finger to pull back the victim's right eyelid. The eye had fallen back in the socket; it was a stew of congealed mucus. He released the lid and had to pull it back down over the socket. "I agree, probably a winter kill."

"So, this is—"

Ash interrupted her. "I'd like to lift the torso, have a glance underneath. Could you help me with that?"

"Okay." She didn't sound enthusiastic about the prospect. "What do you need me to do?"

Ash reached into his pocket and pulled out a penlight. "I want to tilt the torso over to the right. I may have to brush away ground debris, so I'll need you to hold it until I'm done."

"Can't this wait for the ME?"

"It can, but this will give me a confirmation."

Gordon stared up at him, her face serious. She was considering this, and though Ash didn't know it, she was appreciative of the fact that Ash was giving her a nod. That this was still her crime scene. "Okay."

She put on a fresh set of gloves.

They were side by side now, their shoulders touching, kneeling before the body like it was a living being. Ash stole a glance at her. He said, "I'll lift, if he isn't stuck to the ground, and then I'll get you to hold him in place while I scoot around for a look."

"Okay, let's do it."

Ash took a deep breath, placed his left hand under the amputated shoulder and hooked his right beneath the hip bone. He squeezed the flesh gently, making sure he'd found the nubs of bone. He didn't want the torso to dissolve in his grip. Confident, he began to lift. The torso was lighter than he'd imagined and broke free from the ground with the slightest protest. From beneath, two ground beetles skittered and ran between his folded legs for cover. "Okay. You take hold. I am going to scoot around your right."

Gordon placed her right hand beside his, then her left, and took over. He moved back and she moved sideways into his position. A beetle crunched beneath her kneecap.

"Gross," she said.

"I know," Ash said, moving to the other side. "I hate bugs."

Gordon laughed.

Ash did as well, then went down on all fours. He turned on the penlight and shone it beneath the torso. There was a leaf stuck to the place between the shoulder blades. Carefully, he reached in and plucked it away to reveal a much larger hole than anticipated. The insects had gone to work on the puncture. He set the still lit pen light down and said, "Okay, you can lower it."

She lowered the torso as Ash picked up the light and replaced it in his pocket. He was pulling his gloves off, the elastic snapping as he did. He placed them into an evidence bag.

Gordon got up and did the same, then brushed at the crushed insect on the knee of her slacks she said, "So, this is Highwayman?"

"Yep. The Vaseline and the fiber will have to be tested, but I'm confident that testing will come back positive." Ash knelt for a last look, his knees cracked. He stayed that way for a moment considering, then stood back up again. "I'd like to walk the perimeter. After that, your people can take the body out and finish their evidence gathering."

She wasn't sure why he wanted to look underneath, wasn't privy to whatever detail he was holding back and decided not to push. "I appreciate that. Would you like me to accompany you?"

Ash glanced over at her. Normally, he'd say no. But he was warming up to Gordon. She was an astute woman, and there was something he found appealing about her. "Sure, if you'd like."

"I would," she said and smiled again. She had a pretty smile that made her brown eyes light up.

They walked the area in relative silence, Ash looking at the ground, the trees, the brush, for anything suspicious. He doubted he would find anything, but used the exercise as a way of meditating on the things he'd already seen, trying to compartmentalize the facts. He walked down to the shoreline, contemplated the setting sun and said to Gordon, "How did you hear about Highwayman?"

"Off the record?"

"Yeah, sure."

"I have a cousin in the bureau. He doesn't work for you, but we usually chat about cases. I have a voracious appetite for this sort of thing. I've been following the case since Central Falls."

Ash chuckled. "Even federal cops are gossip hounds."

"Why hasn't your forensic guy Simons shown up?"

"You really have been following along," Ash said.

"I read an article about him in *Time Magazine*." Gordon nodded.

"He's no longer on the case. Simons has had some health issues and had to step back. He needs a bypass. Now it's just me and my associate back in Virginia."

"That's too bad. Will he be okay?"

"Yeah, I think so."

"Can I ask you a question?"

"Sure."

"You said that the Vaseline and fibers would confirm it was Highwayman. Wouldn't the fact that he was cut up into six pieces have tipped you off?"

"Sure, but that could be written off to copycat."

"Copycat? That's a bit farfetched, isn't it?"

"It's out there, but it happens. I could probably recite a dozen cases of murder where the perp used another crime to cover his tracks. Better not to jump to conclusions. I like to let the evidence do the talking."

"Really, a dozen? How long you been with the FBI?"

Ash looked at her. "You ask a lot of questions, Detective."

"Keyword: detective. That's what I do, I ask a lot of questions. Sometimes I solve the odd case by asking questions."

"Even personal ones?"

"Especially personal ones."

"I've been with the bureau for thirty-two years. I'm fifty-eight, and they're getting ready to put me out to pasture. Probably this is my last case."

"Thank you."

Ash turned back up the trail and Gordon followed. "Where's a good place to get a bite around here?"

"There's a little restaurant in town that serves a decent steak. I haven't had dinner, I'll buy," she said, "if that doesn't make you uncomfortable."

Ash stopped, turned to face her. "It doesn't, but my boss gives me a bigger operating budget than yours does, so I'll pick up the tab."

"I won't argue with that."

They began walking again, he stared straight ahead processing what he'd seen and thought about what to put in his report. Beside him, Gordon moved quietly. Once they were passed the tent and out of earshot, Ash said. "He immobilizes them by puncturing their vertebrae. We think he uses a pick, like an ice pick or a pointed screwdriver."

"That's what you were looking for?"

"Yeah, and I'd appreciate it if you don't discuss this. I am going to put a gag order on it with the ME."

"Thank you." Gordon smiled. She found Ash attractive; he was twenty years her senior, but he was a dignified looking man who carried an air of confidence. She felt a draw to that and wondered if dinner might turn into something more. "I won't tell anybody about this."

"Including your cousin?"

"Especially my cousin."

"Good."

2

Set to vibrate, the cell phone jittered on the night table. Ash reached over and snatched it up. "Ash."

"We have another one, Lewis," said Michelle Leigh.

He sat up. "Where?"

"Grants Pass, Oregon."

Ash sighed. "That doesn't sound close to an airport, Michelle."

"It isn't. You fly into Portland, and there will be a rental car waiting for you."

"How long?"

"You fly at 10:00 a.m. How are things there? Are the locals cooperating?"

Ash felt a hand caress his lower back, then slide around and between his legs. She squeezed him. "The locals have things well in hand."

Gordon let out the slightest raspy laugh.

"Good. You'll be liaising with Deputy Sheriff Sheryl Landis."

"Where's the sheriff?"

"Her father, Bob Landis, is getting his gallbladder out."

"Okay, has the body been collected?"

"Yes, Portland sent in some crime scene people, identification is pending, but they're pretty sure the victim is a local woman who has been missing for two weeks."

"Okay."

"This one's weird, Lewis."

"Weird? How?"

"The victim, presuming she is who they think it is, went missing after her parents were murdered in their home."

"He killed parents and took their daughter? That doesn't sound like our guy."

The hand that had been massaging him stopped and moved up to his belly. She sat up and pressed into him, her bosom crushing against his shoulder blades. She set her chin on his right shoulder, listening.

"Not exactly," Michelle said.

"The killer may not have been Highwayman?" Lewis glanced at the clock. It was 7:00 a.m; he had a couple of hours before he'd have to be at the airport.

"It's all speculation at this point, but I'll send you over a brief. It's a weird one, that's for sure."

"Anything else?"

"No. I'm emailing the brief now." Michelle paused. "If you have any questions, you can call me when you have your business taken care of."

Lewis didn't know what to make of this. Had she heard Gordon's giggle? He doubted it. She probably just meant a shower and a shave. "Okay, Michelle. I'll call you from the airport."

He ended the call, set the phone back on the nightstand, and brought his hand up to caress Gordon's cheek.

"Duty calls," she said.

He turned and gave her a kiss. "Yeah, I gotta get my butt to the airport. First, I need a shower." He got up and moved toward the bathroom. Then he turned back to her. "You want to join me?"

She smiled, lighting up those big brown eyes. "How are you with multi-tasking?"

He grinned. "Multi-tasking is my specialty."

***

CHAPTER 9 – THE SOUND OF SILENCE

1

22 September 2002

University of Kentucky

Lance went back to school. Advanced computer and Internet studies. It had been five months since he killed the woman in Grants Pass, OR.

He checked the papers regularly, and other than the local rags, there wasn't much mention at a national level about the murders. They knew about him, of this he was sure. He was positive that the FBI was now actively looking for him, but for whatever reason, they weren't reporting on him.

Why?

It was infuriating.

He had killed twelve people. And that excluded the little bartender whore, Wendy, and her bastard kid. So, technically fourteen, but who was counting?

Apparently not the FBI.

He pushed the anger away and picked up the book he had been reading. *The Dark Net: Inside the Digital Underworld* by Jamie Bartlett. This was the third book he'd read on the deep net, and it had spurred him to attend a lecture on the subject by a retired ATF agent who had written the other two books he'd read. The books were *No One is Anonymous* and *The Darkest Corners of the Deep Web written* by G. Howard Stanley. The lecture was called "Understanding the Criminal Aspects of the Deep Web and Individual Privacy."

This should be interesting, he thought and immediately signed up for the lecture. Lance wished that G. Howard Stanley had been FBI instead of ATF.

He wanted to get close to one, see if they commanded the same aura he'd seen and read about in books and movies. He also wanted to kill an FBI agent, strip them of their bravado, and get down to the core, as he had with the others. He wanted to hear one beg for its life.

His thoughts shifted back to his first killing.

He wondered what had become of Detective Hayward. Probably dead of a heart attack. The man was obese after all.

He grinned; that had been a scary time. He'd thought they'd busted him. That Hayward was coming to get him. Even after the fat detective left, he thought he'd be back. But he never did come back, because in his view Lance was a victim, not a criminal. A way station on the route to another case. A case that would hit a dead end and, unbeknownst to Lance, would continue to haunt Hayward.

Now Wendy and her kid seemed ethereal. Like a million years ago, even though it had only been two and a half. And wasn't that strange? Wasn't it supposed to work the other way around?

Seems like only yesterday I decapitated a kid, killed his mom and burned their house, he thought, and the grin widened.

His anger receded, replaced by rationality.

Better to lay low, he thought. *Stay off the radar.*

The urge to kill was still there, but he resisted, telling himself that if it became too overwhelming, he would kill in a different way. One that would not connect to Highwayman. He knew there was a monster inside him, felt it taking over during the ritualistic slayings. In the moments of abduction and killing, Lance Belanger relinquished control to the monster inside. But after the killing, he tethered the monster and pushed it back down into his internal cage. Lance understood the power the creature inside him held. If unleashed, it would probably take over completely. So keeping it leashed was a must.

There were many others with similar entities. Killers who controlled the monster, but in many cases, the monster eventually took over. Ted Bundy had killed with efficient anonymity until he lost control of an abduction and was finally arrested. On his second escape from a jail in Colorado, he made it all the way to Florida. There he melted into society and likely would have avoided capture.

But Bundy was losing control. The dark force that no one except Bundy and his victims had seen was taking over.

On a dark night in January of 1978, the monster inside Bundy took over its master and sent him on a killing spree that would eventually lead to his arrest, conviction, and execution. Lance understood completely how a deliberate and methodical killer like Bundy could suddenly become unpredictable and reckless.

Lance himself felt the urges of the creature within. What Bundy had called "the madness." When unleashed, it took control and as a byproduct of its actions, served up euphoria beyond all belief. Lance could not think of any single sexual orgasm that would compare to the rapture he felt when the monster was let loose. During the rituals, his cock became as hard as tempered steel, but he did not orgasm. The release was at his very core, far beyond that of the thrusting, convulsive finality of intercourse. It was euphoria, ecstasy, super-fucking-nova. The urge to unleash the entity that delivered this feeling was so very tempting.

Tempting, but suicidal, and for Lance, murder was something he wanted to enjoy for a very long time. Sooner or later they might catch him, but he would do everything he could to evade capture.

Lay low, he thought. *Think about the big picture.*

He would keep the monster tethered.

He knew he had their attention, but also knew that he needed to be a pragmatist. If he let his emotions rule him, he would find himself in police custody. Emotions led to mistakes. Sleeping with Wendy had been a mistake. An error that had resulted in him destroying what he had created. Sex could be procured in other ways. He stayed away from the girls who sought him. If he needed sex, he paid for it. Better that way. It was unattached. He didn't want a relationship, wouldn't know what to do with one for that matter. Better to lay a bit of money down and get...

What was the word Homeless Steve had used?

Get serviced.

Yeah, he thought. *Maybe I'll get serviced tonight.*

He closed his laptop and got ready for the lecture.

2

"Hello, ladies and gentlemen, my name is Howard Stanley. I am the author of two books and a retired ATF agent. In the next hour, I'm going to be speaking to you about the workings of the Deep Web. Before I get started, I'm going to ask you all a question." He traversed the room purposely with his gaze. "All right, how many people here have ever visited a pornographic website?"

Nobody raised their hands.

"Really," Howard said and shook his head in disbelief.

This was followed by snickers.

"I was of the understanding that this was a class for Advanced Internet Studies." He walked away from the lectern and opened the classroom door. He cocked his head around at the sign, then closed the door and turned back towards his audience of twenty-five. "Just checking."

"Checking what?" asked a student in the front row.

"That this was the Advanced Internet Studies course, not a religious class on morality."

More snickers.

Howard raised his voice, spoke more slowly. "Okay, I'll ask again. Has anybody here ever visited a pornographic website?" And to encourage them he raised his own hand and said, "I have."

As if tethered by invisible balloons, hands began to rise one after another.

"Man, I thought I was the only one." He wiped his brow dramatically.

More laughter.

Howard pulled out his phone and placed it to his ear. "Okay, send in the team!" Then he put it away. "You are all under arrest for indecent and immoral behavior."

The room erupted with laughter.

Lance smiled but did not join in the collective mirth. He was impatient with Howard's attempt to win them over. It wasn't necessary, everyone here had paid out of pocket for this lecture. It didn't even amount to a class credit.

"Alright, so what we are here to talk about today is the Deep Web. When you're on the Internet, pretty much everything you look at, everywhere you travel, and every purchase you make is tracked. Now, I want everyone to think of the Internet in terms of a large body of water." He went to the chalkboard behind him and drew a single line.

"In this body of water, everyone is fishing." He stopped and gazed back over his shoulder. "Apparently, many are fishing for porn."

More laughter.

"Okay, enough about the porn. So, we're going to picture the Internet as a large body of water, and it has many vehicles moving back and forth, so we'll say fishing boats." He drew a bunch of boats floating on the chalk line water. These boats are trolling for information. Some are Googling Aunt Sally's fried chicken recipe. Some are reading the news. Some are on Amazon, others eBay, or Netflix, or Facebook, or Twitter. Some are surfing porn. I know I said I wouldn't talk about porn anymore, but it's kind of impossible. Porn and the Internet are synonymous, and some might even argue that was why the Internet was created. What people fail to realize when on the Internet, everything they do is tracked, and especially everything that happens on the surface of the Internet is tracked." He drew a long arcing line above the fishing boats, then traced an arrow to each.

A hand went up.

"Even when you're in private browsing?" a female student asked.

Howard's grin widened, his eyes darting left and right. "Especially when you're in private browsing."

"Oh shit," said another student.

More laughter.

"So who do you think is tracking you?" He scanned the room. Hands began to rise. He pointed to a young man in the third row.

"*Five-O?*"

Howard laughed. "Are any of you even old enough to know who Jack Lord was?"

"Jack Lord?"

"Jack Lord. McGarrett? You know, 'Book 'em Danno?'" The kid showed no sign of comprehension. "Ah, never mind." Howard turned his attention back to the rest of his audience. "Meanwhile, back at the discussion, besides the police, who might be tracking you?"

"Spammers," said one student. "Corporations," said another. And, "Hackers."

"Excellent answers! Newsflash, everybody on the Internet is tracking everybody. The spammers want to spam you. The police want to know if you're up to no good. The hackers want to hack you. This is why people get infected with viruses. Has anybody ever had a Trojan or a virus?" Howard looked around again.

Numerous hands went up.

"You people are nothing but a bunch of heathens." Howard smiled broadly.

The room erupted in even more laughter.

Lance thought, *And some of us are killers.* Then laughed himself.

"So where do we go to get away from the spammers, the hackers. The government, the police, and the pornographers?" Howard scanned the classroom and set his sights upon Lance. "Do you know?"

Lance said, "The Deep Web?"

"Exactly. People have been playing in the Deep Web for years. Most people go to play for privacy reasons. Some innocuous, but others have darker reasons for going incognito. We are finding that all sorts of criminals are now making the Deep Web their latest form of communication. And every facet of criminality is using this new frontier. Pedophiles, human traffickers, drug smugglers, and terrorists. This has made the job of law enforcement even more challenging. We used to track these individuals quite easily. They'd go into chat rooms, think they are talking to a minor and wham! Next thing you know, they're on *To Catch A Predator.*"

More laughter.

Howard turned his eyes upon a female student and continued. "In the interest of privacy, some people are going Deep." He stopped holding her in his gaze.

Lance wondered if he was a complete pervert.

"No big brother?" the girl said.

"Big brother is always watching, but in the Deep Web, it is more difficult. Criminal elements who don't want to be looked at in the Deep Web will set up offshore proxy servers. For instance, Mexican cartels were moving drugs to and from a port in New Jersey, and they were using the Deep Web to communicate. ATF was already tracking these cartels, but they had moved a lot of drugs before we got a mole *inside* to intercept the communications. Eventually, there was a large bust off the Jersey Shore, and some suspects were taken into custody. So while some may want to go Deep just to enjoy their privacy, there is undoubtedly a criminal element that uses this new Wild West in some unsavory endeavors.

"But no spammers?" a male student said, and this invoked more laughter.

Lance was thinking now. Thinking about his own little project. He sat up in his chair, scribbled down some notes: **Offshore proxy servers. Exclusivity. FBI.**

The class interaction went on. Howard babbled and flirted with the female classmates, and Lance listened through a filter of epiphanic thought. He needed to explore this further. It could help him access places he'd been afraid to access. He might even be able to contact the investigators or the media without leaving a trail.

Far off, he heard. "Oh God, you're a Trekkie!" It was a male student.

This brought about laughter.

"Guilty as charged," Howard said and raised his right hand in the Vulcan greeting. "Live long and prosper." He then went on to give them their assignments. He referenced two books about Internet studies. The author of these books was G. Howard Stanley.

3

1 June 2005

Quantico, VA

It had been over three years, and Agent Ash was faced with the grim reality that Highwayman had either gone dormant, died, or was in jail. He'd been averaging a kill a month, that they knew of; when that stopped, Ash began to feel sick about the whole thing.

"They're going to shut it down," he told Michelle. "It's just a matter of time."

"Maybe he is dead. Maybe that's why he stopped," Leigh said.

"Maybe." But Ash didn't really believe it.

He and Leigh were having drinks together. She had seen the director that afternoon, and Ash already knew why. She was being reassigned, and he had other things on his mind. The sands of the hourglass were running out. Before Leigh's meeting, he had been pulled in and offered paid leave until his retirement became effective in eleven months. He declined the offer and asked if he could remain assigned to the Highwayman case until his time was up.

"You sure you want to do that, Lewis?" the deputy director asked. "There hasn't been a killing in what, three years? You want to spend your final days beating your head on a cold case?"

A divorcee, Ash had no one to retire with. The FBI was his life, and he really had no game plan for afterward. The dormancy of Highwayman and his impending retirement loomed like the Grim Reaper. Time was running out. The case was already on its way from active to cold. "Yes, sir," Ash said and gave him a smile. "Maybe we'll catch a break. I'd like to close it before my time is up. Or at least try."

"Okay, Lewis, I'll let you ride it out. We owe you that much for all the years of service, but I can't offer much in the way of support. You'll probably end up a desk jockey." Deputy Director Wilkins stood up and shook his hand. He wasn't far from retirement himself. A new younger deputy director was set to replace him. An up and comer named Julian Carswell.

"You think he's still out there," Leigh said, bringing him back.

Ash brought his eyes up to meet hers. "Yeah."

"If he's not in jail, why would he stop?"

"Maybe he didn't stop. Maybe he just stopped here." Ash took a swig of the vodka and tonic he'd been holding. This was his third since sitting down with Leigh. "He could be up in Canada or even down in Mexico."

He thought Canada was a long shot; they were active users of ViCAP. If a similar crime occurred up there, they'd know. American and Canadian officials worked together on serial murder. Of course, extradition for anyone facing the death penalty always became a point of contention, but the Mounties were extremely helpful and left the politics to the bleeding hearts. Lewis wasn't a supporter of the death penalty; he believed they could learn more about these creatures if they were studied.

2

Sitting in his office, he looked at the map of the United States on the wall. Red pushpins marked each crime scene, and beside each pin, a victim's photo. He'd tied a red string to each pin, and in turn, connected all the pins. There was no epiphany in their connection, the locations were random. But the distance and randomness led to a theory.

Eleven victims. Eleven States.

Ten homeless with addiction issues and one encounter that had been bizarre. The mentally ill Sheila Carbone, who had killed her parents and subsequently fallen victim to the Highwayman.

What were the odds on that?

A million to one?

Lewis thumbed through the case file. Noting the similarities and differences in the killings. All victims had been dismembered while alive, their body parts arranged like a starfish. Ten of the eleven had been incapacitated by a destruction of the spinal cord around the third and fourth vertebrae. Ten of eleven had all been stripped of their clothing. The last nine were wiped down with rubbing alcohol after being stripped, thus destroying any conclusive DNA evidence that might have been collected.

The only extrinsic evidence had been fibers, and a few blobs of Vaseline collected in four crime scenes. The Vaseline yielded no DNA, but the fibers were traced back to a neoprene coverall sold by Home Depot. The suit was not exclusive to the store, but it was construed that the suit had come from the building chain. Records showed that Home Depot had sold 2509 of these painter's coveralls nationally in the week that victim number five, Mellissa Hunt, had been found in Central Falls, RI. They worked with the local list of suits sold and compiled 2074 names who had made credit card or debit card purchases. These were investigated, ruling out individuals that did not fit the profile.

As they pared the list down to eighty-five, Lewis became sure that Highwayman would not be among this demographic. He would be in the other four hundred thirty-five, the ones who had paid cash, the ones who did not leave a digital fingerprint on their purchases. The Highwayman was too smart to fall into the other group, but Lewis had investigators run it down anyway. No point in giving this guy too much credit.

Lewis wondered about the machete he used to dismember the victims. Before Wilbur Simons got sick and was pulled off the case, he had a working theory that the Highwayman was using a different blade for each killing.

"Why would he do that?" Lewis said to himself.

There was lots of debate about Highwayman's occupation. He was a cross-country killer, and that led to speculation that he was either a traveling salesman or a truck driver.

Lewis ruled out truck driver almost immediately. While truck drivers moved across the interstate system more frequently than anyone else, truckers were limited in their ability to park such massive vehicles and dispose of their victims. In the case files Ash read, the killers who used their driving occupation to hunt victims dumped their bodies on the side of highways in easily accessible areas like ditches or, in some cases, right on the road. When he thought about it, they were the real Highwaymen.

Ruling out truck drivers was a simple deduction. The plaster casts of eight different tires led Ash to conclude that Highwayman was using different vehicles at each scene.

When stolen vehicles yielded nothing, they started concentrating on rental agencies, and they got a hit, but only one. It was an Enterprise car rental out of Cleveland, Ohio. The type of tire was a match, a Goodyear 70/R15, and Enterprise was using this make and model on all their mid-size cars, and likely the car was a 2000 Chevrolet Impala.

"He's using rental cars," Ash said.

They started running down rental cars and hit another dead end. They thought they could track the tire like a fingerprint, but not only had Enterprise replaced the tires on their vehicles twice, they'd since updated their fleet, and the cars went to auction.

Undaunted, Ash had the investigators chase down all rentals between July 2 and 6 hoping they might get a hit on credit card statements. Unfortunately, this idea fizzled out as well, Enterprise had updated its software system in 2002, and the database they had been using was destroyed.

"If he rented one car, he probably rented eleven," Ash told Michelle, and they began chasing down the rest of the rental car companies, cross-referencing tires, and Ash hoped that GPS coordinates would zero them in on a suspect. Again, they came up cold. Tire castings did not match any of the rental agencies.

Ash's theory was that the Highwayman might not be a highwayman at all. He was beginning to think that the Highwayman was an airport man. The rentals, even if they couldn't prove it, just made sense. You go to an airport, land somewhere else, and what would you need? A car, of course. And didn't most people intended on visiting a place or region need a mode of transportation? That was the first thread of doubt about truck drivers. This guy was using the airways, and when he got there, he needed a new set of wheels. That would account for different tire treads.

So he was a frequent flier.

And that led to Wilbur Simons' theory that every killing was executed with a new machete. It made complete sense. If you fly, you want to travel light and without suspicion. So bringing a weapon onto an airplane was out of the question. Even in the belly, the luggage was x-rayed; sooner or later a weapon of that size would get caught. That would lead to questions, and eventually, they would figure it out. But the Highwayman was smarter than that. He might be an attention whore, but he didn't want to get caught. So he buys his weapon locally and even in that case, it's like trying to find a needle in a stack of needles. In a major city and the outlying towns, purchasing a single machete is not that hard.

"Not that hard," Lewis said. "For him." But finding the purchaser and seller of such an item wasn't an easy task at all. Hoping against hope, they even looked for combination purchases of painters suit and machete, but of the credit card purchases they obtained there was no such combo. The needle in a stack of needles was a goddamned understatement. Ash wondered if the Highwayman was even purchasing machetes. A sharpened lawn mower blade or chunk of steel could accomplish as much if it were sharpened properly.

And here they were.

Or here he was.

All by his lonesome, obsessed with catching someone who had not made an appearance in almost three years. Whose trace evidence stopped dead at a wall without a further clue. A lone wolf that moved on. Most of those involved believed that Highwayman was dead or incarcerated and became less invested. If he was dead, then he was out of business. Never mind the victims. If he's dead, then that meant less business all around. No need to charge. No need to prosecute. And those voids would be quickly filled by any active case that demanded immediate attention. It was never really about the victims, but clearing the case that was deemed clear and present danger.

To the public or to the bureau's reputation? Ash wondered.

He was amazed at how cynical he'd become now that he was at the descending part of the arch. There was a time when he considered himself the most loyal soldier in the ranks. He never would have criticized, but with the clocking winding down, he began to see the shortcomings of his community.

So what was going to happen?

That was a given. Ash would finish the last eleven months of his FBI career in a minimalist position. No field support, no forensic support... just lone wolf Lewis Ash burning out the last of his days trying to solve a case that had gone dead.

***

CHAPTER 10 - THE FOG MAN

1

14 August 2005
Bran Castle
Near Bran, Romania

Lance was neither dead or in jail, and if one were to argue, he wasn't even dormant. He was touring Castle Bran and learning a bit about the greatest serial killer of them all: Vlad Tepes.

Lance enjoyed the castle, but it was the grounds that intrigued him, the bloody earth where bodies were once suspended, impaled on stakes by the thousands. The others on tour had looked around, disinterested at the grounds, except to listen to the female guide explain. Lance was genuinely interested, and as they dispersed, he stood there entranced, imagining the sight, the sounds, and, of course, the smell. Tepes was a god in his eyes, remembered hundreds of years later, immortalized by his actions.

"*S-a* întâmpl*at ceva?*" asked the female guide.

Lance turned to face her, she was smiling. "*Sunt bine*," he said, then unsure of his reply. "I'm okay."

"American, yes?"

"Yes, American."

"The tour has ended." She smiled, her teeth bleached white, eyes blue, hair like corn silk. He thought she might be Swedish or Swiss, certainly not Romanian. Romanians weren't fair skinned. She was a beauty, a specimen that permeated lust. He pictured her laid on the ground, naked and begging for her life. Dismembered and laid out. This gave him an erection. "We must go, sir."

"*Foarte bine*," he said.

"Very well," she parroted in English. "Your Romanian is good."

"*Mulțumesc*. And so is your English."

"You're quite welcome, and thank you."

"How many languages do you speak?"

"Five. I speak Romanian, Italian, German, English and my momma's tongue is Norwegian."

"Five languages, that's impressive."

"I would like to come to America for a visit. I would like to see California and New York City," she said, turning to lead him from the grounds.

"What is your name?"

"Grete," she said but did not ask his.

He took this as a brush off. No matter. He wasn't interested in a date. As he followed, he fantasized reaching out, grabbing a handful of hair and dragging her down. But others were watching. He couldn't, no, wouldn't compromise his plans. But he had a need.

Oh God, how he had a need!

2

15 August 2005

Bucharest, Romania

"I am Andrei Gusa. You must be Mr. Mitchell?" The man in front of him extended a hand and Lance took it. He smiled, his accent was thick but concise. "Please sit down, we have much to discuss."

"Thank you," Lance said, released the man's hand and took a seat.

"Is this your first time in Romania, Mr. Mitchell?"

"Yes, and please, call me Devon."

"All right then, Devon it is. And please call me Andrei, there is no reason that business associates cannot be friends."

"Agreed."

"I trust your visit to Romania has been pleasurable so far?"

"Yes, it has."

"Before we start, Devon, can I offer you coffee or some wine, or maybe some brandy?" Andrei stood, but Lance shook his head, and so he sat back down.

"Thank you, but no. I would prefer to get right down to business, if that's all right."

Andrei smiled. "Of course. My associates informed me that you are looking to set up a secure Internet site. Am I to assume that this will be a webpage which will require discretion?"

"Extreme discretion and advanced security. I would like it to be invisible to the rest of the Internet. Exclusive and invite only. I would also like it to be untraceable. I want to administer it from the US, but I do not want my port of entry tracked. I understand that this can be done?" Lance opened a notebook. "I would like the home site to be in Romania, but you can redirect any IP queries to another country?"

Andrei stared at Lance, sizing him up. "Yes, we can redirect the proxy servers to another country, like Serbia or Hungary, maybe even Slovakia. This will cost."

"How much?"

"That depends. How much traffic will you incur? Is this a download site? Torrents? Or something else with higher risk?"

Lance grinned. "It will not be a download site so traffic will be light. The site will likely host images, have a chat feature for members, but no video. I don't see the membership growing beyond one hundred, and that is being very optimistic."

"What kind of pictures?" Andrei leaned forward on his elbows.

"Do you really need to know?"

"No, but I will need to assess risk, Devon. If the pictures are the type that would alert Interpol, I would have to insist on a higher security rating with possibly two redirects. The first to Hungary and the second to Slovakia. You must also consider the clients who visit; they will pose a risk as well."

"It's not a child pornography site, Andrei."

Andrei smiled. "That is good, but why would you need it in the Deep Web?"

Lance took a deep breath. "I am a businessman, I work in textiles on the West coast, and I may one day have political aspirations. This site is a hobby. Some men surf porn, be it straight, gay, cross-dressing..." Lance sighed and purposely blushed. "I like to look at pictures of dead people. Autopsy photos, crime scene photography, accident scenes. There is a growing community of like-minded individuals with whom I want to share and interact. Not illegal, you can Google all the autopsy photos you want, but you are traceable. I don't want to be tracked."

Andrei opened his laptop and punched a few keys. "This will be expensive."

"How expensive?"

"This is just an estimate, but I would say at least 25,000 Euro to set up and another 28,000 to maintain for one year."

"What is that in US dollars, Andrei?"

"Approximately 55,000 US dollars."

Lance flipped open his phone, did a quick calculation and said, "It's actually 54,156.2. What kind of rate can you give me for two years with a possibility of renewal?"

"Two years? We could probably do that for around $80,000 US, providing your traffic does not increase."

"It won't, but I'll need one thing further."

"Yes."

"Do you know what a fail-safe is?"

"You want a self-destruct option?" Andrei nodded. "That will be included in the original quote. We can set you up and then give you a password that only you can administer. If the need arises, you can use it during login."

"You mean a secondary password."

"Yes, a secondary password. If you log in with that secondary password, it will release a worm that will destroy the site and all of its remote servers."

"How long will you need to set this up?"

"A few weeks. How long for a bank transfer?"

"I can start that today."

"I assume that will be done with discretion."

"Of course, everything will be done offshore."

Andrei stood and extended his hand. "Perfect. I look forward to a mutually beneficial business arrangement." Andrei reached into his pocket, and removed a business card from his pocket and handed it across to Lance. "I am at your service, Devon. If you run into any problems with our arrangement, that is my direct number." Lance gazed down at the card; it was standard white with a single anarchist A. Below that, a European exchange number. "Call that number, a woman will answer, and you say that you need consultation 437. I will meet you on a secure server, not unlike Skype. You will receive all this information in your package."

"Package?"

"A 64-gigabyte SD card. That will contain all the information for your site and how to set it up. Very easy to conceal when traveling abroad, or home for that matter. One other thing, Lance."

Lance glanced up surprised.

"Yes, I make it my business to check out all my clients, but do not let that worry you. I understand why you would want to use another name, and from here on, I will call you Devon, if you please, but understand that I must also protect myself. I will respect your privacy from this point on, but if information about our business or this office ever falls into the wrong hands..." Andrei trailed off staring into Lance's eyes.

"I understand," Lance said.

"I know you do. I don't care what you do, or who you do it to. But do not bring it to my doorstep." Andrei stood, reached out, and shook Lance's hand. "I will be in touch in twenty-four hours. You will be traveling to one more country before this is done. I will give you the details when I call."

"One more country?" Lance asked.

"Yes, Hungary or Serbia. There you will meet with another of my associates to set up an offshore transfer. That will also be the site of your IP redirect. I can't tell you more until I've had a chance make arrangements. In the meantime, enjoy a night in Bucharest, there is much to see and do." Andrei squeezed, his smile widening. "Devon."

Lance felt intimidated.

How did this man know? What did he know?

The handshake loosened and Lance pulled back.

Andrei's words echoed in his mind as he left the little office and made his way down the dank hall. *I don't care what you do, or who you do it to. But do not bring it to my doorstep.*

But what in the hell was that supposed to mean?

It means don't fuck with these people.

3

Gothic was the only way to describe it: fog engulfing the train station, light flickering behind shadows chasing shadows. Lance was still, predatory, watching the comings and goings of the station, wondering what spirits lingered in the darkness, both killer and victim from the past. There had been murder in this place before, he could smell it, taste the copper of blood in the back of his throat.

He had dressed for the occasion. Donning dark jeans, sneakers, t-shirt, and a black hooded pullover. Not far from here, he had stashed a change of clothing. There would not be the protection of coveralls or the Vaseline he applied to keep from shedding his DNA. Killing here, away from his usual hunting ground, was extremely perilous. But the necessity to kill came as it always did. At first, it was a phantom itch, nagging to be scratched. The itch would be elevated by other factors. Lance had thought that he could abstain, resist the urge, but the longer he waited, the harder it became. The monster was demanding to be fed, to be unleashed. Mitigating factors elevated the need. The fact that Andrei knew who he was brought on anxiety, unease only fueled the impulse to abandon his abstinence. This was, he knew, how drug addicts of all walks felt. They shared this common thread, whether they smoked cigarettes, drank alcohol, or mainlined heroin.

Any excuse was excuse enough.

Bad day at work; light up a smoke. Turned down for a date; have a drink. Andrei knows who you are; time to kill.

He wandered through the station grounds. Here, the homeless weren't swept up from the street like so much refuse. In his jacket pocket, he carried a seven-inch blade, part of a newly purchased culinary knife set.

It would have to be quick and without fanfare.

He spotted the man on a bench just beyond the train tracks. Lance thought he was in his mid to late forties, balding, and like the others, he was unclean. The man had spotted him as well. Lance had made sure of that. He looked around and saw no one. Fog floated four feet above the ground, blurring the man's silhouette as he rose from the bench.

Is he homeless, mentally unstable, or both?

Lance approached. When he was face-to-face with the man, he reached into his pocket pulling out a single twenty Euro note which he held up for the man to see. They were gray and colorless in the mist of night. Lance enticed him with the cash and said, "*Dacă doriţi mai multe. Vino cu mine.*" Which meant, *If you want more. Come with me.*

Lance gave him a questioning nod.

The man grinned, wrapped his dirty fingers around the money and Lance released it. The man said, "*Da.*" And followed him from the station and into an alley. As they walked, Lance scanned left then right, up and down. He was looking for anyone who might bear witness.

They were alone.

The nameless, faceless, fog man stuffed the twenty Euro note into his left hip pocket only because there was a hole in his right. He followed the foreigner into the alley, drawn by an itch of his own. He wanted more, would do what was necessary to get it.

Lance again gazed up, looking for those who might be watching. The fog man was behind him, breathing labored, his hunger sweating from every pore. He could feel the impatience of the man, who wanted to get this over with and find a fix. He was purposely slowing, allowing him to get close. He kept his eyes front, took a last cursory glance, and turned to face him.

He thought of Vlad as he unsheathed the blade. He drove it hard up into the solar plexus and heard an elastic snap of gristle separating. He pushed it up beneath the sternum and twisted. The man strained to cry out, but only managed a gasp, swallowed in the thickening haze. Then, his heart pierced, he expired, slumping forward on the blade and Lance's blood-soaked glove.

Impaled, Lance thought.

What logistics would he have to employ to impale a bunch of victims? It would probably be a fucking nightmare. This would have to do. Besides, Vlad would have been proud.

He pushed the fog man back against the wall and pulled the knife out. There was an inconsequential trickle of blood, only gravity: the heart was dead. He wiped the blade down and wrapped it in one of four handkerchiefs he'd purchased after leaving Andrei's office.

Andrei, he thought. *What did he really know?*

He took in his kill, wiping the blood from his hand with the other two nose rags and remembered the twenty note. That would have fingerprints. He checked the fog man and found it in his hip pocket.

He felt better, certainly not as much pleasure, and zero presentation, but it unleashed a bit of pressure. The pressure that had been building since his last, and, as he was learning, the release was an important part of the process.

The monster must be fed, he thought.

Fed and caged or the monster will take over.

He backed away, into the gray and away from the kill. He wished he could spend more time, share some silent time with the fog man. But this was not America, not his hunting grounds. It was time to go back to the hotel.

4

Crowne Plaza Hotel

Bucharest, Romania

The shower water beat against him, a few degrees shy of scalding. In his hand, the seven-inch blade turned under the hammering beads of water. At his feet, the snot rags bloated with water, leaching crimson that swirled in fluid stems that gravitated toward the drain. Satisfied that the knife had been cleaned sufficiently, he impaled it in a bar of soap and stood it upright in the dish. Then he picked up the handkerchiefs and began to ring them out. He thought again about the fog man, and how quickly he'd gone.

This began to excite him.

He had gotten so much better at this. He was becoming a precise instrument, and that was in thanks to his victims. Each a template from which he had honed his craft.

He picked up and wrung the first rag. Thought about the next phase, transportation, and how long before his new plan would take hold.

"I gotta stop renting cars," he said.

They had to be checking with the rental agencies?

"Maybe," he whispered and set the rag aside then picked up the second one. This one was especially swollen. "Maybe I can just buy a beater. Single use, then disposed of."

Maybe, but he'd have to be sure that everything worked, every light, signal, and even the horn. Once used, the car could be driven to the nearest junkyard and scrapped. Presto! No more evidence. He'd probably even get a bit of his investment back for the scrap.

"A murder deposit."

Lance grinned, wringing out the bloody rag, letting the blood flow down over his naked skin. Maybe if he went to Slovakia, he'd visit the castle of that other famous serial killer, Elizabeth Bathory. Europeans had dubbed her the Blood Countess. It seemed she enjoyed bathing in the blood of young virgins. Vampirism. This part of the world appeared to have a fetish for vampires. It was fascinating, but it was also nonsense. They were no different than he, but their acts had made them...

"Infamous," he whispered and turned his face into the path of the beating water. He rinsed, rung the last of the blood from the handkerchief, and draped it over the handle of the knife. The water clear, he exited the shower.

5

Lance didn't need keepsakes; each experience was imprinted in his mind's eye, like a virtual movie. No trophies, but he collected the news clippings of his killings, and that alone would undoubtedly lead to his undoing if they were to fall into the hands of investigators. He also kept a journal, complete with names, places, and summaries of each crime. This was his bible, and he believed it could be a textbook for future craftsman.

Murder & Dismemberment for Dummies.

He grinned at the thought.

In his pursuit of perfection, he chronicled everything. Homeless Steve had run and then fought back, so Lance began reading on how to incapacitate a victim without killing them. The tool he used for this could be bought in any hardware store. It was a screwdriver of sorts, but it had a pointed tip instead of a shaped one. It came in a package of four, which was called a hook and pick set. And conveniently, hardware was located next to the camping goods, which was the best place to buy a new machete. He reread the journal, put in liner notes and wasn't afraid to be self-critical.

He didn't dare bring the journal with him to Europe. If Homeland Security got a look at what was in that book, especially the sketches, he'd be on his way to a federal prison. He hadn't thought he'd need it over here, thought that this was purely a business trip.

In bed, Lance closed his eyes and thought about the fog man. He would sketch him when he got back. Add his kill to the book. He'd have to remember to dispose of the knife and rags separately, in the morning. The pressure relieved, he could feel sleep tugging at him.

Best not to kill again.

His purpose for being here was work, not play. He needed to get his business taken care of. So he could go home and get on with the project.

The monster had been sated.

For now.

16 August 2005

Crowne Plaza Hotel

Bucharest, Romania

That morning his phone rang. He answered it. "Hello?"

"Good morning, Devon," Andrei said.

"Good morning, Andrei."

"You need to head for Serbia, I have booked you a ticket that has been dropped at the front desk. All of the contact information is contained in the envelope. When you get to your destination, you will receive another package. It will come in the manner we discussed yesterday."

"Okay."

"Did you enjoy yourself last night?"

Lance didn't reply at first but scolded himself. *He doesn't know shit about what happened last night. You need to stop being so paranoid.* "Yes, I had a good time."

"You need to leave Hungary as soon as possible," Andrei said. "Remember what I said?"

"Yes, but..."

"But it is time to go. You have overstayed your welcome in Bucharest. Shower and pack, Devon. You have a train to catch."

***

PART II

PARTNERS IN DEATH

"She isn't missing. She's at the farm right now."
— **Ed Gein**

CHAPTER 11 – NORRIS

1

27 May 2006

Quantico, VA

Agent Lewis Ash was boxing up the Highwayman Files for archiving. There hadn't been a murder, which they knew of, in almost four years. All leads had been exhausted, and he could only hope that Highwayman was dead or in prison, because Ash was out options and time. His request for an extension with the bureau had been turned down. Like any government entity, the bureau was in the throes of budget cuts which meant that priorities were being realigned. Behavioral Sciences had taken a backseat to terrorism. Mandatory retirement was being enforced and the old foot soldiers like Ash were being put out to pasture.

Ash set the last file into the container and placed it squarely on the stack of four boxes beside his desk. He was finished, but he didn't feel finished. Dead or in jail, Highwayman was still unsolved and would likely remain that way unless he started killing again.

"Damn it," he said, sighed and leaned back in his chair. He was getting the golden handshake in two days. He was already starting to feel like an outsider. His clearances were being ramped down, soon he would be completely locked out, and any information he got would come secondhand. He ran his hand through his neatly kept silver mane. When the hell had he become an old man? He couldn't remember. There'd been too many cases, too many rundowns chasing the grandeur. He heard it before so many times, years run by like minutes, before you know it, the race had been run. Soon this wouldn't be his world. It would be left to the younger agents like Michelle Leigh.

Leigh had been his protégé, she was still a junior agent, but was ready to move to the next level. She was a hell of an analyst, and she knew it. In some cases, knowing such things was detrimental to growth.

"If someone pays you a compliment, never let it go to your head," he had once told her. This was after they caught the Rudolph Case. Sammy Rudolph was a Virginian beekeeper who was apprehended in Norfolk after the bodies of six young girls were discovered buried in an abandoned slaughterhouse outside Fairfax. The victims ranged between eleven and sixteen. Five were under the age of fourteen and Rudolph would later confess that the sixteen-year-old girl was "too old" for his taste. He had snatched the girl out of desperation.

It was Leigh's detective work that led them to the abandoned slaughterhouse. They already had their sights set on Rudolph, but had no substantial evidence to initiate a search warrant. Michelle Leigh had taken it upon herself to scan Rudolph's property using something as simple as Google Earth, and that was when she got lucky. The still imaging captured the dilapidated building, which had been obscured by trees and foliage, but it had also captured something else. She could see the outline of a man leading a much smaller individual into the building. After confirming that Rudolph was an only child, with no extended family to speak of, they got a warrant and conducted a search of the property. What they found in the slaughterhouse was the stuff of nightmares.

When they apprehended Rudolph four hours later, he had in his company a twelve-year-old girl, bound, gagged and covered with a blanket in the backseat of his PT Cruiser. She was, thankfully, not hurt physically or sexually assaulted. If Leigh hadn't used her initiative, the girl, Deborah Calhoun, would have joined the other victims after being tortured, raped, and filmed. Once word got out about Leigh, the accolades poured in, the bosses fast-tracked her into Behavioral Sciences, and she became the talk of the bureau.

"You're turning out to be a hell of an agent, Michelle," he'd said.

She stared across the table at him, two cold beers between them, listening intently. "I had a good teacher."

He ignored the compliment and gave her a solemn look. "I'm proud of you, but you keep this in perspective. Don't let it go to your head, remember why you came here and remain humble. There's nothing wrong with basking in a little glory, but never rest on your laurels."

"I won't."

"I know you won't." He picked up his glass and clinked it against hers. He was a tad jealous, she was a rising star, and he was on the descent, but it wasn't petty jealousy.

No one gets a do-over, he told himself, and the sand in the hourglass only runs one way.

"Lewis?"

Ash snapped back from memory and looked up. It was Bart Pedersen from Records. Lewis hadn't even heard him. "It's all here." He tapped the boxes and frowned.

"Duplicates too?"

"Sure," Ash said and thought, *Except for the ones back at my place.* He'd known this day was coming and began copying everything, a little at a time. It was against regulations, criminally punishable, in fact, but Lewis didn't see it going anywhere. He could drag that file out from time to time, glance over it and maybe he'd see something he'd missed. If he did find something, he could contact Michelle, tell her to pull the file and...

"I have some forms for you to sign, Lewis," Pedersen said, and set a clipboard down on the desk. Lewis glanced at the paper. He leafed through the papers, perusing the words. The big ones jumped out at him: Classified Non-Disclosure Agreement – Punishable By Law. His name had already been filled in appropriately, and he signed and initialed the pages.

I'm a rogue agent, he thought.

"Something funny?" Pedersen asked.

"Yeah," Ash said. "I was just thinking how everyone said we were going to become a paperless society once we got computers."

"Don't I know it?" Pedersen took the clipboard, scanned it for omissions and after a quick "looks good" set it on top of the boxes. He pushed the handcart under the stack and began wheeling them away. Over his shoulder, he said, "Oh yeah, I'm not supposed to tell you this, but there's a bunch of people with cake and booze waiting for you downstairs."

"Thanks for the warning." Lewis knew about the "surprise" retirement party. Ash stood up, pushed his chair in and worked on his acting chops. Watching Pedersen cart away those files made him sick inside. This was unfinished business, and now it was completely out of his hands. Pedersen swung around to face him as he backed into the crash bar on the door. It clinked. He gave Ash a smile and backed out of the room and into the hall.

Fuck, fuck, fuck, he thought and tried to reassure himself that he had not been the first to watch a case go cold. There would always be unsolved cases, though Ash found little comfort in that fact. He knew that without new victims, the Highwayman case became less relevant. There were plenty of active serial killers out there, and they were being hunted. The ones who were dumping fresh bodies would get priority.

Sadly, the only way Highwayman was going to get traction and renew interest was if he started killing again.

Highwayman might not have been dead, but the investigation and hunt certainly were. The door which Pedersen had backed out closed. The crash bar and locking mechanism clicked shut with the same finality of Lewis Ash's career with the FBI.

It was over.

2

17 July 2007

Louisville, KY

The website was insignificant, a blip in a sea of anonymity. It didn't even have a designation. Just an IP: 19V.41B.65L. Norris wouldn't have given it much thought, except it kept pinging every time he visited his usual sites. He logged into his computer that morning with two intentions: surfing a few extreme bondage websites and rubbing one out; or, depending on what he saw, maybe even two.

The site he was looking at was an exclusive site called Sinister Unlimited. It was, for the most part, a fetish and simulated torture porn site. Mock-ups of women and men dressed in leather, PVC, and rubber made to look like they had been being tortured or had been murdered. The photos were streaked with the inky jet sheen of black latex and the over vibrant splash of human blood. This excited Norris, for reasons he could not explain, but he supposed it was better than the alternative. That being the real deal. Norris was excited by what he saw.

His fetish, if you could call it that, had evolved from cruising Google and searching out images that were of a morbid nature. He viewed crime scene photos mostly, some grainy color, others black and white. Among them, photos of Edmund Gein's ghoulish farmhouse. His hard drive was overstuffed with thousands of these macabre pictures.

In the beginning, he did not equate his fascination with the dead to his fetish for all things bondage. He told himself that he might write a book one day, a real murder mystery, and that was why he sought out such morbid stuff. In fact, he kept the two separate. One file for the departed, another for the BDSM stuff. It was all innocent enough. That is, until last spring; that was when the metamorphosis began to happen. When the BDSM pornography he used for regular masturbation sessions suddenly took a sinister turn. It all changed after he found the body.

3

A year before, he was walking back from the KT National Paper Recycling Plant, following the wood line that separated Chicksaw Park Road from the Ohio River. Norris had worked at KT for the last six years. He ran the paper bailer, and occasionally hopping on a forklift when Amy was off. Amy was a lot older than him, in her forties, but he thought she still looked good. She wore her hair in tightly knit pigtails that looked like weaved corn silk. She always smiled at him from atop the tow motor, waiting for him as he made up bales of shredded paper for her to load on the big rigs that came and went. He wondered how she would look dressed from head to toe in PVC, her corn silk pigtails contrasting the wet shine of black. Sometimes, when he was alone, he thought about Amy. Thought about what it would feel like to be inside her, having her wrap her legs around him as he drew a blade between her bosoms. She would whisper, "Do it, Norris. Do it now!" Tightening her hold on his manhood.

He staggered along the gravel road, dragging the clubfoot that had kept him out of the army. Kicking at stones clumsily, feeling the sun beat against the back of his neck. He walked everywhere, they wouldn't let him get a driver's license. They kept changing the test. Making it harder. They were fuckers. That's what his mom used to say.

"They don't understand you, Norris, don't see the smart little man you are and with a handicap too." Her words were both sympathetic and judgmental. He missed Momma, missed her terribly.

His thoughts went back to Amy.

Amy Pigtails. No, Mistress Pigtails.

He kicked another stone, then he saw something out of his peripheral. He stopped, turned and looked down through the clearing that opened like a yawning mouth to the river's edge. There was an eddy at this point in the river; he used to watch it all the time as a kid. The water's backward flow captivated him. He used to throw sticks into the river, amazed at how they suddenly reversed flow and swam against the current.

"You know what that is, don't yuh?" Uncle Linwood used to say when he brought him down here fishing. "That's the river spirits stopping for a rest." Uncle Linwood had been nice, but Momma said her brother was a lawbreaker. In the fall of 1988, police shot Uncle Linwood dead at a big truck stop in St. Louis. He had just robbed a gas station and been chased into the truck stop by police. He was killed by five bullets. He never got off a shot.

Norris had been eight at the time.

He stared at the eddy, thinking of Uncle Linwood, Momma, and the fuckers who kept changing the test.

"I'm not stupid," he grunted.

And he wasn't—he could use a computer on the Internet as good as anyone else, maybe even better. He knew what an eddy was, not a latent spirit, but a backward current. He just had trouble with questions, and those SOBs down at the DMV made the questions hard to understand. They had hidden meanings, and when Norris tried to interpret them, he got confused.

The current spiraled, dirty foam percolating and dissolving, moderated by the steady hush of the water careening over rocks. Norris was transfixed, unaware that his mouth had twisted into an angry scowl, his hands balled up in hard white knuckled lumps of meat and bone. The SOBs at the DMV still occupying his head. His contemplation lasted minutes, only broken when he caught sight of the waving hand on its second pass. The first time had not been enough to break the angry stupor. Only fingertips crested the waterline, but on the second pass an entire hand emerged like a dorsal fin and drew him from his daze.

Huh?

He stumbled forward, craning his neck. The hand dipped below the current and disappeared. As he approached the water's edge, he could see a naked pale form twisting just below the water's surface. He couldn't make out if it were a man or woman, not at first. When he got closer, a plump breast—not eaten by aquatic life or pulverized by the river rock—ousted the mystery.

The body was ghostly—pale, hypnotic, revolving in Uncle Linwood's spirit current. Her eyes were gone, thin black caverns shrouded by ragged translucent flaps. Norris imagined minnows darting in and taking tiny nips at what was left of her eyelids during a feeding frenzy. As he considered this, the body turned, and he saw her naked buttock, and this sent a quiver of excitement through him.

Paranoia crawled into his scrotum, and he turned to see if anyone else was around, was watching. He did not think about how this woman's naked form came to be in the water. Or that possibly she had been murdered. When she made her third pass, her hand came up again, waved and then she lurched over. Belly exposed, Norris saw the slits, at least ten, and he knew that she'd repeatedly been stabbed. Strangely, this didn't frighten him. The body was only seven feet from shore when the hand dipped back down.

He looked around.

There was no one.

Not her killer, not the police, just the woman's body and him. He should have been afraid, but he was excited. No, that wasn't even close to how he felt. He was thrilled, exhilarated, turned on. Yes, turned on. Absently, he placed a hand into his pocket, and on the body's fourth turn, he began to massage.

He closed his eyes. Pushed against the throb of muscle. In his mind, saw himself wading into the river, cool water slopping over the rims of his work boots, filling them, turning his wool socks spongy. He reached out, felt the cool glib of her icy skin, like a freshwater eel. His fingers traced over that skin, finding her breast, then moving down to her stomach where the multiple punctures were set into muscle. He drew over them, feeling the tears in the fascia pull away and open as he caressed, inviting him to explore.

He did, and his world exploded in orgasm.

His body bucked, and a spasm of release turned the crotch area of his jeans dark. His legs bowed, and he almost collapsed, stumbling backward. He heard a distant whimpering moan of pleasure. Imagined it was her, but when he opened his eyes, she was gone. He limped to the river edge and caught a fleeting glimpse of her floating away as she rolled in the current, milky white against the silty water and disappeared. The spirits of the Ohio had concluded their rest and carried her away. To where? Norris did not know. He watched for another fifteen minutes hoping to catch a glimpse.

Nothing. Norris headed for toward home.

He'd need to change his clothes.

There'd been no mention of the body in the news. Norris thought the Ohio had eaten her, feeding the river spirits on their long journey to meet the Mississippi in Cairo. Maybe

Charon had taken her on his way to Hades. Uncle Linwood would know, he was waiting in Hell. At least that's what Momma said after the cops gunned him down.

4

17 July 2007

Louisville, KY

He clicked an icon on his desktop a program called Cloak Surf, and it began to initiate. In the center of his monitor, an eyeball set into a world globe began to spin. As it did, the words Purging all Trackers began to pulse. Then after a second: All Trackers Purged! After that: It is now safe to surf the Deep Web!

Norris clicked on his web browser. The page Sinister Unlimited opened up. In the top right corner of his browser, the all-seeing globe spun, the eyeball winking occasionally and a small cartoon bubble quantified: You are safe to surf! No trackers!

The page was PVC black, except for the emblazoned blood red logo at the top and a row of navigation buttons in the same color. Norris traced his mouse over the buttons, and they lit up one by one. Photo Gallery – Video – Stories – Extreme Measures – Chat. The pointer hovered on Chat, and he held it there.

Would Devon be on? he wondered.

He clicked the link, and the screen faded from black to gray and then back to black, then, Welcome back to Chat, Barker! Barker was his online persona. There were numerous categories: Murder, Crime Scene, Accident Scene, Autopsy, etc. Norris scrolled down the list until he found the chat room he was looking for. MacabreClub.com.

He clicked on the link. You are now being redirected to MacabreClub.com. And he was, the link was taking him away from Sinister Unlimited and to another page. He'd been worried that the Club might be an attack page, so he ran an IP check on it. The IP always came up the same: 19V.41B.65L. Norris had never seen an IP address which included numbers and letters, he guessed it might be an overseas account because it certainly wasn't American. A lot of what happened in the Deep could not be broadcasted across the mainstream Web. Too many curious people on the mainstream like FBI, or ATF, or even news agencies looking to sting you by making you part of a story. Norris thought about the guy, he couldn't remember his name, from *Catch a Pervert* on channel 27. Every week they'd troll some idiot who had an interest in kids and set him up. Norris had looked at child porno, but only here in the Deep, and only briefly. Children having sex didn't do anything for him. Norris wasn't a pedophile; he thought anyone who would want to have sex with the kids had issues. He did not stop to think that his own perversions might be equally scrutinized. Necrophilia wasn't nearly as bad as pedophilia; the dead were empty shells while children had a soul. Don't mess with the soul, and the boatman won't come to take you to Hades, he reasoned.

The Macabre Club differed from Sinister in that it had a single 3D cube floating in the center of the screen that rotated slightly off-kilter. The rotating cube hung below the pulsing neon banner of Macabre Club, Where Membership is Exclusive. The cube was entrancing; mist filled, it turned, occasionally displaying its contents. Like a crystal ball, there was an occasional fleeting glimpse into the world that showcased what Norris craved.

When he placed the pointer over the cube, it stopped rotating. Then the words **RETURNING MEMBER? Y/N** materialized.

Norris clicked Y and the words Please wait, checking your credentials...

After a few seconds: **HELLO BARKER. ALMOST THERE... PLEASE ENTER YOUR SECURITY WORD.**
Norris typed: **COOPER332.**
Verifying...
Then: **ALL DONE BARKER. COME ON IN...**
Norris clicked on the cube, and the page transitioned.

5

http://macabreclub.com/
   Chat Session #12/Time: 2105/07/17/2007
   Cloak-Surf Enabled (No Trackers)
Devon: I have something for you.
Barker: Really? What?
A box popped open on the Norris' computer with the prompt:
DEVON WANTS TO SHARE A FILE WITH YOU. ACCEPT? Y/N
Devon: It's a gift.
He had been engaged in chat sessions for almost three weeks. They had talked about all sorts of things relating to the Web. Norris confessed about some of his fantasies. Devon had come forward with a few fantasies of his own, and this was the first time Devon had wanted to share.
Barker: What is it, Devon?
Devon: If you don't open it, you will never know.
He hovered his mouse over the **Y/N**, his index finger tremored and he pulled back. What if Devon was a hacker, and this was a ploy to blow up his computer? To this point, all they had done was talk, he about necrophilia and murder, Devon about murder and torture. There was no law against that, not that Norris could think of anyway.
Barker: I'm sort of nervous about accepting anything.
Devon: What have you got to be nervous about?

Barker: I like you Devon, but I don't really know you. And you don't really know me.

Devon: I'm your friend. We've shared secrets... I know plenty about you.

Barker: No, you don't really know me. I'm just a person on the other side of the Internet. I could be young or old. I could be a guy or a girl. You could be...

A police officer?

Devon: You have your cloak surf turned on, right?

Barker: Yes.

Devon: So nothing can be recorded. You can virus scan the shit out of it before you open it, but you are going to want that file, Barker. You are going to want to open it...

Barker: Why?

Devon: ☺ Because ☺

Barker: ☹ I need a better explanation, Devon.

Devon: Because that file is going to be the first step in taking our friendship to the next level. It's a stepping stone, Barker.

Norris hovered the mouse over the prompt and wondered. Devon knew about his fantasies. He even knew about the body in the Ohio, but he had no idea who Barker was. He wanted to keep it that way. There was something about Devon that made him nervous. He was aggressive, pushy, and maybe even manipulative. He could accept the file and quarantine it until he was offline. Then he could virus scan it, as Devon suggested.

He had to admit, he was intrigued. A stepping stone that would take their friendship to the next level. What would that be?

Norris' routine was to first chat with Devon. Then he would rub one out over in the macabre video section. What he knew about Devon was that he was an administrator on the site. He also knew he liked torture and murder, or at least simulated. But Devon had another layer to him. An unknown and that was what frightened Norris.

He worried that Devon might be an INTERPOL cop. Cloak surf or not, they had a way of tracking people.

Never mind that he had once browsed a child porn site, never mind that he regularly jacked to the images of accident, autopsy, and crime scene victims. His compulsion had been stronger than his common sense, and when he decided to switch over to the video section, his excitement trumped his apprehension, and he took it to the next level. In the video section, he'd had viewed three snuff films—real or not, he had no idea—but he was excited at the prospect.

The first video had been foreign. Norris thought it was South American or maybe just plain Mexican. They were talking in Spanish, that much he understood, and it was evident from the outset what they intended to do.

The subject had been a young woman, bound and gagged in an abandoned building of some sort, maybe an old factory or a school. The floor was stained with something dark, the shackles, handcuffs attached to a rusted chain. Her mouth had been covered with duct tape. Mascara from tears long since dried painted her cheeks, and she was naked from the waist up. Her murder must have been a letdown to those who wanted to see that portion of the video. Little or no fanfare, barely a scream, just the wet thud of the knife used to repeatedly stab her. After three hard jabs, she passed out or fell dead, limp.

Norris could not tell. He was too busy getting his track pants down and grabbing hold of himself. The camera zoomed and panned over her dead body as Norris readied for the money shot.

Devon: Are you there, Barker??

Norris pulled focus, found himself staring at the monitor, the prompt still beckoning him. **Devon wants to share a file. Accept? Y/N.** Norris clicked on the Y, and the file started to download.

Barker: I accepted the file.

Devon: You won't be disappointed. I have to get off now, things to do. Once you've viewed it, get back to me, say... Tomorrow and we'll chat about it some more.

Barker: Okay...

Devon: Word to the wise, Barker. This file has a time limit on it. It will become unreadable in thirty-six hours and will self-destruct in forty-eight if you do not delete it. No worries... It won't hurt your computer... And you'll understand why once you view it.

Norris recoiled. What had he gotten himself into? His gaze shot over to the download, **97%** and before he could cancel, **100%. Download complete.**

Barker: Is this safe, Devon?

Devon: There is nothing on there that will harm your computer, but that file is for your eyes only. ☺ Being in possession of it yields responsibility and dare I say, culpability. ☺ **Don't show it to anyone!** ☹ Okay? ☺ Open it, enjoy it, but remember, it expires in thirty-six hours, so plan accordingly.

Barker: I don't even know what that is supposed to mean. ☹

Devon: Yes, you do. You just don't want to admit it. I have to go, Barker. I will be on tomorrow all afternoon and into the evening.

Barker: Okay, bye...

Devon: Ttyl. ☺

Then he was gone, leaving Norris to an empty chat room and to contemplate the self-destructing file. His heart thudded in his chest. Once, a few years back he had downloaded a file which promised sadomasochistic video that was beyond the usual. When he clicked on the execute file, an animated tornado appeared and below that in block letters the words exclaiming, **You're fucked!**

The laptop was decimated by the virus. Norris didn't dare take it to a repair shop. If they had seen what he'd been perusing on the Web, he'd be jailed for sure, or locked up in some institute.

Norris skipped his afternoon masturbation session and went to the bathroom instead. As he defecated, he thought long and hard about what he should do. When he was done, he returned to his computer and forwent the antivirus.

Instead, he found the folder and clicked Open.

***

CHAPTER 12 –THE REGULATOR

1

17 July 2007
Louisville, KY

The file was a zip. A folder which contained more than one item. In this case, three. A text document, a JPEG, and another file, which Norris did not recognize but suspected was the timer or self-destruct mechanism. As the utility unzipped the folder, Norris shook his right leg nervously. In the back of his mind, he could hear a voice warning him to delete the file, delete his account on Sinister, and never return to macabreclub.com. That would have been the sensible thing to do. Sensible, yes, for a reasonable person, but normal people didn't get sexually aroused by the dead.

"Normal," he mumbled, chewing on an already ragged thumbnail, tearing it away and spitting it onto the carpet. "What is that anyway?"

The folder appeared on his desktop, and he stared at it for almost a minute before clicking on it. As promised by the zip utility, there were three files. He almost opened the JPEG first, but the text file had the heading READ ME FIRST! So he hovered the mouse over it and was about to click when he thought, *No, I want to see the picture first.*

He moved the pointer back, clicked on the JPEG titled Dev1.jpeg and waited for it to open. Dev he assumed was short for Devon, or maybe Deviant? No, it was Devon. A spinning hourglass gave him time to reflect as his computer opened the picture software. He was already suffering buyer's remorse, and he hadn't even seen what he had accepted.

I should have read the text, he thought.

A window opened and the picture, at first pixelated, loaded up in high definition. It was too large, and to view it he had to zoom down to 15%. It was what he had guessed it would be. A body, undeniably a murder victim, because the naked body had been dismembered. Head, arms, and legs all separated and laid out like a starfish. Norris took in the photograph with the eye of an art critic, unaware that his analysis had mirrored the police nickname. He was enthralled by the shadows, the pooling of blood and the pale skin. He wished he could touch it and wondered if it was a mockup like he'd seen on Sinister? He didn't think so; this was a legitimate photo. The next question was where did Devon get the photo from? Norris had viewed hundreds of thousands of these types of pictures and had seen so many repeats, but not this one. This one wasn't out there. This one was exclusive. This was from Devon's private collection.

"Did Devon take this photo?" he mumbled.

Did Devon kill the person in this pic? he wondered, and his heart fluttered. He wasn't afraid, not really. It was possible that Devon was a killer, but that wasn't what made him antsy. On the contrary, he was becoming excited. This was like the body in the Ohio. It was better than the stuff he'd viewed, real, if not surreal.

He minimized the photo and clicked on the read me file. As his computer carried out this task, he pondered Devon's parting words after he had claimed he didn't know what it was supposed to mean.

"Yes, you do. You just don't want to admit it."

The text file opened.

Norris began to read.

Hello Barker,

Now we share a secret, and that is the first step in what I hope will be a mutually beneficial relationship. I have been watching you and learned many things about you. I know your real name is Norris and your last name which I will not print. I know where you work. I know where you live. It's okay, **don't be alarmed**. I had to check you out, and trust me, I didn't do it for malevolent reasons. I did it because I have to trust you with my secret.

Trust is going to be the backbone of our relationship.

So, now you know my secret. I am sure that you have a bunch of questions, and I will try and address those when we next get together online. I will continue to call you Barker, and you can carry on calling me Devon. I am not going to go into great detail in this message, even though it will be short-lived. (Remember, thirty-six hours.)

I trust you, Norris. That confidence is based on our online interactions, and the fact that I checked you out. Now, you have to trust me. When we meet again, I am going to show you that I am exactly as I appear.

I will see you at some point tonight. To answer a question that I know is whirling inside your mind. **Yes**, the picture is **real,** and you are the second person on this earth to see it.

Enjoy.

Devon

Norris re-read the message, again and again, scrutinizing every word, every paragraph, looking for a red flag between the lines. Words had always been his nemesis, had been all his life. Words had kept him from getting a license, he had to re-read everything, and they became jumbled sometimes; even turning backward like a mirror.

He wasn't full-blown dyslexic; the doctor said that he had a mild form of the disorder and that he could function normally. "My poor little Norry," Momma exclaimed over the telephone to her best friend, Rita. "Not bad enough that God gave him that deformed foot, but he's made him slow as well."

Momma loved him so much, it was as if she had been afflicted with the clubfoot and struggled with words. Momma would say, "Poor Norry," but, as he would later find out, it was about Poor Momma.

2

At twenty-seven, Norris was working the bailer at KT Paper and supporting his mother, now into her sixties. He saved his money and bought a computer. Amy told him that he could learn all sorts of things about his foot on the Internet. By then, he had trained himself to double back when reading and only found tests hard to comprehend. He was still intimidated by words, but without pressure, he found it easier to understand.

"What do you need a computer for?" his mother had asked, a Camel dangling from her puffy lips.

"To learn stuff," he replied meekly.

"Norry, you have disabilities, you need to come to terms with that." She sucked in a bit of smoke, exhaled, and then pulled the escaping poison back through her nostrils. Each word was shrouded in smoke, she continued. "Aren't you happy working at the paper plant?"

"Yes, but..."

"You have a good job at KT Paper, Mr. Samson treats you well. You have to face facts, Norry. You have limitations."

He did, but argued, "Amy said I can use it to learn about stuff."

"Amy? That tart who drives the forklift?"

"She's not a tart, Momma, she's my friend."

Momma sniffed, then sighed and crushed out the Camel. "You will be on that Web looking at bad things, Norry.

Like the magazines I found under the hamper." She was referring to three tattered men's magazines he thought he'd kept hidden well enough in the bathroom. She stared at him, steely-eyed.

He flushed and said, "I won't. I want to learn things, about the world, about my disabilities. I want to improve myself."

"Whatever!"

This was her shutdown word. She used it as a guilty weapon and to freeze him out. Most times, it worked, but Norris decided to stand his ground. He bought himself a Dell laptop, which was delivered and set up by a Best Buy associate. He paid to have the Internet installed and encouraged his indifferent mother to use the 'Net with him.

He set up an email account, played games on the 'Net and eventually he found his way to the "bad things" Momma spoke of. But along the way, he learned other things.

At Amy Pigtails' suggestion, he went to a Web site called HealthCheck and learned that his clubfoot could have been repaired when he was a child. He also knew there was training to help him with his word problem. He knew this to be true, he was learning to slow down and refocus after doing core exercises on a website about dyslexia. He was reading better every day and learning things that he never would have thought possible. These revelations opened his eyes and changed his attitude on his mother.

She wanted to keep me dumb, he thought. *Wanted me limited.*

Momma wasn't the caring, selfless human being that he always thought she was, but a selfish teller of untruths. He understood that Momma had held him back so that he would not leave her. Norris' father had left. Uncle Linwood had got himself killed, and she had been afraid that Norris would leave as well. While he still loved her and understood her motivation, he felt betrayed at the fact that she had hidden from him the possibilities that he might have a normal life.

That was why she had fought him on the computer, why she had not taken him to a doctor about his foot.

This new knowledge had culminated in a harsh exchange of words. Words that came out of Norris' mouth in a fit of anger when she prodded him about the computer and again brought up the magazines.

"I know why you wanted that box," she said. Norris was quiet at first, hoping she would leave it at that. But she didn't. "Dirty things, Norris. You look at dirty things. Things that are turning your mind into a cesspool of sin."

"I use it to learn things, Momma," he said weakly.

"I'll bet," she snapped.

Norris could feel his anger begin to percolate. Bubbling inside his guts, fueling a rage he had never felt. "You don't know," he seethed. "You don't know what I look at."

"Oh, I know. I know exactly what you're looking at."

And that was it. That was Momma's bluff that unleashed Norris' darkest thoughts. At first, the words came out in a cacophony of stuttering accusations. "You... you... lied!"

"Oh, you best lower your voice in my house," she spat back.

"About... About my foot... that it couldn't be fixed. About my—my—my reading prob—prob—problems!"

"Norris, you are walking on very thin ice with me. I will not..."

"About everything! They could have fixed my foot, Momma. I read about it online. There's procedures, o—p— operations that they can do."

"Procedures cost money," she fired back. "There's no such thing as free healthcare. Where do you think that money would have come from?"

He paused a moment, deflated, but then saw the victory settling in her face in the form of a sardonic smile growing at the corner of her mouth, and he felt his rage grow. "You never even took me to a doctor. How would you know what it cost?"

She flinched, the smile gone, her eyes wavering. "Norris, stop this!" She lit up a smoke, her eyes darting away.

"I got made fun of in school, Momma. They called me Stupe and Gimpy Norris." Tears began to well up in his red-rimmed eyes. "I even got beat up a couple times. You coulda took me to a doctor!"

"Norris, please." She crushed the cigarette out. Her voice hitched, her lower lip quivering. "I don't want to fight."

"I was called gimpy and stupe, and I could have gotten help. It says so on the Internet! Isn't that the real reason why you didn't want me to get a computer? Isn't it?"

"I'm sorry, Norry. We didn't have the mon..."

"I don't believe you!"

"When your father left..."

"Lies, Momma. You just wanted to keep me here!"

"No, no, that's not..." And with those words came defeat, followed by tears. Norris should have let it go, but he was wound up. He held her in his critical gaze, eyes burning until she could take no more. Rising from her chair, she retreated to seek refuge in her bedroom.

"Lies, Momma. Lies!"

The door slammed and the lock clicked.

He sat there, staring at her empty chair, quaking with adrenaline, savoring his triumph. He'd won. He began to come down, listening to her muffled weeps. But he would not give in. Things were going to change. No more Gimpy Norris. No more Stupe. The last thing Norris did before he went to bed was put a password on the computer, just in case she went snooping.

3

The next day he went out the door without saying goodbye and off to work. His resolve softened through the day and thought maybe they could talk it out when he got home. He was mad, but he still loved her. If she would apologize, they could move on.

He put in his day on the bailer, swept up the loading area, and punched out. He walked home, dragging along the bad foot, and the rain fell, cooling the fury even more. She didn't have to apologize if she didn't want to.

When he pushed through the door, he expected to see her in her chair smoking. But she wasn't. He walked down the hall and knocked lightly on her bedroom door. "Momma?"

Nothing.

He tried the lock, it did not move.

"Momma, are you okay?"

Not a sound.

The door handle lock was the type you put on a bathroom door. But Norris knew how to get in. "Momma, please answer me so I know you're okay."

He waited.

One minute, then two, then three, and he began to feel dread. "Momma, I'm going to unlock the door. I'm worried about you." He went down the hall, got a coat hanger and straightened the hook. He came back and inserted it into the hole, pushing against the internal lock release. He twisted the handle and pushed the door open.

Beneath the bedspread lay a motionless form.

"Momma, wake up." She didn't move. So he ventured into the room and touched her. She was cold, her skin hard, like a rock covered in cold vinyl. He pulled back the blanket and saw her face. Her eyes were open, but foggy and vacant, her mouth was also open, her teeth clenched together, an expression of deep concentration on her face. She looked like she was trying to hold on, like something not of this world was trying to drag her away.

"Oh, Momma."

He sat with her for three hours.

During that time, he cried, then told her he loved her, and eventually that he had forgiven her. He confessed to her about the bad things. Worried that she might see him, from the spirit world, tugging on his penis as he scrolled through a labyrinth of pornographic sites. He felt shame, but not ashamed enough to stop. When the tears dried up, and he had nothing left to say, he called 911.

Momma had left him the house, which was paid, but little else. Norris ate mostly prepared foods: Chef Boyardee, Kraft Dinners, and Tombstone frozen pizzas.

With no one to watch him, he deepened his search of the "bad stuff" and began to change.

Now, Momma two years into her grave, and here he was looking at a picture of a murdered woman, feeling excitement and fear.

"You're flirting with the prophet of doom, Norry," Momma would have said. "Riding the slippery slope right into the mouth of the serpent."

Too late, Momma, I'm already there, he thought and clicked back on the picture.

4

25 July 2007

Syracuse, NY

Lance began thinking about the FBI agent, Lewis Ash. How he was no longer on the case. It wasn't how he'd imagined it. Ash wasn't the dogged investigator who followed him to the ends of the earth. He was just a broken down old man now, retired from a bureaucracy that was underfunded and overburdened.

Lucky for me, he thought.

But was it luck, really? Ash had been a part of the game since he started. That he had been taken out when things were just starting to come together was infuriating. With his ability on the Web, he'd been able to glean information from the news agencies and even the NICIC and ViCAP databases. He was able to do this incognito, though he thought that all sorts of people visited these sites, and he had not actually hacked into their databanks. The information about the case was publicly accessible on the FBI site.

His case was mashed in with other cases. A page of small pictures, mostly artist renderings, some photos. On his left, showed a sketch of a man with glasses who had raped four women in Arkansas and killed three in Alabama. On his right, a woman who was now deceased, that had been poisoning old folks in Seattle, Washington. She was a home care provider, and they had linked three murders to her, but the feds apparently thought there were more as they were asking for tips. Then there was his file.

Unknown Suspect

Age: Unknown

Race: White

Summary: Wanted in connection with serial murders of eleven people, possibly more. The victims are male and female. Victims were killed with a blade. Also, the killer committed Gross Abuse of a Corpse.

Lance was horrified to see his case sandwiched in between a serial rapist and a man wanted for a single killing. The accompanying framed picture wasn't even a picture at all. Just a black rectangle with the word Male cut diagonally in white block letters.

He thought he'd be on the Most Wanted list. Thought they'd have a whole page dedicated to him, but he was swimming in a sea of fucking mediocrity! Nothing listed about how he'd methodically lain out the victims! Nothing about his ingenuity in immobilizing them with the pick! Nothing about his nickname! He knew it, he had visited police forums where there were mutterings about the man they called Highwayman, but it was low key. He hadn't even made the Ten Most Wanted list yet. There was a man killing schoolgirls in Michigan who had robbed him of that. Two in Detroit, two in Ann Arbor, and another in Kalamazoo.

The competition. Who would have thought? The Michigan Man had robbed him of national attention, and with only five victims. Apparently, numbers didn't stack up against adorability. Albeit the schoolgirls had all been cute, easily trumping his derelicts.

Is that what I must do? Kill a couple cuties to get some national coverage?

Probably, but hanging out at schools trolling for children would inevitably get him caught, and he didn't want to get caught. The Michigan Man was living in the moment. He would eventually be captured or killed. He wanted to leave his mark and vanish. To do that he had to stay focused, he had to remember the end game.

He smiled now, discerning about Ash, about Norris, and about ways to raise his profile. Norris was going to be a useful tool in that quest, and maybe Ash would be too. He wondered what Ash was doing right now. Down there in Roanoke, Virginia. Fishing? Playing golf? Longing for the days when he wasn't a broken down old man and chasing the scent of a killer? He thought about contacting Ash, that would be interesting and would certainly raise his profile, but it would likely get in the way of his future plans.

Can't have that. There were bigger things on the horizon. Things that would make the Highwayman Killings look like a joke. But there had to be something that could include Ash, if not now, at least for the future. He'd have to give that some serious thought.

For now, it was better to focus on Norris, and what he could utilize him for. He'd already given him a present. Now he would watch him closely to see what he would do. Norris had no idea how close Lance was. He might think that Lance was on the other side of the world, when in fact, he was just a few miles away in a Super 8 Motel. Norris also had no idea that what he did in the next twenty-four hours would determine whether he became Highwayman's next victim.

5

They chatted into the night. A baring of souls, a show and tell that left Norris unburdened and liberated. He told Devon everything, about Momma, about Uncle Linwood, and about Amy Pigtails. Devon listened and gave thoughtful answers to all of Norris' questions. He confirmed that the picture was real, and that he had been the one. There was an exchange of other pictures as well. One from Rhode Island and another from Ohio.

Devon: They call me the Highwayman... ☺ But they're afraid to say it publicly.

Barker: The Highwayman? OMG. I wish I had a nickname like that. You sound like a comic book superhero.

Devon: I've been thinking about that, Barker. ☺ I think I have the perfect handle for you.

Barker: Really?

Devon: Yeah, it came to me when you told me about the girl in the Ohio River. You are a traveling man, Barker... ☺

Barker: What is it? Please tell me? Please...

Devon: What do you think of the Regulator?

Barker: The Regulator? I like it... But... What does it mean? What do I regulate?

Devon: All in good time my friend. Let's take this a step at a time.

Barker: ☹ Okay, sorry...

Devon: Don't frown, I have one more thing for you. A present.

Barker: Another present! ☺☺

When the chat session ended, Norris' thoughts were chaotic and random. He went to bed, but he tossed and turned most of the evening.

26 July 2007

Louisville, KY

The next day at work, he barely noticed Amy Pigtails sitting on the tow motor.

"Earth to Norris," she prompted as he stared into the bailer. "Anybody in there?"

He looked up and smiled, "Sorry."

"It's okay. Penny for your thoughts?"

"Just tired, Amy."

"Well, you better get some sleep, sweetie," she said and raised the forks on the tow motor and honked her horn. Then she backed away and was gone to meet the truckers in the loading docks.

Whore, he thought.

7

29 July 2007

Carlyle, Illinois

The Regulator wore a backpack when he visited the WalMart pharmaceutical section to buy the items he would need. He then took two buses and had to hike a mile. Many thanks to those fuckers at the DMV. But he was serene, and focused and hardly felt the strain on his clubbed foot as he trudged toward his destiny.

By now, the file had begun its self-destruct, but he didn't care. The Regulator, the sidekick to Highwayman, was about to start his real quest and at the end of this arduous march was the beginning of that journey.

"You will need a few things," Highwayman had instructed.

Only a few hundred yards from the site, he stopped to look around. He was alone, the wooded area was secluded, and there were no paths. He opened the backpack as the Highwayman spoke in his head.

"You will need to purchase medical slippers, so you don't leave tracks."

He slipped the neoprene covers over his shoes.

"You will need to dress before you approach the scene."

His hair, now cut down to the scalp, was slicked over with Vaseline.

"This will keep your hair from dropping at the site."

He spread a dab on each eyebrow as well.

"Do not take the backpack with you. Take only what you need."

He unpacked the condoms, guessing he'd need a couple, and hid the backpack in a bush.

As he trekked deeper into the woods, he was careful to break as few twigs and branches as he could. As he did this, his heart thudded in his chest.

"My present to you."

He spotted the body thirty feet out. It was as he had seen in the picture, but it was oh so much more real. He trod toward it, expecting that it would rise from the ground and point an accusing finger, but that would have required the use of its dissected limbs.

Highwayman's final warning: "Never touch the bodies."

Ten feet out, he heard his Momma say, "You are dancing with the Devil, Norry. Turn and leave now! Before it's too late!"

"It's already too late, Momma," he said.

Then he reached into his pocket, pulling out a condom.

***

CHAPTER 13 – HIGHWAYMAN'S SECOND WAVE

1

1–17 August 2007

The body in Carlyle, Illinois, would never be found. After this, Highwayman cut a lethal track from Reeds Spring, MO, to Kalama, WA.

Along that route, he killed in the states of Nebraska, Wyoming, Idaho, Montana, and finally Washington State. The killings were random, and unlike his previous conquests, he used a single vehicle. The number of victims had almost doubled during the month of August, but there was a distinct difference now.

Behind the Highwayman, riding a Greyhound, an odd little man with a limp was following the trail. He was a day and a half behind, and, communicating on a newly purchased Toshiba laptop, the Regulator was receiving GPS coordinates for each dump site. By the time Norris ambled onto the sites, which were far more remote than Highwayman's original body dumps, Lance was on the move again, choosing a location and victim.

All the victims were adults: male and female, all had been subdued with a pick and dismembered, but the demographic had changed. They were no longer throwaway people. Lance was careful not to grab anyone who would be noticed right away. His victims wandered out of bars heads swimming, coordination telltale. Easy pickings.

He knew that this was risky, but it was imperative that Norris made it to the dump sites before the authorities started looking. A little risk was well worth the reward. He'd doubled his portfolio and bumped some white-collar Ponzi-scheming shithead off the Ten Most Wanted list. Highwayman now had national attention. This pleased Lance, almost as much as the killing itself, but the plan was just underway, and the big project was only just being established.

In a wooded area, just outside Jackson Hole, Wyoming, Highwayman stood under a quarter moon. He was a sinister spectacle, hair and eyebrows slicked back with Vaseline. In his right hand, the glint of steel, winking moonlight that flooded the big starry sky with diluted milk. Below him, the man asked drunkenly, "Why?"

He ignored the question.

"Build it and they will come," he said, circling the man, the machete swinging and twisting at his side like a hungry serpent.

"Wha... I did nothing to you."

Twist—swing.

"I'm a fucking genius!" He grinned, the moonlight splashing against the whites of his teeth and eyes. "Build it and they will come."

And then...

Chop!

The blood jetted upward, geyser-like, inky black and thick in the cobalt dead of night. The man did not scream, he was too drunk, but he felt the pain, foretold by an agonized moan. Lance knelt down, watching in fascination as the geyser receded. He reached down, a gloved hand gripping the foot by the big toe and pulled the leg back away from the pooling ink.

The man groaned. "I don't wanna die."

"Shhhh," Lance soothed. "You're already dead."

Chop!

The other leg.

"You should be happy. You will be famous." He dragged the other leg off, inspecting his work. "People will remember..." He stopped; it was pointless. The man had already bled out. That damned femoral artery, it ended the ritual so quickly. He'd have to keep that in mind.

Chop! Chop! Chop!

Once he'd arranged the body, he took in his work. The air smelled of copper. Night creatures sung in his ears, and the power surged through him. It was all coming together now. Not far from the site was a lake. He carried his tools down to the water and waded in, then proceeded to wash away the war paint.

"Build it and they will come." Where had he heard that? Two movies. That baseball movie with Kevin Costner and the other had been *Wayne's World*, or maybe it had been *Wayne's World 2*? He wasn't sure but liked the analogy. Washing away the last of the blood he whispered, "They will come."

And they had.

He took the coordinates and saved them. Then he walked back to the van he'd purchased for the road trip. He'd subdued the victims as they were leaving the drinking establishments. Five of the eight were staggering toward their vehicles when he rolled up and used the pick to get them into the back. He supposed he was performing a public service. Maybe he could become a spokesman for Mothers Against Drunk Driving.

Now dry, he laughed aloud and dressed, wiping away the residue of Vaseline from his scalp and eyebrows. The hunt would intensify now, and he welcomed it.

2

17 August 2007

The FBI did not pick up the trail in Missouri until Lance was boarding a plane out of the Olympia Regional Airport. They did not see the pattern until they were on the third dump site in Gillette, Wyoming. They were behind the eight ball, a new agent had been assigned to the case and was overdosing on information.

By the time they deduced that Highwayman's pattern was bound for Washington State, the unknown man called Regulator was finishing up his business, tying off the last condom and taking pictures to be used in rituals of reliving the experience. No one knew about him or understood the relationship that was deepening between the two men. Nor were they privy to the communications on the Web. The Macabre Club was an exclusive phantom, with a limited community. But it was growing.

Transmission http://macabreclub.com

Chat Session Excerpt:

Devon: Keep the pictures to yourself. I know you're going to need them to get you through for a while.

Barker: I will.

Devon: You are my confidante, Regulator. I depend on you.

Barker: Yes, I won't let you down.

Devon: I know you won't. That is what I love about you. ☺

Barker: So, now I go home?

Devon: Yes, time to lay low for a bit. But I have a project I am putting together that includes you. ☺

Barker: You are an artist. That is what I love about you. ☺ ☺ I have to get back to work. I am saving the rest of my vacation days for whatever else comes up.

Devon: Good plan. Get your butt back home, and I'll contact you on my secure means once I've got this together. You did well. Lived up to your name.

Barker: Okay, I love you. ☺
Devon: I love you too. ☺
Secure Chat Session Ended

3

24 August 2007

Roanoke, Virginia

"Hello," Ash said into the phone. He was groggy, coming back from a nap brought on by an afternoon drinking session that might raise the eyebrows of relatives. Luckily, Ash had none.

"Is this the former FBI agent Lewis Ash?"

"Who's asking?"

"Dave Maxwell, Agent Dave Maxwell, FBI."

"This is Lewis Ash, and yes, I am retired."

"You're in Roanoke?"

Ash felt a sudden burst of anxiety. What was this about? Had they discovered the copies he made? His chest tightened, and then he took a deep breath and thought, *Who really gives a shit?* He was living like a house plant, drinking too much, acting anti-social. What could they really do to make things worse?

"What's this all about Agent Maxwell? You planning on coming down and buying me some dinner?"

"Actually, I would like very much to do that. I have been assigned to the Highwayman case, and I'd like to pick your brain."

He started gathering up the case file sitting on his coffee table. "Has he killed again?"

"I guess you're not much for the news."

"I've been sort of preoccupied."

With booze.

"Well, he's claimed eight more victims in the last two weeks. And those are only the ones we know about."

Ash sat up straight. "Two weeks?"

"Yeah. I was just assigned to the case, so I would really appreciate some insight."

"How many states?"

"Eight." And then, "Can we meet?"

Ash shuffled the papers, set them down. "Sure, when can you be here?"

"I already am."

"In Roanoke? Really?"

"Yes, we're under a lot of pressure, and as much as I hate to admit it, I'm on a severe learning curve here, Lewis. Can I call you Lewis?"

"Sure, where would you like to meet?"

"I just checked into Holiday Inn, the one by the civic center. I saw an Olive Garden about two miles from here. Would you be able to find it?"

Ash smiled. He was a regular at that Olive Garden. They had a weekly martini special he liked. "Yeah, no problem at all."

"Okay, how about 7:00?"

"7:00 works. Will you be bringing the case file?"

"Yeah, everything there is."

"Good," Ash said, feeling a sudden excitement. Maybe they would bring him on as a consultant. "Okay, Dave, I'll be there at 7:00."

"See you then."

4

24 August 2007

West of Kalama, WA

Norris was sliding between the sleeping world and the darkness of his subconscious as the Greyhound hummed along with the highway. He was exhausted; the schedule had been extremely demanding, but he was happy with the outcome. The Highwayman, Devon, had shown him the world he'd only fantasized about, although he craved more with each session.

Not being allowed to touch the bodies had been tough. Devon said that it would be too risky with DNA testing and though this had disappointed him, he obeyed the instructions to the letter. Devon had been completely honest with him, and he did not want to betray that trust.

Nestled into a seat by himself, he lay sideways, his forehead leaning against the cold glass of the window. He wondered where it would go from here. Devon said to avoid the news until they were done.

"Avoid the distraction," he said.

Norris guessed that Devon was more worried that his new apprentice would lose his nerve. And honestly, Norris might just have, but that time had passed. He wanted more, and he was willing to do just about anything to fulfill that obsession.

Even kill?

He turned the thought over in his mind, thought about Devon, no... Thought about Highwayman, because he believed that the two were mutually exclusive. Devon was personable, a good listener, non-judgmental. Highwayman, on the other hand? He was the one out there doing Devon's bidding, dismembering the gifts for Norris. Well, actually he was doing it for Devon. Devon was the master, Highwayman the dark other; but what was he like in real life?

Ruthless?

Definitely ruthless, he had to be. It was a necessary evil when you were a hunter. He imagined that he was like a machine, a predator that lurked in the shadows watching and waiting for that perfect opportunity to strike. Norris wished Regulator could be more like Highwayman.

I'd have to prove myself. Right now, I am just a voyeur.
Then he thought about Amy Pigtails.

5

24 August 2007

Roanoke, VA

Ash showered, shaved, popped two Tylenol, and tried to think what would be best to wear for his meeting with Agent Maxwell. First, he laid out a suit, one of five he wore when he was still with the bureau. After a moment's consideration, he decided that Maxwell would probably be dressed casual. He didn't want to look like a desperate old man trying to relive the glory days. So he pulled out some khaki slacks and a golf shirt, thinking they did not make him look like a depressed old man who had nothing to do, but drink and read through an unsolved case.

Appearances can be deceiving.

He let out a small self-deprecating chuckle.

"Maybe I should go dressed as a house plant."

He decided against that, put on the khakis and golf shirt, settled back into his chair and reviewed the Highwayman file, sipping iced tea while trying not to stare at the clock.

The clock moved at a sluggish pace.

Finally, at 6:30 p.m., Lewis Ash stood up, placed the case file on the coffee table and covered it with a copy of the *Roanoke Times*. He was only fifteen minutes from the Olive Garden, which meant he'd probably beat Maxwell, but he was going nuts, and he wanted to look at the new case file.

He locked the house up and considered calling Michelle to tell her about his meeting with Maxwell, then put it off. She was just getting settled into her new post at the bureau's Pittsburgh office. No longer a junior agent, Leigh would be taking on cases of her own.

"I'll call her later," he mumbled, sliding the key into the ignition. Then he chuckled again because only crazy people talked to themselves. He started the Ram pickup and pulled away from the curb.

Traffic was light, and he made it to the Olive Garden twelve minutes later. He had been right, there was no sign of Maxwell; he was eighteen minutes early. This left him nothing to do but look at his watch, peruse the menu, and drink something non-alcoholic.

When seven o'clock rolled around, and Maxwell still hadn't shown, he began to wonder if the Highwayman had struck again.

An hour later, he was angry. Not only at Maxwell, if that was, in fact, his name, but at himself for not taking down numbers. He was a dinosaur who still had a landline and no caller ID. He had a cellphone, but it was a flip phone, and he barely used it.

Goddamnit, I'm an idiot!

Pissed off, he ordered the sausage stuffed giant rigatoni and a Miller Genuine Draft. He ate half of the meal, had the one beer, and got the rest put into a doggy bag. He hoped that Maxwell had not been a ruse. Maybe some a-hole from the bureau pulling his leg; someone like Harvey O'Neill. O'Neill was a practical joker, and this might have his fingerprints on it, but there was a slim chance Maxwell could be real.

Slim to none.

He could call Michelle now, ask her who was handling the Highwayman file, and if she said Maxwell... Well, that would be good. He decided against calling her, for now anyway. Michelle wouldn't involve herself in this sort of thing, but he wanted to check on some things.

He pulled the truck into a gas station and filled it up. When he was done, he went into the convenience store and saw the headline on a copy of *USA TODAY*: **Cross-State Killer Sought By FBI!** Below that: **8 Known Victims in**

the last two weeks! And below that, eight photographs, presumably the latest victims, lined the page.

It was true.

He picked up the paper, scanned the story, and saw a comment from a Special Agent David Maxwell. "The perpetrator of these crimes has the FBI's fullest attention," Maxwell stated. "We will get him."

Ash reached into the cooler and grabbed a dozen MGDs to take home with him, thinking, *Okay, so Maxwell is real. But that doesn't mean that Harvey fuckhead O'Neill isn't pulling a fast one.*

He was in line behind a big man with severe body odor and thought of unfolding the paper for a full read, but he couldn't stand here reading the newspaper; there were four people behind him waiting to pay for their gas and goodies at the Salt and Sugar Shack. He decided to give it a quick read in the truck, and then boogie home, fire up his laptop, check the Internet and see what he could glean from the FBI site.

This was no practical joke.

Even O'Neill wouldn't pull a stupid stunt like this.

Back in the truck, he started to read the story, but a honk of a horn from behind got him rolling. He was jamming up the pumps.

"Yeah, yeah," he barked and started the pickup. "Impatient asshole!" When he wheeled the truck around to get off the property, he felt like an asshole himself. The lady was driving a van full of kids wearing little league uniforms.

"Shit, sorry."

The drive back to his place was harrowing. Twice, he'd almost rear-ended another vehicle, glancing down at the newspaper. The second time, the beer almost fell off the seat, leaving Ash with visions of fizzing cans and the smell that would come after that.

With that thought, he turned his attention to the road and drove the last two miles without incident. Inside, he was giddy and more than a little excited. There was a possibility, a distinct possibility, that something had happened to make Maxwell stand him up. He'd get home, check his messages and, once he'd figured it out, he'd call Michelle and see if she could raise Maxwell that way. It had to be another murder. He'd stood up a few witnesses in the past himself when a case took a left turn.

And they always did, didn't they?

Of course they did. Killers didn't operate on a timetable, sometimes you had to improvise and double back. He still couldn't believe he hadn't exchanged more information with Maxwell. Or even asked him where he'd cut his teeth. Shit, he'd only been out of the bureau a little more than eight months.

You're losing your edge, Ash.

He pulled the pickup into his drive and put it into park, in the rearview mirror the sun began its descent. He locked the truck and proceeded up the drive carrying beer and paper. When he was on the stoop, he fumbled out his key ring and unlocked the house.

Once inside, he sat down in the kitchen nook where his laptop sat idle. He turned it on, and while it went through its startup, he unfolded the newspaper.

He was hunched over the paper when he heard the footfalls squeak across the linoleum. He never got a chance to turn his head. Suddenly he was trying not to breathe as a rag was being held over his mouth.

Wants to knock me out? he thought and began to struggle.

Then came the fiery sting between his shoulder blades and that caused him to exhale and suck back in an anesthetizing breath. The pain from the stinger receded as quickly as it had come, replaced by a tingling below his neck. Distant aches, muffled by paralysis, but the cords upon which the pain receptors sent signals were still there, humming. Then a hand wrapped around his head and there was an aerosol spray. More of the stuff in the rag. The vapor went straight down his throat, into his lungs.

He went limp, like a man suffering a stroke. His body, or rather gravity, tugged him forward onto the spread out newspaper. Drool spilled from his mouth. The laptop declared its readiness with a cheerful chime. He had only one thought.

Highwayman.

Then the world went dark, but not for long.

***

CHAPTER 14 – ROAD TRIP

1

25 August 2007
Louisville, KY

Amy was waiting for Norris to return to work and tell her all about his holiday. As far as she was concerned, he had gone out to visit family in West Virginia. But on the morning he was supposed to report to work, Norris was a no show. He hadn't even called in, according to the shop foreman Bob Samson. Samson was pissed; he had twenty loads of paper bales scheduled to go out that day and was short because of summer holidays.

"He must be sick or something," Amy said.

"I don't know, but he's left us in a real pickle. I got trucks piling up." Samson scratched his head. "Ah, shit." Samson was rolling up his sleeves. "Looks like I just got demoted."

"Oh wow, management doing the work of peasants." She laughed.

"Very funny." Samson walked over to the bailer and said, "It's going to be a long day." Then he fired up the machine and got to work.

2

Norris was home, had been since the previous evening, but was in no shape to go to work. The evening's activities had been a depraving binge of self-gratification. He printed the pictures he'd taken with his digital camera and pinned them to the walls of his bedroom. From there, Norris embraced the darkness inside him. When the sacrament was finished, the sun was coming up and songbirds called to each other: it was 4:22 a.m. He collapsed onto his bed, naked, exhausted, and without a care. He was supposed to be up and off to work in a little over an hour and a half. He set the digital clock on his nightstand to go off at 6:00 and closed his eyes.

It will be a long day, but I can sleep tonight.

Norris drifted off.

When the alarm sounded at 6:00, he never opened his eyes as his hand floated to the nightstand and shut it down. He would not remember doing this later.

He awoke at 2:04 p.m. that afternoon, exhausted and raw from the night's activities. He felt disconnected and in a haze. Something inside him was different. During his nightly activity, he'd undergone a series of emotional shifts, including ecstasy, shame, anger, lust, and eventually depression. The depression was what was hanging on him now. Like a sandbag.

He wandered into the kitchen and opened the fridge. There was no milk, he'd forgotten to pick any up, so that meant no cereal or coffee.

"Crap," he said, and thought, *There's no going back now.*

He considered calling work, but didn't think he could stand being dressed down by Mr. Samson. He knew he'd have to call in eventually. Just not now. He couldn't deal with it; his mind was a horde of frenzied thoughts.

I need to clean everything up. Take the pictures down. I need...

What did he need? To restore order? To undo his culpability in murder, his acts of necrophilia? Had they been acts of necrophilia? He hadn't touched the bodies, just acted as a voyeur. But he had wanted to touch them. In fact, he had wanted to do more than touch. He desired that which pleased his mentor. Watching and even touching was not enough. He wanted more. To be more like the Highwayman. Without the anchor of insecurity, uncertainty, and self-deprecation.

He closed the fridge door.

Maybe he will take me along next time?

He climbed the eight stairs that lead up to his room. When he reached the short hallway, he stopped at the doorway of his mother's empty room. The door was open, the bed in which she died stripped. He felt an infinitesimal pang of guilt. Small, coin-sized stains of copper dotted the bare mattress. These were not new stains, but years old. Norris knew that they were menstrual but had no idea how long ago that had been stopped and replaced by the change of life.

"I'm sorry, Momma." He looked on a moment longer.

No response. Momma was with Uncle Linwood. He paused another moment and then carried on to his own room.

Once inside, he took the pictures down and had intended on burning them, but instead pushed them between the mattress and box spring.

I'll have to get rid of them, he thought.

It was too dangerous leaving things like that laying around. Too incriminating. He was pretty sure that Devon would be angry that he had even printed them.

"I will burn them in the backyard later," he said aloud as if declaring such a thing was a solemn promise. "I will."

He sat on the bed, staring over at his small desk and wondering where Devon was and wishing that he would come and take him away. He didn't want to be here anymore. He felt empty and doubted that he could ever go back to his old life again.

Norris wondered if he could sell the house, and quit his job. He had no idea how much the house was worth, how long the money would last... or even if Devon would let him go with him. Come to think of it, he had no idea what kind of life Devon lead. He could have a wife and kids. He could have a big family. People around him who would narrow their eyes at the sight of Gimpy Norris.

He frowned and reached beneath the mattress, clamping the pictures between his index and middle finger. He pulled them out and set them on his lap. He didn't have the energy for another ritual. He shuffled the pictures, stopping to pause, reliving each incident which now seemed far off, dreamlike.

3

25 August 2007

US 460 - West of Morgan County, KY

They were on the move, Ash strapped into the passenger seat of his pickup truck while the man who had stabbed him drove. Lewis Ash was upright, but his arms and legs were in some other universe, certainly not attached to his brain. His brain, on the other hand, was pounding, a headache induced by whatever it was the man had used to knock him out. He was just coming back, his lips were parched, a film of chemical residue akin to lacquer wafted up into his nostrils. That was the source of his torment. He doubted it was chloroform; something else had been used to knock him out, something he recognized, but couldn't put his finger on.

Drool ran over his lower lip, down his chin and pooled on his chest, where it was absorbed by the cotton shirt he was wearing. While unconscious, his head had tilted forward, his jaw hanging, leaving gravity to do the rest. As he came back from the chemical abyss, he lay still, head in the same position while he painfully took inventory of his circumstance.

Paralyzed, he thought.

But not completely. He had pins and needles in his arms and left leg. He could only imagine the damage that had been done when the pick pierced between his vertebrae, obliterating the nerves. This thought made him nauseous, so he pushed it away. He shifted his eyes left, taking in his captor, who held the wheel in both hands and had his full attention on the road.

Mid to late twenties, he thought. *Clean shaven. Close-cropped hair, slicked over with something... Hair gel?* Ash suddenly understood why they hadn't recovered even a single follicle at any of the crime scenes. *No skin, no fibers except the neoprene fiber.*

Vaseline, Ash thought. *He slicks himself up and nothing falls off. Not skin, not fiber, and no fucking hair. He's like a magnet, he probably picks up fibers and DNA but doesn't drop a thing.*

Ash opened his left eye and tried to focus on the man driving his truck. He looked sinister in the light of the dashboard, his shiny skin stretched taut against his cheekbones, rimming his eye sockets and outlining his skull like the Grim Reaper.

Not like... He is *the fucking Grim Reaper, and he's here to collect.*

He knew what came next: he'd be driven to a remote location, stripped naked, and chopped into six pieces. Panic rolled through him and the obvious requisite to reconnect with his arms and legs became imperious. He tried to will it, mentally reaching outward, across the static of pins and needles, looking for a toe or a finger to wiggle. All the while, his head bobbed with the contours and bumps of the road, saliva spilling from his mouth.

Nothing. Goddamn it! Nothing.

"You're awake," the man said, still watching the road ahead. Ash said nothing, just opened his eyes wider. "It's nice to finally meet you."

Ash let out a low exasperated laugh.

"Something funny?"

"I can't say I feel the same."

The man turned his head and looked at Ash. "Yeah, I completely understand, but under different circumstances, I'm sure you would have liked to have met me eventually."

"You're in the wrong seat for that."

The man snickered. "Yeah, I guess so."

"Do you have a name?"

"Are you trying to connect with me, Agent Ash? Make yourself more human."

"No. I just want to know the name of the sick fuck who's been killing people all over the country." Ash turned his head up and swallowed.

"Fair enough. I don't offend that easily anyway. You can call me Norris if you like. Or would you rather call me Highwayman? Nah, call me Norris, it's more intimate."

"Where are you taking me, Norris?"

"To an undisclosed location where we can be more..."

"Private?"

"Yeah, private."

"You're going to kill me. Like the others?"

"Yeah, but you'll serve a purpose much higher than the others."

"A purpose, huh." Ash was still reaching out, trying to find a sensation. If he could get the motor action in his left arm, he could grab the wheel and send them into a crash. Except his arms and legs were on vacation in a parallel universe. "So what's your story?"

"Story?" The man looked puzzled for a second, and then a dawning grin tugged at his lips, and he let out an amused laugh. "Oh, you mean why do I do it?"

"Yeah."

"Well, I don't have a story, Agent Ash. My mom never dressed me up as a girl, my dad never diddled me, no creepy uncles to speak of. When I think about it, I am what I am."

"Sure, you're just an average guy."

"No, I don't think it's anything like that. I'm just higher on the food chain than the rest of you. There are many species of fish, Agent Ash, many predators. I guess you could say that I'm a great white shark. Nothing eats me."

He was a predator, one with visions of grandeur. Ash continued his internal search, trying to reach the disconnected nerve endings of his limbs. Any limb.

Nothing.

"So," he said, "what did you knock me out with?"

"Oh yeah, I imagine you have a bit of a headache. I still have one myself." He reached down and brought up a small aerosol can. On it, the words Quick Start. "Ether. I read about it online. Sometimes when normal anesthesia was unavailable during the Korean War, doctors would use it to knock out patients. The only issue is that it is highly flammable and getting the dosage right is tricky. Potentially, the anesthetist runs the risk of knocking himself out." He set the can back down on the seat between them. Lewis eyed the aerosol can, desperately summoning his left arm to come back from its forced vacation.

Just one arm. Damn it!

That was all he would need to derail this.

One arm and a can of Quick Start.

"What's your real name?"

The man looked over, then turned his eyes back to the road, a short derisive grin bloomed on his face. He said, "While you were out, I took the liberty of looking around. You know what I found?"

This broke his concentration.

"I didn't know that you guys could keep official documentation, Agent Ash."

Lewis exhaled and lowered his head.

Norris, or whatever the hell his name was, grinned even wider and even laughed. "Oh, this is good. You aren't supposed to have that case file. Are you?"

"Fuck you," Lewis grunted.

"I should thank you, I guess."

"Again, fuck you, asshole."

"I didn't leave it there, oh no; that would have incriminated you, put a black mark on an otherwise exemplary career. I don't want you remembered as the agent who delivered the Highwayman case file into the hands of the killer."

Don't let him bait you, he told himself.

Lewis tried to resume his quest for motor action. Outside, the landscape rushed past, making him nauseous. He thought of paraplegics and amputees, understanding the madness they certainly would have felt while mentally trying to reconnect with lost limbs.

I'm already dead, he assured himself. *There's no disputing that, but maybe I can stop this bastard, foul up his plans.* All he needed to do was buy a little time and find out where his brain had hidden the keys to his arms and legs.

4

26 August 2007

Louisville, KY

Norris was looking at the basement door thinking, *Oh my, this wasn't a good idea. Not a good idea at all.* And it wasn't, of course; it went against all common sense and decorum. Devon would be angry with him. He placed his fist into his mouth and bit down hard on the knuckle.

Why had he done it?

Why! Why! Why!

"Because I'm sick," he blubbered. "Because I couldn't control myself." This was interrupted by the muffled cries, and he bit down even harder, breaking a blood vessel, copper marauding his taste buds.

He wished Devon were here now, to tell him what to do, how to fix this. Why couldn't he have been content with the pictures?

Why! Why! Why!

More biting, more blood, hot chaotic tears, and from the basement, muted cries that found only his ears. He tried to ignore the sound, to assure himself that he could fix this, that Devon wouldn't be angry. He rose from the chair, wiping the tears with his wrist, feeling the hot perspiration sting the corner of his eyes. Crossing the room to the basement door, he took long, deep, calming breaths. There was no turning back. It also seemed that Momma had passed over to the next world. He no longer heard her repeated pleas that he stop.

When he reached the door, he stopped, gazed down at the glass handle and wondered what to say. He didn't ask for this to happen. If she'd just stayed away, she'd be fine. He wanted to leave, to go to Devon, be the Regulator instead of Gimpy Norris. He touched the door handle and felt the slick sweat on his hand slide over the contours of the glass.

Deep breaths, he thought. He wiped his tears once more, turned the handle, and pulled open the basement door. Once open, the muffling cries stopped, replaced by a hush of consternation. He stood at the top of the stairway for a long time, gathering his thoughts, preparing.

It's coming to an end, he thought. He hadn't even begun to live, and now? *Where are you, Devon? I need you to tell me what to do!*

"You know what has to be done," Devon said inside his head.

I've never done anything like this before.

"But you've always wanted to." Norris stiffened. "It's time for a final transformation."

"Yes," Norris said, and placed a hand on the handrail, and then, "I'm coming, Amy Pigtails."

5

26 August 2007

They'd driven through the night. The trek took them across VA, WV, and KY. Lewis dosed, partially from fatigue, but mostly from shock. He had noted that his captor was avoiding the main interstate and tollways. They were on the Kentucky 15 for several hours, winding northwest to God knew where.

Lewis had given up on his search for feeling. He could only hope that when Norris, or whatever his real name was, moved him, there might be a spark between two severed nerves that would give him the ability to move something. There was another issue as well: a lump was rising in the spot where he had been pierced. It wasn't painful, but it was retarding what little motor action he had in his neck. That was why Lewis dozed. He was hoping that maybe he would just die from the piercing, maybe a blood clot would break free and stop his heart, or give him an embolism or an aneurysm. Lewis felt helpless, but he also felt ashamed. He had given this creep everything they had on him. He was already very smart, and now he had inside details on what they were looking at. Lewis would have loved to interview him on technique. Interviewed him in the confines of a detention center, where he would be in control.

Fat chance that will be happening now, he thought.

During his lapse in consciousness, they had stopped at a poorly lit gas station along the way to fill the truck up. Not just poorly lit, but likely no cameras. Lewis fathomed that his new friend paid cash as well, so there'd be no receipts. Taking a state highway was another way of avoiding detection. No tolls to pay, no attendants or EZ Pass to log their movement.

"Where are we going, Norris?" he said.

The man turned and gazed at him. "Ah, playing possum, Agent Ash?"

"You going to answer the question?"

"To meet someone."

Accomplice? Lewis shifted his head, the lump on the back of his neck making it hard to do so, but he straightened up as best he could. "I would have thought you worked alone."

The man smiled. "I do work alone."

He had the urge to tell this man to fuck off, to lash out, but shifted his approach to get him talking. "We found a glob of Vaseline at one of the dumping grounds, but we—I thought maybe it was a lubricant for self-gratification. You coat your body in the stuff?"

The man smiled.

"That's an effective way to avoid dropping DNA."

"It has other advantages as well."

"Oh yeah, like what?"

"Pretty hard for a Vic to get a grip on you." Lance did not mention that he only greased his face. He left out the part about the experiments, but he wanted to tell. It was an itch that needed scratching. "Anything else you'd like to know?"

"We don't call them Vics, Norris, or whatever your name is? That's the stuff you read about in detective rags. We call them victims." Lewis took a breath, pushed against the lump, which he was sure had grown to the size of a golf ball. "What about the cars? That had me stumped."

"Rentals at first, then I bought beaters. Easy to purchase and even easier to dispose of. Did you guys even look at the rental agencies?" They were slowing down now and he flicked on a signal.

"We did, but we were geared toward stolen cars, we spent a lot of time chasing that. It wasn't until much later that we started thinking rented cars." Lewis thought about some of his earlier cases. He relished conversing with a suspect he'd bagged and learning about their techniques. Those that would talk. Most did, once they realized they had been caught, liked to talk. They were on the exit ramp. Lewis caught sight of the highway green sign that read Louisville. "You flew."

"Yeah."

"You have money?"

He grinned. "Yeah, money isn't an issue for me."

"So, you fly into a place, rent a car, find a victim, return the car, and fly back out?" Lewis laughed; despite himself, he found amusement in how they had missed that. "You have a rich daddy?"

"Not anymore."

Lewis stared at his captor. "You've told me this much, why not tell me your real name? I know it sure in the hell isn't Norris."

"Yeah, okay. You do know that this will seal your fate?"

"Seal my fate? You mean you just stuck me with an ice pick and paralyzed me so we could get more acquainted? Seriously?"

He laughed and said, "Good point. My name is Devon."

"Last name?"

"We don't know each other well enough. Maybe later. When we are more acquainted."

"How many people have you killed, Devon?"

That question hung in the air between them. The Highwayman looked as though he was considering Ash's question. Adding up the numbers, the places, the victims. Finally, his face darkened and he turned to Ash. "Including you?"

6

26 August 2007

Louisville, KY

She was cuffed to a support beam, hands in front. Norris approached her and removed the gag from her mouth, then stepped back. He said nothing, his eyes fixed upon her in a steely gaze. He did not say so, but had decided that if she screamed, he would sink the cleaver into her throat. She did not scream. Instead, she only let out a gasp. When she gathered herself, she said, "Norris, why are you doing this?"

Norris produced a key with his left hand, and said, "I'm going to give you this. Remove the cuffs and set them on the floor." He leaned forward and placed the handcuff key in her hand. Then he stepped back, raising the cleaver as a warning. "Just remove the cuffs, nothing else."

"Norris..."

"Just do what I say!" His voice cracked. Taking in a measured breath, he gathered himself. Then, through gritted teeth, "Fucking do it!"

She fell silent, not wanting to enrage him. She worked the key into the cuffs and turned. While he'd been upstairs, she had twisted and pulled, trying to free her hands, but to no avail. Now her wrists were bruised and swollen. There a click and the right cuff unsnapped. She brought her eyes up to meet his, seeking approval.

He nodded.

She inserted the key in the left cuff and it unlocked. Slowly, she stepped from behind the support beam and obediently placed the cuffs on the floor. With that done, she stood back up, hopeful that Norris was coming to his senses.

"Let me go, Norris."

His eyes were far off, robotic.

"Please, I'm your friend."

"You should have stayed away."

"Norris, this isn't like you. Please..."

"Take off your clothes. Place them by the cuffs."

And there it was, the one thought Amy had suppressed. He was going to rape her. She had always known that he had a crush, had even teased him a time or two, but always thought it was harmless. Like a kid's crush... But Norris was not a boy, he was a grown man holding a meat cleaver. Amy decided at that moment that she would do whatever he wanted. She needed to pacify him. If she could do that, she had one saving grace in the back pocket of her jeans. All she needed was a minute alone and she could call for help.

She carefully removed each article of clothing, folding and stacking it upon the floor. He did not have to prompt her to remove her underwear and bra. The cleaver he held, the look in his eyes were enough to quell any thought of resistance.

When she was done, she stood before him naked.

"I'll do whatever you want," she said. In the back of her mind, she began to numb herself and prepare for the horror of being raped. Just a minute or two alone, that's all she needed. She was terrified that it might ring. Then all chance of rescue would be lost. "Whatever you want, Norris. Just don't hurt me. I'll do anything."

Norris' brow furrowed. She had said anything. She had no idea what he wanted. No idea at all.

"I'm sorry, Amy. You can't be here for this."

Then he came at her.

7

26 August 2007

Louisville, KY

They traveled the outskirts of the city, traffic still very quiet in the early hours. At one point, a big rig passed on the left, but Lewis was powerless to alert the driver of his situation. *This was hopeless.*

"Where are we going, Devon?"

"I have a safe place on the other side of the city. That's where we'll conduct our business."

Lewis felt weak like he was going to pass out. "Business. You mean that's where you're going to kill me."

"Yeah, but not right away. I'd like a chance to go over that case file, maybe talk a bit more. Maybe answer some questions so that you'll at least know. Maybe you can answer some of mine." He turned the vehicle. The sound of wheels suddenly changed from humming to crunching. They were on a gravel road. Rocks pinged off the undercarriage of the truck.

"You want me to enlighten you about FBI procedure? You're kidding, right? I'll never do that." Despite his circumstances, Lewis laughed. "Not in a million years, asshole."

Lance felt anger churn in his stomach. He wasn't used to the insubordination. The way he saw it, Agent Ash should be begging for his life, bartering everything just to gain a few more minutes of breath. "You got a lot of nuts for someone who has no way of defending yourself. The FBI teach that, Agent Ash?"

Lewis said nothing. Just grinned, as he desperately tried to move an arm, a leg, anything. If this guy could see through the false front, he would see Lewis' desperation and fear of the unknown. He didn't want to die, not like this, but he refused to serve that fear up to his captor. He was going to die, of that he was sure, but he would not go out begging or screaming. Because that was what this ghoul of a human being fed on.

No way, he thought and forced out a defiant laugh. "I'm sort of tired, Devon. Can you wake me up when we get there? I don't want to miss anything."

Lance tightened his grip on the wheel, forcing his own painted smile, but his mind was whirling madly. This wasn't going how he planned, not at all, and he felt powerless to change the course. He was supposed to take Ash out to the factory, they were supposed to converse like adversaries, showing mutual respect. Like generals meeting on the battlefield for the last time. But this man, this beaten down old man wasn't cooperating. "You know," he whispered, his voice slicing the air between them, "respect is a two-way street."

Ash chuckled. "Respect?"

"Yes," Lance seethed, but regretted letting the words out.

"You think I respect you? What do you think, we're all characters in a novel? You're a malcontent who can't assimilate with ordinary people. A freak. You kill people, because that's how you achieve some mental orgasm, because... I'm guessing you can't—"

Muscle crunched against bone, followed by a zenith of pain on the left side of Lewis' face, cutting him off mid-sentence. His head twisted painfully on his neck, pulling the muscles and tendons taut. White spots floated before him. Through all this, he heard the commanding growl of his captor.

"Shut your mouth."

The pain receded, leaving in its wake a numb, clay feeling that spanned from eye socket to cheekbone. He rolled his head slowly back, wincing at the thought of another blow, but still, it was a small victory. He'd gotten under this creep's skin. That was something. Wasn't it? When he focused, he saw the Highwayman massaging and shaking out the knuckles on his right hand. The blow had come from a closed fist; his knuckles weren't bleeding, but they'd sustained damage.

Maybe I can beat his fist to death with my face, Lewis mused and even laughed. When the Highwayman turned his head, Lewis decided to push a little harder. "Does your hand hurt, asshole?"

The confident mask had slipped, revealing the monster beneath and now he was scowling, eyes ablaze. Branches whipped against the window. The truck began tilting over to the right, and the scowl suddenly fell away from his face. In its place, blossomed panic. Gravel smattered beneath the truck, thrown from the wheels in operatic unison with the tree branches lashing against the passenger window.

Maybe we'll crash, Lewis thought.

But the thought was short lived. After a quick correction, the truck was righted and the pinging of gravel on the undercarriage lessened to the odd pop and knock. Along with that, the mask of supremacy began to return, flowing back onto his face like wax. He kept his focus forward, and said, "Here we are, Agent Ash. The end of the line."

Lewis turned his head to see the goliath of stone and steel looming in the opening at the end of the road. They were slowing. Ahead a chain crossed the road, and Lewis felt his heart first sink, then start to beat against his chest cavity like a man buried alive.

The truck stopped and Highwayman glanced over, a smirk dawning and overcoming the panic. "Don't go anywhere, I'll be right back."

Lewis said nothing.

The Highwayman, Ash could not think of him as Devon, climbed out of the truck and as he watched him walk toward the chain, he thought, *I'm really done. No escaping this.* Then, morosely, *Fuck it, I'm a head on a stick. The sooner we get this over with the better.*

But was it really?

Lewis didn't know for sure. His uncertainty of what lay beyond this world was what held him back. Would his wife be over there? Would his daughter? His mother and father, all waiting in the great beyond?

On May 31, 1984, Lewis Ash lost everyone who mattered. His parents were driving his wife, Candice, and daughter, Paige, down to their cottage in Virginia Beach when a passing fuel tanker blew a front steering tire and crossed the line. Everything in Lewis Ash's life was erased in a matter of seconds. According to witnesses, the big rig swerved across the line just as it met the opposing Oldsmobile 88 his father had been driving. The head-on collision killed all occupants of the car, but the truck driver was unharmed.

He hadn't been with them that day. He was supposed to be, but got called back in after six death row inmates from the Mecklenburg Correctional Center, in Mecklenburg, VA, escaped. Ash had told Candice to go with his parents and that he would catch up with them after the escapees were apprehended.

"These guys don't usually get far," he'd said. "You and Paige can ride with Mom and Dad, and I'm pretty sure this will be wrapped up in a day or two."

He was riding shotgun with another agent, Barry Kay, when he got a message on his beeper. Urgent: Call in. They were just outside of Richmond. The message had come from Gene Sydney, the special agent in charge: SAC for short. Ash figured Sydney was going to redirect them, maybe take control of the manhunt.

When he checked in, Sydney gave him the bad news and pulled him off the case. Barry Kay had also been pulled and ordered to escort Ash down to the city morgue in Newport News, VA, where the bodies had been transported after the accident.

The six inmates would all be recaptured, while Ash buried his entire family and took special leave to mourn. All would meet their scheduled appointment with execution. Ash was left to wonder if Candice and Paige would still be alive if not for the escape changing their plans.

He turned his head slightly, watching his captor. Raw with emotion brought on by the memory of the accident.

The Highwayman was unclasping the lock, carrying the chain off to the right. He glanced back over his shoulder, his eyes meeting Lewis'.

He set the chain down.

Maybe there is life after death, Ash thought. *Maybe they're all waiting for me.* That would make it easier. If there was something beyond this madness. Beyond the dungeon of horror in which he was now imprisoned.

Highwayman was coming back now.

Or will my world simply blink out and cease to exist?

The driver's door opened. For a second, the Highwayman just stood there, a perplexed look on his face. Lewis stared forward, not wanting to engage him, afraid that he would be able to consider his soul. Instead, he hardened his stance, and said, "Come on, asshole, let's get this done."

The Highwayman said nothing, fascinated by the fresh tears glistening on the old man's cheeks. No longer enraged by the verbal assault, he climbed in and put the pickup in gear. Once they pulled through the gate, he stopped the truck again and got out to replace the barrier.

Lewis was unaware he'd been silently crying until the first coursing tear rolled over his upper lip and into his mouth, then another. Comprehension that he'd exposed himself to this monster sliced through him, resulting in convulsive shudders. Hiccups of anxiety hurtled up and his head lolled right, banging against the passenger window.

I can't even wipe away the tears! Oh God! Oh God!

The driver's door opened again, and then they were rolling up the dirt road toward the towers of steel. The Highwayman said nothing. But if he glanced Ash's way, he wouldn't have known. His gaze was fixed, willing the tears to stop, preparing himself for what was to come.

Holding on to the only thing he had left.

8

26 August 2007

Louisville, KY

Finished, the Regulator stared at his work and wondered what to do next. Nobody had come looking for Amy, but eventually someone would. She had a husband who would call the police. The police would go to her work and find out who she knew and talk to their supervisor, Mr. Sampson.

"Yeah, Amy mentioned she was going to check in on Norris. To see if he was feeling any better. Norris? Yeah, he works the bailer, but he never came in. He and Amy are sort of friends," Mr. Sampson would say.

The trail would lead right here. He didn't have much time. He had to get a hold of Devon. He wouldn't be able to stay here anymore, but would Devon be mad? Maybe Devon would turn him out for being so impulsive.

"You really fucked up," Devon would scold.

Norris began to cry.

"I shouldn't have done this."

"No, and now... I'm going to have to cut you loose."

He wouldn't be the Regulator, just Gimpy Norris.

This isn't fair!

He got up off the cold concrete floor where he had been sitting cross-legged and staring through Amy. He didn't have much time. They would be coming soon. He climbed the stairs, gathering his thoughts as he did. He had to get online and track down Devon: he would know what to do.

9

Blood flowed deep black across the scarred concrete toward the slotted drain by the hot water tank. Without the beating heart, it had been a deliberate affair, first pooling at each point of separation, then succumbing to the call of the gravitational slant. The body had been arranged like a starfish, then separated with a cleaver. It hadn't been as clean as the Highwayman's cuts, especially in the case of the meaty thighs. Norris had to take three hard swipes to separate them from the torso, but his work was done now, and he thought he'd done a fair representation of his mentor's work.

He watched the blood trickle down the drain, thought it would eventually make its way to the Ohio and onto Hades, where it would join the other floating entity. A sacrifice to the boatman as it welcomed her spirit. Standing over her, considering the frozen stare, he no longer thought of her as Amy Pigtails. He did not see the woman who had treated him as a friend, did not hear her pleading, "Please, please, Norris" or her high screams as he punctured her again and again. That part of her was gone, making her inanimate, waxen.

The basement was lit by the repeated strobes of a camera flash as he took pictures to add to his collection. Then he stared down into the black ichor that pooled between head and neck. He had one last thing to do before checking to see if Devon would be there to tell him what to do. Kneeling he dipped his fore and middle finger into the coagulating blood, and then he began to write in bold block letters.

HIGHWAYMAN

***

CHAPTER 15 – ESCAPE

1

26 August 2007

Norris' Residence

The blinking cursor pulsed against the empty screen, drumming a cadence that parroted the throb behind Norris' eyes.

Pulse—fade—pulse—fade.

With each silent beat, anxiety grew. Norris could hear his own voice calling, an abysmal ghost, banished to the far reaches of his insanity.

Pulse—fade—pulse—fade.

You've gone too far.

Pulse—fade—pulse—fade.

Momma was right.

Pulse—fade—pulse—fade.

There is only one path to redemption.

Kill yourself.

"Stop it!" he screamed. "Shut. Up. Shut. Up. Shut. Up. Shut. Up!" And then, he really did scream, standing up quick enough to knock the chair over.

Kill yourself.

"I will not!"

Kill yourself.

"No!" He pulled at his hair, spittle frothing at the corners of his mouth. "I will not. I will not." He began to blubber, expelled a labored breath, his head pounding mercilessly, and he held that way a long time as if to expel the ghost inside him.

The voice retreated.

Only silence and...

Pulse—fade—pulse—fade...

He darkened, a manic grin tugging at his face and he moved back in front of the computer, kicking the overturned chair aside. Eyes fixed to the screen, fingers crawling over the keyboard with tarantula grace.

Devon: Barker? Are you there?

Barker: Yes.

Devon: Are you alone?

Barker: Yes. Where are you?

Devon: Come to the window.

Norris turned, looked at the window which faced out on the street and felt his heart race. Had Devon come to him? He turned back toward the computer screen, waiting for another message, but there was none. Heart clawing against the inner cavity of his chest, he stepped away from the monitor and moved to the window.

He eased the curtain back. Expecting to see a lone vehicle idling below, but was disappointed to see nothing except the same cars that were usually parked there: the Andrews' dilapidated Safari, the Scullys' Chevy pickup, and that was it. The street was empty this late in the morning; most folks were at work, keeping up appearances. He scanned the neighborhood just the same. There was nothing, nobody.

Was this a stupid cruel joke? Was Devon leading him on? For the first time, he could feel resentment bubbling up. He whispered, "This isn't funny, Devon. I'm in real trouble here."

He made his way back to the computer, ready to type just that. He never saw the door glide quietly open, never saw the shadow in his peripheral and when he reached down to type a new message...

From behind, "Hello, Regulator."

2

The basement was dank, earthen, and the smell of blood intermingled with the foundation's decay hung in the empty space. He barely spoke, taking in the entire scene, staring at the corpse, his face vacant. Behind him, Norris stood back, waiting for a reaction. Terrified at the prospect of Devon's possible anger.

"How long has she been here?" he finally asked, his tone without emotion. He was looking at the word scrawled in blood, shifting his eyes from that to the body. "Who is going to come looking?"

Norris shifted uncomfortably, from one foot to another.

"This is important. How long?"

"Ten hours, maybe eleven."

"No one has been here yet?"

Norris began to shake. "I fucked up. I'm sorry."

"Answer the question." His voice was low. "We don't have much time."

"No. No one has been here."

He was hunkered down, careful not to step in the blood, his own heart beating faster. "You need to pack a bag. You need to do it as quickly as possible, ten minutes tops. They will be coming very soon, and we need to get out of here before they do. Do you understand me, Norris?"

Norris didn't respond. Not at first. He was just staring, his face contorting, tears welling up. He began shaking, "You're taking me with you?"

Then he began to cry.

Lance stood up and walked around the scene, careful not to step in the blood. He spoke as he crossed the floor.

"You need to decide what you want to take, and it can't be much. One bag. Only the important stuff. We are going to be running at first, people will be looking for us."

Norris wiped his nose, sniffled and said, "Oh... Okay. Should I bring my computer?"

"No, but I'll need to look at that while you pack."

"Okay."

"Get moving, the clock is ticking."

"Yeah, um... Okay." Norris pivoted and clunked up the stairs.

Lance didn't follow. He gazed back at the body, admiring the work and feeling like a parent of sorts. Was this what it felt like, to have a child? He was so dependent, and he wanted to please. Taking in the block letters, HIGHWAYMAN, that had at first infuriated, leaving him to think it might be a ploy to implicate him in the killing, but that just wasn't the case. This was an emulation. No, not just an emulation. Norris did not want to be Highwayman. It was a tribute, a first killing for the master. He had really embraced his persona, become what Lance had made him. He really was the Regulator. *He'd probably follow me to the ends of the earth,* Lance thought. *Do whatever I ask.*

Yes, whatever he asked, but he'd already deviated from the game plan. *He was supposed to cool off, lay low. He sure as hell wasn't supposed to murder anyone.*

Lance thought about Agent Ash, who was incapacitated at the Ironworks. Agent Ash, who still had to be dealt with. And now? They had to move fast, because Norris knew this woman, which meant there'd be questions. The bread crumbs would lead investigators here. If she were discovered, they'd put up roadblocks. He felt an urge to abandon Norris, but he knew too much.

Better to take him along.

Gotta move!

He climbed the stairs, careful not to touch anything, and when he got into the kitchen he grabbed a dishtowel and closed the basement door. After wiping the knob down, he was moving again, up more stairs where he could hear Norris rummaging around in his room. He entered the bedroom, reached into his pocket and slipped on some blue surgical gloves.

Norris stopped packing and watched him. "Should I be wearing gloves too?"

Childlike, Lance thought and said, "We gotta move. The clock is ticking. Finish packing."

Norris went back to stuffing a duffle with articles of clothing and keepsakes. There was a framed picture of Amy and him at KT Paper on the dresser. He reached up, looked at it sadly, and then put it into the duffle.

Lance unplugged the home computer and opened the side with a screwdriver, which sat conveniently on a shelf above the desk. Once opened, he removed the hard drive and pocketed it. "Any other computers in here? Anything? Smartphones? Tablets?"

"My laptop."

"What about photos, digital camera?"

"My camera, it has the pictures on it."

"Go get it, put it in your bag. Laptop too. We gotta be out of here in five minutes. Also, I need you to do something before we leave, but first, go get the camera and laptop. Okay?" Lance was becoming frustrated, but kept his voice even. There was no point in panicking even though he was sure he'd hear a knock at the door at any moment. A knock accompanied by badges. *Take it easy, she hasn't even been missing twenty-four hours. Shit, they might not miss her for a day or two.*

He doubted that. He was pretty sure this woman was married, and that she might have told someone she was coming to see Norris. He glanced around the room looking to see if there was anything else he'd missed. On the desk, next to the computer, there was a pad of paper. On it were doodles, scribbled passwords, and next to that macabreclub. com.

He tore the page off, balled it up, pocketed it and grabbed the pad of paper. "You got any Scotch Tape?"

"No, I have masking tape and—"

"Masking tape will do, meet me in the kitchen."

3

Ten minutes later, the Ram pickup rolled down the alley and was gone. It would be a full day before anyone came knocking.

Amy's husband Jeff wasn't home that day; he was up in Cleveland with a couple buddies attending an Indians game, which would lead to the attendance of a strip club and beer.

As the pickup rolled away, leaving behind the house with a note firmly attached to the front door window, a cell phone rang in the basement of Norris' house.

It rang four times and went to voicemail. On the other end of that voicemail prompt was Amy's intoxicated husband.

"Hi, sweetheart, me and the boys got carried away and had a few too many. We're gonna split on Motel 6. I love you, thanks for being such an understanding wife. I'll make it up to you when I get back."

He laughed mischievously and hung up, unaware that her cell phone was tucked into the hip pocket of her denim jeans, which were folded neatly in a pile only a few feet from her dismembered body.

4

27 August 2007

KT Ironworks

Cold, dark in here.

Lewis Ash opened his eyes, pain bore behind them, aching pinpricks brought on by another ether-induced trance, leaving him hungover, nauseous. He was on his back, staring up into the darkened rafters of the factory, and though he did not have the strength to lift his head, he knew that he had been undressed and prepared. He was in a steel mill; there was a pungent fragrance of welder's rod. Bits of slag on the floor.

Well, at least I slept through that indignity. He blinked, turned his head, first left and then right. There was a sliver of light which cut a vertical line to his left. A door. *Too bad I'm a fucking cripple. That could be my way out.* But even if he were able to move, he guessed it would be chained or locked. *What was that old saying? "Up shit creek without a paddle?"*

The Highwayman was gone. *Where?* he wondered. Maybe to get them a bite and some sodas, but he doubted it. He laughed aloud at this, a hopeless, dry crackling hiccup of a laugh.

God, I'm parched.

He listened to the darkness, waiting for a tell brought on by a scurried foot or the breath of a voyeur. He listened so intently that it hurt his head. Using his sense of hearing like a dragnet, trawling the darkness for any presence.

Nothing.

Maybe Highwayman got scared and took off. Maybe this place wasn't as secure and safe as he thought. Lewis doubted it, remembered what the Highwayman had said before putting his lights out for a second time. Where were they going?

"To meet someone."

An accomplice? Was that it? Had to be. But a full-time accomplice? Ash didn't think so, everyone in this guy's life was currency. He didn't believe in partners. He was an alpha, a loner, so what was the deal? *Whoever it is, they're expendable.* Yeah, expendable or disposable, a dupe or a mutt for this creep's endgame. But what was his endgame?

"To chop me up, of course," he grunted morosely.

Stow the fatalist crap, Ash, and start detecting.

"Sure, why not."

What is his endgame?

"He wants to be remembered."

But what is his ambition here?

"He wants to kill me and..." Lewis stopped. In the distance, he could hear an approaching vehicle. The drone of an engine, tires crunching on gravel. Ash turned his attention back to his body, reaching out one last time for a sense of feeling or the cool touch of air on his skin.

He wants to kill me, but he wants to disappear.

Yes!

He seeks credit.

There had to be something, realignment of nerve endings. Something that might give him the ability to crawl away, to hide.

I don't want to die!

The vehicle was close. Crunching tires slowed and then stopped. The engine cut out. Vehicle doors closed.

Kachunk, kachunk.

Lewis pushed harder, felt a tingle in the index finger on his left hand. His heart bumped and quivered, tightening his chest, constricting his breathing.

Focus!

Muffled voices, barely audible footfalls. Two men.

He pressed harder, furled then unfurled, and suddenly life found its way into the nerve endings of his thumb and ring finger. Pins and needles, but still, his hand was coming back to life.

A door, outside the room he was in, opened and shrieked on its metal track. Lewis was making a freakish fist now. If only he could get that arm to work. It might be enough to roll over, to drag himself to cover. He ignored the voices, the sliding metal door, and the footfalls of the Grim Reaper.

Focus! Bend your elbow! Bend your elbow!

He raised his arm, still fuzzy, still pins and needles, but the feeling was coming back. He bent his elbow, and with that, feeling started to come back in other places. His big toe on his left foot, his elbow on his right arm began to ache miserably, but he could feel it. Ignoring the pain, he pushed harder trying to reestablish communication with his limbs.

The voices were becoming clear, the footfalls closer.

Come on, come on!

Lewis made his first attempt to roll over, got halfway into a pitch, and rolled back. He sucked in a deep breath and held it and tried again, ignoring the approaching voices, trying to zone out like an athlete. On three, he told himself. *On three, I roll this body over and get into the doggy position.* He inhaled and exhaled again.

One, two, three...

He pitched over, coming down hard on his left elbow, the right still not quite there. His awakening was not limited to his limbs, his scrotum contracted into a hard plum, a reaction to the cool warehouse air. His penis had also tightened and under any other circumstances he might be self-conscious, but his bareness seemed inconsequential in the blue-gray gloom of the warehouse. He might have to fight this way, and in all honesty, it hardly mattered because he was in the match of his life. It was simple, very simple: fail and be killed.

They were coming. Closer than ever. Voices now audible.

Now I gotta move!

Lewis attempted to do the one thing he'd thought impossible only an hour before. He crawled like a drunk crab across the concrete floor. Scuttling toward the shadows, his mind a maelstrom of emotions: terror, anxiety, even giddiness. Behind, he could hear the switch of a door lock being turned.

Come on! Come on!

His bare knees scraped against rough concrete, his head turned awkwardly on its axis, drool spilling from his mouth. There was a gap between a stack of pallets, shadows in which to hide; that was where he was scrambling, and that was the Alamo.

Behind, a door creaked.

Lewis didn't look back, instead focusing on the opening, pushing his body, ignoring the scraping pain, keeping the terror at bay. The calling voice of gloom, the one that told him he wasn't going to make it.

The door slid across a rusty track.

The opening was only six feet away and from behind...

"What the hell! Hey!"

***

1

"Hold it! Hold it right there," the voice called. There was an air of surprised panic in that voice, but Lewis gave it no thought. He was only feet away from the opening, scrambling for his life, feeling insect-like. Then he heard something that made him stop. "Paul! There's a naked homeless guy in the warehouse!"

Paul?

"Holy shit," a second voice, presumably Paul, said. "Hey, buddy, take it easy, man. Albert, get your cell out. We gotta call someone about this."

Lewis froze.

"He's got no clothes on. What the fuck?"

Lewis turned and faced them, slanting to the right like a wounded chimpanzee. He was panting, more drool spilling from his mouth, his eyes wide and unpredictable.

They think I'm a crazy person.

"I can't get a signal in here," Albert said.

Both men were dressed in coveralls; the one named Paul was in his mid-fifties, sporting a rat's nest of gray hair on his head. There was a deep look of concern on his face. "Okay," he said, locking eyes with Lewis. "Can you understand me?"

He's talking to me.

"He's probably a schizoid, Paul. Don't bother, I'm going outside to see if I can get a signal."

"No," Lewis blurted. "We have to get out of here."

The guy named Albert stopped, looked at his buddy. "What's he talking about, Paul?" And before Paul could answer. "What are you talking about, mister? And why don't you have any clothes on?"

Lewis attempted to get up. "We have to leave now."

"How did you get in here?" Paul asked. "The door was latched from the outside. What in the name of God is going on here?"

"Kidnapped." Lewis tried to stand and felt himself shift suddenly. He stumbled backward against the stack of pallets he'd intended to use as shelter.

"Kidnapped by who?" Albert was shifting now, looking over his shoulder in panic. "What the fuck is he talking about, Paul?"

"How the hell should I know?" Paul barked. "Mister, you gotta fill us in here. What happened to you?"

"We gotta go now, he'll be coming back."

"Who?"

"Listen to me!" Lewis raised his voice. "I am an FBI agent, my name is Lewis Ash. I was kidnapped by a man I was tracking. He took me from my home in Roanoke."

"Roanoke, Virginia," Albert interrupted.

"Shut up and listen to me. We have to leave now. He's coming back. And he might be bringing a friend." Lewis was becoming faint, and the damage inflicted by the ice pick paralysis seemed to be returning. His knees began to buckle, he was going down. In desperation, he said, "I know how I look... Please, we are in grave danger. We have to get out of here."

Then he collapsed.

2

His chin was resting against his chest, the ground rushing by; in either ear, he could hear the labored breathing of two men. Paul and Albert were carrying his naked form through the corridors of the warehouse.

God love them.

His toes were dragging along the concrete as they sped him along and though he knew the skin on the top big toe, along with the nail, were being ground down by the friction, he didn't dare ask them to adjust their grip.

No time! We gotta get out of here.

And they were getting close; he could smell the fresh air flowing into the corridor, see the purple hues of enclosure withdrawing from the impending daylight. They were panting, but they weren't slowing down. Lewis knew that they believed him.

"Thank you," he said.

"You're welcome," Albert said.

"Hang on, mister," Paul said, wheezing. "Just a little further." Paul was the older of the two, the senior guy. He was the decisive one, Albert his ward. "We'll get you to the work van and then..." He wheezed, a cacophony of raspy coughs. Then he inhaled catching his breath. "We'll get you to the work van and call the cops."

Lewis didn't answer, not yet, he was raising his head, taking in the rectangle of light ahead. They were almost there, his big toe on his left foot was on fire now, rubbed raw, but he didn't care. He could see the van. All they had to do was get to it.

"Goddamn it, Paul. I still don't have a signal." Albert was looking at his phone with his left hand. "What the fuck is it with this place?"

"The Ironworks blocks the Verizon tower," Paul said. "We have to make it back to the river." He leaned into Lewis' ear. "We're going to have to put you in the back."

"Okay," Lewis said. "Just get us out of here as fast as you can."

"Who is this guy?"

They were crossing the threshold now, the abrasiveness of the floor replaced by weed and stone. "He's a serial killer."

A twisted sound came out of Albert; there were no syllables or words, just a croak. Lewis knew that sound. It had manifested itself in him a number of times in his early years with the bureau. It was accompanied by a tightening in the chest, a whirlwind of anxiety, a feeling of utter helplessness. It was the sound of fear.

"Jesus, Murphy," Paul muttered and they were on the driver's side of the van, setting him down on the ground. The other guy was fiddling with his phone, raising it in the air, trying to capture a signal. "Albert, get that goddamned door open! You're not going to get a signal here."

Albert croaked again, but he moved to the side door and slid it on its track. The floor was littered with tools, boxes of parts, Lewis wasn't going to fit. "I... I got to make some room."

"Goddamn it." Paul came over and started heaving stuff out of the van.

"What are you doing? That's my toolbox!"

"We'll come back for it when we're not trying to outrun a serial killer." Paul hurled a box on the ground, its contents clanging metallically.

Albert croaked again, but helped him unload.

3

Lewis was on his back again. The rubber floor was cool, and it smelled of dirty grease. He was going to need a bath when this was over. The floor was filthy and sticky. Paul was driving, and he was aiming for every pothole and bump in the road, because Lewis was taking a pounding.

Just lay still, he told himself. *Maybe when we get out of this, they can fix whatever it was that he did to me.*

"How far?" Albert was hysterical now, the croaks replaced by a whiny child-like tantrum. "Shit! I still got nothing, Paul!"

"Another mile," Paul yelled back. "We'll be there soon enough, kid. Just keep watching for a signal! Once you grab one, call 911."

They hit another bump. Lewis caught air, then slammed back down on the rubber-coated floor. He still had feeling in his arms and legs, but there was a fuzz that surrounded that feeling. A white noise that dampened the transmission to his synapses, buzzing over it like a horde of insects. Lewis could hear that sound, thought of the snow he used to see on the television, long before cable and satellite.

"How you doing back there, mister?"

But before Lewis could answer, he was sliding forward and slamming against the aluminum wall that separated him from the driver's compartment.

They had come to a full stop.

"Oh fuck," Paul said.

Albert croaked again.

Crunched against the separator, his neck warped hideously, a band of muscle rising beneath the skin like a finger, and with it, spasms. "What is it?" Lewis managed, but he already knew.

Paul said, "What kind of vehicle did the guy who kidnapped you drive, mister?"

Lewis felt his heart sink. "Dodge Ram." Lewis tried to push over, get back on all fours. "A black Dodge Ram, it's my truck."

"Back up, Paul!" Albert was screaming frantically and before Lewis could ask anything, he heard the growl of the Hemi and felt the impact, followed by the crunch of metal and plastic. Then he was knocked into the separator again. Paul didn't have to back up because they were being pushed.

A second before this happened, in the cab of the van, Paul and Albert were staring into the windshield of the Dodge;

behind the wheel, a man glowered as he held the wheel tightly in what Paul like to call a "Mexican standoff." Paul's heart was beating so hard, he could feel it in his ears, could barely hear the questions he was asking the man in the back, but he heard his response. And so it would seem the driver had heard the response, because his face tightened into a mask of fury and with that, the engine revved and the pickup truck came barreling forward. The collision was loud, the impact jolting, and a moment before they began rolling backward, Paul could hear Albert screaming to back up.

Too late for that, Paul thought.

The driver of the pickup was smiling, his passenger looked as surprised as they and was saying something to the driver. Paul had no idea, he was trying to hold his own against a much bigger vehicle, and even with the brake pressed firmly into the floor, they were being pushed back up the road.

Back the way they had come.

4

"Shit," Lance said, as he and Norris rolled up the gravel drive which led to the factory. Norris had asked what it was, but Lance didn't answer. He was enthralled by the piece of chain that lay in the road. The chain he had hooked and locked. The lock was open now, its shackle cut by a bolt cutter. Cut, because Lance had changed the lock after cutting the original off himself.

"What is it?" Norris asked.

"Be quiet." Lance rolled down the driver's window and pinned his ears back.

"Wha..."

"Shut up and roll down your window," Lance said, then turned to Norris like a patient teacher. "We have to listen now, Regulator."

Norris nodded and opened the passenger window.

At first they couldn't hear it; just the call of birds, wind whispering between the trees, and purr of the Ram's idling engine. Then? Far off.

The crunch of tires on gravel, a vehicle engine wound up and coming fast. Norris turned toward Lance and without a word, he acknowledged Norris with a raised hand. Ahead on the trail, there was a corner and beyond that a rise, but stretched out before them was one hundred feet of straight hard road.

Coming fast, Lance thought. *They've found him.*

But who were they?

Norris shifted his gaze from the oncoming sound and back at the man sitting behind the wheel. This was not Devon, but the specter that hid below the surface. Devon was gone, transformed in the passing seconds, replaced by something cold, predatory. This was the Highwayman.

"Listen to me," the Highwayman whispered. "They're coming and this is where the Regulator proves himself. Do everything I tell you. If you do, this will be over quick." His knuckles whitened as he clamped down on the steering wheel.

Terrified, Norris gave a nod of acceptance.

The approaching vehicle rounded the bend, it was a mini work van, and it did not look official. Probably a subcontractor sent out to the site to do some plumbing or electrical. They were coming fast, seemingly unaware that the road before them was blocked by a huge 4x4 pickup. But coming fast probably meant that they had found Agent Ash.

"Get ready," he said.

They were coming right at them, fifty, then twenty-five, and then the driver of the van, who Lance thought was going to run right into them, locked up his brakes and they skidded to a halt, not fifteen feet away.

Dust swirled up from the road, engulfing both vehicles in a haze, diminishing but not obscuring all visibility. Norris again shifted his gaze between Highwayman and back to the vehicle in front of them. He could feel his pulse pounding in his temples, wanted but didn't dare to say anything. He was along for the ride.

As the nylon haze began to recede, Lance watched the expressions of the two men. They were talking, and then he saw the man in the driver's seat turn his head just slightly. He was not addressing the passenger, but someone else.

"Agent Ash," the Highwayman said.

"What?" Norris said.

"Hang on to something," Highwayman said and shoved the accelerator into the floor. The Ram truck lunged, snapping Norris' head back. Before Norris could respond, his head snapped forward from the impact. He let out a small squeak. He clamped his right hand onto the dashboard and held on. They had connected with the work van and were shoving it backward up the trail.

5

Albert was screaming. Paul was yelling at him to try and get a signal. Lewis was struggling to turn over. All the while, the van had stalled, its transmission locked up. But they weren't slowing down. In fact, they were speeding up.

"Goddamn it!" Paul yelled. He was trying to get the van into neutral, restart it, and with any luck, get it into reverse, but the gear lever was locked. Everything was locked, in fact. The power steering had locked up as well, and to make matters worse, they were veering backward to the right off the path.

In the back, Lewis managed to get himself turned over onto all fours, he was pretty sure he had whiplash, but he still had some feeling. He had only one thing in mind.

Find a weapon.

"We're going to crash!" Albert cried. He was fumbling with his cell phone, trying to get a signal, dialing 911 again and again, but the phone kept saying No Service. "Why is this happening?"

"Hang on, mister! We're going into the rhubarb!" Paul yelled. Then they were bouncing off the road and down an embankment, listing over to the right. Lewis lost his balance then, collided with the van's sliding door, and remained glued there, unable to fight the gravity.

The van rolled down a twenty-foot embankment into the dense bush, cutting a path as it went. It hadn't come to a stop when the Highwayman stopped the pickup and unbuckled. He turned to a stunned Norris and said, "Now we have to act. Get out and give me a hand."

Norris unlatched his belt, the events of pushing the van backward up the road and down into the bush were surreal. He was becoming disconnected, much in the way he had when he killed Amy Pigtails. He thought that this must have been how Devon felt when the Highwayman took over. That had to be it. And now, Highwayman expected Regulator to join him and carry out the deed at the bottom of that embankment.

He opened the passenger door and stepped out.

Highwayman worked his way around to the truck box, began rummaging around, pulled out two neoprene white coveralls and handed one over to Norris. "I had to guess, but this should fit."

Norris stared at it dumbly.

"Grab a hold of it, Regulator." He was already putting on coveralls. "We haven't got a lot of time. They're going to run. I'm going to go down the bank and get started. You join me as soon as you're suited up, okay?" He pulled a jar of Vaseline, slicked his hair down, his eyebrows, and applied a coat to his face and neck. Then he set the open jar on the tailgate and lifted up a long homemade machete. He looked it over, then back at Norris. "In the tool bag, there's a hunting knife and a hammer. Take your pick and meet me down there."

Then he marched up the road and down the embankment as Norris tried on his new outfit. He was making his choice between hammer and knife when the first scream cut through the morning air. He decided on the hammer.

6

They were lodged against a tree and Albert had gotten out to try and free Paul, who had suffered a sprained arm in the crash, but worse, the bucket seat had broken off its track and pinned him forward beneath the steering wheel.

Albert was fumbling with the seat belt, trying to use it to dislodge the bucket seat, but the headrest was bending. "I wish you hadn't thrown out my toolbox, Paul."

"Yeah, me too..." Paul was smiling, trying to hide the dread that was cooking inside him. He placed his good right hand on Albert's arm. "I think you better get the tire iron out of the back."

Albert looked at him, knowing he didn't want it for leverage or to use as a tool. He said, "Yeah, maybe you're right."

Yeah, do it quick, kid, Paul thought. *Real quick!*

He backed out of the cab and started for the side door when he felt a hot sting just below the elbow. He heard a dull thump and looked down to see an arm laying on the ground. It didn't register at first, not until the ropes of blood began to spill from the stump where his arm had been. He gazed up to see a man wearing white painter coveralls taking another swing with what looked like a machete. He ducked and the blade pinged metallically off the van's roof. Albert then did the unexpected; he lunged at the man with the machete and knocked him off balance.

As the machete-wielding man fell backward, Albert made a run for it, but did one heroic act to counter his retreat. He kicked the passenger door of the van shut and screamed, "Lock it, Paul. I'm going for help!"

Paul did just that, watching Albert as he passed the van, leaking out gluts of blood with every step. Paul looked on, his heart breaking; the kid wasn't going to get far, not at the rate he was bleeding out. "Keep going, kid!" Paul cried. Then he heard the naked guy in the back say something.

"Find a weapon," Lewis said through the separator.

Paul would have responded, but the man in the white coveralls was standing at the passenger window. They locked into a frozen stare, which Paul broke to examine his legs and the seat for something, anything to fight back with. The cab was barren. Although he didn't want to say it, he knew he was worse off than the retreating Albert.

The man in coveralls tapped the handle of the machete against the window. He smiled and said, "I believe you have something that belongs to me." Then he drew back his arm and brought the butt of the handle into the glass. It shattered in a rain of square crystal pebbles.

Albert was working his way up the embankment, feeling weaker as every heartbeat hemorrhaged another glut of his lifeforce out onto the ground.

Just a few more steps, he told himself. Then he would be on flat ground again. He lifted his right leg, then his left, his head swimming. He'd get his second wind when he reached the flattened ground, be able to tourniquet off the wound. Four steps, then two, then...

Norris was waiting at the top of the hill, hammer raised high, waiting to bring it down in a lethal arc. He watched the bleeding man coming up the trail with fascination. He'd lost an arm, the Highwayman had done that. He was probably finishing the rest of them off.

But this one was for him.

Albert looked up, saw the strange little man at the top of the trail, and said, "Who are you?"

"I am the Regulator," he said and brought the hammer down on top of Albert's skull. There was a crack, like splintering of wood, a fleck of bone and a piece of the guy's scalp splatted against the white coveralls. Simultaneously, the guy dropped to one knee, fell to the right, and rolled back down the trail.

Highwayman reached through the broken window, unlatched the passenger door, and put out his hand to Paul. "Keys." In his other hand, the machete was held as leverage. "Now."

Paul reached down, pulled the keys from the ignition and dropped them on the floor. He was about to say that the vehicle was broken. That it really couldn't go anywhere, but it was cut short by a hot sting in his neck. He did not realize that the man had thrust the blade forward, severing his windpipe. Not until the blade withdrew and the blood began to milk out. He then understood that the keys were for another reason. To retrieve what had been his all along. The naked man in the back of the van. Paul's head lulled upon his chest. His gray coveralls darkened as the last of his life flowed down upon them. His last thought was whether or not Albert got up the hill.

Lewis lay in the corner of the van listening to the chaos play out, knowing that it was over. He could barely move his left arm and his legs were rubber. There was no escape, no way to fight back against what was coming.

The Highwayman had won.

There were two of them now, and they would drag him out and chop him up with little or no resistance. Dying wouldn't be the worst of it. It was the mortification he feared, the contempt in which he would be found. Cut into naked puzzle pieces and left for someone to stumble across. That was what he feared, likening it to the indignities he had come across his entire career. Victims who had been ejaculated upon, defecated upon, dismembered by the foulest of humanity in order to fulfill some unspeakable need for release.

He refused to surrender to that.

Norris ambled toward the van just as the Highwayman was opening the sliding door. The sleeves of his coveralls were splattered with blood. In his right hand, the machete glistened claret; he looked ominous to Norris. Godlike.

"They're all dead," Highwayman whispered into the door, a leering grin cut across the expanse of his face that personified evil. It was a grin only the Devil himself could possess. "Can you hear me, Agent Ash?"

Nothing.

Norris looked on as Highwayman slipped the key into the door lock and turned it. There was a successive click. He gripped the handle with his left hand, readying the machete in his right, then he slid the door open.

Lewis Ash heard the door slide across the track. Heard the clunk of the lock and faintly saw the light flood in. He was in the back corner, in a sitting position, his back against the driver's side wall. He only saw the silhouette fill the square of light, his vision had blurred. In an act of self-dignity, he pulled a piece of cardboard up over his crotch area; it wasn't much, but it would have to do. That was when he found the utility knife on the floor, and had he not been a puppet without its strings, he would have made a last stand, but he didn't stand a chance.

In the final seconds of Paul's life, Lewis Ash made his decision and sliced into the one artery he knew would be quickest. The femoral would bleed him out before Highwayman could have his way with him. Making the cut had been easy, almost painless, thanks to the nerve damage he'd sustained from the pick attack. He tried to sit up as best he could and leaned back against the cold steel. As the Highwayman stood outside the door taunting him, he grinned, feeling his world darken. When the door slid open, he was already looking out through a filter of black and white and he had two thoughts when the man screamed angrily.

You lose, asshole.
And before things went completely dark.
Don't touch the cardboard.

***

CHAPTER 17 – THE FUG GAME

1

27 August 2007

Outside Shelby County, KY

The drive on I-64 between Louisville and Frankfort, KY, took the better part of an hour and a half. They would have driven north on I-71, all the way up to Cincinnati, but Lance had to get rid of Ash's pickup, and he had a new car waiting in Frankfort. He'd purchased the car in Lexington, driving it back to an abandoned strip of land just outside the city limits.

As they pushed east, the late afternoon sun rode high, leaving them vulnerable to detection. The ride was quiet, Norris afraid to disturb the Highwayman's brooding silence feeling he was the reason for the intense silence. Norris wondered if had he been too slow in coming to help? He had killed the fleeing man, but he wondered if he'd been faster getting down to the van if Highwayman would not have been cheated of his prize.

When the Highwayman discovered the dead man, he went crazy. First, he stepped back, dumbfounded. Then a metamorphosis began. Every muscle in his body tightened, his shoulders bunched and the tendons in his neck pulled taut beneath the skin. Norris thought it was like watching a volcano getting ready to explode. He stood statuesque, processing what he had found. Computing the loss.

An eruption of words began. First soft, a temperament of shocked disbelief... "No. No. No."

Then, through gritted teeth, they began to climb in decibel. "No! Fucking no! Fuck! Fuck! Fuck!" This was followed by an angry roar, the machete twisting and turning at his side. His knuckles whitened on the blade's handle. His breathing became erratic, and he let loose another incomprehensive growl.

Something horrible was coming. Norris could feel its electricity. If Devon were ever there, he was gone, and the Highwayman had taken over.

He cut through the air with the machete. Twisting and chopping invisible ghosts in every direction. The long, bloodied blade clanged off the roof of the van's door jam, and when it missed the intended targets, it sliced through the thin air again and again. Each swing followed by a *whoosh*.

"No!" ***Clang!*** "Fuck!" ***Clang!*** "No! No! No!" ***Whoosh!***

Highwayman spun in circles, like a machine wielding a lethal blade striking out at invisible foes. Norris thought of the Tasmanian Devil cutting through trees, rocks, destroying everything in his path. This was how Highwayman looked. Norris stood back from the deadly arc, afraid that Highwayman might look to him as a consolation prize.

Norris didn't know it, but he was bearing witness to the monster unleashed. The raving madness that was Highwayman, untethered by the master, and if he had gotten too close, he would certainly have paid with his life.

"I hate you!" screamed Highwayman. ***Clang!*** "Damn you!" ***Whoosh!*** He turned and swung, turned and swung for what seemed an eternity. Perspiration broke through the Vaseline coat, his eyes darted angrily, and finally, exhaustion began to slow him down. The tornado slowed, the chopping arcs lessened, and finally, with the machete at his side, he looked skyward as if he were addressing God, or Agent Ash himself. "You can't do this! I wasn't finished! I wasn't... This is bullshit," he cried. "Fucking shit! Fucking bull. Shit."

Exhausted, he dropped to his knees, and brought the machete up and drove it down into the earth. "Fucking bullshit!" Tears filled his eyes, those of a child who has been told there will be no dessert, or that it is time for bed. When it seemed there would be no more, he extracted the blade and stabbed the earth again and again. "I hate you! I fucking hate you!"

He thrust the blade into the earth one last time, burying it halfway, and then dropped his head down onto the grip. He stayed that way, looking like King Arthur preparing to extract Excalibur from its penal stone, meditating in a sequence of unstable, melodious snorts.

Minutes passed, the wind rustled the trees, and the screaming murderous tantrum subsided. Taken by the afternoon breeze. Then, as if waking up, came calmer words that were more Devon than Highwayman.

"We have to leave," Devon finally said. His voice was emotional, off-kilter, but it was Devon. He took three deep breaths, shivered, and pulled the machete from the ground. He glanced around, never brought his eyes to meet Norris', perhaps afraid that the vulnerability he felt would be seen. He set the blade down and started pulling off the coveralls. There was uncertainty on his face, a sense of panic. "Get your suit off and let's get out of here before someone else comes looking."

Norris stared at him dumbly.

"Come on, Norris, we don't have much time."

"Okay, Devon." Norris dropped the bloodied hammer and reached for the zipper. He thought that Highwayman might kill him at that moment, but this wasn't the dark figure, this was his friend.

He handed Norris the tools. "Take all of this up to the truck. I'm going to sweep the area and make sure nothing has been left behind."

Norris didn't question. He worked his way back up the bank and waited for Devon.

Five minutes later, Devon came up the bank. The coveralls were stowed in a bag, tools of death wiped and replaced in the satchel.

Once inside the truck cab, his mood darkened, and Devon was gone again. Before the Highwayman started the truck, he turned to Norris, his face emotionless and said, "Soon, they are going to be looking for you." He paused a moment on those words, his face like stone, eyes piercing orbs that penetrated Norris. Then he spoke. "You're a liability now."

2

They reached Frankfort and pulled the vehicle behind a building that was part of an abandoned strip mall. They were out of sight. Norris was mute, stealing glances at the driver trying to decide if this was Highwayman or Devon. Meanwhile, the stranger held the wheel with both hands staring out into the vacant lot. He stayed that way for a long time, letting out an exhausted sigh, and turned to face Norris.

"You have to stay here, Norris. I am going to get us another ride, but I need you to keep an eye on things." He smiled when he said this. Devon had returned.

"Okay," Norris mumbled.

"I won't be long. I have another vehicle a few blocks away. You stay here and gather up everything: the gear, the tools, and the coveralls. Put it all at the tailgate and have it ready. Use a rag to wipe the inside of the truck. Handles, seats, anything we might have touched."

"Devon?"

"Yeah?"

"You're not going to leave me, are you?"

"No, I wouldn't have brought you this far if that was my intention." He opened the driver's door. "I'll be fifteen minutes, tops. Then we're heading east, and I am going to let you in on a secret." He reached out and took the little man softly by the shoulder. "Gather up our gear, and be ready to go in fifteen minutes." Then he got out of the car, walking away at a brisk pace across the dusty lot.

Norris did as he was told. He gathered the clothes, the tools, and everything that he thought might be incriminating. He used a rag to wipe down the inside of the truck, and though he tried not to think about it, the wait was an eternity. He anticipated a police car to roll into the dusty lot. The first thing they'd do was run the plate and ask for identification. He didn't even have a license to show them.

By the fourteenth minute, the combustion of anxiety was kindled by the summer heat. Norris could feel the sweat running down the small of his back, between his butt cheeks, causing an uncomfortable itch that was begging to be scratched. He ignored the temptation, knowing it would only be worsened by probing fingers.

By the sixteenth minute, he was going out of his mind, and he had begun rehearsing his confession to the police on the matter. "I didn't mean it. I am sick," he mumbled aloud. He was holding his duffle with his left hand, the right digging into his nostril for a dried kernel of snot.

The car, a gray-blue Cavalier, rolled into the lot just as he was eating the newfound treasure. The window lowered and revealed Devon smiling. The trunk popped and he said, "Need a ride?"

Norris swallowed the nugget and grinned. "Yes."

Devon got out, took Norris' bag, and left the other items.

Once they had everything, he took a container of lighter fluid and doused the carpet and seats. Norris didn't ask, but wondered why he'd had him unload and wipe the truck down if he was just going to burn it up.

He placed the bloody coveralls along with the tools back into the pickup and then produced a second can of lighter fluid and saturated them. He went back to the driver's side of the truck and said, "Get in the car, Norris."

Norris moved around and climbed into the passenger side of the vehicle while Devon lit a match and dropped it into the cab of the truck. There was no sound and just a hint of smoke. He tossed the second can onto the seat, and as he made his way back to the car, there was a sound. *Farump*!

The smoke thickened in the cab, orange and yellow light danced in its mirage. By the time he was again seated behind the wheel, it was ablaze.

Norris watched the fire hypnotically.

"My name's not Devon," he said.

Norris drew his eyes from the fire and back to the driver.

"My name is Lance."

"Lance?"

Lance cut him off and said, "I had to be sure, Norris. Sure that you were the one. I am now, so that is why I am telling you my real name. That is why I am risking bringing you with me."

Lance? Then Norris asked, "Where are we going?"

Lance gazed back at the cab of the truck, which was now engulfed in flame. The interior had caught, sending up plumes of black smoke. Fire licked through the window cracks. Soon, others would be drawn to the fire. Lance turned to Norris again and answered his question. "Pennsylvania."

"What's in Pennsylvania?"

Lance put the car into gear and began rolling out of the lot. He checked the rearview mirror and watched as the Ram's paint began to bubble from the heat. It would be a charred mess before anyone of any authority got to it. He turned east down the road and saw no one.

That was good.

"I have many secrets, Norris, and I have shared the biggest one with you so far, but there is much more to come. For now, let's get clear of this place and chew up a bit of road." He turned and gave a reassuring smile. "Okay?"

"Okay, Lance."

Lance pushed down on the accelerator, the little Cavalier picked up momentum. Behind, the dirty smoke of the Agent Ash's pickup tarnished the Kentucky skyline. There was a bang, one of the truck's tires had exploded from the heat. Then there was a second bang. Lance turned left up a road, keeping his speed at thirty-five mph.

When they were three miles out of Frankfort, they heard sirens. The skyward plumes of smoke were farther away, but easy to spot. Lance checked his rearview repeatedly. Norris glancing back over his shoulder.

"I've got a blanket on the back seat. If we come across anyone, you'll have to hide under it," Lance said.

"Okay," Norris agreed.

"No one can see you. If someone sees you, we'll be caught. Do you understand?"

"Yes, Dev- I mean, Lance."

Then Lance asked one more question. "Did I scare you?"

Norris didn't hesitate. "Yes, very much."

Lance grinned. "Good."

3

27 August 2007

State Route 850 - Landisburg, PA

Had they taken the main interstates, their travel time to Lawrenceville, PA, would have been a little over ten hours, not including gas stops and bathroom breaks. But Lance avoided the big interstates and even the US routes. The turnpikes and interstates had cameras, and some even had toll booths. So, when he could, he used the secondary highway and state roads to navigate from Kentucky through Ohio and into Pennsylvania. It was a long, exhaustive process and not without risk. He understood small boroughs sometimes had overzealous law enforcement looking to supplement their budget with unwarranted traffic stops.

They were into their eleventh hour of driving and still had one hundred and sixty miles to get to Lawrenceville. Lance was exhausted. Throughout the drive, Norris had several naps. At first, Lance found this humorous. It was very possible there was a nationwide manhunt on for Norris Connelly, and he was sleeping like a baby. Lance didn't know if they had found the body at Norris' house or if they had come across the bloodbath at the Ironworks. How could he? The shitty radio in the Cavalier wouldn't pick up anything except some evangelical fool espousing the *"word of Jesus"* through a sea of static.

They needed fuel; the gas gauge had dipped below one-eighth of a tank, and he had hoped to fill up in Landisburg, but the little town apparently rolled up its sidewalks after midnight. He didn't want to go into Duncannon, but decided it would be the only option. The small boroughs in this part of the state wouldn't have an open gas station after midnight. He was again driven off route just to get gas. This annoyed him almost as much as Norris' snoring.

He knew there was a small Sunoco in Duncannon, but thought it might be closed. A small gas station would be best, it would likely mean less possibility of working surveillance. He decided to try for that first.

The Sunoco was indeed closed, and as a bonus, a Pennsylvania State Trooper was using it as a hiding spot to nab speeders. Lance's heart jumped in his chest when he saw the car, but he kept moving, and the police car remained stationary.

"Dueling Rivers Travel Center, here we come," Lance said, stealing glances in the rearview mirror. The state cop hadn't moved, which was good. Norris woke up then and asked where they were.

4

"Keep your head down, I have to get fuel," Lance said. "And get under the blanket." He was turning off the highway and into the fuel islands. Norris was in the back seat.

"It's hot," Norris complained. "Can't I just duck down?"

Lance stopped the car just short of the glowing white lights and leaned in close, grating his clenched teeth into a carnivorous smile. "If someone sees you, it'll be a lot hotter in a holding cell. So, do me a favor, Norris, get your goddamned head down and keep out of sight." He reached around the seat and pushed Norris down under the blanket. Then he patted him on the shoulder and said, "I'll bring you back some ice cream. That'll cool you down some."

"Okay," Norris said.

It was hot, the night air humid and thick, beads of sweat ran down his lower black, but he knew that Lance would be angry, so he kept his head down. As he did, he heard the amplified sounds. Car door closing. Gravel crunching beneath Lance's feet. The compartment door for the gas cap snapping open. Norris tried to focus on these sounds, tried to ignore the claustrophobic heat beneath the blanket. Gas cap unscrewing, nozzle clunking as it penetrated the car's orifice, a sudden gush of liquid.

Norris abruptly needed to pee.

What was an eternity for Norris amounted to seven minutes in real time. The flow of gasoline ended with the *click-click-click* of the last ejaculation of fuel. Finished, the nozzle was withdrawn, clunking against the outer lip of the orifice.

He was overheating, it was horrible.

Gas nozzle being replaced. *Clunk.* Cap being screwed on. *Clickety-click-click.* Compartment door snapping shut. Then Lance.

"I won't be much longer. You want an ice cream or a popsicle?"

"Popsicle," he whispered. "And could I get a Mountain Dew?"

"Sure, why not?"

Lance shuffled away, toward the store. Norris listened. Until... The bell jingled, the glass door clamped shut, and Norris came out from under the blanket on the rear passenger side of the car. He was covered with perspiration, and he was hyperventilating. He sucked in great gasps of breath, stealing a glance over his shoulder to the driver's side, where Lance was, to make sure he wasn't coming back.

Occasionally, an event occurs that seems almost preordained. This was the case when Lance was hovering over a laydown freezer considering different flavors of popsicles. Meanwhile, outside, Norris was rolling down the window of the Cavalier. At that very moment, a girl named Jennifer Potter was texting with her friend Mina Carberry, and they were playing a game they had invented. It was a game neither of the girls' parents would have approved. The game was called Find the Fug, which really was short for *Find the Fucking Ugly*. The name of the game alone would have horrified both the twelve-year-old girls' parents, that they had been active in playing it for almost six months and had compiled three albums of pictures would have been an even tougher pill to swallow.

Jennifer was in the back of her parents' truck; they were heading home after visiting with her grandmother. Mina was up one Fug after a visit to the local WalMart two days before. The Fug in question was a woman of considerable girth, who was wearing flower print spandex pants and a red bra outside her wife-beater t-shirt. Her hair was green, orange, and dirty blonde. Even worse, her makeup appeared to have been applied by an orangutan with a paint roller. She was the best Fug so far, but Jennifer was looking to beat it.

She spotted the pudgy-faced man as they were exiting the parking lot. He was in the back seat of a crummy car, rolling down the window. Her parents, who were talking, seemed not to notice. But Jennifer was getting her camera phone ready. As they passed, she didn't think he was a contender for Mina's Fug. She snapped the picture and watched the man who followed her and the vehicle with his eyes. Their eyes were locked, and though she knew she'd been caught, there was no anger in the face of the strange, ugly man. He looked confused and maybe even a little sad. He continued to track her until her parents exited the parking lot in their Ford F350 Super Cab.

Once they broke contact, she leaned back in her seat and looked the picture over. The pic wasn't that great. Clear enough to see the man. See his eyes hold the camera lens frozen in his gaze. His face was doll-like, part of it shrouded by the car window frame, and over his head was a hood or maybe a blanket, which made him look like an ugly hobbit. This might have given a person a moment of pause, to reflect on the cruelty of the game they were playing. But Jennifer Potter was a pre-teen girl, and she didn't even know the definition of empathy.

She sent it, along with a text that declared **fug Alert!**

5

Lance returned to the vehicle, where he found Norris tucked beneath the blanket. He fumbled the door open and said, "Just stay low until I give you the word, it shouldn't be more than a minute longer."

"Okay," Norris replied. He wanted to tell Lance about the girl and the picture she'd taken, but he was afraid. Lance had told him to stay under the blanket, and he hadn't listened. This was his fault. If he told Lance, it could end badly. There was a real possibility that the girl had no idea who he was, and the police might never see it. She might even delete it.

Why take the chance of upsetting Lance?

Exactly, why take the risk?

The car was moving now, sliding into a left turn. The gravity tugging Norris to the right.

"Just a few more seconds," Lance said.

The car bumped out of the lot, and they accelerated.

Norris lifted the blanket and waited.

***

CHAPTER 18 – MAXWELL

1

28 August 2007

KT Ironworks - Louisville, KY

It took a day before the carnage at the Ironworks was discovered. This discovery was due to the persistence of Mrs. Albert Shimkus, who dogged the contract company and the police about the whereabouts of her husband. She was insistent that her husband was neither a drinker nor a womanizer. Like clockwork, he was always home in time for dinner.

"There's something wrong," she said to Gordon Koss, the supervisor at Jumpstart Contracting. "You need to go out and find them."

Koss went out to the Ironworks that morning. Driving his pickup right past the crime scene to the main warehouse. He never paid any attention to the broken brush on the side of the road. When he got to the warehouse, he found the pile of discarded tools, electrical parts, and boxes.

"What the hell?" he said, picking up a circuit breaker that he knew cost at least a hundred and seventy-five bucks, and that was one of four, not to mention the copper wire, the tools; it ran into the thousands. "Why would they throw all the tools on the ground?"

After that, he walked the perimeter of the building and again found nothing. He went inside and noted footprints in the cumulative dust, but still no sign of Albert or Paul. He left the warehouse and went back outside to look around. Before long, he found himself standing over the pile of tools and parts again, and decided that Mrs. Shimkus had been right. Something was wrong. He pulled out his cell phone, tried to make a call and found he had no service. "Man."

Koss got back in his truck and started back toward the service road. His thoughts kept returning to that pile of tools and parts.

It's like they were abducted by aliens, he thought and let out a bemused laugh that instantly made him feel guilty. He reached over rechecked his cell. No bars. "Fucking Verizon!" Then he saw the break in the bushes, and the tracks he had missed on the way in.

Koss drove just past the break, stopped his truck, and got out. When he did, he felt the hairs on the back of his neck bristle and a flutter of moths in his stomach.

"There's something wrong," Mrs. Shimkus whispered in his subconscious.

Koss shook it off, pushed Albert's wife out of his thoughts, and went to the bank. When he looked down, he saw the body at the bottom, and it didn't register that it was Albert's helper, Paul Perron. In later recollection, Koss would remember two things about that discovery: the moment he saw the body, and driving like a maniac to get out of there. He would never remember how he got back into his truck. Whether he walked calmly or ran. That part of his memory blacked out and would remain so until the day he would die the following year of a stroke.

2

28 August 2007

FBI Headquarters - Quantico, VA

Supervisory Special Agent Hugh Bailey was summoned by Deputy Director Julian Carswell that morning. Bailey was overseeing the Highwayman Murders from Quantico, but he had a field agent named Dave Maxwell following the trail. Bailey didn't much care for Maxwell because he didn't always follow the chain of command. Bailey hadn't assigned Maxwell to the case, that had come directly from the deputy director. Maxwell and Carswell had come up together, and when Highwayman became active again, Carswell told Bailey to assign Maxwell to the case. While Bailey didn't appreciate it, he didn't protest. He had a career to think about.

Typically, the case would be assigned to an FBI field office, and an agent from the National Center for the Analysis of Violent Crime (NCAVC) would liaise with local law enforcement. But Highwayman wasn't like other stranger killers. He was a traveler, which meant they had to assign a field agent who could move from state to state.

Bailey arrived at the deputy director's office at 10:25 a.m., where he was greeted by his secretary, Patti. "Good morning, Hugh. Grab a seat, and I'll see if the deputy director is ready to see you."

"Thanks, Patti." The informality of the deputy director's secretary annoyed him at first, but he learned to ignore it. She was a pleasant woman and had the ear of an influential member of the bureau. He was in the process of sitting on the couch when the office door opened. Out came Carswell and another man Bailey didn't know.

"Thanks for coming by, Keith, I appreciate the information." He shook the man's hand and turned to see Bailey, who was now rising from his half-sitting position. "Just the man I want to see. Come on in, Hugh," he said, then to the other fellow, "Thanks again, Keith, I'll have Patti set you up with another appointment."

"Okay, sir," Keith said and turned to Patti.

"She's the one that actually runs this place anyway," Carswell said and nodded to Bailey to go on into the office. Bailey went in and stood behind one of two leather chairs that sat in front of an oak desk. Behind him, Carswell talked briefly to his secretary, then stepped back in and closed the door. "Take a seat, Hugh."

Bailey sat down, and Carswell took the chair beside him, rather than sitting behind the desk. Bailey didn't know if this was a good thing or a bad thing.

"There's been a triple murder in Louisville, Kentucky," Carswell said. "You heard anything about it?"

"No, sir."

"Where's Maxwell?"

Bailey thought about it. "He's in Hollister, Missouri. He sent an email that he would be interviewing family members this morning."

Carswell placed both elbows on his knees and made a steeple with his hands. He leaned into that steeple, hooking his thumbs under his chin like he was praying. This was a mannerism that all his subordinates recognized: the boss was thinking. This went on for a few seconds, and then Carswell unclasped his hands, slapped his knees, and let out a loud sigh. Another well-known mannerism. "You need to get Maxwell on a plane to Louisville, Hugh."

"Sir, I don't understand. You want me to pull Maxwell off the Highwayman case?"

Carswell stood. "No." He moved behind his desk and sat down now. "We're keeping Maxwell on the case, the trail now leads to Louisville." He reached in and pulled out a thin brief and held it up for Bailey to take. "None of this is public yet."

Bailey took the brief and sat back down. As he opened it and began to read, the deputy director filled him in on the Louisville massacre.

28 August 2007

Louisville, KY

FBI Special Agent David Maxwell landed in Louisville, and after renting a car, proceeded directly to the scene. The bodies had already been collected.

The call came from newly-appointed Supervisory Special Agent Hugh Bailey. "Dave, we have a strange one in Louisville that might be related to your case," Bailey said.

Maxwell had been on the hunt. Chasing a phantom across the nation. He'd hardly had time to catch his breath over the last two weeks. His days, it seemed, were spent visiting crime scenes, riding airplanes and renting cars to visit new crime scenes. The last victim had been a woman in her late thirties, Jennifer Gilmore, snatched from a bar in a small town called Branson. Jennifer had one thing in common with all the other victims. She was a frequent barfly and drank religiously after work in a bar called Craig's. So far, that was the only thing they had learned. Maxwell was standing on the front porch of her sister's house, cell phone pressed against his ear.

"When did it happen?"

"Local investigators put it at late afternoon, yesterday. Multiple killings, three victims."

"That doesn't sound like our guy at all."

"One of the victims is a retired FBI agent."

"You have my attention, sir, but I'm not sure how..."

"The FBI agent's name is Lewis Ash, your predecessor."

"I'm on my way."

Now, the Chrysler 300 he'd rented was bouncing up the same beaten track that led into the steel plant. When he rounded the bend, he was stopped at a checkpoint, where he produced his ID and was flagged through. After parking, he walked three hundred yards up the roadway and passed technicians taking plaster castings of the tire tracks. Ahead on his left, he saw a broken bush where it appeared a vehicle had gone over the bank. Standing next to the opening was a tall, thin man. In one hand, he held his jacket draped over one shoulder and was smoking a cigarette with the other. Maxwell pegged him for the lead investigator.

"You the FBI man?" He had a slight southern accent. Maxwell guessed he had worked most of it off. He heard a hint of "youse" when the investigator said "you."

"Special Agent Maxwell." He extended his hand.

The detective placed the smoke in his mouth and shook. "Welcome to the shit show." The cigarette bounced up and down between his lips. "Detective Lonnie Perkins."

"What have we got here?"

"Let's take a walk down, and I'll tell you what we knows." His accent had thickened a little, and Maxwell thought that if this man were among his own, the drawl would come more naturally. Maxwell, a native of Oregon, hardly had an accent at all. When he traveled the country, sometimes picking up on the nuances of dialect and comparing, he found Bostonians and New Englanders the hardest to decipher. Southerners generally talked slow and deliberate while New Englanders bastardized words to no end. Car was *cah*. Park was *pahk*. Perkins crushed out his smoke on the heel of his shoe and tucked it into his hip pocket. From there, they walked the crime scene, and the detective filled him in.

Perkins explained where they'd found the first worker, pointed to the area where his body had lain, and surmised that he'd climbed the grade and had been struck down. "Looks like they were making a run for it when another vehicle shoved them off the bank. The guy on the hill was missing an arm, but we're pretty sure blunt trauma to the head was what killed him. We found his arm over there." Perkins pointed to the rear of the van.

Maxwell checked out the ground; there was dried blood everywhere, staining the brush and earth in rich copper hues. He gazed onto the driver's seat, it was a mess of blood.

"That's our second victim. He was stabbed with a large object in the throat. The only other trauma was a broken leg."

Maxwell looked over the scene. Blood had splashed up onto the dashboard and pooled there. It had since coagulated and hardened.

They then moved to the cargo section of the van.

"This is where we found your man." Perkins pointed into the back. "He never had a stitch of clothing on."

Naked? Maxwell ducked his head into the van. The cargo section floor was also covered in blood.

"We printed this one first, and his name came up immediately. Best we can figure is that our other two guys found your man and were trying to get him to safety when they were pushed off the road and slaughtered."

"How was the agent killed?"

"That's the odd thing. We think he took his own life," Perkins said, and before Maxwell could answer, continued. "He had a box cutter in his hand. Looks like he cut his femoral before they could get to him."

"They?"

"I would have thought two guys because our first man, who had his arm chopped off, made a run up that bank and was struck down. I'd bet the farm he was met by a second assailant, just based on the carnage, but also the way he was killed."

"Two assailants." Maxwell thought about it. *Makes sense.*

"There's something else that drew us to that conclusion."

"What's that?"

"Follow me." Perkins moved away from the van and toward a large yellow modular tent. "We've been placing all the evidence in here until the techs are ready to transport." Maxwell followed him into the tent.

Inside, there were three six-foot folding tables covered in plastic. On them were many items contained in plastic baggies. Perkins had donned a set of gloves when they entered, and Maxwell followed suit. "This led us to the conclusion that there were two killers." He reached down and lifted a piece of a cardboard box encased in a large evidence bag. "Your man had this over his crotch area. Presumably to hide his nakedness, but..." He turned the cardboard over, and scrawled in blood were two words stacked on top of each other. The words were written hastily, likely with a finger, and smeared from being pressed against Ash's body. But they were legible.

Devon
Norris

"Shit," Maxwell said.

"We put out a BOLO on a Devon Norris, just in case. But given how the first victim was killed by blunt trauma... I think we're looking for a team. I think these are the first or last names of our killers." Perkins placed the cardboard back on the table.

"I'm inclined to agree. Also, the names are stacked, if it had been one man, they would be side by side. I'll have these names expedited into the ViCAP database. If there's a Norris or a Devon, we should start getting hits."

"We've photographed everything."

"Good."

"My boss tells me that this is the work of the Highwayman?" Perkins looked directly into the eyes of Maxwell. His face was serious, it said *Don't bullshit me.*

Maxwell nodded and said, "There's an awful lot of coincidence. It's probably him. But I want to wait for the autopsy on Ash."

Perkins raised an eyebrow. "What will that show?"

Maxwell took a breath. "He incapacitates his victims by stabbing them in the upper spine with an ice pick."

"You think he did this to Ash?"

Maxwell didn't answer his question directly. "We haven't released this to the media. He sticks them, either before or after he takes them to a remote location. Strips them of all their clothing, washes them, then chops them into six pieces."

"Starfish," Perkins said.

"Yeah, starfish."

The search for the Highwayman had become as troubling as the hunt for the Green River Killer. When the murders ramped back up, the FBI decided it was time to go public, and Highwayman was now being written about in the media. Maxwell had played a part in that initiative. Coincidentally, it had also been his intention to contact Lewis Ash, and bring him back on board as a consultant.

Ash hadn't been wrong after all.

But Maxwell hadn't gotten to calling Ash, he was chasing the killer state to state. He would be following leads from one crime scene and get a call for another one. They were talking task force, but Maxwell hardly had time to get that done either.

He should have called Ash first. If he had, he might be alive now. He might be back in Hollister with the former FBI agent interviewing the Gilmore family, but maybe that was presumptive garbage?

"All done?" Perkins asked, breaking Maxwell's trance.

"Yeah, I'd like to take another walk over the crime scene. When I'm done, could you recommend a good place to get some dinner?"

"Sure, we can do both. I've been here since morning. I could use a bite as well. We can talk about the case."

Maxwell realized that Perkins had just invited himself to dinner. For some reason, this made him smile. "Sounds good."

They exited the tent, and Maxwell revisited all three scenes, again trying to imagine the melee that had gone on. He took notes, and when he gazed into the back of the van, where Ash had been found, he was overcome. The poor bastard knew he was done, but he'd taken his own life to cheat the creep of his kill. Even better, he left a clue.

Way to go, Agent Ash.

There was no doubt in Maxwell's mind. This was the work of Highwayman.

4

28 August 2007

KT Paper – Louisville, KY

A missing person had been filed by her husband, and a female police officer named Rachael Javaris was sent out to her place of work to follow up. The supervisor made mention that she might have gone to see a sick employee.

"What was the employee's name?" Javaris asked.

"Norris Connelly," he said and added, "He runs the paper baler. I think he's always been sort of sweet on Amy."

"They date?"

"No, nothing like that. Amy is always real nice to him, but even if she wasn't married, I doubt she would have much to do with him."

"Why is that?"

"Norris is handicapped, has a deformed foot, but he's also kind of, kind of slow, not completely retarded, but he's definitely a few bricks short of a full load." The supervisor looked down, ashamed of his statement. Even if it was true, he didn't like talking badly about Norris, because he genuinely liked him.

"You got an address on this Norris?"

"I can get Kathy in HR to pull the file. You don't think..."

"At this point, we're just covering all the bases; my guess is that she will turn up before the day is out. Maybe this Norris fellow can point us in the right direction." She jotted the name down on her pad, and then proceeded upstairs to see Kathy in HR.

Pulling up to the house an hour later, she found a note attached to the front door saying that Norris had left town.

"Shit," she said. It was a dead end. Something was bothering her and she wasn't sure why. Something felt wrong about this. She went around to the back of the house, looked in through the window on the back porch. Nothing, no sign of life. She opened her notebook, flipped back two pages, and reread the notes she had taken when talking to the husband.

The husband first called on the 26th, and after six rings, it had gone to voicemail. After returning home on the 27th, he found the house empty. He tried calling again three times. The phone rang six times and went to voicemail. He checked out the house and noted that Amy's work clothes were not at home. He had called this morning, and the same thing. The phone wasn't going straight to voicemail, so she could get the service provider to ping it. That would take an authorization from upstairs, and it would take time. Right now, she was just an absent wife whose husband had done an overnighter in Cleveland.

Something feels wrong about this, she thought.

The service provider was Verizon. She reached into her pocket, pulled out her cell, and punched the number in.

What the hell, why not take a chance?

Maybe the woman would answer, hungover in some hotel room after partying a little too hard with a fling. Instead, it rung unanswered, and it wasn't until the fourth ring that she heard a faint ringing coming from inside the house. She ended the call before it could go to voicemail. She'd already left one. Then she listened.

Nothing.

So she dialed again. This time, she cupped the earpiece and listened intently. There was ringing coming from inside the house. She checked the phone. The rings were in unison.

"I'll be damned."

She ended the call a second time. The ringing stopped.

She grinned, feeling exhilarated: the phone was in the house. She stepped back up in front of the back door and knocked. "Hello? Louisville Police. Is anyone home?"

Nothing.

Now what?

She couldn't enter the place without probable cause, and a ringing phone would not be enough. She was a uniformed cop, not a detective. A judge wouldn't be handing over a warrant without the word of someone more official.

Javaris listened, and after a minute of silence, she called the one detective she knew she could trust.

"Perkins," the voice answered curtly.

"Hi, Uncle Lonnie, I hate to bug you, but I need some advice." She squeezed the phone tight against her ear, a nervous mannerism she'd developed when expecting to be told no or fuck off.

"Hi, Rachael. What's going on?"

"I'm following up on a missing person." She took a breath, afraid she might sound nervous, but she was. "I am outside the residence of one of the people on my list to question. Anyway, the homeowner is out of town, but when I dial the missing woman's phone number, I can hear it ringing inside the house."

There was a pause, Lonnie was thinking. "Have you spoken to the homeowner? On the phone, I mean."

"No." She glanced down at her notebook. She had scribbled UTL, short for unable to locate, next to the name Norris Connelly. "He left a note saying he'd gone out of town."

Lonnie was quiet again. "Hang on, Rache." He covered the phone and was talking to someone, and that's when bells started to ring. Muffled, but still audible, she heard him say, "Keep an eye out for the names Devon and Norris. Anything comes back first, last, any variation."

"Lonnie."

"I know it's a long shot..."

"Hey, Lonnie!"

To the person, he was talking to, "Hang on a sec." Then to Javaris, "I need a minute here, Rache."

"My homeowner," she said. "That's his name."

"What?"

"Norris. Norris Connelly."

There was a momentary pause as Perkins processed this, and then he said, "Rachael, I am getting my coat on. I want you to go back to your cruiser. And stay on the line."

"What's going on?"

"The triple down by the Ironworks. One of the suspect's names is Norris. Get to that car and wait until we get there."

"We?"

"Yeah, I'm bringing an FBI guy with me."

"Okay." Javaris was making the way down the back stoop, the gravity of what might be beginning to sink in.

"What's the address?"

She gave it to him and then, clearly nervous. "I'm heading for the cruiser."

"Keep the engine running. Don't try and take anyone on yourself. We'll be there in ten minutes, and I'll see if you have another uniform in the area for backup."

5

Perkins was moving to the duty sergeant's desk, waving to Maxwell, who was coming up the hall, coffee in hand. He caught his attention and leaned on the duty desk. "Bob, I need a favor."

"What's up, Perk?"

"I need you to see if we have a uniform in the Chickasaw Park area. If you do, can you send a backup to this address?"

"Sure, what's going on?"

By now, Maxwell was at his side, listening.

"We might have caught a break with the triple. But we have a lone uniform officer down there, and I want to make sure she has backup. Tell them to roll in quiet, no lights or sirens. Just pull in behind and observe. No action until we get there."

"Who's the officer?" Bob asked.

"My niece, Rachael." He then turned to Maxwell. "Let's go, I'll explain on the way. I'm hoping that you got a judge who might fast track a warrant."

"I do," Maxwell said.

***

CHAPTER 19 – GIFTS

1

28 August 2007 - 1:12 a.m.
Off US 15 - near Trout Run, PA

North of Williamsport, Lance fell asleep behind the wheel. He hadn't dozed long, a micro-sleep really, but it had been enough to jolt him. The rumble strips on the side of the road were what snapped him back. Not on the right side, where Lycoming Creek snaked along the winding highway, but on the opposite side of the highway. In the seconds he lost consciousness, his hand loosened on the wheel. Then the car began to veer over the centerline. Now, they were riding the opposite shoulder.

He awoke when the chiding vibration below the wheels exclaimed the warning for which they had been embedded in the first place. To their left, the road dropped away, at least twenty feet, maybe even thirty, to a merciless grave of rock and trees. Lance tightened his grip on the wheel, careful not to overcompensate and eased the car back across the centerline to its rightful place on Highway 15. He held his position, contemplating how close they had come. Then he squinted into the rearview at the man he had been chauffeuring. Norris had slept through the entire incident.

Unbelievable, he thought.

He rolled down the window to let in some fresh air. It wasn't cool exactly, but the Cavalier didn't have AC, so it would have to do. The swirl of oxygen caused Norris to shift and snort. He let out a choking gasp. This pleased Lance.

We almost crashed! How the fuck can you sleep?

But that was sort of a silly question, because Lance himself had drifted off while in the driver's seat, and he couldn't even remember closing his eyes. They still had an hour of driving ahead of them.

Fatigue, he thought. *I've been burning the candle at both ends.* The events of the last few days, the constant racing of his mind and the schedule of killing over the last month, was finally taking a toll. He was crashing, like a drunk after a week-long bender. But the binge of killing had lasted a month. Maintaining a schedule, coordinating with Norris, and the others had been grueling.

Lance was burned out. He needed to get his head down for a power nap. He managed to keep going for another ten minutes until he found an unpaved road off US 15 that looked unused and relatively remote. Lance thought it was probably an old logging road, so he followed it almost a mile until it was overrun with wild grass. The Cavalier creaked and groaned as they went deeper into the woods. Stolen glances in the rearview revealed a comatose Norris, jostling back and forth, gulping and gasping, but never opening his eyes. When Lance finally found a suitable area where they could turn around and use the canopy of trees for cover, he brought the car to an abrupt stop, catapulting Norris forward and finally stirring him.

Lance got out of the car and urinated by the back wheel. There was a slight breeze. For this, he was thankful. The bugs wouldn't be as bad with the breeze. Lance zipped up and got back into the Cavalier. Norris was in the back on the passenger side, so Lance reclined the seat and tried to get comfortable.

"Where are we?" Norris asked.

"Near Trout Run," Lance said. "I gotta get some sleep. We'll stay here for a couple of hours, then finish the trip."

"I'm not really sleepy," Norris said.

At that moment, Lance seriously considered killing Norris and being done with it. He could go into the trunk of the Cavalier, get the tire iron, and beat Norris' brains in.

Instead, he said, "I am fucking tired, I've been doing all the driving while you've been doing all the napping. I need to lie down for a while."

Lance closed his eyes.

"What do you want me to do?" Norris said.

Lance opened one eye and said, "How about you stand fucking guard?" Then closed it again.

"Okay," Norris said, and started to open the rear door of the car and get out.

"Norris," Lance said, eyes still closed.

"Yes?"

"Where are you going?"

"I have to go to the bathroom."

Lance exhaled. "Don't go far, and wake me if anyone comes around."

"I will," Norris said, and closed the car door behind him.

2

28 August 2007

Louisville, KY

After meeting on the street with Rachael Javaris and another uniform cop named Sullivan, who had come to back her up, Maxwell made a call to Federal Judge Walter Poke and explained the situation. That they were investigating a triple murder that included a retired FBI agent, and they had reason to believe that a missing woman, Amy Hill, was inside the house of Norris Connelly. That Connelly was a person of interest in the triple homicide. Maxwell gave him the condensed version of the events, but it was compelling enough for the judge to give the go ahead.

"Sounds to me like the ringing phone is plenty for probable cause," Judge Poke said. "You get in there and do what you have to do, and just to be safe, I'll authorize a warrant."

"Thank you, Your Honor," Maxwell said.

"Good luck," Poke said and hung up.

Maxwell placed his phone in his pocket and started laying out the plan. "Here's what we are going to do. I want you two at the back of the house, just in case someone tries to run. Me and Perkins will go in through the front. Be ready for anything, but do not shoot anyone unless you are in danger of being shot." Maxwell looked at Javaris and Sullivan real hard. "This is a situation that can turn on a dime. So I am throwing out a warning before we proceed. If you shoot someone and they're unarmed, your career is over. So I want your weapons out and at the ready, but don't discharge it unless you are certain."

Perkins chimed in. "Don't you hesitate either. If anyone looks hostile and has a weapon..." He paused to look at Maxwell. "You take him the fuck out! We'll figure it out after."

Maxwell wondered what Perkins meant by "figure it out later" and if he was he referring to planting a throwdown gun if things went sideways. It was a possibility, although Perkins didn't strike him as a dishonest or dirty cop. Maxwell didn't dwell on it. He wasn't above getting a story straight after a takedown that went completely off the rails. Bending the truth, especially when the greater good was the endgame, was better than being a martyr.

"Everybody ready?" Maxwell asked.

Javaris, Sullivan, and Perkins all nodded.

Maxwell got out his gun and racked the slide. The others followed suit. "We'll give you two a minute to get behind the house. Set up on either side of the back steps, close to the house. If someone comes out, they'll run right past you, and that's when you evaluate the situation. Check the individual's hands."

"Try not to shoot anyone in the back," Perkins said.

"Yeah, that would be good too."

The mood between the four was electric. Maxwell could feel the adrenaline coursing through his veins; this was not new to him. He'd kicked in his fair share of doors over the years, but it was always an unnerving experience. Maxwell didn't know anyone with nerves of steel, except maybe the stupid ones who got killed along the way.

He and Perkins gave Javaris and Sullivan a chance to get into position. He watched Perkins staring after his niece, saw the concern in his face. He could only imagine what Perk must be thinking. When the two disappeared around the corner, Maxwell said, "Let's hope nobody's home."

"Yeah," Perkins said, flipping off his weapon's safety.

3

28 August 2007

Four hours later - Louisville, KY

It had become a media circus of epic proportion. CNN, FOX, MSNBC, and even foreign press, like the BBC and the CBC, set up on the barricades of what had once been Norris Connelly's street.

The woman's body had yet to be removed, the street was cordoned off, and the house was being swept by forensic specialists. Maxwell and Perkins were looking down the street where a sea of vans and RVs were lined up. Antennas and satellite dishes pointed skyward. Someone had leaked. Now, Highwayman dominated the headlines.

Javaris had been whisked away to give her statement to the Major Crimes Unit. A task force was being formed, but Maxwell doubted if he would be a part of it. Highwayman was on the move again, and Louisville was in his rearview mirror. No sooner they would put a static task force together, and he would strike again elsewhere.

"Goddamned media," Perkins muttered.

"Now the pressure is on," Maxwell said.

Perkins was lighting one cigarette off the other. "Well, at least we got his mug out there. Shouldn't take long before someone spots this clubfooted creep."

"Maybe," Maxwell reached up and pinched the bridge of his nose, his sinuses were filling up. The heat of the day was inflaming his allergies. "but this is a double-edged sword, Perk."

"Yeah, I know."

"If we don't get these guys fast, that mob over there is going to turn on us. We'll be tripping over the assholes, they'll be sympathetic for a while, but if we don't find them, they will turn their fake outrage on us." Maxwell felt his eyes puffing up and begin to itch. He reached into his pocket and pulled out his pills and took one. His phone rang. "Maxwell?"

Perkins couldn't make out the voice on Maxwell's phone, but he knew that it was an update of some sort.

"Yeah, okay. How long ago? Where? Okay, I'm on my way. Email me the address, and I'll call you back with an ETA." Maxwell closed the phone.

"What is it?" Perkins asked.

"They found Lewis Ash's truck up in Frankfort." Maxwell was standing up. "You want to come along?"

Perkins crushed out the smoke. "You really need to ask?"

"No, but I thought I would anyway."

They climbed into the 300 and drove off.

28 August 2007

Outside Tioga, PA

The power nap lasted two and a half hours, and Lance got moving again. Norris, to his credit, had dutifully stood watch without bothering him.

A Kentucky boy his whole life, Norris watched the rise and fall of the Pennsylvania hills under the light of a half moon with claustrophobic fascination.

The state was quite beautiful, the trees were in full bloom, but the thing that struck Norris was the duality of Pennsylvania. As they wound north on US 15, he had seen plenty of signs that said things like, No One Comes To The Father Except Through Me - *Jesus Christ*. This was Bible country, but you also couldn't drive more than twenty-five miles without seeing an advertisement for an adult store. There was a great abundance of adult stores in what seemed to be the most unusual place. If Norris had been driving, he would have stopped in for a look, maybe there would be a pretty woman behind the counter. Maybe someone like Amy Pigtails.

They exited the US 15 in Tioga, ran parallel on the PA 287 until the junction of PA 328, and then they went east. The road was rougher; overhead, the trees shouldering both sides, clasped hands cutting the moonlight into moving puzzle pieces across Norris' face.

"Don't you want to know where we are going?" Lance asked. He turned to Norris, a smile spreading across his face, widening into a big, toothy grin.

"Sure," Norris said.

"I own a cabin out this way, used to be my father's before he and my mother died in a fire." The grin did not falter and that struck Norris strange. "It's stocked with canned goods, so we will be able to hide out there for a bit."

"Do you think they are looking for us?" Norris watched the light flicker on and off Lance's face.

"They have always been looking for me. Now, they will be looking for us, but there will be one difference." The smile melted back into Lance's face.

"What's that?" Norris asked.

He turned to Norris. "Once they find what is in your basement, you will be on every news channel in the country." He slowed the car, turned left onto Burrows Hollow Road. "We have to hide you from the world, Norris."

"I'm sorry, Dev... Lance."

The smile returned.

"It's okay. We'll get you up in the cabin and sit tight for a while. Maybe there will be a terror attack or someone might go on a shooting spree, the twenty-four-hour news cycle has a short attention span."

"Yeah?" Norris sounded hopeful.

Lance sharpened his smile. "We can change your appearance as well. Maybe you can grow a beard." He was lying, of course. Norris was a huge liability and the others would be coming soon.

"I've never had a beard. Do you think it would really change how I look?"

"Ah, here we go." He turned right up an unmarked drive, tree branches brushed against the side of the little car, and the canopy became like a tunnel. "My place is about a mile up."

5

28 August 2007

Pittsburgh, PA

Special Agent Michelle Leigh got the call from the Quantico office after they identified Lewis Ash. The FBI Deputy Director, Julian Carswell, told her as much as he knew.

The conversation was surreal, his words came through a filter of disbelief; she agreed with him when he said that she would have to depend on her fellow agents to track the killer down. She listened intently, knowing that they would not assign her to the case.

"Maxwell is one of our best, Michelle. He's a tracker, this is what he does. I've known him a long time. There isn't a better man to be assigned to the case."

"Yes, sir. I know of him."

"He will find the killers; the bureau has made this their top priority."

"Yes, sir." *Killers?*

"Lewis was one of our best. We'll get the bastards."

"Yes, sir." *Bastards?*

"I'll have my special assistant put together a brief for you this afternoon. Maxwell is on the case, the bureau is on the case, we are on this. No one takes one of ours and..." Carswell went on with accolades for Lewis, mock concern for Michelle, and the hollow promises of keeping her in the loop.

When the call ended, Michelle set her phone down on the kitchen table and heard Lewis inside her head. "You're one hell of an agent," he said. "I'm proud to have served by your side."

She felt her body tighten. Her hands balled up into fists. Her face became flush hot. Then the blur of tears drowned her vision. She was frozen, staring into the void, and feeling disconnected, could not hear her own weeping.

They wouldn't keep her in the loop. She wouldn't suddenly find herself on the hunt for the person or persons who killed her mentor. Although she wished it were true, the reality was that they would keep her as far away from this case as possible.

28 August 2007

Frankfort, KY

The pickup was burned beyond recognition. As Maxwell and Perkins approached it, neither could really tell its make. When the fire department arrived, it was just a smoldering hulk. The tires were gone, the interior reduced to ash, white-hot springs replaced the leather seats. The only part of the truck left unscathed was the back bumper and the Virginia license plate, which brought about a quick identification by the state cops.

Maxwell spotted the head of the claw hammer first, and then the machete blade. "They left us some gifts."

Perkins looked in from the passenger side. "So they did."

"That's a first, this guy is pretty thorough."

"He doesn't leave things behind?"

"Just a body, but his MO has changed, probably due in part to his new buddy, Norris." Maxwell stuck his head further into the burned-out hulk, careful not to touch anything and hoping to see something that had not been destroyed by the fire. It was a fruitless effort. "You know what I think, Perk?"

"You think Norris is a liability for this guy."

"Oh, he is definitely a liability, and I also think he's living on borrowed time." Maxwell pulled his head from the window and came around beside Perkins. "I don't think that all this carnage was part of his plan. He has been way too careful up to this point, and this has just been way too messy."

"Maybe we'll get lucky, maybe they'll be spotted on the turnpike or in a toll booth." Perkins reached into his jacket, pulled out a smoke and lit it. "Norris is a nationwide celebrity by now."

"If he isn't a corpse already."

A crime scene van pulled up and stopped outside the taped perimeter. The driver and his passenger got out, began suiting up.

"Why do you think he went after Ash?"

"Ash ups the ante."

"You think he wants the undivided attention of law enforcement? That seems sort of reckless, given what you have told me about this guy." Perkins flicked the cigarette ash into his hand, and they began walking back up toward the van.

"This guy is all about presentation. Every corpse was methodically laid out for us. He wants to be known, and until now, we have cheated him of that. Ash managed to keep the Highwayman handle out of the public eye, actually, our boy was doing that unintentionally as well." Maxwell stopped halfway to the van. The two men were removing equipment from the back. "This guy would kill and then go dormant. The fact that he was doing it in different states was deliberate. He wanted the FBI involved, wanted to find his way onto the Most Wanted list."

"Still, wasn't he achieving that? He killed eight people in what, the course of a month? Why go after Ash?"

"Ash was a trophy and a message for us."

"A fuck you?"

They began walking again.

"Yeah, maybe that, or a message that no one is safe. That even an FBI agent could be taken." Maxwell started walking again. "The real question is: Why Norris?"

"A dupe. Someone to take the fall for him?"

"Maybe, but this guy is smart enough to know that the evidence would never add up. Norris took and failed the driving test six times. He couldn't have possibly done all the killings."

"So why?"

"I don't know, Perk. Maybe to get his numbers up. Maybe to throw us off the trail. A temporary diversion. Highwayman is a narcissist. He derives pleasure from this."

They reached the crime scene techs. Maxwell addressed the older of the two, pulled out his card, and handed it over. "In the front seat, there are two items, a claw hammer and a machete. Both items are burned up, the handles are gone. We have good reason to believe that these are the murder weapons. Can you process those first?"

"Sure, doesn't look like there's too much to go over, so we'll get that first and rake the ashes for anything else." The technician handed the card back to Maxwell. "Leave your card on the seat of the van, and I'll call you when it's processed."

Perkins lit a smoke.

Maxwell took the card back. "Thanks."

Perkins said, "Yeah, same goes for me."

Maxwell got into the Chrysler 300. Perkins was about to crush out the cigarette when Maxwell said, "Go ahead and finish your smoke, Perk. I gotta make a call."

The phone rung twice and was answered up by a woman's voice. "Special Agent Leigh."

"Hi, this is Special Agent Dave Maxwell, I took over the case from Lewis Ash."

"I know who you are."

"My boss told me to give you a courtesy call. I understand you and Ash were pretty close."

"Yes, he was a good friend and mentor."

"Look, I'm sorry for your loss. I'm in the field right now, we have Ash's vehicle, it was burned. I have forwarded a brief to my boss in Quantico, and he's is going to pass it to your boss in the Pittsburgh office. As you can guess, I am moving at a pretty fast pace, so..."

"Thank you, Maxwell. I understand you're in the field. I worked this case from Quantico when it was under Ash's watch. I will not keep you, I'll read the brief as soon as it's processed, but I won't impede your investigation by harassing you."

Maxwell relaxed a little and said, "Thank you for that. I may want to call you to pick your brain. Will that be okay?"

"Sure, my line is open 24/7." She sounded unconvinced and rightly so. Maxwell had no intention of calling her. He was on the hunt. Maybe after the fact, although he doubted she would have much to add.

"Okay, well, I have to get back to this."

"Maxwell?"

"Yeah."

"Find the bastard."

"I'm working on it." He hit the end call button and took in a deep breath. "You finished that smoke yet, Perk?"

Perkins opened the driver's door and climbed in. "Ready when you are, Max."

Maxwell started the car and they headed west, back to Louisville. They chatted, the two-hour ride a solemn one. Both knew they would be parting ways. Perkins would continue to work the case in the city, while Maxwell would take up the hunt of Highwayman into whatever state he next turned up.

***

CHAPTER 20 — HOT BROWN

1

28 August 2007

Lawrenceville, PA

Even under the moonlight, the cottage was appealing to the eye. It was a single level bungalow, painted charcoal gray with shutters to match. At its front, a circular drive made it easy to get in and out. Off to the side, there was a free standing carport. Inside and to the right sat a vehicle that had been draped with a beige tarp.

Once parked under the port's canopy, Lance cut the engine, turned to his companion, smiled, and said, "Home sweet home."

Norris gazed out in awe. "You own this?"

"Yes." He pulled the keys from the ignition and pushed the car door open. The interior light washed them in yellow light, and the door gave a guttural misaligned protest. Lance got out of the car. "Come on, Norris."

"Coming." Norris opened his door, got out of the car and stared about in wonder. It was beautiful. He could live out the rest of his days in a place like this. "You are fortunate, Lance."

Lance remained silent. His gaze vacant, his face expressionless. Norris had seen that look before; it was the look of transition. Before his other took possession. "We better cover the car," he said, more to himself than Norris. He moved around the covered vehicle, and said directly, "Give me a hand. We'll take the tarp off, and put it over the Cavalier."

Norris shuffled over and took up a position, and the two lifted the tarp up and off of the vehicle it had been protecting and onto the Cavalier. With that done, Norris turned his attention back to the car that had been cloaked. It was a car he recognized immediately because Uncle Linwood had had one just like it. The car was a jet blue 1968 Chevrolet Impala, and to Norris' eyes, it was a thing of beauty. Uncle Linwood's car had been red and not restored as well as this, which was complete. He gazed inside at the interior of two-tone blue leather and cloth. "Wow. Nice car, Lance."

Lance leaned in beside him. "It was my father's car. I don't drive it much."

Norris did not know how much Lance disliked the car. Or his father, but he could feel the vibe.

"We should probably get inside. I'm going to junk the Cavalier in a day or two and look for another vehicle." Lance left him standing there, and Norris soon followed.

The path leading to the front of the cottage was raised gray flagstone. Moss grew between the cracks, crawling over the surface of the rock, threatening to swallow each piece from all sides. It was spongy beneath Norris' shoes, moist from the evening rain.

When they mounted the porch, Lance turned to the left, and walked until he came to a planter box whose inhabitant had long since passed. He dug a finger into the soil, rooted around and produced a single key. He brushed the dirt away with his hand and opened the door.

The furnishings in the main living area were old-fashioned. Most were from the '60s and '70s, laminate dominated the wood furniture, and the seats printed with flower patterns. All were coated in a blanket of dust. The main living area had a sofa, loveseat, a leather recliner, and a round coffee table. The focal point of all seating was the forty-two inch LG plasma television mounted on the wall above the fireplace. The youngest piece in the ensemble, it stuck out considerably.

"You can put your bags in the back room," Lance said.

"Okay."

They moved out of the main living, Lance acting as a tour guide. "The kitchen is stocked with canned goods, survivalist stuff mostly, Spam, canned soup, stew. I'll go into Tioga later tomorrow and pick up a few things, like milk and eggs, maybe some burgers." They moved past the kitchen into a hall. "There's two rooms and a shared bathroom." Lance opened each door as he gave the tour. "This one is mine." The room was dark, in it was a king-sized bed, a solid wood clothes hutch, and above the bed, a ceiling fan sat dormant. The room served one purpose only.

"Does the television work?"

Lance looked confused, "Television?"

"In the living room."

"Yes, I have a satellite dish. We'll check it out later." He led Norris to the next door and opened it. "This will be your room."

Norris looked in. There was a queen bed and a small dresser. The smell of musk hung in the air, dust particles floated in currents of air caused by the disturbance of the door being opened. The room was bigger than his own, back in Louisville. It suddenly occurred to him that that house, Momma's house, was never going to be his again.

"Don't unpack, keep your stuff ready."

"Ready?"

Lance sighed. "Norris, when they discover the secret you have in hidden in your basement, if they haven't already, your face is going to be posted on every news agency in the country."

"I shouldn't have—"

"Let's not talk about that right now. Put your gear in the room and have a shower. You're smelling sort of ripe." He smiled, but it was a reedy smile, one of impatience. "There's towels in the closet and bars of soap below the bathroom sink. I am going to have a shower right after you, so leave me some hot water."

2

31 August 2007

Media briefing – Louisville, KY

The briefing room was full: a clutter of boom mics, television cameras, and recording devices. Most of the reporters were seated, but not all. There weren't enough seats to go around, so some were forced to stand. At the head of the room, there was a podium with a microphone set up. An officer in uniform was adjusting it by speaking a low "Test, test, testing, one, two, three." To the left and right of that were chairs set up for speakers to take their place.

The mood inside the room was electric. Some of the reporters were on their cell phones while some of the others checked their media uplinks. In the audience were all the major players, CNN, FOX NEWS, MSNBC, *The New York Times*, and Louisville's local news media including, WDRB 41 and *The Courier Journal*. There was blood in the water, and a feeding frenzy by the press was about to ensue.

Behind closed doors in the adjacent hall, Maxwell, Perkins, and the lieutenant overseeing the Homicide Division of Major Crimes. Also present were the chief of police and his deputy. Even Perkins' niece, Officer Rachael Javaris, was present. She wouldn't be speaking about the investigation, but acting as a spokesperson, introducing the mayor and the law enforcement personnel. She looked nervous; Perkins had spoken with her, told her that this was her first step in moving on from patrol into a detective position. In her hand, she held briefing notes. Maxwell thought she'd do okay, she had handled herself well during the entry into Norris Connelly's house. She hadn't thrown up when they discovered the dismembered body of Amy Hill. The other cop, Randy Sullivan, had to go outside and puke. They weren't even in the basement that long. They backed out once they determined the house was empty and Norris Connelly was gone.

Now, all were waiting for the mayor to arrive. Everyone looked tired, especially those in the ranks of leadership. Perkins had said, "Welcome to the shit show" on the day Maxwell had arrived. This was the real shit show. The media would be breathing down their necks from here on. There would be security issues, fear of leaks, and overzealous reporters looking for an exclusive. Perkins was put in charge of the highwayman task force along with another detective named Jessica Hood. Although Perkins didn't say it out loud, Maxwell got the vibe that Lonnie Perkins didn't like Hood much. She was a tall, slim, boney, unattractive woman, who had a voice which could only be described as shrill. She had talked to Maxwell briefly and gave him the impression that she didn't care much for the FBI.

"Ladies and gentlemen," the chief of police announced, "the mayor is here. We'll be starting very shortly. Officer Javaris, you should take your place."

"Yes, sir," Javaris said and glanced at Perkins.

In turn, he gave her a smile and a nod of confidence. She started for the doorway, looking like a scared kid. When she got there, she took a deep breath, checked her uniform, and straightened out. She was all business now. There was a job to do. She jettisoned the nervous look and went through the door.

The mayor came in then, and the chief of police called for everyone to pay attention. There were handshakes, and finally, the mayor asked everyone to gather in a semi-circle.

"Good morning, the chief has informed me that all of you have been working very hard on this case. I want you to know that you have my fullest confidence. I will only be giving a brief statement and then handing it over to the chief. I will not be taking any questions from the media, that will be the job of you people. Keep your answers short and to the point." He smiled at them, a politician's smile, then turned to the chief of police. "Bob?"

Chief Robert Knetter said, "Thank you, sir." And then turned his attention to his command and lowered his voice. "There are things on the brief highlighted in yellow that are off-limits to the press. Detective Perkins, Agent Maxwell will follow our address and give statements. They will answer the questions, no one else." Maxwell glanced at Detective Hood for a reaction. There was none. "Lonnie, could you add your bit here?"

Perkins stepped up beside the mayor. "We've got four murders on our hands and two assailants at large. The media is going to dog us, but those highlighted points are off limits. The state of the body in Connelly's house, the photographs that were found in his room are not to be discussed. If anyone leaks sensitive information to the press and we find out about it, make no mistake, it will be career altering." Perkins scanned his eyes over the group, and let them rest on Hood. She stared back and broke contact. Maxwell found that very telling.

"Agent Maxwell, you have anything to add?" the chief asked.

Maxwell stepped up next to Perkins. "Thank you, Chief Knetter." He cleared his throat and said, "This is a federal investigation, but it is also a joint venture. I won't rehash what the chief and Detective Perkins said about leaking. I will say that the unknown assailant who is with Norris Connelly has evaded apprehension for quite some time. He is smart and extremely dangerous, and to my estimate, uses the media and the Internet to his advantage. I'm an outsider, but I'm also a member of the law enforcement family. Agent Lewis Ash was a decorated member of this family, and our killers have sent us a direct message. No one is safe. Not me, not you, not your family members or friends. No one. Let's not give him... Correction, give *them* anything that will aid in their ability to stay at large. Direct all press queries to the media relations officer." Maxwell turned to the mayor. "That's all I have to say."

"Any questions?" the mayor said and paused. No one responded. "Okay, let's get this over with."

Maxwell leaned into Perkins and said, "Welcome to the shit show."

Perkins elbowed him lightly and smiled.

3

31 August 2007

Trout Run, PA

The FUG Alert arrived on Mina Carberry's cell phone two and a half days after it was sent. The reason for its lateness was Mina's father, Jack Carberry. He took the phone from his daughter as a form of punishment when she failed to get home before curfew. Mina was furious with her father, but he would not accept her lateness. Her father turned it off, put it into his pocket and said, "You will get this back when you learn to follow rules, young lady. But if you give me a bunch of guff, I'll make it a week."

Mina protested, but the threat of two days without her phone was, to Mina's line of thinking, equivalent to having her arms amputated at the elbow. The protest was short lived. Her father pocketed the phone only minutes before the text and picture were sent by her friend. This resulted in the FUG Alert hanging in limbo until 8:35 p.m. on August 31. Her father, who sat next to her watching CNN on the sofa, watched his daughter as she watched the news with keen interest. She was enthralled by the ongoing press conference out of Louisville, Kentucky. She didn't see her father staring at her intently. He did this often when he saw her in extreme bouts of concentration. It was at moments like this he felt overwhelmed with pride. Mina had already chosen her career path, even if at the tender age of twelve, her seriousness about that was steadfast.

My daughter wants to be a cop, he thought. Not a ballerina, not singer, not a movie star, but a cop.

"Maybe a government agent," she told him. "Like FBI."

Jack Carberry could have been worried, but he wasn't really. He could see the seriousness in Mina's eyes, had perused her growing library of true crime which included authors like Jack Olsen, Ann Rule, and other authors in the genre. She even had a copy of Truman Capote's *In Cold Blood.* She was extremely serious about her future, and was engrossed in a world most girls weren't. Jack Carberry was proud of his daughter's commitment, and thought that such dedication would inevitably lead her to success in whatever field she chose. This news conference out of Louisville had her full attention. He reached over and touched her shoulder. Mina gave a brief smile and turned her eyes back to the television.

"I guess you've learned your lesson," Jack Carberry said, and set the cell phone down beside her on the couch. She glanced at it, then back at the television, taking in the conference that spoke of murder and an ongoing manhunt.

Mina took the phone and said, "Thank you, Daddy."

He leaned over and kissed her on top of the head. "Pay attention to curfew, and please, if your mother comes in, change the channel."

"I will." She absently pushed the power button on her phone while listening to the FBI agent, Dave Maxwell, talk about the nationwide manhunt. Then on the screen a man's face appeared and below it scrolled:

Norris Connelly Is Being Sought On A Nationwide Warrant In Connection With Four Murders That Occurred In The Louisville Area.

A female anchor narrated, "Police are warning anyone who might come into contact with the suspect that 'Connelly is to be considered armed and extremely dangerous. Citizens are not to attempt apprehension, please notify local law enforcement by calling 911.'"

The phone beeped and then chimed. In a messenger bubble, she saw the words: FUG Alert! At first, she ignored it, but when the news conference began to wrap up, she picked up the phone and looked at Jennifer's message (Check out this sorry FUG), which was accompanied by a picture of Norris Connelly.

4

31 August 2007

Louisville, KY

With the press conference behind them, Perkins made good on a promise of some food, and he and Maxwell found their way to a restaurant called Kirbees Café. It was a quaint little restaurant with a '50s throwback feel. The tablecloths were checkered red and white, the walls were covered in memorabilia relating to Kentucky's world-famous racing derby. Pictures of horses with their jockeys covered the wall. The latest to hang was 2007's Derby winner Street Sense and jockey Calvin Borel. Maxwell looked closely at the print, and thought of Dan Fogelberg's song "Run for the Roses." Atop the dark brown horse sat jockey Calvin Borel in yellow and blue, wearing the smile of a man on top of the world, his lap covered in a garland of roses.

"You like horse racing?" Perkins asked.

Maxwell turned from the picture and shook his head. "No, I'm just absorbing some of the local histories." He paused then, caught Perkins in his sights and said, "You like the ponies?"

Perkins grinned. "Nah. My dad was a degenerate gambler. Blew the rent, the gas, the food money all on horses that were crazy longshots. I watched my mom struggle to keep us fed and disliked horse racing as a result."

Maxwell laughed. "Strange place to come for dinner."

"We're not here for the horses."

"Oh?"

The waitress was approaching.

"I guess we better grab a seat," Perkins said. "Here comes Charity."

"Lonnie Perkins, how are you?" The waitress was a lovely woman, in her mid-forties, with shoulder-length dyed blonde hair and carrying a sizeable bosom inside her floral print dress.

"Hi, Charity, this is..." Perkins started.

"Agent Dave Maxwell," Charity finished and gave him a seductive smile. "I saw both of you on the news tonight."

"Nice to meet you, Charity." Maxwell put out a hand, and she took it gingerly.

"Likewise." She squeezed his hand and smiled even broader. Maxwell wondered if this might be a prelude to a come on, then thought better of it. "What can I get you, boys, to start?"

"I'll have a double Jameson on the rocks and a glass of water," Perkins said.

"Sam Adams, with a glass, please," Maxwell added.

"Coming right up." Charity floated away to get their drinks, and Perkins touched his breast pocket absently. They'd only sat down, but he was already thinking about a cigarette.

"Did you..." Maxwell made a smoking gesture.

Perkins grinned, a little embarrassed. "That obvious, huh?"

"I smoked for about fifteen years," Maxwell said. "I get it."

"You used to be able to have a cigarette inside most places. Not anymore. City ordinance."

"Well, I can't say I disagree. I used to frequent places like that, and it's kind of unfair to the staff who aren't smokers," Maxwell said.

Perkins sniffed. He hadn't been converted.

Charity returned with their drinks a minute later, and set them down. "Will you need menus, Lonnie?"

"Nope, Dave's here for a bit of Louisville culture."

Maxwell looked at Perkins, confused, who gave him a reassuring nod.

"Ah, okay. And you'll have the same, Lonnie?" Charity said.

"Absolutely. Is the alley behind the can still okay for a smoke?" Perkins asked.

"It is, but if you're going to take your drink, keep it out of sight," Charity said.

"Thanks, will do."

"Your dinner should be up in about twenty-five minutes."

Perkins got up, drink in hand, and said, "Come on."

He led him down a corridor, past the washrooms and to a steel door with a push bar on it. Perkins leaned down, picked up a piece of cardboard and used it to keep the door from automatically locking. They were shielded by a green Dumpster with a WM logo emblazoned on the side. Perkins lit his smoke, and said, "Where do you think they're going?"

Maxwell thought about it for a second, and said, "I'm hoping that they've gone up toward NY state, but I can't be sure."

"You think Connelly is dead?"

"He might be, I think the Highwayman would be a fool to keep him around. He's a significant liability." Maxwell took a sip of his beer. "I believe that we'll get him, Highwayman I mean, but I don't think Norris Connelly has too much sand left in his hourglass."

"I can't figure out the whole Norris thing. Based on what I've read about your boy, it seems sort of out of character. He strikes me as a meticulous planner."

"My boy," Maxwell mused. "There are no master villains, Perk. At the core, they are defective, and that is why they do what they do. Hollywood has done an excellent job of portraying them in a manner that seems superhuman, but Highwayman will get caught."

"You have to admit he's a little smarter than your average bear. Tracking down a retired FBI agent isn't exactly the work that gets assigned to Henry Lee Lucas."

"I attended a lecture on Ted Bundy a few years back. It was conducted by one of the investigators involved, his name escapes me right now, but anyway, that detective talked about the duality of the serial killer. In Bundy's case, he was the ultimate planner, and because of that planning, he was very successful. Bundy killed women in several states. And even after he was in custody, he managed to escape twice. The first time by jumping out a courthouse window. He was apprehended a few days later. He escaped a second time through a broken light fixture in his jail cell. When he broke out, he fled to Florida. When he got to Florida, he could have laid low and went back to snatching women, but Bundy had been building up pressure while incarcerated. That need to kill had to be relieved. Each of his killings fed the monster, calmed it, kept it in its cage. I believe that the entity that hides inside these men slowly takes control. When Bundy got to Florida, he started to unravel, lose his battle against that inner monster. Gone was the well-dressed, charming Ted Bundy, replaced by a creature of an insatiable appetite."

"I know the story," Perkins said.

"So you know he lost it, and went on what was more like a killing spree than his usual methodical kidnap-murder. He lost control of the monster." Maxwell took a large swig of his beer.

"You think that's what happened at the Ironworks? You believe the Highwayman lost control? Went on a killing spree?" Perkins lit a new cigarette off the old one.

"No, I think he intended on upping his ante by killing Ash because he wants celebrity. I believe that those two poor guys that found with Ash were simply collateral. In the wrong place at the wrong time. But I also think that Highwayman has lost some of the control he has maintained over the last decade. We are benefitting from that."

"Devon?" Perkins looked at his double. It was getting low.

"Yes, Devon. If that's his real name. I'm sort of doubtful it is." Maxwell finished the last of the beer. "My only hope is that we'll get a Norris sighting, and as a result, we'll be able to track them."

"One can hope." Perkins exhaled a plume of smoke, and the door opened. It was Charity.

"Your dinner will be served in about five minutes." Charity was peeking through the crack in the door, looking left and right to see if anyone was watching. There wasn't. "You want a fresh drink, Lonnie?"

Perkins examined his cigarette, which was half-burned, and said, "Sure, but I'll take it with my meal. I'm pretty sure Dave here can use a refill as well. We'll be a minute more, Charity."

"Okay, Lonnie." She closed the door, but not before setting the cardboard back in place.

"Nice looking woman," Maxwell said.

"Second cousin," Perkins said.

Maxwell laughed. "You people certainly get around."

"Her husband was in Vice, got shot last year by some banger. It ended his career. The bullet is still lodged in his spine. Didn't completely cripple him, but he was pensioned off. Charity works here to help out."

"Now I feel like a heel," Maxwell said.

"Don't. Charity is flirty for tips. Just leave her a nice tip."

"Okay," Maxwell said. "I will."

Perkins crushed out his smoke, and they re-entered the restaurant. When they reached their table, two fresh drinks waited, and before they were seated, Charity was coming with two steaming plates. She set down Perkins' plate first and then Maxwell's.

The aroma was fantastic; blended cheese, tomato, bacon, and turkey brought Maxwell's saliva glands to life. The dish looked more like a breakfast meal than supper, but Maxwell wasn't above having bacon and eggs in the evening. He said, "It smells delicious."

"Wait until you taste it," Charity said. The front door chimed, and customers began to shuffle in. Acting as the host as well waitress, she set off to meet them.

Maxwell lifted his fork and said, "What is it?"

Perkins said, "That, my friend is a piece of Louisville culinary history. They call it The Hot Brown, and aside from The Brown Hotel, Kirbees makes the best hot brown in Kentucky. Dig in, you won't be disappointed."

Maxwell cut into the dish, releasing an even more intense potpourri of delicious aroma. He squared off the first steaming bite of the dish and placed it into his mouth.

Louisville had much to be proud of.

5

01 Sept 2007

Trout Run, PA

It was after midnight. Mina, who considered Jennifer her very best friend, was still looking at the photo with great interest, and perhaps even a bit of terror. Because she positively recognized the man in the picture. When the picture came up on her phone, she at first thought it might be a joke, but when she went back to her room and visited cnn.com and compared the photo to Jennifer's FUG... *Oh my God*, she thought. *It's really him.*

Then she texted Jennifer.

Mina: As soon as you're alone, we have to talk

Jennifer: WTF?

Mina: It's serious

Jennifer: Ok, give me 10 mins.

Mina: Hurry!

Eight minutes later, they were on the phone.

"That picture you took, where was that?" Mina said.

"I took it at the Travel Center, why?" Jennifer said.

Mina took a deep breath. "Jen, you have to dump all your FUGS, except that one. I'm going to do the same."

"Why? Why would I do that?"

"Because you took a picture of Norris Connelly!"

"Who?"

"Norris Connelly, he's a killer from Louisville. There's a nationwide manhunt for him on CNN."

"Don't be ridiculous," Jennifer said, but she felt her heart flutter. She knew Mina, and she wasn't kidding, but she asked anyway. "Mina, you're serious?"

"Super serious! We must dump our FUGS, and then we have to get our story straight. We got to tell our parents, and they will have to call the police."

"When?"

"Right now. I've already dumped mine. You do the same. Get rid of your text messages about the FUGS, make sure you delete them all."

"Mina, there are hundreds!"

"All of them."

"That could take hours."

Mina thought about it for a minute. "Okay, dump all the texts, including the one you sent me. I'll do the same. Then you resend that pic and say something like, *Take a look at this creepy guy.*"

"Oh my God. This is scary."

"I know. Just do it, and resend the pic, then call me back."

"Okay."

"Make sure you're thorough, Jen. The cops will probably want to take both our phones. And there are going to be questions. Once you're done, call me back."

"I will." Jennifer felt cold and afraid, her hands trembled as she set about deleting the amassed photos and string of texts. If her parents found out about the Fug game, she'd end up grounded until she graduated senior high.

When she was done, forty minutes later, she had erased all of her FUGS except one. It hadn't taken the hours she had originally thought, but it still had been a task. She had one thing left to do. She typed Check out this creepy looking guy! After that, she attached the picture she hadn't deleted.

Then she held her breath and pushed send.

***

PART III

LOOSE ENDS

"If they were dead, hollow vessels,
they couldn't hound me, call me
names. No more Gimpy Norris."

- Norris Connelly, the Regulator

CHAPTER 21 - DICK 101

1

01 Sept 2007

Wellsboro, PA

He could have gone into Lawrenceville to buy the items he needed, but something told him venturing out would be safer. Now, standing in the line at the Stop-n-Go convenience store, Lance was trying to contain himself. He was balancing the shopping basket on the edge of the conveyor, waiting to get a bit of real estate for the items he'd purchased. The female clerk, an older woman in her late sixties, had short gray hair and a mouth that was just a tad too chatty for his liking. Lance wished he'd brought the Impala, but the battery was dead.

Fucking battery!

He could have shopped in Lawrenceville if the Impala was up and running. People in Lawrenceville knew him, knew his car, but not the Cavalier. He didn't want them equating that car to him. So, as a precaution, he stayed off the US 15 and took PA 287 and drove the thirty odd miles down to Wellsboro. He could have gone up to the WalMart in Painted Post, NY, that would have been quicker, but a lot of folks from Lawrenceville shopped in Painted Post. There were cameras in the parking lot as well. People who knew him might see him behind the wheel of this car, and he didn't want that. He made a mental note to stop at the Interstate Battery on the way back.

He'd wished he'd gone down the road to Dollar General, they might have had more than one cashier, and odds were that at least one of them would not have been in slow motion like this old girl. He felt antsy and giddy, he was tired, and wanted to get back, he didn't like the idea of leaving Norris alone. He sighed impatiently. The two people ahead of him glanced back, but the inept blue hair seemed not to notice.

"Patience, young fella," said the old man in front of him.

Lance smiled, nodded and thought, *Maybe if I cut your fucking head off and set it on the conveyor, Chatty Cathy might shut her pucker hole and pick up the pace.*

The conveyor moved six inches. The old-timer smirked, placed a divider stick behind his ten cans of Purina Cat Chow, thus reducing the real estate to five inches. "There you go," he said. "That ought to lighten the load a little."

"Thanks." Lance reached in, placed a loaf of Wonder Bread on the conveyor and voila, the little ground he gained was again gone.

He smiled, but inside, he was a torrential rage. What a fucking mess this had become. The loss of Ash, that was what hurt the most. He had wanted to draw that out, make it last, talk about the case file, develop a rapport with the agent even if it was adversarial. Ash had screwed that right from the beginning, refusing to cooperate, clinging to some ridiculous perception of moral superiority.

How fucking dare he!

The conveyor moved three inches. Lance placed a jar of jam, a bottle of Heinz ketchup, and a package of Oscar Mayer wieners down. Outside the eddying of his fury, he faintly heard Chatty Cathy continue her psychobabble rap of pleasantries.

He had to calm down. After all, this was a model, a test stage before the main event; there were bound to be hiccups. He tried to relax, to calm, to push back the growing foolishness that fucking demanded *Kill everyone in this fucking hick convenience store! Kill them now!*

The cash register clanged.

The conveyor moved another four inches.

Chatty Cathy declared, "Well, how are you today?"

A rather plump lady in front of the Cat Food Man replied, "I'm fine, Jenny, how are you doing?"

Correction, he thought. *Chatty fucking Jenny.*

Lance ground his teeth together, reached into his basket, and placed the last of his items on the faded black belt. He set the basket into the stack and felt even less in control. At least before he had the basket to hang onto, but now, when he turned back to face them, he was surprised to see everyone was looking at him.

"Are you okay, son?" Cat Food Man asked.

What the fuck? Lance inhaled and said, "Yes, I am fine." He took in another deep breath, looked at Chatty Jenny, and the plump woman she was serving.

What did they see?

He forced himself to smile; it was a mechanical gesture, completely unconvincing, so he said, "I'm sorry, I got some bad news today, and I am just a bit anxious. Please carry on."

Cat Food Man began picking up his cans from the belt and said, "Jenny, you take care of this young man before me. He has to be somewhere."

Lance shook his head. "No, that's not necessary."

"I insist." He waved him forward.

Oh, for fuck's sake!

The Plump Lady smiled pleasantly and said, "Hon, you pick up your stuff and get it paid for. We have all day."

I ought to kill every fucking one of you!

"Really, it's..."

"Not another word," Plump Lady said.

Lance grabbed the basket, replaced his items and moved to the front of the line. He felt like an amoeba under their dissecting eyes. Grudgingly, he said, "Thank you." He couldn't look at them, felt the embarrassment chewing him up, but still, he placed the basket atop the mountain of useless shit Plump Lady had set down for purchase. The only one who was not looking at him with sympathetic eyes was Chatty Jenny. She had a look of disdain. He had upset the balance in her mundane, useless existence, interrupted her continuum of perpetual small talk.

"Would you like a box or a bag?" she asked.

He brought his gaze up to meet hers.

Would you like me to cut off your right arm or your left?

"Box, please." He had no idea what expression crossed his face, but Chatty Jenny dropped her own eyes and began tallying up his order, minus the chat.

2

01 Sept 2007

Louisville, KY

Norris Connelly sent the twenty-four-hour news cycle into a frenzy. The big networks - CNN, FOX, and MSNBC - lined up experts including former FBI agents, true crime writers, and psychologists often called upon to testify at trials. News networks, who espoused themselves as the hallmark of media integrity, misreported, sensationalized, and completely ignored fact checking.

First reports claimed that Norris Connelly was, in fact, the Highwayman, that he might have killed as many as twenty-five people over the course of the last decade. Networks contradicted each other, and two major networks got into a media war on who had the goods. Both completely ignored the fact that Norris didn't have a license, ignored the fact that he was disabled, and that there was no way he could have been in the states where he was supposed to have killed.

Then the unthinkable happened. Homicide Detective Lonnie Perkins, annoyed at the coverage, asked a reporter at CNN if he had attention deficit disorder. Perkins' callous insensitivity to the afflicted children of the world became their focus.

"Norris Connelly is involved, but no one in the Louisville PD or the FBI has stated that he is the Highwayman. I'm beginning to think you folks have attention deficit disorder. Because you certainly aren't listening to me or any other goddamned investigator."

This off-handed remark provoked a campaign of fabricated outrage, and the network wanted Perkins to apologize to the sitting president of the National Society for Attention Deficit Disorder, who was demanding Perkins' firing. He caught hell from his superiors, but the running joke among his fellow officers was that they would eventually forget about it.

And they would.

In the meantime, just to avoid future insensitive remarks, Perkins was not allowed to talk to the press anymore, which suited him just fine. Louisville assigned a female spokesperson who met and addressed the media with updates that were vetted and rehearsed.

Retractions in network news are as rare as an albino moose, so the media did what it did best. It moved on and conveniently forgot what it had misreported. Norris Connelly became the face, but the Highwayman remained an enigmatic sinister unknown.

Tips came in from all over the country. Norris was spotted in Boulder, CO, Newport News, VA, and even in Porcupine Plains, Saskatchewan. All leads were followed up by local law enforcement, but all proved to be fruitless.

One misstep by the FBI came in the form of a press release declaring, "It was just a matter of time before the two suspects were apprehended. The killers would be brought to justice."

The release made Maxwell cringe.

"The goddamned idiots are playing right into their hands," he said in a phone call to his boss, Deputy Director Julian Carswell. "Now the media is going to turn on us if we don't track them down."

"I spoke to the director, and she is not happy about it either, but the pressure is on," Carswell said, and added, "Do the best you can, Dave."

"We are, Julian."

"I know you are. Every FBI office across the country has their radar on."

"For all we know, Norris is dead."

"Jesus, let's hope not."

"Did you see the idiot they brought in as an expert panelist on the news?" Maxwell was referring to Casper Simpson. Simpson was a retired LA Detective who had a reality show on the R Channel called *Dick 101*. The show, like most television reality, was scripted nonsense directed at the lowest common denominator of America's television viewing public. *Dick 101* touted itself as a weekly docudrama following the exploits of veteran LAPD Detective Casper Simpson, turned private investigator. No longer controlled by the bureaucratic nonsense of "Yes Men," Casper did what others couldn't. "Sometimes you have to bend the rules," Simpson can be heard in narration during the opening credits. "Casper Simpson takes you on the hunt. Doing what most cops can't do. Tracking down criminals and leading you to their hiding places. This is *Dick 101*."

Aside from the fact that *Dick 101* was a complete joke among real cops who used the title as phallic fodder when, pun intended, busting each other's balls. Casper Simpson's hunt entailed tracking down small-time criminals who were wanted for petty crimes. He was like Dog the Bounty Hunter without the mullet and chest hair.

Maxwell watched the show one night in his hotel room after seeing Casper stating his expert opinion as to how law enforcement was going after the Highwayman. Maxwell let out the odd snicker, exasperated sigh, and finally a barrage of expletives. He was into the mini-bar not long after, pouring Jack Daniels over ice and talking sarcastically to the television.

"Oh yeah? Why didn't I think of that? You, sir, are a fucking genius." On his fourth mini bottle, he ran out of Jack and started on the Bacardi.

His phone rang, and he picked it up.

"Maxwell."

"It's Perk, what are you doing? Heard anything?"

"He's in Saskatchewan. I hear the Mounties will have him in custody at any minute. Casper Simpson will be overseeing his extradition."

Perkins laughed. "You drunk, Max?

"No, but I'm working on it. What are you up to?"

"I'm just leaving the station house, was going to head home."

"You want to grab a drink?"

"I don't know. I got an early morning."

"Oh, come on, Perk. Sometimes you have to bend the rules."

"Dick..."

"101."

"Yeah, okay."

"Okay, I'll meet you in the hotel bar."

3

01 September 2007

Lawrenceville, PA

Norris heard the car coming back up the drive. He was sitting in one of the recliners facing the television, his jaw hanging open. He was looking at himself; it was a blown-up copy of his identification badge from KT Paper. Below his picture, in block letters, rolling across a red marquee were the words breaking now! Nationwide manhunt underway for norris connelly and another unknown suspect!

It hadn't taken long; Lance had been right.

The anchorman said, "A source within the Louisville Police Department has told us that a nationwide manhunt is underway for Norris Connelly, who is a suspect in at least four murders and quite possibly more." The anchorman paused, listening to some unheard voice. "We are now getting unsubstantiated reports that this mass killing in Louisville may be connected to the Interstate spree that left dead in the states of Oregon, West Virginia, and..."

A key slid into the lock, and the deadbolt switched over, then the front door opened, and Lance entered the room carrying a box. He used his foot to close the door.

"I'm on television," Norris said.

Lance stopped and looked up at the big screen. Now they were hovering above the street in Louisville where Norris lived. That faded and a picture of Norris filled the screen.

A commentary said. "We are coming to you live from Louisville, Kentucky, where yet another murder has been connected to the triple murder that occurred at an abandoned steel plant. Police have a nationwide search going on for Norris Connelly, who they believe might be the Interstate Killer."

The screen switched to a street-level view and a blonde female reporter standing in front of an MSNBC van.

"On location, outside the street where Norris Connelly lives, we have Tina Chance situated," the anchorman said. "What is happening at the scene, Tina?"

She paused, made that face that all reporters make. "Well, Jake, a source within Louisville PD has said that Norris

Connelly was a worker at KT Paper for over five years. A woman's body has been found in the basement of his house, and they believe it is directly connected to the triple homicide at Kentucky Ironworks."

"Have the police given any details as to how they have come to that conclusion, Tina?" anchorman Jake Beckerman asked.

Another pause.

"They are not giving specifics, Jake. Except to say that the similarities in the crimes have led them to that conclusion."

"Is there anything else you can tell us about Norris Connelly? There is speculation that he may be a spree killer involved in over twenty murders stretching across the continental United States."

"Details are still coming in, Jake, but we will be doing an exclusive interview with his employer, Robert Sampson, who works at KT Paper Plant, later this afternoon."

Suddenly, the soundbar appeared on the television, and it muted. Norris looked up to see Lance holding the remote. There was an angry scowl on his face, but his voice was low and pleasant. "I think we need to talk about some house rules, Norris." He was staring at the television screen, his head shaking left and right, left and right. "I'm going to make us some lunch. You hungry?"

"Yes."

"I figured you might be. Hot dogs okay?"

"Sure. Are you angry with me, Lance?"

Lance was still staring at the television screen. "No." He shut off the television and wandered into the kitchen, carrying the remote with him. "How many hot dogs you want, Norris?"

"Um, five, I guess."

"Five?" Lance laughed, and then in a sarcastic tone. "Being a fugitive is a hungry business." There was a clambering of pots and pans. A pipe thumped in protest somewhere in the wall as the water turned on. The pan clunked on the stove. "Ketchup and mustard okay?"

Norris looked at the blank screen. "I guess."

As the water boiled, Lance came back into the living room and sat down on the sofa. He looked thoughtfully at his companion, who cringed uncomfortably in the recliner. That uncomfortable silence lasted an excruciating thirty seconds until Lance finally spoke up.

"We've come a long way together, haven't we?"

"Yes," Norris said. Only a few months ago, he had been harmless Gimpy Norris; now he was probably on the FBI Most Wanted list. "I feel like you're mad at me."

"No. I'm not mad at you. You have been a good friend and confidante. Any mistakes made to this point have been all mine." He reached across and patted Norris gently on the knee. "Right now, they are looking for two men, Norris Connelly and the Highwayman. You know, you really should have written *Regulator* next to the body. That would have added to the mystique. Made you even more legendary."

Norris shifted uncomfortably. "Maybe they think I am the Highwayman, and it will take the spotlight off you."

"No, that won't work. Once they start digging, the timelines won't match, and besides, you don't have a license." Lance rubbed his thumb against the index on his right hand, thinking. "Do you know how many people I have killed, Norris?"

"I'm not sure, twelve people?"

"I have killed twenty-six people in the last seven years. The first killing was a woman and her young boy, my first failed effort at notoriety; it was a messy killing, especially the boy. The innocent little boy who had no idea that his mommy had invited a monster into their home. Nobody except you knows about that one; I had to cover it up. I left too many clues."

"It sounds like you did a good job."

"Did you always know that you were different?"

Norris thought about this. "I felt normal enough when I was a kid, but when I went to school, everyone was mean to me, calling me Gimpy Norris. Especially the girls. That's when I had thoughts, thoughts about how they would look when the meanness was gone. If they were dead, hollow vessels, they couldn't hound me, call me names. No more Gimpy Norris."

"Did it make you feel powerful?"

Norris leaned forward. "No, it was more like I was free. I think most people are cruel inside. Even my momma and Uncle Linwood could be mean sometimes. Momma would say I was handicapped, that I couldn't do the same things other kids did, but then I read that there was an operation I could have gotten to fix my foot. When I asked her about it, she said it was too expensive, that we needed insurance to cover it. I believed her, but she was lying."

"How do you know that?" Lance leaned in, his mood lightening. "How do you know that she lied?"

"People think I'm dumb, because of the way I look. Because of my limp. I'm not dumb, Lance. I might be broken, but I can read, and after my momma died, I got a payout on her health insurance. I read the policy, and she had full coverage. My operation wasn't too expensive; she wanted to keep me that way. She needed me to take care of her, so she let me stay this way."

There was a sizzling crackle from the kitchen.

"The hot dogs," Lance said and got up. "I'll be right back." He disappeared and could be heard moving the pot off one burner and onto another. A minute later, he re-entered the living area and sat back down. "Please continue."

Norris sat motionless as if wondering what else to say or where to pick up. "Do you miss your parents?"

He regarded Norris thoughtfully. "Do you know what separates us from the animals?" Norris opened his mouth to say something, but Lance cut him off. "Irrational connectivity. When a bear raises her cubs, she gives them the essentials of life. How to survive and keep oneself fed; basically, momma gets them through childhood, and once they are grown, she cuts them loose. They leave their mother and strike out for new territory to hunt. Once that bond is broken, she will never again be attached, and might someday even kill one of them should they wander into her territory. Only people seem to have this need of a family, to surround themselves with those they say they love. Did you ever ask yourself why, Norris?"

Norris thought about it for a second and said, "No."

"Take a family man and transplant him onto a battlefield, and he will kill to survive. Leave a man on a mountain with no food among the dead, and sooner or later he will eat his own. Two drug addicts will cut each other to pieces for the last pebble of crack cocaine. A man will fuck his brother's wife if he gives in to lust. A mother will leave her son an invalid, to suffer a lifelong handicap, to be called horrible names, if she knows that he will take care of her for the rest of her life."

"I still miss my mom."

"Why? By your admission, she used you."

"I don't know."

"It's a weakness, Norris. Society looks at people like me and you and thinks we are freaks, but once you unload all the ridiculous insecurities and embrace what is inside of you, that is when you are purest of heart. When you watch a tiger or an alligator take down its prey, you don't think that animal is evil. Why?"

"Instinct?"

"Now you're getting it." Lance stood up. "Let's grab some lunch, and we'll talk about this some more."

4

01 September 2007

Louisville, KY

They were well into their cups. Maxwell four or five drinks ahead of Perkins, and his words were edging into slow, syllabic slurs. They had stepped out of the bar and were standing outside the Holiday Inn so that Perkins could smoke. The air was cooling off, heavy dark clouds blanketed the impending dusk, threatening rain.

"Where do you think he is?" Perkins asked.

"I think he went north. May-maybe NY state, or Mass, but what the hell do I know? He could be holed up in Frankfort or West Virginia." Maxwell stared at the smoke in Perkins' hand and resisted the urge to ask for one.

"Maybe we should ask Casper what he thinks?"

Maxwell sniffed. "Maybe."

"Fucking media."

"Yeah, fucking media."

Perkins crushed out his smoke, and they went back inside for another drink. Perkins said this would be his last, and Maxwell agreed. Neither of them should be drinking, if something in the case broke, they'd be hooped. If something did happen, Perk looked like he'd have an easier time recovering.

"One more," Perk said.

"One more," Maxwell agreed.

They each had a double.

"What do you think?" Perk asked.

"I think that we lost the initiative when the media got onboard. I think our friend the Highwayman is now in self-preservation mode, and that if Norris Connelly isn't dead, he will be very soon."

"Fuck."

"Yeah, and that isn't the worst of it. You know what else I think, Perk?" Maxwell didn't give him a chance to answer. "I think I am about to suffer the same fate as my predecessor."

"As Ash, you don't think..."

"That he'll come after me? No, I didn't mean that. I mean, he is going to go underground. He's going to go dormant and wait until things quiet down before he rears that ugly fucking head of his again." Maxwell took a sip of his drink. "Maybe he'll come for me after I retire like he did Ash, but I don't think so. I think he's regretting doing that."

"Maybe we'll get lucky."

"Maybe." Maxwell finished the rest of his drink, and set it on the table. "As much as I'd like to get shit-faced, I guess we better knock it off."

Perkins downed his drink.

Outside, it had begun to rain, and Maxwell followed him out for one last smoke. They chatted, but not about Highwayman; the mood had become somber and uncomfortable. Neither addressed the fact that Perkins really shouldn't be driving. After he crushed out his cigarette, he got into his car and drove off. Maxwell went up to his room, set the alarm on his phone to go off in five hours and backed it up with a wakeup call.

5

01 September 2007

Lawrenceville, PA

While Lance and Norris should have been wired for sound and action, both gave in to the exhaustion after scarfing down hot dogs and Diet Cokes. Neither went to their respective rooms. Instead, they sacked out in the living area after Lance closed the curtains on the picture window. They slept most of the afternoon, and Lance awoke to snoring.

He opened his eyes to see it was almost 4:45 in the afternoon. Wiping away the sleep, he gazed over at Norris, who was fully reclined, feet elevated, and mouth agape. Norris snorted, swallowed, let out a strangled whispering whistle, and stopped breathing. Lance thought he might asphyxiate before the gasp came, and the process resumed.

He reached for the remote and turned the television on which opened with a photo of Norris front and center. The television was still muted. Rolling across the CNN marquee, at the bottom of the screen came rolling bulletins.

CNN... *FBI: The nation is on high alert for fugitives...* **CNN...** *Norris Connelly wanted for killings with an unknown assailant. He is thought to be in the company of a man going by the first or last name of Devon...* **CNN...** *Anderson Cooper to interview the family of Amelia Hill...*

Devon? How the hell did they know that?

He sat up, splitting his gaze between the news, and sleeping Norris in the chair, who was gasping every thirty seconds or so. He would have to do something very soon; the whole country was looking for him. If anyone spotted him, they would swoop in, and it would all be over. He wondered how long it would take Norris to crack if the cops got him.

I bet he wouldn't he even last an hour, he thought.

He could get up, go into the kitchen, grab a knife, and cut his throat right there in the recliner. Do it right in mid-snore. That would be messy, and he didn't want to kill Norris. He liked the strange little man. They had an intimacy, understanding, and shit, if his mom hadn't been such a bitch and not left him an invalid, he could have recruited him for the next phase of his project. Norris had all the right traits; he'd proven he could kill, and he was loyal.

Loyal, yes, but reckless.

The woman hadn't been part of the plan. The plan was to go quiet and keep a low profile. Lance brought his eyes up the flat screen.

And not end up on the fucking news.

Norris snorted, gurgled.

He wasn't exactly innocent; the woman was only part of it. The steelworks had been a royal disaster, and how did they know about Devon? He already had the answer to that.

He'd let that name slip with Agent Ash; he must have left a clue for the feds. Something that hadn't been noticed in the spur of the moment.

Or maybe Norris left an unintentional clue at the house?

Lance thought about the notepad he'd torn the pages from; it wasn't unthinkable that Norris could have had other things written down somewhere. They would be taking the house in Louisville completely apart looking for clues. They would be tearing up the floorboards, ripping out the drywall, looking for other victims.

I can't leave this for too long.

He left Norris' cacophony of snorts and gasps behind and went to the bathroom. He closed the door behind him and did his business. Finished, he washed his hands and opened the medicine cabinet. Sitting between a bottle of Pepto-Bismol and a can of Foamy shave cream was a small prescription bottle. Lance picked it up.

RX 675489 Belanger, Wallace

Dr. Hall, Karl - LJD - Issued 16 Nov 1998

40 Tab Oxycodone 30 mg

TAKE 1 TABLET TWICE DAILY

He shook the bottle, there had to be at least twenty pills in there, but they were over nine years old. Would they work, and would that be enough? Did pills lose their potency as time went on? He held the bottle up and examined the contents, some of them had already degraded into powder.

It would be the most humane way.

Just send him off into the big sleep. No blood, no fuss, no muss and no more Norris. The pills would probably stop his heart. Then all he'd have to do is bury him out there in the woods. He shook the bottle, pills clicked against one another and crumbled even more.

6

01 September 2007

State Police Barracks - Montoursville, PA

State Trooper Corporal Billy Leeman brought the phones into the troop and turned them over to Lieutenant Cole Abraham. The supper hour was upon them. Abraham was annoyed, his wife had pot roast waiting, and he was on his way out.

"I'll have a look at this tomorrow," Abraham said.

"I think you better look tonight, Lieutenant," Leeman insisted. "I think this is about that Norris fellow. The Louisville killer."

That stopped Abraham in his tracks. He looked at his trooper and said, "Come into my office."

Leeman followed him, and they closed the door.

"Okay, Billy. Fill me in."

So Leeman did. He spoke about the call he'd received from a Jack Carberry of Trout Run. He explained about the text his daughter received, and how he'd gone up to interview the family and took the phone. He also recounted his interview with the girl who had sent the text, Jennifer Potter, and that was why he had two cell phones in his possession.

He turned both phones on for his boss and brought up the texts and accompanying photos of Norris Connelly. To add to that, he set down the ViCAP alert between the phones as a comparison.

Cole Abraham looked at both pictures then at the identification picture attached to the alert. "Where was this taken?" he asked.

"Duncannon," Leeman said.

"Last night?"

Leeman opened his notepad and checked. "I interviewed both girls and the girl who sent it, Jennifer Potter, says she took it three nights ago and forgot to send it until last night. The other girl, Mina Carberry didn't receive it until after midnight. I put in a request to review both their phone records; something isn't adding up. But I think this is Norris Connelly, and I think he was in Pennsylvania."

Abraham looked up from the photos. "He may still be."

"Yes, sir."

Abraham looked down again. Picked up the ViCAP alert and checked the number on it. At the bottom, there were two names: Detective Lonnie Perkins of the LPD, and FBI Special Agent David Maxell. He picked up his phone and hung it on his shoulder. "Billy, call my wife, tell her I'm sorry but I'm going to be late. Then get on the horn, and call in for a large meat lover's from Pizza Hut."

"Okay, anything else?"

"I'm going to contact the FBI. I want the Carberry and Potter girl in here right away for re-interview."

"Okay, I'll get right on it." Leeman was about to step out.

"One more thing, Billy," Abraham said.

"Sir." Leeman looked in expecting another order.

"Good work, Corporal."

***

CHAPTER 22 – INTO THE THIRD ROOM

1

01 September 2007
Louisville, KY

The call was just after 8:00 p.m. that evening. It came from Hugh Bailey, and it was the first real lead they had. "One of our operators picked up a call from the state cops in Montoursville, PA. We've got a Norris sighting in Duncannon, PA," Bailey said.

"How long ago?" Maxwell asked.

"Four days. A young girl snapped a picture of him with her phone in Duncannon, Pennsylvania. I just emailed you the picture."

"Okay," Maxwell said, opening his laptop on the hotel room bed. "Where the hell is Duncannon?"

"Harrisburg area. We've sent the photo down to our facial recognition people, and they have already confirmed it's Norris. They got a 98.5% match. It's him."

Maxwell was staring at the photo that Bailey sent him. He studied the face, but his focus was on what framed Norris Connelly. The window of the car, its color. "We got a make on the car yet?"

"Shouldn't be too long. NCIC is dissecting the photo as we speak. They think it's a GM or Dodge, and they're querying both companies for input. Hang on a second." Bailey covered the phone, there was muffled chatter, and then he came back. "I want you to get up to Duncannon and start poking around. Maybe they're holed up somewhere."

"Okay," Maxwell enhanced the photo size and continued to study it. "What about the task force?"

"I've assigned an agent from the Louisville office. Right now, what I want is you out there beating the bushes. I've already arranged for you to meet with a Lieutenant Cole Abraham, and he is going to organize an interview tomorrow morning with the girl who took the photo and her friend. I've emailed you addresses and timings. Abraham said there was something fishy about both girls' stories, so they pulled their phone records from Verizon, and it appears these girls were playing some game."

"Game," Maxwell said. "I'm not following."

Bailey ruffled some paper. "Find the Fug. They take pictures of ugly people and share them via text. It was a contest between the two. Always trying to one-up each other."

"Nice. Whatever happen to sock hops and cheerleaders?"

Bailey sniffed. "Teenage girls can be pretty vicious, check out YouTube sometime."

"I'll take a pass."

"We were lucky to get the texts. Verizon is the only cell provider that hangs onto texts and only for three days. The records of transmission are there for eighteen months, but the texts get wiped. We made it in just under the wire."

"Do they know we know?"

"No, use that to your advantage."

"Any issue with me keeping the parents out of this?"

"No, as long as you can do that without ending up on CNN or fucking *Fox and Friends*."

"Okay, anything else?"

"That covers it. You can start there. I've got a communication out on the wire that all law enforcement are to report anything unusual."

"That's good. Okay."

"Max, I'm going to put you on with my secretary. She's got your flight information and car rental details. There's a second email coming to you with info on the Montoursville state cops and the girls. They'll be expecting you."

"Okay. Anything else?" Maxwell got up, set his suitcase on the bed and opened it.

"Not yet, keep the line open. Once we have the car make, I'll contact you. I got to get my butt into a Homeland Security briefing that I'm already late for. I'll put you over to Katie. Keep me updated."

"Okay..." Maxwell didn't get to finish his sentence because Bailey had already transferred it. The phone began to beep, and Katie came on.

"Hello, Agent Maxwell." Katie Heller's voice was pleasant. "I have you flying out of Louisville and into Harrisburg at 10:00 p.m. tonight. There will be a car waiting for you at HIA. I'm emailing you the details now. It's a ninety-mile drive from Harrisburg up to Montoursville, so I thought you would rather drive than wait on a connector flight. The connector doesn't depart until 2:00 a.m."

"Yes, I'd rather drive than sit in an airport. Thank you, Katie."

"You're very welcome. Your contact in Montoursville is a Lieutenant Cole Abraham of the Pennsylvania State Police. I've also booked you a room at the Williamsport Comfort Inn. Those details are in the package I'm sending."

Maxwell thanked her again and ended the call. He began packing his suitcase and inventorying the room for anything he might have forgotten. Once he'd done this, he made one more phone call.

"Hello?" It was Lonnie Perkins.

"Hi, Perk. I just called to say I'm leaving town."

"Oh?"

"We got a Norris sighting up in Pennsylvania. I'm going up to see what I can shake loose. The bureau is sending over another agent to help with your task force." Maxwell scanned his email. "I don't have a name for you."

"Shit, I wish I could come along."

Maxwell didn't say anything. He liked Perkins, but he moved faster on his own.

"I was just starting to like you, Max."

"Same here. I'll keep in touch."

Perkins laughed. "No, you won't."

2

01 September 2007

Lawrenceville, PA

With Norris asleep, Lance locked his bedroom door and knelt in the middle of the room before the rectangular throw rug centered on the floor. He pulled it away and revealed the surreptitious reason for its placement. The floor was smooth hardwood, and at a glance, the trap door was almost seamless. Lance had spent considerable time designing the trap door. He counter-synced a single spring-loaded board that set into the floor flawlessly. He brushed his hand across the floor and once reaching the spot, he pushed down. There was a click, and the chameleon floorboard lifted four inches revealing its true identity: a handle. Below the handle, on either side, entrenched in the door were two sliding bolts. Lance slid them over.

With that done, he stood and went to the door to double check the lock. He didn't want Norris seeing this, at least not now, and possibly not ever. He returned to the spot on the floor and carefully reached down and lifted the lid. The trap door was rectangular, but the hardwood boards that covered it lifted in the same staggered cuts that lined the floor, rendering the seams almost invisible. Almost, but not quite, and that is why he covered it with the throw.

It gave a faint creek, but not loud enough to wake the snoring Norris. He then reached over and flicked on a light switch located on the left side of the first step. The ten stairs descending into darkness became discernible in the fluorescent glow.

Lance listened for Norris, heard the choppy gasp of his snore and descended the stairs. The stairwell ended in the center back of the room. The chamber was almost a perfect square, 14x14 feet with an eight-foot-high ceiling.

This was his secret place, building it commenced not long after the twin towers in New York City fell. He had done all the construction himself, had even poured the concrete floor. Lance educated himself on construction that fall, taking online classes and attending a few home depot seminars on weekends. The walls and ceiling were made from sheetrock, properly sanded and painted eggshell white. At the center of the room was a glass desk, and upon it, a very large computer monitor. All wiring plugged directly into the floor; this was a piece of engineering Lance was particularly proud of. He had run the conduit and wiring across the floor before pouring the concrete. He'd even installed the GFA breaker on the wall to which the conduit ran. He tested this and made sure that everything worked before pouring the concrete. There were no issues to date.

He crossed the room, admiring the news clippings and pictures that plastered the four walls. The computer, monitor, and a LaserJet printer were the only items on the glass desk. Sitting down in the chair, he pushed the power button on the computer, and it went through its startup. Reaching into his pocket, he pulled out a digital camera and plugged in the USB cable attached to the computer. The monitor on the screen pulsed while a single orb of white light spun on an invisible access.

Below that, the words greeted, **Hello, Devon.**

Devon. This made him smile; he couldn't even be honest with his computer. The screen came alive, and he punched in his password. Then the desktop appeared. It was as organized and uncluttered as everything in Lance Belanger's life.

The computer prompted him by opening a folder which led to the digital camera. He opened the photos and started scanning through them. He'd been taking pictures after he killed the Fog Man in Budapest. There were four shots in the camera. The first was of Lewis Ash, very much alive and stretched out naked on the warehouse's concrete floor. The other three were after death shots. One of Ash slumped over in the back of the van. The other of the driver slumped over the steering wheel. And the last one was the younger guy that Norris had killed. He had taken these after sending Norris back up the hill to the Ram pickup.

Lance moved his mouse and highlighted the four pictures, and prompted the computer to print them. As they printed, Lance got up from his seat and looked for a suitable place to hang them.

Each wall had a purpose. The south wall was for photographs, the only trophies Lance kept. The east enshrined in news clippings about Highwayman. The west had a 4x8 map of the United States mounted on a slightly bigger framed cork board. Each kill site on the map had been marked with a red pushpin. A bookshelf completely covered the north wall, and the books were all reference material for the modern-day serial killer.

He had books by authors like Ann Rule, Jack Olsen, Robert Ressler, John Douglas, and Mark Olshaker. He had a total of two hundred and seventy-five books dedicated to true crime from the perspective of FBI profilers, psychiatrists, and investigative reporters. He supposed, that if he were to die before being caught, this room would become a time capsule for future investigators to crack and puzzle over.

He knew it was foolhardy to keep the trophies, but whether he wanted to admit it or not, these things were important to him. For him, they were like a musician's gold records, or an actor's Academy Awards. For years, he told himself it was all about the presentation and not really about the killing. That was just a lie he was telling himself, and in between the outbursts of violence, the times when he would go dormant, he would sequester himself to this room and meditate on everything it contained.

3

02 September 2007

Duncannon, PA

Maxwell drove the same stretch of road Highwayman and Norris had. He knew that they'd been in Duncannon and took the rental into the Travel Center for a look. He stopped the vehicle and got out at the fuel pump. He topped up the car and looked up. Hanging above each pump was a security camera.

Security, he thought. *Why hadn't Bailey mentioned this?*

He decided to go inside.

Behind the counter, a stout man reading *Maxim* magazine ate powdered donuts out of a package of six. Maxwell noted that there were three missing. He also caught a scent of marijuana and Axe Body Spray. Maxwell deduced the guy probably used the spray to cover up his marijuana breaks.

Overall, the place was quiet, except for another middle-aged man, who Maxwell thought might be a truck driver, perusing the potato chip rack. Maxwell stepped up to the counter and said, "Is the manager available?"

"Manager," the man puzzled for a second, giving the open donut pack a guilty glance, wondering if he was in trouble.

"Manager's off until the morning. Is there something I can help you with?"

"Maybe." He leaned in closer, produced his identification and said, "I need to know about your security cameras out there on the pumps. Are they operational?"

The counter guy was staring at the FBI logo, and then up at Maxwell. "Are you chasing someone?"

"What do you think?" Maxwell felt annoyed, not only at the question but the fact the guy had white donut powder in the corners of his mouth. He could have the manager called in and avoided dealing with this mope. He was tired, from the road and from the drinks he'd had the night before. Before he could say anything else, he felt a presence behind him and turned around. The guy perusing the chip aisle was waiting to pay for his goods. "You go ahead," Maxwell told the guy and stepped aside.

"Thanks." The guy moved around Maxwell. Then set the items on the counter. As they were being punched in, Maxwell inventoried the store for more cameras. If they bought fuel, there was a good chance he might get some video of the Highwayman. He noted three cameras: one at the entrance, one in the corner overlooking the merchandise and another pointed at the cashier.

The clerk bagged up the guy's items and sent him on his way. Maxwell stepped back up to the counter and said, "The security system here. Does it work?"

"Yes," the counter guy said. "I don't have the keys for it, though. All the equipment is in Roger's office; he's the manager."

"You have a number for Roger?"

He reached below the counter and got a pen and a sticky note, then scribbled the number down. Below that, he wrote the name *Roger Carlisle.* "You can get him at this number... best to call in the morning. Roger turns his phone off at night."

"Seriously?"

The counter guy shrugged and whispered, "He's sort of a dick."

Maxwell reached into his jacket and produced a business card wallet. "Do me a favor, when the manager comes in, have him call me immediately." He handed the guy one of his cards.

"Okay."

"What's your name?" Maxwell asked.

"Rodney..."

"Rodney what?" Maxwell pulled out a pen and notebook.

"Gyzel."

Rodney looked worried. "Why are you writing down my name?"

"When I first came in here, you asked me if I was chasing someone. The answer is yes, I'm chasing a very bad someone, and your manager may have evidence that will help me catch him. The answer to your second question is, that if your manager doesn't call me as soon as he gets in, I'm coming back to you, Rodney Gyzel."

Rodney said, "I didn't do nothing. Why are you acting this way?"

"Look, I don't care if you want to sneak out for a toke on your break. But I do care whether you pass this information along. I want the message passed. You do that. We're all good." Maxwell smiled, but it was a carnivorous smile, one that said *I'm not fucking around.*

"I'll pass the message. You can call him right now if you like, but I doubt he'll answer." Rodney then added, "But I'll make sure he gets the message."

Maxwell turned to go. "One more thing, Rodney."

"Yeah?"

"Stop stealing donuts."

"I paid for these."

"Yeah, okay." Maxwell left the store and went back to his rental. If there was any place they were going to get a picture of Highwayman, this was the place.

If the fucking security system works and doesn't roll over every twenty-four hours, he thought.

He wondered if the state cops already pulled the security system. Maybe Rodney, who was a stoner with a penchant for contraband donuts, was too inept to know or care.

"Fuck it," he said and called the dick manager.

The phone rang twice, and a woman answered. "Hello?"

"Hello, sorry to call you so late. My name is Agent Dave Maxwell, I work for the FBI. I need to speak to Roger Carlisle."

"Just a minute," she said and then muffled, "Roger, wake up, there's an FBI agent on the phone."

Then, "Huh? FBI? I'm up. I'm up." And then, "Hello."

"Hi, is this Roger Carlisle who manages the Travel Center in Duncannon?"

"It is."

"My name is Special Agent Dave Maxwell. I need to talk to you about your security system."

"I already went over this with that state trooper," Roger said. "I told Trooper Leeman. The security system is down; the hardware crashed a week ago. I'm waiting for an IT guy out of Harrisburg to come and fix it."

Fuck, Maxwell thought and said, "Rodney said it worked."

"Rodney's a chronic pothead. Nice guy, but dumb as a bag of hammers."

And a donut thief too, Maxwell thought. "So you're telling me you've had no surveillance for a week?"

"We had an electrical storm. Lightning hit a transformer and the surge fried our mainframe. I'm not happy about it, but I'm at the mercy of the geeks out of Harrisburg."

Maxwell thanked the manager and told him he'd want to follow up. Maybe there was a witness in the store who could connect Highwayman to the car or Norris. He started the rental car and got back on the US 15.

03 September 2007

Williamsport, PA

Maxwell drove north, from Duncannon to Williamsport in a little under an hour and a half. The US 15 snaked north along the Susquehanna River and provided a challenging drive of twists and bends. He pushed the car up to 80 mph on the highway's straight-away and dropped down to 60 where the road cut left and right. Maxwell liked driving roads like this.

He was pulled over just outside Sunbury by a state trooper who clocked him doing 78 in a 45 zone. When he flashed his identification, the trooper seemed unimpressed and was going to write him a ticket. That is until the light bulb came on as to why FBI Agent David Maxwell was in Pennsylvania. This epiphany came when he called in Maxwell's license, and the dispatcher filled him in.

Maxwell was sent on his way and told to ease up on the accelerator. The trooper would have given him the stock speech about the accidents he'd had the pleasure of overseeing on the US 15 but decided not to.

It was 1:20 a.m. by the time Maxwell got checked in and opened the door to his hotel room. He was exhausted, but he had a full plate for the next day. He would be meeting with Cole Abraham at 8:00 and with the two girls at 9:00. He took a quick shower and laid out a fresh set of clothes for the morning meetings. He set his alarm for 6:30 and climbed into the bed.

He lay thinking about the make of the car and the route the two had taken. The security issue at the Travel Center was maddening, but maybe something else would shake loose. There had to be other cameras, other fuel up points along the route, something that would push them in the right direction. Once they had the make, they could start beating the bushes.

By 2:30 a.m., Maxwell began purging his thoughts. He needed what sleep he could get. "Maybe I should have grabbed a joint off Rodney," he said to the darkness and chuckled. He continued to meditate, pushing the thoughts out, willing himself to sleep and drifted off soon after.

5

03 September 2007

Lawrenceville, PA

The online conversation had gone on for about an hour in the shadow of Norris' stupor. There were four participants: Dusk, Steel, Larry, and Devon. The conversation had become heated. Up until the disaster in Louisville, his plans were on track, and they were all on board. Now?

Lance stared at the monitor, watching the blinking cursor, his nerves were frayed; he had to get rid of Norris and soon. But he also worried about the online name he was using. That would have to change, Deep Web or not.

http://macabreclub.com/
Group Chat Session #44/Time: 1:44/09/03/2007
Cloak-Surf Enabled (No Trackers)
Dusk: You have a lot of heat right now.
Devon: I know, but I have it under control.
Steel: You are all over the news, Dev.
Devon: It's under control. I'm going to deal with my problem very soon.
Dusk: When.
Steel: ??
Devon: Leave that to me.
Larry: Sooner the better. He's going to fuck everything up.
Devon: I have a few things to get rid of. Remember who started this. Remember who's leading this parade.

Don't think for a minute that I haven't looked at every contingency. I have, and before long, they won't know where to look. I haven't stayed three steps ahead of them by being complacent.

Larry: That might be, but we are all in this together now.

Devon: I understand that. Look, I'm going to take care of it. In the meantime, I'm going to need you guys to do something for me.

Dusk: ??

Steel: ??

Larry: What do you need?

***

CHAPTER 23 – CAR TROUBLE

1

03 September 2007

Montoursville, PA

Maxwell was parked outside the of the Pennsylvania State Trooper barracks. It was 7:03 a.m. now. He'd been up since 5:30 and couldn't get back to sleep. He decided to head down to the barracks early, go through his emails, and get up to date before the meetings. As he perused the FBI communications, he saw one marked urgent from Evan Ferguson, SA.

He opened and gave it a read.

To: David Maxwell SA, FBI

Hello, I am Evan Ferguson, SA. I have been assigned to the task force in Louisville, KY, by Hugh Bailey, SAC. I will be meeting with the lead homicide investigator Lonnigan Perkins. That meeting is scheduled for 11:00 a.m. I will be consulting with him this morning to discuss the aspects of the case and strategy. I would like to speak with you via telephone before my liaison, if possible.

I understand that you are in Pennsylvania, and the SAC suggested that we should communicate so that I am brought up to speed. I am available all morning from 6:00 a.m. and can be reached through the Louisville office or on my cell provided below.

Good hunting.

Evan Ferguson, SA, FBI

Louisville Field Office

"Lonnigan?" Maxwell laughed. "I guess Perk isn't that bad." He'd never heard of Agent Ferguson, so he didn't know what to expect. Maxwell considered himself a career special agent. He tended to speak his mind, and sometimes that got him into trouble with his superiors. He knew Bailey didn't like him because of this, and his direct line into the deputy director didn't help. In the last incident, Julian Carswell called him into his office and said, "Max, every other year, you piss someone off, and I end up having to smooth it over."

Maxwell nodded. "We all have our talents, sir."

"Hugh Bailey calls you a problem child. He says you're on the cusp of insubordination, that you deviate from protocol, and that you're an accident waiting to happen."

"Hugh Bailey is..."

Carswell raised a hand cutting him off. "Is your boss."

"Yes, sir."

"Your record for clearing cases is exemplary. That is your saving grace, but it's not enough. Like it or not, this is a bureaucracy, and even though I know you are a first-rate field agent, sooner or later you are going to piss in the wrong bowl of corn flakes."

"Yes, sir."

"Cut the *sir* shit, Dave, and listen to me."

"Okay."

"I told Bailey that you are a top-notch field agent and that if I could, I would tie you to a post in the field and leave you there until we need you. That would certainly keep you out of trouble. Unfortunately, human rights being what they are, such a scenario, as appealing as it is, just isn't plausible. I know Hugh Bailey is a bit of a tightwad, but you really need to cool it with the mouthing off. Every time you're not on a case, you piss someone off. You got to knock this shit off."

Maxwell said nothing.

"You know what I think, Dave?"

"What, Julian?"

"I think you do it on purpose. I think you purposely sabotage yourself because you want to stay in the field chasing bad guys. Is that why you do it?"

"No, I want to be sequestered to an office." Maxwell smiled.

Carswell also smiled. "Get out of my office, Dave."

"Yes, sir." Maxwell turned and left.

The memory of that meeting faded, and he glanced at his watch. It was 7:20 a.m. He read the cell number Ferguson provided and dialed through. It rang three times, and a voice answered, "Agent Ferguson."

"Hi, Dave Maxwell calling. I'm following up on your email. How can I help you?"

Ferguson took a breath, "Nice to hear from you, call me Evan."

"Okay, Evan. First things first. Call him Lonnie, not Lonnigan, that could be a bad first impression," Maxwell said.

Ferguson laughed. "Is that what you call him?"

"No, I call him Perk, but you might want to wait and get to know him a little better. He's a good guy, solid investigator. He doesn't have prejudices against the bureau like a lot of homicide cops."

"Good to know. How are things developing at your end?" Ferguson muffled the phone and let out a cough. "Sorry, summer cold."

"I'm in Montoursville waiting to meet with the stateys. Oh shit, how much do you know?"

"Pretty much everything in your files, I'm still working my way through the Ash files; about three-quarters through."

"I'm impressed."

"Don't be, I've had the case file since the carnage at the Ironworks. As I understand it, they didn't know whether they were going to pull you out of Missouri. Bailey called me directly, sent everything over and told me to bone up. When they brought you into Louisville, I didn't think I'd be coming over, but reviewed the files just in case."

"Good thinking." Maxwell could smell Bailey's bullshit maneuver. Why wouldn't he come to Louisville, it was his goddamned case. *Maybe Bailey just wanted a backup in case I did something that was on the cusp of insubordination.* This was the kind of shit that pissed him off. *Fucking Bailey!*

There was an uncomfortable silence that Ferguson finally broke. "Look, Dave, I don't like muscling in on a case. So I'll do everything that is needed of me with the task force, but I understand that you are still the lead investigator."

"Thanks." Maxwell softened. "I appreciate that."

"I'm going to need to lean on you a bit anyway," Ferguson said. "I know you've been at this awhile."

"Okay, I'll give you all the support you need. But I'd appreciate it if we can keep a direct line of communication open. My boss informed me that he just assigned an agent yesterday, we don't exactly see eye to eye on some things."

"Welcome to the bureau." Ferguson laughed.

"Exactly, so if it's all the same to you, I'd like to be the first to know about anything that comes to light. I don't want to hear about it on the news, and I don't want it vetted through the SAC. I'm not telling you to withhold; I just want to know first. If you do that for me, I'll do the same for you." Maxwell hoped Ferguson was stand up. If he went to Bailey with this, he'd be well beyond the cusp of insubordination.

"I can do that. I won't withhold, but I'll certainly put you at the top of my contact list." Ferguson seemed a little more relaxed.

"Any word on the car make?" Maxwell asked.

"Not yet, but when I know, you'll be the first to hear."

"Thanks. My guess is that LPD will want to release that to the media along with the photo of Norris. I don't have an issue with it, but please let me know in advance. Once that goes viral, it might be enough to panic Highwayman and Norris." Maxwell checked his watch. 7:35 a.m. He had twenty-five minutes before his meeting, and still more to do. "Keep me in the loop, and I'll do the same for you."

"I will." Ferguson sounded sincere.

I hope so, Maxwell thought.

They wrapped up the conversation with Maxwell telling Ferguson he'd email the picture of Norris up to him as soon as the interviews were finished. Apparently, Bailey hadn't done that yet. After Maxwell hung up, he started to scan his email then stopped and said, "Bailey, you fucking backdoor-humping piece of shit!"

Suddenly there was a knock on the car window. Towering over him was a big man in his early fifties wearing a Smokey the Bear hat. His uniform was light gray, with a darker patch on the shoulder emblazoned with gold lettering: Pennsylvania State Police. Below that: Trooper. On his collar was a single bar. The nametag above his right breast pocket read Abraham. "Good morning, you're early."

Maxwell rolled down the window.

2

03 September 2007

Lawrenceville, PA

Outside, the birds, still unmindful of the coming fall, sang to each other that September morning with marked enthusiasm. Norris awoke at almost the same time as the FBI agent who was chasing him. 5:29 a.m. He got out of the bed and crept to the bathroom, fearful of waking Lance. He sat down and did his business, pondering his dilemma. With his name all over the news, he was aware that Lance might decide to do away with him. It was almost a certainty. He shouldn't have done what he had to Amy Pigtails. That was a huge mistake. But he couldn't help himself; he wanted to touch, wanted to please, wanted that which he was not allowed.

"Never touch the bodies," Lance had said.

I should have listened.

"You should have stayed away from this devil," Momma whispered inside his head. "I tried to warn you."

She had, but he had a want. Not just for fantasy, but to cross that line. *What do I do now? I don't want to die. Lance is going to kill me.*

"You need to protect yourself, Norry," Momma said. "Sooner or later, the Devil will come to collect."

Yes, I need to protect myself.

Norris got up, checked his stool, and flushed.

For a man with a disability, he moved quietly from the washroom, dragging his deformed foot gingerly across the hardwood. He reached the kitchen without waking Lance and inventoried the room. The dishes were neatly stacked in the drying rack; everything had its place. Pots and pans hung below the cupboards, glasses neatly stacked on counters, utensils in a tidy array of steel bowls, and knives set into butcher block.

Knives...

Norris ran his fingers over the handles, feeling the density of the wood that sheathed the cold steel. His heart pounded in his temples as he considered the consequences of his actions. He could remove a knife, knock on Lance's bedroom door, and drive a blade into his stomach. It would be that simple. But he didn't want to kill Lance. He listened to the songbirds, tears glistening in his eyes, threatening to spill over, and touched the blade in its sheath.

How had he gotten to this place?

03 September 2007

Louisville, KY

HIGHWAYMAN Task Force Meeting

Ferguson had found his way into the building when the call came through. He answered on the first ring.

"Agent Ferguson," he said.

A woman's voice said, "Hello, Agent Ferguson, my name is Karen Rothstein, I work in the NCIC, and we've got a make on the car you've been seeking."

Car, Ferguson thought. "Oh yes, go ahead."

"We have pinpointed it down to a 1991 Chevrolet Cavalier; the paint code for that particular model is WA8970, which is dark sapphire blue."

Ferguson laughed. "I'm not up on my color coordination. I assume you have a picture."

In the background, there was the clicking of computer keys. "Yes, we do. I can send over a photo spread of the model and color, but keep in mind that this vehicle is sixteen years old, and the paint will have aged, and quite possibly there may be other colors."

"Other colors?"

"It's an old car, Agent Ferguson. Old cars oxidize and rust. Sometimes they end up with new fenders from junkyards. Based on the photo that was sent to us, I'd say that the car's paint is, at the very least, very faded."

"I understand. Can anyone there do an aging effect on the photos?"

"We already thought of that. We'll be sending you two separate profiles. Four photos as the car would look new, and composites with aging." Rothstein sounded very pleased with herself.

"That'll be great. Do you need my email?"

"I already have it. I also have two other contacts on my list. SAC Hugh Bailey and Special Agent David Maxwell, do you want me to carbon copy them as well?"

"Send it directly to me, and I'll forward it to Maxwell and Bailey," Ferguson said.

"Sounds good, I'm sending you the email now."

"Thank you."

4

03 September 2007

Montoursville, PA

With introductions made, Maxwell, along with Abraham and Leeman, awaited the arrival of the two girls. It was just before 10:00 a.m., and Maxwell was filled in by Leeman on how they had figured out the girl's FUG game.

"Something wasn't adding up with their stories. The gap between when the photo was taken and when it was received seemed extensive. Also, the Potter girl was lying to us from the get-go. She kept looking off and to the right when we pressed her about the picture and why she'd taken it."

Leeman was talking about what detectives referred to as "a tell." Often when someone being interviewed was untruthful, they would display a mannerism. Breaking eye contact, speaking faster, crossing arms, something out of the norm which most investigators see right off.

"My supervisor updated me on this. Good catch. The girls still don't know that you're onto their game?" Maxwell felt his phone vibrate in his pocket. He pulled it out, looked at it, and said to Leeman and Abraham, "Will you excuse me for a second?"

Both men said, "Sure."

Maxwell got up and stepped into the hall. "Maxwell."

"Hi, it's Evan Ferguson. We've got a make and color on the car."

Maxwell felt a torrent of exhilaration. "Fantastic!"

"I just got the email from NCIC. I'm forwarding it to you and calling as a courtesy. I'll have to inform the SAC."

"Of course, and thanks, Evan," Maxwell said. "You're a man of your word."

"Yeah, well, I said I would. Anyway, there are two sets of pictures coming through. The first is the car when it comes off the line and the second is an age enhancement. They think it's a sapphire blue '91 Chevrolet Cavalier, which is technical for the dark blue shit box."

Maxwell laughed, and Ferguson joined him.

"I'm just about to interview the girl who took the picture. Can you email those immediately? I'm going to see if I can put together an array with a couple of different cars."

"Sure. I guess the task force is going to want to release these to the media ASAP." Ferguson took a breath and said, "Hang on a second, Dave."

"Okay," Maxwell said and could hear Lonnie Perkins in the background.

"You're the FBI man who's come to replace Max," Perk said. Maxwell smiled. He'd become fond of the Kentucky investigator.

"Special Agent Evan Ferguson. Can you hold on a sec?" Ferguson asked.

"Sure," Perk said.

Ferguson came back on. "I got to go, Dave. I'll forward the email when I get off and inform the SAC."

"Let Perkins in on this as well."

"Will do. Hopefully, this will aid you in the hunt."

From behind, a door opened, and two teenage girls accompanied by their parents entered the barracks. "Thanks, my interviews just showed up. I expect we've both got our work to do. Thanks again, Evan."

"No problem, Dave."

The call ended and a moment later the email prompt on Maxwell's phone chimed. He stepped back into the office where Abraham was. Leeman had gone to collect the girls and their parents.

"Lieutenant Abraham, I've got pictures of the suspect's vehicle, but I want to set up an array for the interview. Can we Google some photos of cars similar to a dark blue '91 Chevrolet Cavalier?" Maxwell was opening his laptop and brought up the email attachment. "I'd like to print them out, and have the girl see if she can make an identification."

"Sure," Abraham said. "No problem."

Fifteen minutes later, they had five separate pictures of cars much like a '91 Cavalier. In fact, two of the models were from the same manufacturer. Maxwell placed the pictures into his briefcase. He went out into the waiting room and looked at the two girls. "Who's Jennifer?"

"I am," said a blonde girl sitting with her father and mother.

"You're up first," Maxwell said.

Jennifer and her parents all started to get up.

"No," Maxwell said. "I'm afraid that we are going to have to talk to Jennifer alone, if that's alright."

"What is this?" her father protested. "She didn't do anything wrong."

"Mr. Potter," Trooper Leeman said. "Nobody is accusing Jennifer of anything. But we need to talk to her alone."

"Maybe we better call a lawyer," Mrs. Potter said.

Maxwell turned and faced Jennifer straight on. "You don't need a lawyer. Jennifer, we need to talk to you about what you saw that night and the man you photographed. Do you have a problem with that?"

The girl looked scared; she wanted her parents there. "I think maybe..."

"You know what we call a situation like this," Maxwell said. "We call it a 'Fugly' because the guy we're chasing has done some pretty ugly things prefaced by a word that begins with F." He looked at her, not them. "Do you understand what I mean, Jennifer?"

"Yes," she squeaked.

He turned to face Mina Carberry. "You girls understand my dilemma? We have to catch these guys, or things can get really fugly."

"Is that sort of language necessary?" Jack Carberry complained.

"Dad," Mina Carberry said, "we need to go in alone."

Maxwell smiled, but not enough for the adults to see.

"Yeah, it's okay," Jennifer agreed.

"Mina will go with Trooper Leeman, and Jennifer will accompany Lieutenant Abraham and me." Maxwell shifted his eyes between the parents of both kids. "They're not in trouble of any sort, but we need to talk to them without distraction. We're looking for some really bad guys."

The parents reluctantly agreed.

When they sat Jennifer down in the interview room, even before the closed-circuit camera was turned on, she said, "Please don't tell my parents about the FUGS."

"You be honest with me, and they'll never hear a word," Maxwell said.

"I will," she urged.

Then the interview got underway.

5

03 September 2007

Lawrenceville, PA

It was almost three in the afternoon. Lance was scanning the Internet for wrecking yards in northern Pennsylvania and southwestern New York area.

He had to get rid of the car. He'd held onto it for too long as it was. He'd only been up for five hours, his nocturnal meeting running into the late hours of the morning. He felt refreshed and ready to deal with his logistical problems. First, he'd find a wrecker and unload the shit box Cavalier, then he'd deal with the second liability. The second chore made him feel sad. But he couldn't keep him here, and he certainly couldn't leave him alone for too long. He might murder a neighbor and have sex with their remains.

For reasons Lance could not fathom, this made him smile.

"Something funny?" Norris asked.

"Yeah," Lance said, but didn't share what. Instead, he said, "Turn on the news, Norris. I need an update."

Norris crossed the room and turned on the television which was already set to CNN. A banner declared **breaking news** and the words Suspect Picture And Car Identified In A Nationwide Manhunt. On the screen, Jennifer Potter's FUG picture was being broadcasted along with the make and model of the car they were driving.

The split screen flashed to a man standing behind a podium. His suit and demeanor gave away his occupation almost immediately. Below the video was the agent's name. Special Agent Evan Ferguson. "The FBI, in conjunction with the Louisville Police Department, is making a call to the public to be on the lookout for a 1991 dark blue Chevrolet Cavalier. They are warning the public not to approach individuals in the suspect car as they are to be considered armed and extremely dangerous."

Lance said nothing, watched the screen images flip from the car to a picture of Norris in the car, and at first, it wasn't registering.

Where did they get that picture? he thought.

Norris, on the other hand, knew exactly what was going on and regretted not pulling a knife from the butcher block. Out of the corner of his eye, he could see Lance rising from behind his laptop like a meerkat.

"What the fuck?" Lance said.

Norris cringed.

"How did they get a picture of the car?" His voice rose slightly. "Of you? What the fuck?" A wave of panic rolled over Lance. How would he dispose of the car? Where had that picture been taken? Were there more?

"Lance, I made a mistake."

"A mistake." Lance blinked, and the confusion and panic exchanged for rage. "A fucking mistake!"

***

CHAPTER 24 – BEATING THE BUSHES

1

03 September 2007
Montoursville, PA

The girls were let go, their Fug Game kept secret, but with a warning. Maxwell told Mina Carberry, whom he thought was the smarter of the two, that if he found out the girls had held out on anything, he'd have them back in and talk to them about the FUG game in front of their parents. Mina said they had not, and for the most part, Maxwell believed her.

"What now?" Cole Abraham asked.

"Good question," Maxwell said.

Maxwell stood outside the barracks looking up at the gray overcast sky, trying to think of what to do next when the troop lieutenant asked him the question he had been asking himself again and again.

What now? What fucking now?

Abraham lit a cigarette, leaving Maxwell to think that he was the exception, not the rule when it came to healthy living. He turned to Cole Abraham and said, "Can I have one of those?"

"Sure," Abraham said, shaking the pack mechanically, and a single cigarette popped out. Maxwell took it, placed it between his lips, and Abraham lit it for him.

He took a small drag and exhaled. The smoke tasted terrible, so he took a second drag knowing he could quickly pick up the habit once the nicotine deadened the taste buds in his mouth. "You from here, Cole?"

"Born and bred."

"If you were on the run and passing through Duncannon, where would you go and why?" Maxwell tried another drag and looked over at the big trooper.

Abraham thought about the question, and said, "I'd take the US 15 north."

"Why?"

"Couple reasons. First, the interstates are monitored by cameras, and there are toll booths on the turnpikes. Also, there is a larger police presence on the interstates." Cole Abraham flicked the ash off the cigarette. "The US 15 has been around a long time, truckers use it regularly to get around the tolls and fudge their logbooks, and it has escape routes."

"Escape routes?"

"There's plenty of places to get off and disappear. People mind their own business in these parts. Even the shit box car you're looking for isn't all that uncommon in these parts. So, if I were on the run, looking for a place to hold up or hide, I'd use the 15 and look for a place to get out of sight."

The cigarette, which Maxwell regretted taking, burned absently in his right hand. "And if you just wanted to keep going?"

"I'd stay on the 15. It takes you up to Painted Post, NY. From there, you have all sorts of options, east to Binghamton up into Syracuse and onto all points north." Cole Abraham knocked the cherry off his smoke and slipped the butt into his pocket. "You think they're making a run for it?"

"No, I think they're still in Pennsylvania, holed up in one of the little towns you're talking about," Maxwell said. "I'm hoping they still have that car."

"What do you need from us?"

Maxwell extinguished the cigarette and thought about it.

2

03 September 2007

Lawrenceville, PA

"A fucking mistake!" Lance had Norris pinned by his shoulders in the chair, his face was so close that bits of spittle peppered Norris' face. A bit had actually gone into his mouth when he tried to explain. "I told you to do one simple thing! One simple motherfucking thing! Stay out of sight! That's all you had to fucking do." Lance dug his fingers into Norris' shoulders and through gritted teeth, shouted, "Are you fucking mentally retarded?"

Norris opened his mouth to respond. To explain that it was hot, that he hadn't meant to be seen, but Lance cut his words down.

"How the fuck do I unload the car now?" Lance roared. "Do you have any idea how much you've crippled us? You fuck!" Lance's eyes were bulging and red-rimmed, like the tantrum at the Ironworks. He began shaking Norris, beating him against the chair back, accompanied by, "You fuck! You fuck!"

"I'm sorry," Norris wept.

Lance released him and began pacing. His face flushed, on the edge of tears. "I ought to have my head examined! The car, how do I get rid of the car?"

Norris said nothing.

Lance turned up the television and listened to the broadcast. The FBI agent, who wasn't Maxwell, was talking to the media. He told them where the picture had been taken, that investigators from the Pennsylvania State Police were now involved.

They know we're in Pennsylvania.

Before this revelation, he was looking for a wrecking yard to unload the car. If he had made that call before turning on the news, he most certainly would have been caught.

They know we're in PA, and they know the car.

Meanwhile, Norris sat in the chair like a fucking sloth, offering absolutely nothing in the way of help. He'd have to get rid of him, but he needed to get rid of that car. Needed to make it disappear.

But how?

He could dump it in a lake, but it would probably be discovered. There were a few small lakes up the back roads in the area. There was one up Buckwheat Hollow Road about eight miles away. Eight miles of road where he might meet a state trooper.

"Norris," Lance said.

Norris didn't respond and continued staring at the television.

"Norris, I'm talking to you."

He turned to face Lance. "I'm sorry, Lance. I really am."

Lance steadied his voice. "We need to get rid of the car. Now that the cops got an all-points bulletin out on it."

"Okay?"

"So, seeing that you created this mess, you are now responsible for figuring out how to clean it up. Put your fucking thinking cap on and start coming up with ideas. We have to make it disappear!" Lance looked genuinely scared, and there was desperation in his voice, something Norris had never seen nor heard before.

"Yes, Lance. We need to get rid of the car. It's my mess, I need to clean it up," Norris said.

Lance turned off the television and took the chair next to Norris. "The clock is ticking. I've driven that piece of junk around these parts. Someone may have seen me. Now we can't drive it fifty fucking feet. So, how Norris, how the fuck do we get rid of it?"

"I'm not sure yet," Norris said.

Lance leaned over and whispered, "You better come up with something soon." He inhaled. "Or I'll bury your ass along with that car in the back of my property." Then he recoiled to the chair, leaving Norris to consider his options, which were very limited.

3

04 September 2007

Montoursville, PA

What Maxwell wanted from the PA state police, or more specifically from Cole Abraham, was an ear to the ground. "What are we listening for?" Abraham asked.

"We're listening for crazy," Maxwell said.

Abraham chuckled. "Agent Maxwell, this is Pennsylvania, there's plenty of crazy for anyone who's buying."

"I think the guy we're hunting is losing control," Maxwell said.

"Why?"

"Prior to Louisville, he was methodical, controlled, and he was a planner. He didn't leave a trail. No evidence at a single scene. But he posed the bodies for one reason only. He wants to be known." Maxwell looked up at the taller cop. "He's making stupid mistakes. It started with hooking up with Norris, who we now know was visiting the crime scenes after the Highwayman finished with a victim."

"How did you determine that?"

"Norris told us."

"Huh?"

"When he printed the pictures of each crime scene, the digital date marking, when the picture was taken, was embedded into each photo. We also know that he used Greyhound as his mode of transportation, so we were able to track his movement right across the country. He was visiting dead bodies left for him by the Highwayman."

"You'd almost think he was working for us," Cole said.

"That's the thing. Up until now, Highwayman didn't make stupid mistakes. Bringing Norris in was foolhardy. Then, if that wasn't enough, he kidnaps the FBI agent who was tracking him."

"That doesn't mean he's losing control. In fact, that sounds calculated. You said he wants notoriety." Cole said.

"Fair enough, but I started connecting the dots after the massacre at the Ironworks in Kentucky. Those murders were different than the Highwayman killings. The Ironworks was complete bedlam. More like a spree killing. Then I ask myself, 'Why not just kill Norris too?' He could have finished him at the Ironworks and disappeared. Instead, he does the irrational and takes Norris with him. I think this guy is unraveling. For almost a month, he's been on a binge of murder. Sooner or later he's gonna do something that will draw attention."

"So, we listen for the crazy," Abraham said.

"That's right, and we follow every lead," Maxwell said. "He's going to make a mistake, and I want to be there when he does."

4

The crucial tip came in around 10:00 a.m. that morning. It was put into a file folder for review along with three hundred other strange stories that ranged from a disturbed man in Cogan Station, who was shitting in public, to a guy in Muncy, who took out a victim's eye with a screwdriver.

Two troopers were given the task of extracting tips new and old. They began compiling a paper database as tip after tip rolled in from different parts of the state involving the US 15 running from Duncannon to Lawrenceville, PA.

Maxwell became mindful of Cole Abraham's earlier laughter as the stories started piling up. Police reports and complaints were logged after the sighting on the 28th of August in Duncannon up until the present. Maxwell leaned into Abraham, when the complaint list was at three hundred and two, and said, "What kind of fucked state is this, Cole?"

"Welcome to Pennsylvania, Max."

They'd moved past the formalities. Abraham was okay, he still preferred Perk, but he was a long way from Louisville.

Ferguson was running Louisville now. With Perk. This stirred resentful embers toward Bailey, and how he had tried to sandbag him. Although not surprising, it still pissed him off.

Maybe I should get out of the field. Do some instruction, maybe work on getting promoted. I can't do this forever. He could do all those things, Maxwell was a very capable instructor, and he had the connections to make promotion. "But first, I've got to catch this fuckhead."

"Pardon," Cole said.

Maxwell smiled, realizing he'd spoken that last thought out loud. "Nothing, just thinking out loud." Then he smiled at Cole, and said, "I think Pennsylvania is rubbing off on me."

"Bound to happen," Cole said and picked up the file folder and said, "Come on in my office, and we'll start chiseling away at this."

Maxwell followed and closed the door behind him. They put the complaints into two piles. One was Of Interest, the other Irrelevant. The defecating homeless guy found his way onto the Irrelevant pile immediately. He was joined by a complaint from a sex store where a man with a double-ended dildo was demanding a refund. When the clerk refused, he began swinging the two-headed snake and knocking over displays, which prompted a call to the police. There was also an incident with quarreling brothers, a hatchet, and a trip to the emergency room with two fingers on ice. Then there was a woman who beat up another woman in a bar bathroom, knocking out her teeth and pissing on her for good measure. What the fight was over was a mystery, but a recurring one at that. The two women were regulars who would get physical when the beer started flowing.

"Lesbians?" Maxwell asked.

"Sisters." Cole smiled. "And might I add that was pretty damned presumptuous of you."

"Forget it." Maxwell picked up the next complaint and began reading. This latest incident did not have the drama of swinging dildos or defecating crazies, but it had a vibe. Maxwell read on.

Type 1 Incident Report
Filed by: Trooper Ben Arquette
Date: 01 Sept 2007
Location: Wellsboro, PA

At 16:35 I was dispatched to the Stop-n-Go convenience store in Wellsboro, PA, to investigate a minor disturbance.

Stop-n-Go employee Jennifer Manley (DOB 7-12-1957) reported that there was an individual in the store who was extremely agitated.

Manley told me:

-The individual was scary. Looked almost psychotic.

-Other than extreme agitation, the individual did nothing of a violent nature. Individual described as "creepy."

-Outward appearance, well kept. Clean clothes, short hair (buzz cut), clean shaven.

Additional witnesses.

Patron: Larry Moore (not available at time of interview)

Unknown patron: (female) mid to late 40s, possibly a tourist.

Additional information

-The individual was driving a small, dark blue car, no tag recorded. Described as possibly late model 1990s Pontiac Sunfire or a four-door Dodge Neon.

Maxwell grabbed a yellow highlighter and traced it over the words *scary* and *psychotic*. He also highlighted words *small blue car*.

"Possible," he said and placed the complaint in the Of Interest pile. He picked up two more files and scanned them. One was Irrelevant and the other Of Interest.

Maxwell and Abraham reviewed all the complaints. It took almost five hours and forty-five minutes. In that time, three hundred and two had been pared down to twenty-two.

At 4:00 p.m., they broke for supper, Cole opting for a Big Mac meal combo, while Max had the Filet of Fish. Maxwell tried to convince himself he was making the healthy choice but failed miserably. After dinner, they returned to the pile of twenty-two and began paring it down even further.

By 7:00 p.m., the Of Interest pile had been reduced to six. The Stop-n-Go incident was still in the mix and Maxwell traded reports with Abraham, who said, "Could be something. Probably isn't, but it could be."

Maxwell thought it was. "I'm going to head over to Wellsboro in the morning, and check it out myself."

"I could come along, but it wouldn't be until afternoon. I have to meet with the Montoursville city council in the morning."

"That's okay, I'll go up solo." Maxwell was exhausted, his eyes were sore from all the reading, and he was getting restless from being cooped up in an office. A road trip would do him good. "You're right, it's probably nothing, but I'd like to rule it out."

"Suit yourself," Abraham said.

04 September 2007

Lawrenceville, PA

The property surrounding Lance's cottage was rural and extremely private. Private enough to conduct experiments on animals, but sound carried, even in the Pennsylvania woods. Norris did come up with two ideas. The first was to chop the car up and distribute it over the three acres. This idea got shot down very quickly. Cutting a car into pieces was a noisy, time-consuming endeavor; it would draw questions for sure. This brought them back to dumping it into a lake. Lance was concerned about driving it anywhere, even under the cover of darkness. Cars traveling back roads at night drew unwarranted attention. This had been Lance's initial idea, but Norris had a better one.

"Rent a truck," Norris said. "A big truck from U-Haul or Penske, and you drive it up here, and put the car in the back. You can take the car somewhere else and dump it."

Lance thought about it. "Still pretty risky."

"It could work. You could take the car anywhere and dump it, but it would have to be at night." Norris sounded more confident, and judging by the look on Lance's face, he had a good reason for the confidence. "It's a good idea, Lance."

The smallest of smiles crept across Lance's face. "It has potential. How do we get the car into the back of the truck?"

"When I worked at KT Paper, we had portable ramps for loading trailers outside. You could run a forklift up into a fifty-three-foot trailer, I guess you could rent a ramp."

"Or build one." Lance's grin widened. "Renting a ramp to load a car is just one more piece of potential evidence. I have wood and tools here. We could build a set of sturdy ramps that would support the car and take them along to unload it."

"You could just rent a car-carrier trailer, hook it to a pickup, and use that. That might save some time." Norris was just full of ideas.

"No."

"Why not?"

"I don't want anything connecting my name to moving a car. If I rent a full-size truck, we can get the Cavalier out of here. I can also use it to pick up a vehicle from my place in Syracuse, New York. I have a '97 Oldsmobile Intrigue that is dark green. It used to be my mother's car."

"You have a place in Syracuse?" Norris said.

Lance waived the question off and thought, *The Intrigue isn't the exact color as the Cavalier, but given some time, it might be mistaken for one. I could bring it back, even drive it around the same route I used the Cavalier on. If I'm questioned, the car is clean.*

Lance went back to his laptop and began searching for truck rental places on the Web. He couldn't rent locally, and decided to drive up to Syracuse and grab a truck from there. He could take the Impala and switch it out for the Intrigue, then he wouldn't have to load it up. If he could get rid of that car, dump it somewhere else where it would be found, that would work well with his plan. Once the car was gone, he could figure out what to do about his other problem.

6

It was almost midnight, and he decided that he would drive up to the place in Syracuse so that he could get the rental in the morning. He was ready to go, and Norris looked nervous about being left alone. Not as edgy as Lance was about leaving him alone, but taking him was out of the question. He could kill Norris now and then take care of the car business after, but for reasons he couldn't explain, he kept putting it off.

"You're going to have stay here," Lance said. "There's lots of food, and I'll be back by tomorrow afternoon with the truck."

"Okay." Although not showing it outwardly, Norris was relieved that he wouldn't have to go, thinking his fate might find him chopped up like the others.

Lance gave Norris a hard look. "You need to stay out of sight. Don't go outside. Don't answer the door, and keep the shades pulled."

"I will."

"You better. This is your mess. If you'd kept your head down, they wouldn't be looking for that car." Lance took him by the shoulder. "I've been patient to this point, but I won't be if you don't listen to me."

"I promise, I won't go outside." Norris then added. "I'm sorry I fucked up. I won't..."

"You better not."

They were standing at the door, Lance holding an overnight bag, Norris anticipating being left alone. He was in mortal fear that his life would be ending tonight, that Lance would just kill him and bury him on the property.

"Lock the door behind me," Lance said and stepped out onto the porch. The Impala was already idling in the carport. The Cavalier had been moved to the back of the property and re-tarped. "It'll take me a couple of hours to drive up. I'll get right down to the rental agency in the morning and come right back."

"I'll be here," Norris said.

"You better be." Then he turned and walked away.

Norris locked the door.

***

CHAPTER 25 – CAT FOOD MAN

1

05 September 2007

Wellsboro, Pennsylvania

Maxwell entered the Stop-n-Go, produced his identification and got down to questioning the two people inside. The one Lance had called Chatty Cathy, whose real name was Jennifer Manley, was helpful. "I remember him, he had a buzz cut, and he was fidgety. Like he was upset about something, and his car was just like you described. Cavalier or maybe it was a Sunfire, but it was blue, that's for sure. What do you think, Larry?"

Larry Moore, the one Lance had called Cat Food Man, said, "I only saw the back of it, but I'm pretty sure it was a Cavalier. My daughter had one. The biggest piece of shit car Chevy ever made, if you ask me." Then he looked at Jennifer embarrassed. "Sorry, Jennifer."

Jennifer smiled.

"Did you recognize him," Maxwell asked.

"Recognize him? Why would I recognize him?"

"I mean, is he a local, have you seen him around?"

"No," Moore said. "Can't say I have. Is he the one you're looking for with that business in Louisville?"

"He might be; right now we're following up all leads."

"Uh huh. That's nasty business."

Maxwell shifted the questioning. "Was there anybody else in the car?"

"He was all alone, but he had to be somewhere, there was no doubt about that."

"What about outside the store? Any unusual characters loitering around?"

"If you mean that Norris fellow, no."

Maxwell stopped and said, "You seem to know a lot about what happened in Louisville."

"I've been watching Fox News around the clock, and if I had seen that Norris character, I would have remembered. This guy was alone."

Maxwell wrote down: ***Call state cops. Get separate statements.*** "Okay, I've sort of jumped ahead here, but I'd like to jot down a full description, head to toe. You said he had a brush cut. What color was his hair?"

"Brown, maybe even black. He didn't just have a brush cut. It was down to the wood."

"Do either of you remember his eye color?"

Moore said, "No."

Jennifer said, "He had blue eyes. Pale blue, almost gray." Maxwell could feel the cashier's eyes inventorying him. She was developing a flirtatious tone. "How long you been an FBI agent, Mr. Maxwell?"

"Too long," he said, managing a smile. "What was his build?"

"Build?"

"Yeah. Was he tall? Short? Thin? Fat? Muscular?"

"He wasn't all that tall, but not short either. Maybe five ten, and he was slim," Moore replied.

"Would you say he was ex-military?"

Jennifer said, "Maybe..."

Maxwell started to write. ***Milit***

But then, Moore said, "No. He never served."

Maxwell turned his attention back to Moore. "Why do you say that?"

"I was in 'Nam, did three tours with the Rangers. I spent ten years in the army after that. Call it what you will, but I have a sixth sense about military guys. You develop a feel for them. Pick up on their mannerisms. This guy didn't have anything like that. He wasn't regimented."

"Regimented?"

"Most ex-servicemen are able to contain their feelings. We get this stuff drilled into us. You know what I'm talking about, Agent Maxwell. The FBI can't be much different. You guys go through a boot camp, don't you?"

"Yes, we do, and I think I understand what you're saying, but I want to hear it from you if that's alright."

"Sure." He paused to think for a second, and said, "In 'Nam, but even after that, I met some guys that were certifiable, if you know what I mean. Some guys are borderline nuts in the military, but most of them are able to contain it. Except maybe the ones who go off their rocker. This guy, he looked like he wanted to kill everyone. It was written all over his face. He says, 'No, I'm fine,' and 'I'm sorry,' but his eyes. I'm not sure how to say it. There was something in those eyes."

"Something? What?"

"I don't want to say in front of Jennifer."

"Oh, Larry."

Maxwell said, "Would it be better if we stepped outside?"

He nodded. "Sorry, Jennifer, I'm old school. I don't like swearing in front of ladies."

She shook her head and smiled. "That's okay, you gentlemen step out. I think you're just itching for a smoke, Larry."

They stepped outside.

05 September 2007

Ithaca, NY

It was coming down hard, rain beating off the asphalt of Interstate 86. Lance was on his way back to Pennsylvania driving the biggest truck his license would allow: a twenty-six-foot moving truck. The size of the truck for the cargo was overkill, but he didn't want to come up short, and knew he'd need enough room for ramps to load and unload the Cavalier. Lance's level of paranoia had elevated to the extreme since leaving Norris alone at the cottage.

I should have just killed him and buried him in the back, he thought. But he couldn't. He needed Norris to help get the car in and out of the truck. Besides that. *The little fucker should help. He created this goddamned mess.*

The rain intensified. So Lance turned the wipers up to full, and they went back and forth, sounding like an uncalibrated metronome. Angry as he was, he had to admit that Norris' idea about the moving truck was a good one. "Points for Norris," Lance said. "Gimpy fucking Norris, who couldn't keep his head down for five minutes." He could not see the angry scowl on his face but felt the stress in his clasp on the steering wheel. Lance let out a breath and loosened his grip. His mind was racing.

I have to start cleaning this up and shutting down. Norris is one thing, but the car is a whole other problem. Get rid of the car, get rid of Norris, and close down macabreclub.com, he thought.

It was time to push the self-destruct on the website. It might be in the Deep Web, but it was still a liability. He would do that after getting rid of the car and Norris.

But first, he had to go to home depot and buy wood.

05 September 2007

Lawrenceville, PA

Norris was doing a little speculating of his own. He grabbed a four-inch paring knife from one of the drawers in the kitchen and wrapped the blade, first in paper, then with medical tape from a first aid kit. Once done, he'd created a sheath for the little knife. He didn't want to use it, thought of it as a last resort, but considered it a practical weapon of self-defense.

He also set about the cottage and decided to break into Lance's bedroom. It hadn't been a difficult task. There were no jams on the door, and he was able to use the paring knife to draw back the deadbolt. The lock on the bedroom was only there for one purpose: to keep an honest man honest. Norris decided that, in this case, honesty wasn't the best policy and pushed the door open.

What he found was puzzling, to say the least. The room was as mundane and boring as his own. It had a king-sized bed, a dresser, a nightstand, and a throw rug. No books, no pictures, no television or radio. The chamber was for sleeping, and Lance appeared to be a man of straightforward needs.

Norris stood in the doorway, looking around the room, inventorying what little was there. Then it occurred to him that Lance had brought back a camera and a ragged-looking binder that had the FBI logo on it. Where had these items gone? He took three steps into the room, knelt on the throw rug, and looked under the bed.

Nothing. Just dust bunnies.

Then he heard the faintest chime.

He cocked his head, listening.

Then the chime sounded again. But it wasn't a chime at all. It was the sound a computer made. It was an alert. Norris stopped breathing, traversed the room with his eyes, then closed them and listened.

Where was it coming from?

And there it was again, but more refined. It sounded like a xylophone. Definitely a computer alert of some sort, and it was coming from below. Norris opened his eyes and looked down at the throw rug.

He moved off the rug and began to roll it up, taking note of its position for replacement. Beneath it, more hardwood; presumably, the carpet was there to offer warmth to the feet upon getting out of bed.

With the rug out of the way, Norris placed his hands square beneath him, like he was going to attempt push-ups, then lowered his head, and put his right ear to the hardwood. Again he stopped breathing, but this time, he kept his eyes open while he listened.

The sound came again, up through the hardwood and into Norris' right ear. It wasn't a xylophone, it sounded more like *ta da*, and Norris recognized it.

"Vista," he whispered and waited for it to chime again.

Ta da came the sound, and Norris' heart beat a little faster. It was an alert for the operating system Windows Vista. Norris lay like that a moment longer, and it came again. *Ta da.*

"Where?" he said, and his palms were suddenly searching the hardwood. He ran them across the polished surface. Then found the slightest imperfection with his left hand.

Ta da, the computer prompted.

Norris kept his hand on the edge, and got up on his knees, eyes focused on the spot. He could see the thin pencil line now, following its pattern with his free hand.

"Ta da," Norris said and laughed.

05 September 2007

Wellsboro, Pennsylvania

Larry Moore lit a cigarette and offered one to Maxwell, who declined. "The wife thinks I quit. I shoot down here twice a day and sneak a couple. Jenny doesn't say anything, God love her. I should quit them, but old habits die hard."

Maxwell prompted him. "You were saying?"

"He kept insisting that he was okay, kept apologizing, but those eyes. They were intense. I could feel the way he was staring at Jenny, like he wanted to hurt her. There was nothing but malice in those eyes. He could have been singing 'Happy Birthday,' but his eyes told a different story about what he was thinking. This guy was a madman, I could feel it coming off him. I'm not kidding when I say he had a look in his eyes, and I'm not exaggerating when I say he looked like he wanted to hurt Jenny."

"You keep saying that. Why?"

"There was a guy I did my training with before we went into that godforsaken jungle. His name was Ricky. I won't tell you his last name. I guess you could look it up, it's a matter of record now. But why would you?" Moore took a drag and exhaled. "Anyway, Ricky and I were fire-team partners when we did our pre-deployment training down in Louisiana. They put us through our paces in the worst imaginable conditions. They really fuck your head up when you do that training. Sleep deprivation is the worst, but the weather down there plays a part. It's not the Vietnam jungle, but it's close. I think back and all I can remember was out there in the Louisiana swamp... one minute you're cold, the next you're sweaty, and you're on an emotional roller coaster of paranoia, anger, giddiness, you name it. Ricky, he was quiet most of the time, but when they really started putting the screws to us, he started getting weird. The sergeant would come and yell at us, sometimes he'd hit us or kick us to get us motivated. The first time he kicked Ricky, I saw the look. He had rattlesnakes in his eyes, but his manner was passive. He just looked at the sergeant and said, 'Yes, Sergeant. I'll pay more attention, Sergeant.' This would appease the sergeant some, but I started getting really scared around Ricky because I started picking up on that weirdness.

"We finished our training and deployed. Ricky didn't say much, didn't go whoring with us in Saigon; some guys got the idea that maybe he liked guys instead of girls. A big gorilla in our unit named Holly started pushing Ricky, calling him a gearbox and a faggot. Ricky would smile, but I saw the same thing I'd seen back in Louisiana. On our last night in Saigon, after a few too many whiskeys, I told Holly to lay off, and he cleaned my clock. 'You a faggot too, Moore?' He was saying this over and over after he knocked me down and kicked me in the ass five times. All I could do was curl up in the fetal position and protect my face. A few of the other boys pulled him off, and I left the bar. We caught a ride with the air cav the next day, and Ricky was sitting next to me in the chopper. He leaned over and said, 'Moore, Holly is going to pay for what he did to you.'

"'Let it go, Ricky,' I told him. 'We got enough to worry about.' Ricky said nothing, but his eyes were burning.

"Four hours after we arrived at the LZ, they kitted us up and sent us into the bush. Our mission was to set up an ambush for NVA operating in the jungle. Holly was the point man, cutting our path with a machete, M16 clutched tightly in his left hand. I caught a glimpse of his face, and I knew then that he was just as scared as the rest of us. We stopped for a few minutes while the LT and the sergeant looked over the map. They had us in all-around defense. Holly was about twenty feet to my left taking a dump. Ricky, crouched on my right, was watching him, a grin on his face, and he said, 'Watch this, Moore.'

"He got up and stepped over me, heading straight to where Holly was pinching a loaf. He picked up the machete, and before Holly could get a word out, he reached out, grabbed him by the front of his helmet, and swung the machete. It was that quick. Holly's headless body fell over and continued to carry out its bodily function. Meanwhile, Ricky was coming back to me carrying Holly's head, which was still in the helmet, held by the chin strap. He was smiling when I heard the shot ring out, and then he fell over dead. The sergeant shot him. The mission was aborted, and we went back to the firebase."

Moore took a last puff on the cigarette and looked grimly at Maxwell. "The guy in the store, he had the same look as Ricky. If we hadn't stepped back, let him move up the line... He looked like he might melt down and start killing people. Especially Jenny." He crushed out the smoke. "It frightened me. I think she was sort of oblivious to this, but I saw it."

Maxwell studied the old guy. "Anything else?"

"Yeah, he was wiry like a runner, but not muscle-bound. I think he was maybe twenty-nine or thirty. Shit, he could have been thirty-five. It's hard for me to gauge people's age nowadays. Everyone looks between twenty and thirty years old. Part of getting old I suppose."

"This is helpful," Maxwell said. He felt mild exhilaration and wrote *Intense* and underlined it. Then he wrote *suspect composite*. "Larry, I'm going have the state cops send down an artist, see if we can work up a composite of this guy." "Can you tell me anything more about the car? If it had any distinguishing dents or scratches, broken taillights, cracked windshield?"

"No dents or scratches, but the paint was oxidized from the sun. It was a shit box, but the boroughs are full of shitboxes." Jennifer tapped on the window. Moore looked at her. She made a phone gesture with her hand. "My wife, she's probably worried."

"You don't have a cell phone?" Maxwell was writing *oxidized paint* on his pad.

"I managed to live through Agent Orange, Agent Maxwell. I'll quit while I'm ahead."

"I don't get you."

"Radio waves. Those things give you brain cancer."

Maxwell ignored the urge to say that cigarettes caused cancer too. He pulled out a card. "Okay, this is my private number. You think of anything, call me collect. Day or night."

"I don't think I've got anything else, but if I remember something, I will." Moore stuck out a hand, and Maxwell shook it.

"The state police will be coming with a sketch artist, and will want to re-interview you both separately. They're gonna ask all the same stuff I did. It's part of the investigative procedure, so try not to get annoyed by this."

Jennifer rapped on the window again.

"Okay, that'll be my woman." He released his hand. "I hope you get him, Agent Maxwell."

"Thanks for the information."

Maxwell went back inside, and handed another card to Jennifer and told her the same thing. He then went out to his car, intent on calling Cole Abraham, but remembered he was in a meeting this morning. He called in anyway and got Corporal Leeman, the one who'd investigated the Norris sighting.

"Pennsylvania State Police, Corporal Leeman speaking."

"Good morning, Corporal. Agent Maxwell calling. Have you got a minute to chat?" Maxwell had never really clicked with the young corporal. There was an air of awkwardness between them, mostly on Leeman's part. Perhaps it had been Maxwell's fault; he had gravitated toward Lieutenant Abraham and ignored him, even though he'd brought them a significant piece of evidence.

Maybe the kid was put off.

"I'm going out on patrol in fifteen minutes, but I can talk," Leeman said. "What can I help you with?"

"I'm wondering if your troop has a sketch artist."

"No. We use the Identi-Kit program."

"That's what I thought." Maxwell didn't care much for the Identi-Kit program. It used images from a database, piecing them together and making up composites, but it was too generic, and, Maxwell believed, inaccurate. Most police organizations used the program because it was cheaper than employing an actual sketch artist. "Okay, is there any chance we could get someone up here with the kit to make up a composite?"

"You have a lead?" Leeman sounded excited.

"Maybe, not a hundred percent, but I'd like to get a composite done."

"Okay, can I call you back? I'll have to check with the shift sergeant, and see if we can get a guy up there."

"Sure," Maxwell said, and they ended the call. He then put in a call to Hugh Bailey.

"Bailey."

"It's Maxwell, I've got a possible sighting on Highwayman in Wellsboro, Pennsylvania."

"Really, that's good news. What do you need?"

"The state cops are probably going to send out an Identi-Kit tech, but I'd like to have a certified sketch artist." Maxwell heard the call waiting on his cell begin to beep. "Can you hang on for a second? I've got the state cops calling back."

"Yeah," Bailey said.

"Thanks," Maxwell put Bailey on hold and took the call. "Maxwell."

"Agent Maxwell, Corporal Leeman calling back. We can send someone up there right away." Leeman sounded excited. "As a matter of fact, the trooper who took the original complaint is trained on Identi-Kit. Trooper Arquette just came on shift. He could be there in about an hour."

"Send him. I got my boss on the other line. Can I get back to you?"

"No problem."

Maxwell ended that call and went back to Bailey. "I've got the state cops coming up with an Identi-Kit tech."

"But you'd like a sketch artist." There was a hint of skepticism in Bailey's voice. "You haven't really told me what you got."

"Yeah," Maxwell said. "In all honesty, right now it's pretty circumstantial. The car is identified as a possible, and the individual has been described as psychotic. No one knows where he's from, but my guess is Pennsylvania. I'd like to throw the dice, and run a sketch out in the media. See what we can shake up."

"Let's stick with the Identi-Kit. If it's a wild goose chase, we can blame the technology."

And the state cops, Maxwell thought. *You fucking asshole.* "I think this might be our guy. I'd like an accurate composite."

"It's not solid enough, Maxwell. Use the state cops. You can run whatever they come up with on all the majors. If you get something more solid, I'll send out an artist."

Maxwell tried to hold his frustration back. Bailey was a fucking bureaucrat. The whole point was to run an accurate description. He considered calling Julian but pushed it away. *Check your temper, Max,* he told himself and said, "Okay."

"Once you have the composite, send it out to me for approval, and I'll have the task force in Louisville put it out in a press conference."

"Louisville? Why not hold a press conference in Montoursville? This is where we want to shake things up." Maxwell's words were measured. He could feel the anger building.

"We will announce it using the task force. We will credit the Pennsylvania cops with the composites, but I don't want multiple press conferences." Bailey's voice was firm, authoritative.

Maxwell eased his temper. This was a battle he would not win. "Okay, I'll send you the composites once they're done."

"Good. I've got a meeting. Anything else?"

"No," Maxwell said. "I'll contact you once we have something."

"Alright, bye for now," Bailey said, then hung up before Maxwell could respond.

"Bye for now, you fucking idiot," Maxwell grumbled into the dead phone.

5

05 September 2007

Lawrenceville, PA

Norris checked the clock in the kitchen. It was 10:30 a.m. The trap door was open, inviting Norris to descend. He was a bundle of anxiety. His throat clicked. His ears closed but for the beating of his heart. He shouldn't do this. He should go into Lance's room, close the trap door, roll the rug back over it, and leave the room.

But...

He wanted to see.

What is down there?

Wanted to know.

Why is that computer calling out?

The necessity tugged at him, drawing him toward its inevitability. Deadening the calls that he do the contrary, that he stop this before things got worse than they already were. A final question came to him, solidifying his resolve.

Why didn't he tell me about the secret hiding place?

That broke the deadlock of paralysis and sent him into the living room. He went to the front door and checked the deadbolt on the front door.

Still locked.

But Lance had a key and would be home in the early afternoon. That was if Lance was telling the truth. He had kept the secret place to himself. Had introduced himself as Devon. Norris stared down at the deadbolt, contemplating. *He is deceptive. A liar, and he's probably going to kill me. So what do I really have to lose?*

Norris found himself standing over the trap door.

I have nothing left to lose.

From below, he was summoned by the computer. *Ta da.*

He descended into the secret place.

***

CHAPTER 26 – DEVIL'S WORKSHOP

1

05 September 2007

Wellsboro, PA

As planned, the state trooper vehicle rolled up an hour later, but accompanying Trooper Arquette was Corporal Leeman. Maxwell met them outside. He said, "Glad you guys could make it." Then to Leeman, said, "I thought you had to go out on patrol."

Leeman smiled. "I asked my sergeant if I could come along."

"And he said yes," Maxwell said.

"He did so," Leeman agreed. "This is Trooper Ben Arquette." Maxwell came around to meet the trooper while Leeman carried on with introductions. "Ben, this is Special Agent Maxwell of the FBI."

"Nice to meet you," Arquette said. He was a big guy, at least six foot seven and, Maxwell thought, at least two hundred-seventy pounds. Even bigger than Abraham. Arquette's noteworthy features were the cluster of rusty red hairs on his head and the freckles on his pale skin. That and the fact that his massive hand swallowed Maxwell's in a dry, loose grip.

"Likewise," Maxwell said. "I guess we should get this show on the road."

Two hours passed, and it had gone much better than Maxwell expected. In working with each witness individually, Trooper Arquette was patient and methodical. He made multiple changes, switching eyes, noses, and even face shape as he listened to each.

While Arquette worked on the composites, Leeman, along with Maxwell, re-interviewed Moore and Jennifer individually. The story about Vietnam did not come up in the second interview with Moore. After Jennifer had finished her interview and Moore was finished with his composite, they brought both of them in and compared.

"I want you both to look at the composites. First, look at your own, then look at the other and tell me if there is anything we need to switch," Arquette said, looking at both Jennifer and Moore. "Take your time." Both studied the pictures on the laptop screen, while Maxwell and Leeman looked on. Moore spoke up first.

"I think the nose on Jennifer's picture is closer." Arquette switched the nose. "Yeah, much better," Moore said.

"That's it?" Arquette asked.

Jennifer made a sound like she was about to say something, then relented.

"Jennifer, you want to say something?" Maxwell asked.

"Um..." She hesitated. "I think the eyebrows might be thicker. I'm sorry."

"Don't be sorry," Arquette said. "It's normal to make changes." He used the mouse to bring up a dropdown menu containing different sets of eyebrows. "Just tell me what you think, and I'll switch it up. If you think it's good, say so. If not, we can change them again."

05 September

Lawrenceville, PA

His jaw agape, Norris stood at the bottom of the stairwell. He was in awe of the room. Taken by its orderliness and how utterly concealed it had been. The news clippings on the walls, the giant map of the United States, the library. It looked like a historical time capsule, a mini-museum. The map with all its beautiful red pushpins that could mean only one thing.

It's incredible, he thought.

Norris began to pace the wall, examining the news clippings, the map, the library, and, of course, the photos.

The photos were...

Glorious, he thought and felt himself stiffen. *Not now! I will not let this get in the way. Not yet.* He ignored the expanding need and continued his tour.

Why had Lance not shown him this?

He would not have even found it had it not been for the call of the computer. He stopped, turned toward the center of the room.

"Ta da," he said, and observed the computer monitor on the glass desk to see if it would respond.

Ta da, the computer responded.

He moved a little closer. Was this a trap? Had Lance purposely left his computer to snare Norris? He reached down, his hand quivering, and touched the mouse. The screen came alive, and the hard drive in the tower below the desk began to purr and click.

It opened up to a page Norris immediately recognized.

Welcome to macabreclub.com

ADMIN C-PANEL

Login

Username: Devon

Password: *********
ENTER

"Shit," Norris said. Lance had left his computer logged on. Username and password both saved. He would have never believed that Lance would do such a thing. But there it was.

Ta da, The computer replied.

Norris brought his left hand up to his mouth to stifle the terrified laughter. While he used his right to slide the mouse and hover the pointer over the enter button. Then he clicked. The screen went dim for a second, then transitioned to a page Norris had never seen on macabreclub.com. It contained no images, no video, or titillation. It was an administrative page for making changes to the site. At the top of the page were five buttons: **Home - Member Profiles - Upload - Rooms - Gallery.** Norris hovered the pointer over **Member Profiles** and double-clicked.

Again, the page transitioned, and this time a list of members came up.

Devon. Barker. Dusk. Steel. Larry.

Below each name was the word *Logs*.

Norris clicked on the Logs button under his name, and a drop-down menu opened up revealing dates and times. He understood immediately what he was looking at. They were chat sessions that he had engaged in with Lance.

He clicked on one date and a second window opened.

http://macabreclub.com/

Chat Session #4/Time: 265/05/09/2007

Devon: Hello, Barker.

Barker: Hi, Devon.

Devon: What would you like to talk about today?

Norris clicked an earlier date and scrolled down.

Barker: I like... Dead things. They excite me.

Devon: What kind of dead things?

Then he turned his attention to the others. Before opening the log, he wondered, *Who are they?* He hovered the pointer, trying to decide whose name to click on. *Dusk, Steel or Larry?* As he did, each name lit up, and Norris began to feel the sting of jealousy. He'd thought he was the only one.

Apparently not.

"What have you drawn me into, Lance?" Norris said and clicked on the Logs below Dusk. A drop-down menu with dates appeared. The last chat session had been two days ago. He clicked on that, which brought up a joint chat.

Then he began to read.

3

05 September 2007

Painted Post, NY

Lance was loading the wood into the back of the moving truck. He'd also purchased four-inch straps at the home depot which he hoped would help stabilize the car once he had it in transit.

Strangely, Lance was in a good mood; the anxiety regarding Norris and the car had calmed. Perhaps it was because he had a purpose, a project. He liked projects, whether it was building a hidden room below the cottage, planning a killing expedition, or building ramps that would put a hot Cavalier into the back of a moving van.

He was even considering bringing Norris outside to help in the construction of the ramps. After all, idle hands were the Devil's workshop. Norris, it seemed, needed to be occupied all the time.

"That's an understatement," Lance said to himself as he loaded the last 2x4 into the van. Then looked around to see if anyone had heard him. No one had, so he lowered the door and latched it. The drive from Painted Post to Lawrenceville was less than half an hour. He was sure he could get the moving truck into the back of the property and out of sight.

It would probably take an hour or two to construct the ramps and then maybe a half hour to load and secure the car. He decided to wait until dark before moving the car. Less chance of being pulled into a roadside inspection by the nysdot, who made it a habit of using rest areas when doing an inspection blitz.

He started the cube van and got moving. He hadn't wanted to go to home depot in Painted Post, but there was nothing after Ithaca. There were security cameras all over the parking lot, but Lance thought the risk was minimal. How many people who are moving use a rental truck to pick up lumber for some reason or other? He guessed that plenty did.

Lance got back on US 15 south and started for the cottage. Simultaneously, Norris had closed the trap door on the hidden room and was rolling the throw rug out to conceal it. He left the computer as he had found it, on the C-Panel login page, pinging it's repetitive *ta da*.

Lance was thinking, *What to do about Norris? If I bring him along, I'll have to kill him after we dump the car. I can't have him riding back in Mom's Oldsmobile.*

Lance looked up at the sky; it was gray, still threatening rain. He hoped he'd seen the last of the showers. Rain would make the ramp construction miserable, and it would also create hazards. The last thing he wanted was to get stuck. "Don't rain."

4

05 September 2007

Montoursville, PA

Maxwell put in a call to Bailey, but Bailey was unavailable, and this angered him. Bailey's secretary told him that the SAC would be in meetings all afternoon, and that he could try back around 4:30 p.m. He thanked her, hung up, and put in a call to Ferguson.

"Special Agent Ferguson," he answered.

"Hi, Evan. It's Dave Maxwell."

"Hey, how are things going down there?"

"What time are you meeting with the press?"

"We're going to do an update at 16:30, but in all honesty, there's not much to update. You have something?"

"I have a composite, but you can't run it until the SAC signs off on it."

"Hmm. Well, why hasn't he signed off yet?"

"He's in a fucking meeting."

"Perfect. The wheels of justice stop spinning for no one, except bureaucrats. I guess the composite is of our mystery man?"

Maxwell took a breath. "In all fairness, putting it out is sort of a gamble. I'm not a hundred percent, but I've got a strong suspicion."

"Jesus, Dave. What if you're wrong?"

Maxwell wanted to tell him that his gut feeling was that the man in the composite was probably the Highwayman. But it was very circumstantial. "What if?"

"Is that why you're waiting for the SAC? You don't want to get burned for throwing the dice?" Ferguson waited.

Maxwell thought about it. If he released the composite without authorization and they made an arrest, all would be forgiven. If they didn't, he was finished. Bailey would throw him under the bus in a heartbeat. "Something like that," he said.

"I wish I could help you, Dave. Can you send me the composite? I won't release it, I'd just like a look at it."

"Sure," Maxwell said. "Apparently, the SAC is tied up until 4:30 P.M.. Can you prepare a statement, and have it ready in the unlikely event that the SAC finds time to pay attention to the case he's overseeing?"

Ferguson laughed. "Yeah, I can do that. But this conversation will sound a whole lot different if I get pulled in for a talk."

"It won't be on you, Evan. I'll take the heat if that goes down. You can say I sent it to you with the understanding that the SAC had already signed off."

"Alright. You could just get the Pennsylvania cops to do a press conference."

"No, I can't. That's what I wanted to do, but Bailey won't allow it. He wants everything through the Louisville task force."

"Huh?"

"Exactly. Huh. My guess is he wants to take credit if we are onto something, but also wants an exit strategy if it doesn't amount to anything. That's why he wouldn't give me a sketch artist."

"I'm getting the distinct feeling you don't much like the SAC."

"Yeah, what would give you that impression?" Maxwell laughed, and Ferguson joined him. "I'll forward you a scan in your email. I'll keep on Bailey, and hopefully you can use it in your briefing. Be sure to say that you received this composite, that way it doesn't fall at your feet if it goes sideways."

"If the SAC approves?"

"Yes, if he approves. If he doesn't, I'll find another way."

"That's a risky endeavor, Agent Maxwell."

"Danger is my business, Agent Ferguson."

"Good luck."

"Thanks." Maxwell hung up and checked his voice messages and email. No messages or emails from Bailey. Maybe he was going the wrong way with this. It was circumstantial, but it was all he had. That, and a feeling that he was onto something.

What if I'm wrong?

"Then I'm wrong," he said and found Ferguson's email. He wrote a quick note, attached the interview transcripts and composite, and sent it.

What if Bailey doesn't get back to me?

He could leak it to the press, or have the Pennsylvania cops leak it. It would be career-ending. Even Julian Carswell wouldn't be able to save him after that.

Maxwell knew he only had two options. Release the composite and hope that someone recognized the man from the Stop-n-Go or wait for another body.

5

05 September 2007

Lawrenceville, PA

Tree branches scraped the roof of the moving truck as Lance maneuvered it behind the cottage. The threat of rain was still present, but for now, the ground was dry and he hoped it would remain that way until he got the car loaded inside. The prospect of getting stuck worried him.

Inside, Norris watched from his bedroom window. His invasion into Lance's secret room would remain a secret. He had replaced everything as it had been, leaving no clue of the break-in. Except for a thin pencil score on the bolt catch of Lance's bedroom door. This had been caused by the paring knife when he pried it back to enter the room. Norris looked at the scratch and dismissed it. He wasn't worried about Lance discovering it. His priority now was to stay alive.

With the truck parked, Lance got out and made his way to the back door of the cottage. In his left hand, he was carrying a plastic WalMart bag. He removed his key from his pocket. Was about to insert it when the lock turned over. The door opened, and Norris was standing there staring at him.

"You want to give me a hand?" Lance asked.

Norris stared at him, wide-eyed. "With what?"

"I'm going to get some tools, and there's lumber in the back of the truck to be unloaded. We're going to build some ramps out of the wood and load the car up." Lance was stepping into the house. He handed Norris the WalMart bag. "Here."

Norris took the bag from him and gazed inside. "What's this for?"

"It's a hair clipper and box of hair dye. I think we might want to change your appearance slightly. Maybe shave that mop down and change your hair color." Lance was down the hall, opening a closet, looking for his toolbox.

Norris lifted the box out of the bag and scrutinized it. The color on the carton said Born Red. After four days holed up in Lawrenceville, his facial hair had started to come in. "Red? Wouldn't that make me stand out? Why don't I just shave it all off like you?"

Lance came back with a big steel toolbox, set it down, and took the box from Norris. "No, I think we should use a number three setting on you. Maybe shape and trim your beard. Then we'll use the color on it." He handed the box back to Norris. "First, give me a hand unloading the wood."

Norris started for the door, still carrying the WalMart bag. He reached down into his pocket and touched the paring knife.

"Norris?"

He stopped and turned. "Yes?"

"Nobody is going to see us back here, and you can leave that inside. We'll change your appearance after we build the ramps and load the car." Lance was smiling.

"Okay," Norris said and took the bag to his room.

Lance watched him. Something didn't feel right. He took three steps down the hall and checked his bedroom door. It was locked. "Everything okay, Norris?"

"Sure." He was coming back now.

"You sure?"

"Yeah, I'm sure. I mean, I'm feeling bad about the car and..."

"What's done is done. The moving van was a great idea. Let's get it done, and we'll move on." Lance broadened his smile. "Okay?"

"Okay," Norris said, scurrying past him and into the yard. He didn't look back; he just made his way to the moving van.

Lance lifted the sliding door open, and they unloaded the wood. After that, Lance assembled the tools and ran an extension cord from the back of the cottage to a sliding miter saw he had set up behind the van. With that done, he measured the height of the van floor and made some calculations. "I love projects," he told Norris. "Pass me a 2x6, and we'll get this done." Norris handed him the first piece of wood, and Lance marked it. Then another and another. Once he'd scored the boards, he began cutting them to length.

Two and a half hours later, the ramps were done. Lance then went on to construct braces that would keep the car from shifting once it was loaded into the van. This took an additional fifty minutes. Throughout, Norris remained pensive, doing as was asked, but clearly distracted.

Lance set up the ramps and brought the Cavalier around to line it up. He looked on, beaming with pride. Aside from killing and dismembering people, carpentry was his passion. "What do you think?"

"You're an excellent carpenter," Norris said.

"Thank you, Norris. Now, let's get this baby loaded, and we'll have a bite to eat." Lance moved toward the car while saying over his shoulder. "I'll need you to direct me, Norris."

"Okay."

After loading the car, it took another thirty minutes to secure it. Lance used the straps and some homemade wheel chocks to keep it in place. Satisfied, he brought the moving van back around the front of the cottage and parked it. He padlocked the back and went inside to eat an early supper.

Lance put two TV dinners into the oven and perused Google Maps for suitable dumps sites. To the east, approximately two hundred and ten miles away, off Interstate 88, was a town in New York state called Cobleskill. Lance thought that would be the furthest he would want to drive. Along that stretch of highway, there would be plenty of forest, and hopefully, a place to quickly unload the Cavalier. He wanted to conceal it, but not permanently.

It had to be found.

Norris stole glances at Lance, turning over the knowledge he had acquired this morning. There was no doubt in his mind that the man he was looking at was a cunning liar. *Liar intent on killing me,* he thought. He wasn't just projecting anymore. The chat logs had confirmed it. He was a problem, and the others wanted Lance to dispose of him. Even worse, Lance agreed with them. His words: "It's under control. I'm going to deal with my problem very soon."

"Norris," Lance interrupted. "You got something on your mind?"

Norris looked up from his dinner. "Um... I was just wondering what the plan is from here." And *Are you going to kill me before or after we dump the car?*

"After dinner, we'll cut and dye your hair. Once that's done, it should start getting dark. So we'll get on the road, and look for a place to get rid of the car."

"Where will I be riding?"

"There's nowhere to hide you in the cab, so you'll have to ride in the back with the car."

"I don't want to ride in the back."

"I imagine you don't, but that's where you'll have to ride. Everyone is looking for you. We don't need you being seen again."

Norris said nothing. He thought that he should have called the police and turned himself in. He might have ended up down in the Kentucky State Prison in Eddyville. That was where they executed killers. Maybe right next to Marco

Chapman, who was waiting to be executed for murdering two kids. Maybe. Or perhaps not. If he had agreed to turn on Lance, he might have been able to cut a deal.

"Are you listening to me, Norris?"

Norris brought his eyes up to meet Lance's. *It's too late for deals now,* he thought. "Yes, Lance, I'm listening to you."

"You sure? You seem sort of preoccupied." Lance scraped the last of his dinner up with his fork and put it into his mouth. He chewed it and waited for a response.

Norris kept his eyes down, afraid they might betray him. "I just feel bad that you have to go to all this trouble. I should have stayed under the blanket."

"What's done is done," Lance said and thought, *Yeah, you should have kept your fucking head down.* While adding, "At least you came up with the idea for the truck."

In the chat log, Lance had said, "I'm going to take care of it. In the meantime, I'm going to need you to do something for me."

What was that something? Norris wondered. *Will they be waiting when we drop the car? Waiting to kill me?*

Norris' heart stammered.

"Get that dinner into you, we've got a bit of a ride ahead of us." Lance got up and moved into the kitchen.

"Yeah, okay." Norris stared down at his half-eaten meal and began scooping up forkfuls of food and filling his mouth. The meal was tasteless, the mashed potatoes like mucky sawdust, the turkey was wet cardboard. Norris wondered if the lack of taste had been tainted by his nerves. Regardless, he shoveled in every bite and chewed for good measure. He was going to need his energy tonight.

6

05 September 2007

Williamsport, PA

At 4:45 p.m., just as Ferguson was fielding questions from the media on television, Maxwell's cell phone rang. He muted the TV and picked up the cell. The number was blocked, but he knew who it was.

"Maxwell."

"Agent Maxwell, I'm returning your call." It was Bailey.

"Yes, sir. I'm looking for a go-ahead on the composite."

Bailey sighed. "I looked at the composite you sent and the fact sheet. There's not a lot there, Maxwell."

Maxwell took a breath, "I know that, but..."

"You have a feeling."

"It's more than that, sir."

"Okay, I'm listening."

"Highwayman is still in Pennsylvania. We have had no other sightings on the car. No murders. Norris hasn't turned up, which means he's still around."

"Or lying in a shallow grave."

"Maybe, but I think we need to turn up the heat."

"What if this composite looks nothing like the Highwayman? Have you thought about that?" Bailey wasn't condescending. If anything, he was pragmatic.

"Then I'm wrong, but that could work to our advantage as well."

"How?"

"If he thinks we got it wrong, he may venture out or make a mistake. He has to get rid of the car."

"That's a leap, Maxwell. If we're wrong, this will reflect very poorly on the bureau, especially if he commits another murder. I can't authorize this."

"It's all we got, sir." Maxwell was gritting his teeth together.

"Get more."

"I have a witness in Duncannon who saw Norris, including a photograph. We have the make and color of the car. We have eyewitness accounts who put a strange man with a similar car in Wellsboro, Pennsylvania. My police contact in Montoursville agrees that Highwayman and Norris are probably holed up somewhere along the US 15. What more do you want?"

"A positive sighting."

"That's not going to happen, sir. Right now, the Highwayman is probably considering his options."

"And what are they?"

"Kill Norris, if he hasn't already, dispose of the car, and go dormant as he did with Ash."

"I agree, but if this composite is wrong, the media is going to roast us on a goddamned spit," Bailey said. "I want to help you, but..."

"What do you suggest, sir?" Maxwell said.

Bailey was quiet, contemplating.

Maxwell waited.

"Okay," Bailey said. "This is all off the record. If anyone asks me, I will deny it. Do you understand?"

Here comes the fuck over, Maxwell thought, but said "yes" anyway.

"If the composite were to be anonymously leaked to a media outlet, we could claim outrage. Let them run with it, and if something shakes loose, good. If it doesn't, we blame it on the leak."

Maxwell thought about it. "So your official position is that we need to gather more evidence?"

"Yes, and unless you bring me a positive ID, I'm not changing that position. I'm not endorsing a release, nor am I suggesting it be leaked. But if it did, it might shake something loose."

Maxwell didn't think Bailey would ever suggest such a thing, but the pressure was on for him as well. They needed to catch the Highwayman. Ash's murder had elevated the serial killer to the number one spot on the FBI's Most Wanted list.

"I understand." Maxwell felt like he was signing a pact with the Devil.

"I hope you do, Agent Maxwell. My official position on the composite is that we do not have enough evidence to present it to the media. I have sent a formal email to you and to my superiors stating that. I expect an email back from you acknowledging my position."

"I'll get one back to you immediately."

"Good."

"Anything else, sir?"

"Yes. Find them."

"Yes, sir."

"Contact me if you hear something." Bailey hung up leaving Maxwell to ponder his situation.

7

05 September 2007

Lawrenceville, PA

Norris' hair was rusty red. Even the beard and mustache he'd started growing were strawberry blond. Lance had clipped his hair down to a length that wasn't quite military, probably closer to the standard of police regulation. He then trimmed and cleaned up Norris' beard and mustache with the clippers and a comb.

The stench of the hair color had taken up permanent residence in his nasal cavities, even after repeated rinsing. He felt nauseous, but his appearance had changed considerably.

"Look at that," Lance said. "You're a ginger."

Norris stood up and considered the mirror. "Holy."

"Jesus, Norris. I can barely recognize you." Lance giggled.

It was after 6:00 p.m. They had to get going. "Can I ride in the front now?" Norris asked.

"No, still too risky. Besides. I want you to keep an eye on the car, in case it shifts." Lance was leading him to the front door. "Stay here until I get the back open."

Lance went down the steps and opened the sliding door on the van. "Let's go, Norris."

He hesitated. If Lance was intent on killing him, why go to such lengths to disguise him. Maybe he'd been wrong. Maybe Lance had a change of heart.

Maybe if he stops somewhere, I can get out of the back and make a run for it, he thought. That was an option.

"Norris?"

Norris moved quickly from the porch, down the steps, and into the back of the van. Once inside, Lance gave him a flashlight. He was standing at the rear of the Cavalier. "How long will this take?"

"At least a couple hours, maybe more. I've gotta find a place with relative privacy where we'll be able to dump it very fast. If the car starts moving, I want you to bang on the wall. Okay?" Lance was reaching for the strap to pull down the door.

"Okay," Norris whimpered. If the moving van stopped, he was going to bail out. He'd rather take his chances with the cops. Hair color or not, he was sure he would not be returning to the cottage.

"Hang in there, Norris." Lance pulled the sliding door down and clamped it. Norris turned on the flashlight, pointing the beam at the inside latch. He'd be able to open it from the inside.

He heard something then. A rattling sound, metal against metal and then a distinct *click.*

"What was that?" Norris asked.

"Padlock," Lance said. "We don't want anyone opening the back door until we get where we're going."

Or getting out, Norris thought.

Lance banged a hand on the door. "Sit tight. It'll be bumpy until we get on the highway."

Oh no, Norris thought.

The van started and Lance called, "Hang on to something. It'll be bumpy for awhile."

Norris slid down the wall onto his butt.

"Now what?" he said.

***

CHAPTER 27 – LAWYER BOB

1

05 September 2007

Williamsport, PA

Maxwell was sitting on the bed in his hotel room staring at the composite. Was it worth the gamble? The composite could be some guy who was having a bad day. He might enter a police station and say, "Why, yes, that was me. I was having a fight with my girlfriend that day. I just lost my job. Or, maybe, my father was just diagnosed with..."

It could be any of those things, but the story Larry Moore had told him and his belief that the guy in the store was a complete psycho had been compelling. The car, while not positively identified, still fit. They were in Pennsylvania, somewhere along the US 15 corridor. Maxwell could feel it in his bones.

But not for long.

No, not for long. Time was running out. Norris was probably dead, the car hidden somewhere in the woods or at the bottom of a lake or a reservoir.

If he didn't do something, the opportunity would be lost, and Bailey wanted him to do it. "Where are you?" Maxwell whispered. He tapped the composite and reviewed the notes.

Suspect described as between twenty-five and thirty years old, driving a car like the one Norris Connelly was photographed in at Duncannon. His head was shaved down to the wood, no facial hair. The description of the suspect is that he has pimples on his face.

Pimples? Between twenty-five and thirty? Why?

No hair or DNA found at any of the crime scenes.

The only foreign evidence at the scene was dried globs of Vaseline. Lewis Ash had thought it might be used as a lubricant for self-gratification. But if it had been for pleasuring himself, there would have been DNA in those globs, and there was none.

Why?

Maxwell minimized the case file and brought up Google on his computer. In the search box, he typed, *Does Vaseline cause pimples?* Then pushed enter.

The search returned information from the company itself which stated that Vaseline does not cause acne and that the skin disorder is actually caused by bacteria trapped in the pores. Maxwell scrolled down, and avoided the company site, and began reading anecdotal information.

He found a forum on skin care and started reading. The contributors, mostly female, claimed to use it for hydration. Many of the responders said that it fought acne, but as Maxwell scanned the responses, there were complaints about skin irritation. While the petroleum jelly might not cause acne, it certainly sealed what would be in the pores.

Sealed?

"He dresses in a set of coveralls and brings petroleum jelly to the scene. But the jelly contains no DNA. Why?" Then it hit Maxwell. "He coats his face in jelly to avoid dropping DNA." Then asked himself, *But why wasn't there DNA in the jelly we found? Maybe that Vaseline never touched his skin? Maybe that was... spillage?* Maxwell scrolled down, reading the comments on the forum.

Sally wrote: "I don't care what they say. My face broke out in a bunch of pimples. And that was the night I was supposed to go out for my fifth wedding anniversary."

Peggy responded: "Maybe you had an allergic reaction? I use it all the time and have never had an issue."

Sally wrote: "Fuck them and their fucking wonder jelly! It's made out of petroleum, and it screwed up my complexion."

Maxwell went back and read the manufacturer article and laughed when he saw the words *Wonder Jelly*. After that, he read two more pieces. The subject matter of the first was filled with recommendations by a dermatologist not to use Vaseline. He claimed the petroleum jelly was toxic. The second article from the same website had been revised to include the refining process of the product and paint a friendlier picture. The article also had been retracted.

Must have gotten a call from a lawyer, he thought. He closed the page and went back to the composite. "If I leak this and I'm wrong, Bailey will definitely throw me on the woodpile."

And if I don't, Highwayman will remain at large.

2

05 September 2007

East of Binghamton, NY

Lance drove east on Interstate 86, and by the time he was through Binghamton, darkness had fallen. On the passenger seat, a laptop was propped open, washing the interior of the truck with hard white light. On the computer, a map up of lower New York state followed along as they drove. Lance had purchased the program Microsoft Streets And Trips the year before and had been using it to navigate his way across the country. The program came with GPS, but the signal faded as the Appalachian Mountains enveloped them.

Lance checked on Norris, calling to him from the cab. "How's it going back there? Anything moving?"

There was no response at first.

"Norris? Everything okay?"

"Yeah," Norris said. "How much longer?"

"Maybe an hour." Lance waited for a response, but there was none. So he added, "I think I found the perfect spot." He guessed Norris was sulking in the darkness and that was fine by him. *Brood all you want, my little friend. This will all be over very soon.*

Inside the box, Norris was sweaty, nauseous, his nerves a horde of twisting worms. He was holding the paring knife in front of him, though it was too dark to see anything. The motion of the vehicle coupled with visual impairment had made him physically ill, to which he surrendered by vomiting in the back-right corner of the box.

That was not going to please Lance.

Tears spilled down his face, over his upper lip, and into his mouth. He could still smell the taint of chemicals used to color his hair. He wondered if that was what was really making him sick.

Maybe?

Norris thought back to what he'd read in the chat site log. About the others insisting he be put down, about Lance's agreement with the suggestions. He still didn't know what part Dusk, Steel, and Larry were playing in Lance's labyrinth of serial murder. He hadn't the time to read the entire log because he'd panicked. The last thing he'd read was Lance saying that he needed them to do something for him.

Then came the interruption of an approaching vehicle, it's diesel engine rumbling. It was a truck. Norris went into a panic. Closing pop-up windows, trying to put the PC back precisely as he had found it. He had backed out of the room, toward the stairwell, as if turning to run might harken the murderous spirits contained in the hard drive.

When he'd reached the top of the stairs, the sound was even closer. Winding its way up the road to the cottage. He lowered the trap door, engaged the locks and snapped them back into place. The rumbling had been just down the road. He rolled out the carpet, covering the trap, adjusting it to look exactly as it had before he displaced it.

Jesus—Jesus—Jesus.

Then he was backing out of the room. Scanning it for anything he'd missed. The sound was right on top of him when he closed the door, seeing the scratch caused by the paring knife on the bolt.

Nothing I can do about that. No time.

He closed the door, jiggled the handle to make sure it was locked, and that oncoming truck drove right past the driveway and was gone. Norris let out an anxious moan.

Not Lance. Not the moving truck. Probably just a neighbor going home. He wasn't finished reading; there had been more, and he had no idea what else was written in the chat log.

He left the hall, went to the kitchen, and looked at the clock. It was only 11:09 a.m. Lance had said that he would return around noon. He still had time if Lance hadn't lied about his estimated return. But Lance did lie. He lied about his name, about the others, about the secret room. He had used Norris, and now that he was finished, he was going to dispose of him.

Oh Momma.

"I wasn't finished," he'd said.

But he was. Because he couldn't bring himself to re-enter Lance's secret place. Couldn't muster the courage. Defeated by his cowardice, Norris returned to the living room and dropped into the recliner. His final thought that morning was *He's going to kill me.*

Now, he was locked in a box, like a piece of livestock being herded to the slaughterhouse. The minutes counting down until they were parked in Lance's perfect place.

Oh my God, please save me.

3

05 September 2007

Louisville, KY

It took three hours for the story to go viral. The headline, **Person Of Interest**, was accompanied by the composite drawing. The story did not go to a major news organization; it was instead leaked to the online home of *Crime Scene Examiner*.

Lonnie Perkins found out about the leak after he got a call from his lieutenant. "Perk, what do you know about this composite of a 'person of interest' in Pennsylvania?"

"Nothing," Perkins said, getting out of bed and making his way into his living room. "You want to fill me in, LT?"

"Turn on the news, it's on every fucking channel. Get your ass in here. We need to get in front of this before it blows up in our faces."

"Okay, I'm on my way in." Perkins started for the bathroom. He'd only been asleep an hour. He went back into the bedroom. Gathered his clothes for the next day, his gun and badge.

"What's going on, Lonnie?" his wife murmured.

He leaned over and kissed her temple. "Not sure yet. Go back to sleep."

She brought a hand up and padded his face. "Love you."

"Love you too." He kissed her again and got up.

Ten minutes later, he was on his way in. He was listening to the news and checking his messages as he drove.

There was a message from Evan Ferguson. "Lonnie, this is Evan, I need you to call me as soon as you get this."

Perkins told his lieutenant that he didn't know about the lead, but that wasn't exactly true. Ferguson had shown him the composite, and said it was for his eyes only.

He tried calling Maxwell, but it went straight to voicemail.

Perkins left a message. "Max, call me back."

He called Ferguson.

"Ferguson" Ferguson answered.

"It's Lonnie. What the hell is going on?"

"It's not confirmed, but there's been a leak," Ferguson said. "Where are you?"

"On my way in. My lieutenant is pissed."

"Yeah, well... We should probably chat before the shit hits the fan."

"Meet me in the parking garage in ten minutes. I have a reserved spot on level two." Perkins turned the corner.

"Okay, I'll be there."

"One more thing, Evan."

"Yeah?"

"In case you didn't realize it, the shit has already hit the fan, and we're standing right in front of the air stream."

"See you in ten minutes."

Ferguson was waiting in the parking garage when Perkins arrived eight minutes later. He parked his car and got out. "You want to fill me in, Evan?"

"Someone leaked the picture," Ferguson said.

"Someone? Any idea who?" Perkins lit a cigarette.

Ferguson smiled. "I have my suspicions."

"Jesus Christ, we're going to be dancing like politicians with our dicks out over this," Perkins spat. "I checked my office phone on the way in, and it's jammed with calls from reporters."

"My boss is on the way in as well. I see a witch hunt in our future. When we aren't fielding questions from politicians, we'll be getting grilled." Ferguson hadn't broken eye contact with Perkins throughout the entire exchange. "You talk to Maxwell?"

"I left him a voicemail." Perkins flicked his ash, and the cigarette broke between his fingers. "Fuck." He dropped the smoke on the ground, crushed it out, stabbed another between his lips and lit it. "Do you think it's him?"

"The Highwayman?"

"No, Maxwell."

Ferguson's expression stiffened. "That, I don't know. What I do know is that if I am asked officially, I will not be making such speculation."

"Okay, do you think it's the Highwayman?"

"Again, I don't know. Obviously, somebody does."

Jesus Christ, Max. Why don't you call me? Perk looked at his watch; it was 11:20 p.m. He took another puff on his cigarette and checked his phone. "Well, I guess we better get our asses up there. Time to get this dog and pony show underway."

"If you insist." Ferguson followed Perkins to the entryway. He felt a need to say something else. The best he could come up with was, "I hope it is."

Perkins crushed out his second smoke and scanned his pass over the electronic sensor. The door buzzed, and they pushed through. "Who broke the story?"

"*Crime Scene Examiner* broke it on the Internet."

"What the hell is that?" Perkins was pushing the button to the elevator door.

"It's a true crime magazine. They publish weekly in print, but have a website that runs a 24/7 news feed. The story broke on their website just after 9:00 p.m. They are citing the source as anonymous." The elevator door opened, and Ferguson stepped through first.

Perkins joined him and pushed the floor button. "Well, that will slow down the people who are looking for someone to throw under the bus."

"Who knows, it might be a blessing in disguise."

"Only if they catch him," Perkins said.

4

05 September 2007

Colchester, NY

The spot Lance found was a semi-secluded gravel road off NY 17 and bordering the Cherry Ridge Wild Forest just west of the Catskill Mountains. The place had already been figured out in advance, but Norris didn't need to know that. The less Norris knew, the better.

He drove the moving truck about a mile down the gravel road, and then made a three-point turn so he was facing back toward NY 17.

He cut the engine and the lights, and moved around to the back of the van. "Norris, we're here."

No response.

Lance unlocked the padlock and put it into his pocket. He reached down, flipped the latch over and lifted the door. It rattled as it went up, and suddenly Lance felt the full force of being driven off balance. "Wha..."

There were two thumping sensations against his left shoulder, and he thought they were poorly placed punches. He was going down, and Norris was wrapped around him like a rabid mongoose. They crashed into the gravel, a cloud of dust kicking up into the darkness. Yolky liquid spilled onto Lance's face and into his eye, blurring his vision. He had yet to understand that this was saliva spilling from Norris' open mouth. The area where the punches had been struck began to sing a painful tune, while wet, sticky warmth moistened the inside of his jacket. It was then Lance realized that he had been stabbed twice in the meatiest part of his shoulder.

Norris straddled him, raising the blade, concentrating on a target that would do the most damage. Lance's right hand shot up, seizing Norris' wrist.

He stabbed me. Holy shit, I've been stabbed!

"What the fuck are you doing?"

Norris ignored the question, taking great gulps of air, trying to break his wrist free so he could stab Lance in the throat. He heard Lance ask him what he was doing, but stayed silent. He had to kill him or at least disable him to a point where he couldn't fight back. Twisting against Lance's grip, Norris tried to unlock his arm, wanting to drive the knife home. Bits of drool spilled from his mouth and onto Lance's face.

Lance began squirming then, back and forth, and suddenly headlights came on, freezing both in their death struggle. Norris was blinded, but he held tight, feeling Lance's grip on his wrist begin to loosen. It didn't matter that they were now in full view of someone. This was a fight to the end.

"Norris, stop," Lance said. His shoulder was now sending pulses of agony down his arm and into the hand that held the hand of death at bay. He was losing his grip.

Norris grinned, more drool spilled down onto Lance's face, making him shift uncomfortably. Although Norris never spoke, his thoughts were blazing.

You're not as tough as I thought. Are you?

He twisted his wrist again, feeling Lance's grip loosen and knowing that he only needed to put the knife in his throat. From the car, he heard a door open, then another and another.

"He's killing me!" Lance shrieked.

Feet came crunching on gravel.

Norris brought his knee down on Lance's shoulder, and that did it. Lance shrieked in pain. The grip which held him back loosened enough to break free.

Silhouettes broke the headlight array.

Norris brought the blade up.

One of the silhouettes called, "Stop, police!"

Norris ignored them. He had to kill Lance, had to finish him or...

Norris' world shattered; blinding white streaked across his vision as his brain jarred against the inside of his skull. He was tumbling sideways, knife still in hand, and Lance scrambling out and away from him.

5

05 September 2007

Syracuse, NY

Robert Hawkins was watching the news when he saw a ghost, or so he thought. MSNBC was running a story about the fugitives out of Louisville who had killed four people, including a retired FBI agent.

It sure looked like him, he thought, and the news said that they were probably in the Pennsylvania area. Hawkins went to work that morning carrying the image in his head. When he arrived at the firm, Hunter, Hawkins, & Webster, LLP, he was very distracted.

Could it be him?

His partner in the firm, Eric Hunter, was on vacation; the other partner, Dan Webster, had been killed in an accident on the I-90 in 1999. The three had been partners, but also close friends for almost forty years. When Webster died, both Hawkins and Hunter decided to keep his name on the firm.

Hawkins wished Webster was here now. But if Dan Webster had been alive, Robert Hawkins, Bob to his friends, wouldn't be distracted by the sketch that was all over the news. Because Dan Webster had overseen Wallace Belanger's estate, not Bob Hawkins.

Hawkins didn't know Wallace Belanger all that well. On occasion, he attended functions in Syracuse where both Webster and Belanger had been present. What he remembered about Wallace Belanger was that he was an outspoken man and had taken to calling Hawkins "Lawyer Bob," which Hawkins detested.

"I can only take about five minutes of that idiot," he had told Webster.

"He's actually not that bad, Bob," Webster had told him. Dan Webster had known Belanger since college. He was the stereotypical alpha, sending feminists off the deep end. He was a loud, bombastic womanizer, always with an inappropriate comment at the most unfortunate time.

On the other hand, Wallace Belanger's wife, Sheila, was a real looker. Hawkins remembered her very well. She was long and lean, but still curvaceous, and man, she had a great rack. She was a natural beauty as well, with dirty blonde curls, light gray-blue eyes, and full lips that were intoxicating. Bob Hawkins was caught by his own wife checking out Sheila Belanger's D-cup breasts at that same function.

"Put your eyes back in your head, Hawkins," she'd warned.

"Huh, what?"

"What, nothing."

Bob Hawkins did as he was told. He loved his wife and was embarrassed to have been caught checking out another woman. But Sheila Belanger was a thing of beauty and very hard not to look at. Especially those eyes.

He would not see Sheila Belanger again until he took over the Belanger estate. Hunter detested Belanger and could care less about his beautiful wife because he was gay.

When Webster got killed in 1999, both Hunter and Hawkins began divvying up the files to send out notices to Webster's clients.

When they got down to the Hawkins file, Eric Hunter had said, "I think you should take this one, Bob."

"Gee, thanks. Nothing better than being called Lawyer Bob by Wallace fucking Belanger for the next twenty years," Hawkins had said.

"He's got a hot wife," Hunter had said.

"How the hell would you know, Eric?" Hawkins leaned in. "Besides, I see hot women all the time, it's not really a game changer. This Belanger idiot was Dan's friend, and I use that term rather loosely because I think even Dan didn't much care for him. Why don't we just send out a notice of withdrawal?"

"He's worth almost nine million bucks, Bob."

"Then you take him."

Hunter sighed. "Let's flip a coin."

"Are you kidding me?"

Hunter pulled out a quarter, flipped it in the air, and said, "Call it."

"Heads."

Eric Hunter caught the quarter, and slapped it on the back of his hand. When he revealed it, a smile spread across his face. "He's all yours, Lawyer Bob."

"Fuck."

Thankfully, Bob Hawkins only had to deal with Wallace Belanger twice, and he never saw Sheila Belanger again. Both she and her husband had died in a house fire in the spring of 2000. It was a tragedy, and Hawkins did his best to settle the estate and steer their only son, Lance, on a path that would not leave him broke. Lance Belanger had his mother's gray-blue eyes, but he was as narcissistic and disrespectful as his father.

"Just tell me where to sign, Bob," Lance Belanger had said, and Hawkins had wanted to punch the little puke right in the mouth. If he'd called him "Lawyer Bob," he probably would have.

Now, sitting at his desk, Hawkins called his secretary. "Judi, could you come into my office for a minute?"

"Be right there," she answered.

She came in carrying a steno pad in her right hand and twirling a pen in her left. "What do you need?"

"Can you dig me up the files on the Belanger estate? It'll be in the archives, probably 2000."

Judi wrote the name and date down. "Are you looking for anything particular?"

"I just want to check something that's been bugging me."

"Okay. You have a meeting with Jack Walton at 10:15, you want it after that?"

Hawkins looked at his watch: it was 9:30 a.m. "If you can get it to me before the meeting, I'd appreciate it. If I'm already in conference with Jack Walton, just store it behind your desk."

"Okay."

"Thanks."

"No problem." She left the office.

Ten minutes later, the Belanger file was sitting beside his desk. He didn't have time to go through it. He had a meeting with Jack Walton. Walton was a British transplant who'd become an American citizen. He liked Walton, thought he sounded a bit like Roger Moore. Walton was a retired photojournalist, who now owned two art galleries in Albany and Syracuse, NY. Both were worth millions.

He looked at the news feed on his computer. There was that sketch again, jumping out at him. The eyes and forehead were what made him think of Wallace Belanger's creepy kid.

He thought back to when he first heard that word. *Creepy.*

"Wallace is okay," Dan Webster had said a week before the accident on the I-90. "His wife is incredible, and once you get to know Wallace, he isn't that bad. But his kid. The kid is creepy."

"Creepy?" Hawkins asked. "How?"

"I can't explain it. Okay, you know how everyone is bonkers over his mother's eyes?"

"Yeah."

"Well, the kid has the same eyes, but he's got this look. Like one of those creepy kids from that movie, *Village Of The Damned*."

"Jesus Christ, Dan. You crack me up." Hawkins laughed.

Webster got serious then. "Not just that. Wallace once told me over drinks that the kid was trapping, torturing, and killing animals. Wallace said, and these are his words not mine, that his son sometimes was more like a robot. Emotionless."

"Are you saying the kid is a future Jeffrey Dahmer?"

Webster didn't smile. "The kid is creepy."

"Well, I'm glad he's yours and not mine."

The phone on his desk buzzed, bringing him back. "Go ahead, Judi."

"Mr. Walton is here."

"Send him in." Hawkins looked at the box sitting beside his desk. It was probably nothing. Lance Belanger was probably screwing young women and blowing his inheritance. *But the property he inherited in Pennsylvania. Where was that again?*

Hawkins wanted to be sure.

He got up and opened the door to his office.

"Come on in, Jack."

He took one more look at the box marked Belanger.

After, he thought.

***

CHAPTER 28 – MACDONALD TRIAD

1

05 September 2007

Colchester, NY

Lance held his left shoulder, the pain was incredible, but the three of them were bearing down on Norris. He hadn't even caught his breath, yet he barked the order, "Don't kill him."

They stopped, hanging over him, wanting to fill their collective need. In the looming dust of the headlights, they looked more like predatory animals than men.

That was when it struck Lance that he didn't know one of these men by looks. He hadn't checked them out like Norris, hadn't had time. He thought that if he tried hard, he might be able to distinguish them from their words, but there wasn't time for that, and they had seen him at his most vulnerable. Standing up, he gathered himself and formulated a growl. "Somebody turn off those fucking headlights."

"He was going to kill you," the taller of the three said.

"Steel, shut off the lights before we attract someone," Lance snarled. "I'd rather not have to kill a cop tonight."

The heaviest and shortest of the three withdrew from Norris and marched back to the car. A second later, they were in darkness, and Steel came back.

"Dusk, check if he's breathing," Lance said, closing ranks. The tall man dropped down into a crouch and Lance was among them, his confidence growing. "He better not be dead."

Then there was low sarcastic laughter coming from the middleman, the one Lance now knew to be Larry. "Sorry for hurting your precious friend. I guess we could have just let you die underneath his knife."

Lance turned to face the man. His face barely distinguishable, the white of his eyes catching the starlight with sinister intensity. He was in the company of wolves, and he should have been afraid, but he wasn't. He could feel his influence over them and moved to reinforce it.

"Wouldn't that have fucked things up." And in spite of the pain in his shoulder, Lance laughed and hunkered down, picking up the paring knife, bringing it up for them to see and without saying so, he recognized it from his kitchen. He'd used it, that little blade, for slicing up apples, pears, and once, he'd used it to dissect a squirrel. "He didn't stick me that bad."

They were focused on the little blade.

Lance gave Norris a nudge with his foot, not to hurt him, but to check if he was playing possum. "Wake up, Norris, you dumb shit."

There was no response, but Lance knew better.

He leaned down and whispered, "I wasn't going to hurt you. But I needed you gone. Now quit pretending, or I'll get Dusk to put you in the trunk of the Cavalier before we torch it."

"Liar," Norris mumbled and opened his eyes. "I was in your secret place. I saw what you wrote. What they wanted you to do."

Lance's grin faltered. "You were in my room? You know something, Regulator, you are just full of surprises." He got back up and said to the others, "Nobody touches him. I don't want him hurt." Then he kicked Norris hard in the right side.

"Oof," Norris said, and began to cry. "I loved you."

"And I love you, Regulator." Lance kicked him again. "The first one was for stealing, and that one was for stupidity."

Norris had no words.

"Get him up," Lance ordered.

Dusk and Steel got down and picked the little man up by the arms and held him, feet dangling an inch above the ground. His chin dropped to his chest. He looked as though he might pass out until Lance brought his hand up and gave Norris' testicles a twist, then yanked. Norris' eyes shot open, his guts filled with broken glass.

"Please. Please, Highwayman, just kill me," he begged.

"I'm not going to kill you, Regulator. I'm just teaching you a lesson for being bad." Lance released his grip.

The other man was there beside Lance, a looming sentient puppet waiting to be directed. He had something in his hand, and Norris realized that he had only one chance. The sound of tape tearing from its roll filled his ears, and he began to scream for help.

But it was short lived.

They bound his hands and legs, then carried him to the back of the car they'd come in. Norris twisted perversely, trying to fight, but it was futile. He could hear Lance giving them orders.

"I don't want him beat up anymore," Highwayman said as if he were a foreman on a job site rather than a wanted serial killer.

"Alright," the man who had taped his mouth said.

"He's been punished," Highwayman said.

They were putting him in the trunk of the car they'd come in. "I understand," the tape man said.

"Dusk, Steel? No turning him into a plaything," he ordered, and then he leaned down to look Norris in the face. "These men were here to pick you up. It's true, they wanted to kill you and that I was going to let them, but there was a change of plans. You shouldn't have attacked me, Regulator. If you hadn't, you'd be riding in the back of this car instead of the trunk." He turned to the other three. "Make sure you clean him up."

"We will," the tape man said.

"And go easy on him."

"No worries," the tallest said.

Lance turned his attention to Norris one last time. "You're going to go with our three new friends. Behave, and when you get there, they'll clean you and treat you right. Understand?"

Norris nodded.

Then the trunk closed and there was darkness.

2

06 September 2007

Syracuse, NY

Robert Hawkins was sitting in an underground garage behind the wheel of his Lincoln. Beside him, a box was unpacked, its contents scattered across the leather seat.

"State Police Trooper Radcliff speaking," said the officer answering the telephone.

"Hello, I'm calling regarding the sketch you guys are running on the news about the murders in Louisville," Hawkins said.

"Yes, sir, do you have information, and could I get your name?"

"I'm not giving my name, not now. If you arrest him, I'll come forward, but for now, I'm going to keep this anonymous."

"Okay." Hawkins knew the trooper would be checking the caller ID, which would come up as a NY state number. He'd be jotting it down. "What information do you have?"

"There is a young man who owns property in Lawrenceville, Pennsylvania, just below the New York border, who fits the description you put out."

"Do you have a name?"

"His name is Lance Belanger. I'm not positive it's him, but he looks a lot like the sketch, and he inherited that chunk of property back in 2000."

"What relation do you have with this Lance Belanger?"

"I'm not going to tell you that. Look. I might be wrong, but I've heard stuff about him. Stuff that might make you want to look at him." Hawkins bit his lower lip.

"What kind of stuff, sir?"

"I was told that he had a proclivity for torturing little animals when he was younger."

"Who told you that?"

"A colleague of mine who was close to this guy's father said that he'd confided in him. That same colleague said that the kid was creepy, emotionless."

"Do you have a name or number for the father and your colleague? I'm sure we'd like to speak with them as well." The trooper sounded skeptical.

"The colleague and the father are both dead," Hawkins said. "Look, I don't know for sure if this is your guy, but it might warrant a visit, and at the very least you can cross him off your list."

"Have you met this Lance Belanger?"

"Yes."

"And what was your impression of him?"

"He's a creepy bugger. He might just be an asshole, but there's something off about him."

"Off? Can you elaborate."

Hawkins thought about it. "I can't say, he's just sort of weird and intense."

"Do you have a phone number or an address for this Lance Belanger?"

"I do," Hawkins said, and gave him the address. "I don't have his number. I haven't seen him in seven years."

"Seven years." Trooper Radcliff's voice became skeptical again. "That's a long time, sir."

"It sure is, but worth checking out."

"We are following all leads in this matter. Are you sure I can't get your name just so we can follow up?"

"No. I'm not giving my name and just so you're aware, the phone I'm calling on is a throwaway. I bought it this afternoon at a Rexall." Hawkins winced. Why had he said Rexall? "I'm going to hang up now."

And before the officer could protest, he did.

Hawkins had done his duty. If that little prick Lance Belanger was involved in this, then so be it. If he wasn't, then this was karma coming full circle.

He started the Lincoln and exited the garage.

3

07 September 2007

Syracuse, NY

The bleeding from his left shoulder had ruined his shirt. Norris had punctured him twice, driving the paring knife all the way into the muscle. The bleeding had been stopped, but the damage was going to put him out of commission for a while.

Initially, he took off his shirt, tearing it into strips, and dressing the wound. Larry had helped him with this, using duct tape to keep the cloth in place, then he put on his old Syracuse University hoodie. The bottle of oxy he'd intended for sedating Norris was now being used to control his own pain. This was after they put Norris into the trunk. With that done, he popped what he estimated to be two pills, and after going separate ways with his newfound friends, he started back to Syracuse.

The ancient pills worked, and he was able to drive the one hundred-thirty miles back to Syracuse without much difficulty. He parked the truck at the Syracuse place and went inside.

There, he cleaned his wounds with peroxide and used crazy glue to seal the lesions. A doctor would have sutured the muscle, but that was out of the question. He'd just have to tough it out.

The temptation to stay in Syracuse and rest was quashed by the need to tidy things up in Lawrenceville. He still had Norris' stuff at his house, and he needed it gone. But he had to wait for the rental place to open in the morning. He unloaded the homemade ramps, dragging them with his good arm, and placed them in the garage.

At 1:34 a.m, he collapsed on the couch after popping two more pain pills.

He woke at 6:07 a.m., throbbing, stiff, feeling like his shoulder had been tenderized by a meat hammer. The pain was almost unbearable, he could barely move his left arm, and the muscles on the left side of his neck hummed like rusty barb wire. Unloading the ramps hadn't helped his cause. All the pills did was mask the pain. In doing so, he must have worsened the knife wounds that penetrated the muscle.

He eased into a sitting position, staring at his reflection in the dusty television. The likeness staring back at him was an exhausted, empty shell.

"I need a vacation," he said, thinking of Arnold Schwarzenegger in *Terminator 2*. He repeated it, but this time with a horrible Austrian accent.

Then he let out a moan and said, "Fuck me, it hurts."

He stood, went to the bathroom, and opened the medicine cabinet. There were two more prescription bottles with his father's name on them. Both bottles had the same pills, but

Lance had no idea what they were or what they did. So he removed the pill bottles, carried them out to the living room, and opened his laptop to see what the drug was for.

He typed in *Vicodin* and the search came back.

"Oh Father," he said. "It seems you had a bit of a painkiller addiction." He read the bottle; it said one or two pills every four to six hours. Lance took three and made his way to the shower, thinking that hot water would loosen his neck muscles.

Or unseal the crazy glue you used to close those lacerations, he thought. "Better not chance it."

He opted for a bird bath instead.

He filled up the kitchen sink, and using a facecloth, he cleaned himself up. Before long, his skin began to prickle and itch, and the pain slithered away, back to whatever cave it went to wait out the drug. He felt better, could wipe himself down, overcoming the barbs of tenderness that webbed out across his shoulder, down his arm, across his chest and back. And now he purposely took his time, knowing that if he took it easy, he'd be back in top form in no time.

The sky outside had begun to lighten.

Lance returned to his place on the couch and sat down. He hoped the lethargy would come off before he returned the rental. Leaving things unfinished at the cottage was nagging at him. He had to get back there, burn or bury Norris' things, maybe even the stuff he kept in the third room.

"Just in case," he said and floated off.

4

07 September 2007

Montoursville, PA

"Hello?" Maxwell said.

"Hi, Max," Perkins greeted.

"Perk. You must be on a smoke break."

"I am. How goes the hunt?"

This made Maxwell chuckle. "So far, nothing. How are things on your end?"

"Well, we are being inundated with calls, and the media isn't letting up, but I think the bad guys are closer to your neck of the woods."

"I sincerely hope so, Perk. I've run out of ideas. How do you like working with Ferguson?"

Perk sniffed. "He's okay, but he's sort of a stiff G Man; all business, no play. I'm not going to ask you how that sketch ended up on the news."

"Less you know, the better."

"Listen, your boss. Bailey."

"Yeah?"

"He, along with my boss, grilled us about leaks to the media. Bailey was on the warpath, said if he found the leaker, his career was finished." Perkins inhaled, then said. "Watch your ass, Max."

"Yeah, I will. You too."

"Okay, I gotta get back in. Good luck."

"Thanks."

5

07 September 2007

Lawrenceville, PA

"Fuck," Lance said.

This was in response to the sketch he was looking at on CNN. It didn't look a lot like him, but still, he wondered, *what was the source*? There was a resemblance, and that sent terror he hadn't felt since facing down that fat cop Hayward back in his dorm room.

His shoulder was still very tender, and he was buzzing from the drugs. He'd heard a report about the sketch on the radio while driving back.

How? Who reported him? Then it struck him. It must have been the stoner in Duncannon. The place where Norris had revealed himself. *Had to be.*

"Better start tying up loose ends," he said.

He went in and gathered Norris' stuff, took it outside and around back to the burn barrel. There wasn't much, but it had to be incinerated completely. He would have just buried it, but he was too stiff from the attack.

Thank you, Norris.

He emptied the contents of Norris' bag into the barrel and went to the storage shed to get some gasoline. He thought about the place in Duncannon; he'd purposely worn a hoodie to conceal himself. If they'd made the connection there, they would have had video footage. There were cameras in that place. He'd made a great effort not to engage them. But if they'd seen, there'd be footage of him all over the news.

Then where?

And suddenly it dawned on him.

"Chatty fucking Cathy." It had to be there. It was the only place someone would have gotten a good look at him. "Shit." He was back at the barrel, unscrewing the cap from the jerry can. He poured gas over the clothes and the duffle, soaking them. He turned and walked away, about twenty feet, and set the can on the grass. All the years of being so careful, and now they had a faint description of him. "Goddamn."

There was nothing he could do about it. He could not undo the past, he could only prepare for the future. This one was his fault, bought and paid for.

He reached into the kangaroo pocket of his Syracuse University hoodie and pulled out a box of strike anywhere wooden matches.

Considerate of the amount of gas, he stepped back from the barrel and struck a match. The smell of sulfur caught in his nostrils. He tossed the lit match into the barrel, and nothing happened.

"God fucking damn it!"

He tried again, and this time it ignited.

Whump!

Flames licked the rim of the barrel, black smoke billowing upward into the overcast sky. Lance had always liked fire, always been hypnotized by its consumption and unpredictable nature. He watched the smoke morph as the appetizer of gasoline was consumed, and the main course of cloth caught fire. The smoke darkened, and the aroma took on a chemical scent. He glanced back at the cottage.

Maybe I should burn it all.

The idea appealed to him. He could light the cottage up and maybe the whole forest. He could go up and find his nosy neighbor, Donny Williams, and chop him up. They didn't know who he was, not yet. If he lit the place up, he could get on a plane to Europe and disappear.

The monster was looming, wanting to be fed.

Let's do it, he thought. *Let's march up to Donny Williams' place and kill the old drunk.*

"No," he said. "I've come too far." The sketch hadn't been that good, and if they vetted all the evidence, there was nothing that could connect him to the crime.

Something in the barrel crackled, and Lance stepped forward to look. Most of the clothing had burned, but he'd have to soak it down with more gas, just to be sure. Lance left the barrel and returned to the cottage.

Inside, he entered the third room and tried to decide what he should do with this place. The website MacabreClub had to go. He brought it up and looked at the logs he'd been keeping and wondered how much Norris had discovered.

It was strange; he didn't want to dump the site, but if someone came along and reported it, well, that might lead right back to him. No matter the assurances by Andrei in Bucharest that the site was impenetrable by the authorities;

he doubted that it was. He had read a book on the Silk Road and how the feds eventually found their way to the criminals moving drugs via the Deep Web. Nothing was infallible.

He signed out of the website and returned to the log-in page. His name and password auto-filled the log-in boxes. He highlighted the password and clicked delete. Then he typed in the auto-destruct password he had assigned to the account when it was set up.

He typed *Patrick* and pushed enter.

There was no warning or secondary prompt asking if he was sure. The screen just went black. When he tried to refresh it, a white screen appeared with the words *Oops, invalid address* sitting dead center. His computer then went *Ta da*, and a message appeared: *Bookmarks updated*! He checked, and that was gone too. The MacabreClub was now permanently closed, or so he thought.

6

07 September 2007

Bucharest, Romania

Andrei Gusa was looking at his own computer when the notification came in that the site was being deactivated. A prompt came up in Hungarian. The English translation was: **User Wishes To Deactivate. Do You Want To Archive? Yes/No.**

Andrei clicked **Yes** and the Hungarian word for **Archiving** appeared on the screen, while an animation showed the progress. Andrei archived every site he had brokered. If his colleagues in Hungary, Slovakia, Czech Republic, or Serbia knew about this practice, he would be a dead man, but it was his insurance policy in case he ever got into a jam with Interpol. Five seconds after he initialized the archive, it was done.

"Just in case," Andrei said.

7

07 September 2007

Montoursville, PA

Maxwell was seated at a desk Abraham had provided in a makeshift office cubicle. He was sitting behind his laptop, vetting the tips they had received so far, which wasn't much. He felt desperate, thinking he'd been boxed in by Bailey's suggestion of leaking the composite. The reaction from Abraham was lukewarm. He hadn't been angry, but it had taken them back a few steps. Now, after the call from Perk, he began to think that he was in serious trouble. That was when another one of Abraham's goliath troopers appeared at the entrance to his office, holding a steno pad at his side. This guy was six foot four at least, leaving Maxwell to wonder if they bred these guys on a farm close to a nuclear power plant.

"Agent Maxwell," the trooper said.

"Yes?"

"My name is Trooper Radcliff. I have a tip I would like you to look at."

"What have you got?"

"It was an anonymous tip. The guy who called it in was pretty antsy, but the stuff he said made the hair on the back of my neck stand up." Radcliff frowned, regretting the last part of what he said. *Had that sounded contrived?*

Maxwell picked up on the awkwardness and said, "Come on in, Trooper Radcliff. Sit down and tell me what you have."

Radcliff entered the cubicle, took a seat, crossed his legs, and placed the writing pad on his lap. He looked down at the pad and said, "The individual is supposed to live in

Lawrenceville, Pennsylvania. Just on the New York state line, right on the US 15 corridor."

"Okay, you got my attention." Most of the tips they were vetting were coming in from all over Pennsylvania, from Pittsburgh to Philadelphia. He hadn't specified the US 15 corridor in the leak on purpose. "Tell me more."

"The tipster said the individual's name is Lance Belanger, and he looks very much like the composite. But what really got me was that he said that this Belanger had a proclivity for torturing animals when he was younger."

"Zoosadism," Maxwell said.

"Huh?" Radcliff looked up.

"Deriving pleasure from the torture of animals. It's part of a theory based on a study by a psychiatrist named J.M. MacDonald. The theory was that people who tortured animals in their youth, lit fires, and wet the bed had the potential of becoming serial killers. They called it the MacDonald triad. You didn't have to exhibit all three behaviors, but at least two."

"I've heard of the animal torture thing."

"Did you run a background on this Belanger?"

"I did, he has no record of arrest or unusual activity. He's university educated, and he's a trust fund baby. Both his parents died in a fire back in 2000. His father was a rich guy, worth millions. When the parents died, the kid inherited everything."

"Was the fire suspicious?"

"No, it was electrical. Lousy contractor according to the papers. The contractor was charged with manslaughter and did some time."

Maxwell was sitting up in his chair. "Did the tipster say anything else?"

"He said that Belanger's father had mentioned the animal cruelty. That he thought his son was like a robot. Without emotion. He used the word 'creepy' a bunch of times. I think the tipster must have been a family friend or an associate."

Radcliff looked over his notes to see if he'd missed anything; he hadn't.

"Okay." Maxwell felt mild exhilaration. This might be something. At the very least they could pay this guy a visit and check him out.

"So where do we go from here?"

"Dig up everything you can on him. Everything. News articles about the fire. Everything. Once you think you've got everything, bring it to me and I'm going to give it a read."

"Alright." Radcliff was getting up, and he looked eager.

"What's your first name, Radcliff?"

"Mike."

"Good job, Mike. We might have something here."

***

CHAPTER 29 – THREE ACTS

1

08 September 2007

Montoursville, PA

Maxwell had been up most of the night, reviewing what Radcliff had dug up on Lance Belanger. Which wasn't much. The contractor who'd wired the Belanger house was out on parole, and Belanger was leading a normal life. Of course, they'd only just scratched the surface; there wasn't enough to start seeking warrants or pulling records.

He got out of his car and started into the troop when Abraham pulled in. He stopped and waited. Both he and the lieutenant had discussed it the night before, and though there was little to go on, they had both agreed to take a run up to Lawrenceville and take a look.

"Morning," Abraham greeted.

"Hey, Cole." Maxwell watched the big man climb from his personal pickup truck and pull out a briefcase. Maxwell felt sick with anxiety. He was second-guessing himself, thinking that they were on a wild goose chase. Worse, one he had organized. But there was that other half, the pragmatist who told himself that cases and suspects were caught by chasing down every lead.

"I'll be ready to roll in ten minutes," Abraham said. "Are you going to alert your people in Louisville?"

This was something Maxwell had struggled with. He didn't want to raise the alarm until they had a look, but Bailey would want to know. "Yeah, I'll put in a call while you're getting ready."

"Okay."

"Who are we taking?"

"Well, I figured that Leeman and Radcliff could back us up when we go up there. Seems only right." Abraham pulled the door open and held it for Maxwell.

"I agree. What about Trooper Arquette?"

"Arquette's wife went into labor last night. They had a boy, no complications, he'll be off for the next week."

"Oh, good for him. Send my congratulations."

"I will. Anyway, I think two cars is probably best. We don't know what we're dealing with. It could be a dead end."

"Could be," Maxwell agreed.

"And if it's not, I think the four of us can handle it." They were at the door of Abraham's office. "Let me make some calls, Max, and then we'll get this show underway."

"Right." Maxwell turned and made his way to his desk. He sat down and put a call into the SAC.

"You have something?" Bailey asked.

"Person of interest. The name is Lance Belanger. He's twenty-eight, single, and lives in Lawrenceville, Pennsylvania. We received a tip about him yesterday. He looks somewhat like the composite, and the tipster said he liked to torture animals when he was a kid. Also, his parents died in a house fire. The fire wasn't connected to him, but that's not to say he didn't do it. Oh, and get this. He's worth a ton of money."

"Really, how much?"

"Maybe seven or eight million."

"So what's the plan?"

"Myself, Abraham, and two troopers are going to go up for a look. The troopers will hang back in reserve, while Abraham and I talk to the guy and size things up."

"Anything we can do?"

"Well, if he looks good, I'd like to start digging into his comings and goings. Internet, travel, purchases, that sort of thing."

"And if he doesn't?"

Maxwell sighed. "I don't know. We keep looking."

Bailey sighed. "If you don't shake something loose, I'm going to pull you out of there."

"Where will I be going? Back to Louisville?"

"I haven't figured that out yet. I don't think you're needed in Louisville. Ferguson has things well in hand," Bailey answered.

"Really? What lead is he working?" Maxwell asked, his tone somewhat sarcastic.

"Special Agent Maxwell, dial it back." Bailey's voice was rigid. "Follow this lead; if it looks promising, I'll give you what you need to dig deeper. But we're in a shit storm here with the media, the pressure's on. They're making Green River and BTK comparisons. Some asshole actually wrote a column about how incompetent we are."

"Fuck." Maxwell felt the anxiety rising in his chest. "We'll be heading up in about ten minutes. I'll keep you advised of our progress."

"Everyone is watching, Agent Maxwell."

Maxwell resisted the urge to tell Bailey that it was his idea to leak the composite. "Yes, sir."

2

08 September 2007

Lawrenceville, PA

Lance awoke around the same time Maxwell and Abraham were going over plans with the troopers for a visit. He'd changed his dressing and popped another Vicodin. One instead of three. The pain in his shoulder was still bad but manageable. He ate a bowl of cereal while watching the news and perusing the Web for any new information.

There wasn't anything new. The sketch was still being broadcast, but the news did what it always had when they needed filler; they brought in panelists and so-called experts to offer opinions. He considered packing up and heading to Syracuse, but he needed to sit tight. If they were coming, he had to protect this place and himself.

They're coming, he thought.

Sooner or later, they always came, and he knew he'd have to face them. In his head, he heard a paranoid fusion of sound. Approaching vehicles, faint sirens, the crunch of military boots on underbrush. In his mind's eye, he could see a tactical force in black cutting across the wood line behind the cottage, weapons tucked into their shoulders, fingers on trigger guards. Leapfrogging, covering and moving again.

This is what you wanted, to be the most wanted.

He grinned.

Yes, it was what he wanted. The killing had only been part of it; the infamy was what he'd desired.

He finished the bowl of cereal while a commentator on Fox News talked about Dennis Rader and Gary Ridgway, making comparisons to the Highwayman.

There was no comparison.

Rader and Ridgway had been lucky. The science had not been there, that was why they'd managed to evade detection. He was far better than them. He'd left nothing behind but the masterpieces of his portfolio. Even the mother of all serial killers, Ted Bundy, wouldn't have been able to avoid detection acting in the manner he had. No, Lance had studied and learned, the student becoming the master.

"I'm better than all of them," he said.

He got up and carried the empty cereal bowl into the kitchen. There, he rinsed the milk from the bowl, ignoring the shakes he'd developed in his hands. This had come with the paranoia.

Calm down, he thought.

He tried to relax.

If the cops came knocking, which he thought they might, he had to keep it together. Had to maintain his confidence.

But something else was eating at him.

The monster needed to be fed and put back to sleep. It craved the copper scent of spilling blood, the song of a pleading voice, the art of dismemberment. Maybe he should have killed Norris instead of sending him away with the others. With a fresh kill under his belt, he wouldn't feel himself unraveling and fantasizing. Of course, if the cops came knocking, he could lay in wait and ambush them. There was a shotgun in the shed out back and two boxes of shells. He could retrieve it and...

Stop it!

Lance hated guns, mostly because his father loved them, but also, there was no sport in that type of killing. A real hunter didn't hide behind a machine to do their bidding. In Lance's opinion, hunters who used guns were cowards.

3

08 September 2007

US 15 - 5 miles south of Lawrenceville, PA

They were coming. Cole Abraham was driving the lead car, with Maxwell sitting shotgun. Behind, Corporal Leeman and Trooper Radcliff followed in a marked cruiser. The morning was overcast, the sky decorated in deep shades of charcoal clouds that threatened to burst and rain down upon them. For most of the eighty-three mile trip, Abraham and

Maxwell spoke very little, each meditating, contemplating what the day would bring.

As they crossed the Tioga Reservoir, Maxwell said, "When we get into Lawrenceville, I want to pull off in a place where we won't raise too many eyebrows."

Abraham thought about it for a moment and turned his head to Maxwell. "I've got just the place. There's a pull off just south of town. It's secluded. We can get out there and have a chat before we go up."

"That's good." Maxwell gazed into the passenger mirror at the state cruiser. "We'll need them to hang back, but not too far."

"Norris?"

"Yeah, just in case. If Belanger is the Highwayman, I don't want to spook him. We should be ready for anything."

"I understand."

"Do they?"

"Leeman's a solid officer. A good investigator and he's been in a scrape, so he's no virgin."

"What kind of scrape?"

"Drug store robbery in Williamsport. He took down a guy who killed a male pharmacist and a female cashier. Leeman took a bullet in the shoulder but still managed to take the guy out. He's got a Purple Heart and a Letter of Commendation for Bravery. He's a damned good officer, and I expect when they send me off to the glue factory, he'll be taking my command." Abraham turned to face Maxwell reinforcing his words. "He's solid."

"What about Radcliff?" Maxwell asked.

"He's never shot anybody, but I have confidence in him. He'll follow Leeman's lead if we get into a jackpot."

"Well, let's hope it doesn't come to that."

"Let's hope."

They went silent again, the road to Lawrenceville humming beneath their wheels as they closed the distance. Maxwell never asked Abraham if he'd been in a scrape nor had the lieutenant returned the question. As far as both were concerned, it went without saying.

Maxwell's mind alternated between two streams of thought. If it was the Highwayman up there in Lawrenceville, he hoped for a little action. Not an outright gunfight, he wanted the killer alive, but a dramatic takedown appealed to his needs. Although it almost never went that way, of the three serial killers he'd arrested, all surrendered without much of a fight.

And then there was the alternative.

If it isn't the Highwayman, I'm probably fucked.

"The pull off is just ahead," Abraham said.

"Good." Maxwell felt his chest tighten.

They pulled off into a roadside jug handle. The pavement of the pull off was overgrown, weeds pushing up through cracked asphalt, and trees sheltered them from the road.

They parked and gathered at the trunk of the lead car. Maxwell pulled out a map, unfolded it on the trunk and said, "Let's hope that this goes smoothly, but if it doesn't..." He purposely engaged Leeman and Radcliff. "You two are the cavalry."

Radcliff and Leeman nodded.

"Get your sidearms ready first." Maxwell upholstered his Glock 23 and jacked a round into the chamber. The state troopers removed their P227s and did the same. Abraham unlocked the shotgun in his car and told Radcliff to do the same. Maxwell turned his attention to Abraham and said, "Whenever I start an operation like this, I like to know the men I'm standing shoulder to shoulder with. If it's all the same to you, this is where I'd like to be a bit more personal."

Understanding, Abraham smiled. "Sure."

Maxwell turned to the troopers. "What are your first names?"

"Billy," Leeman said and stuck out his hand.

Maxwell took his hand and shook. "My first name's Dave, but people call me Max."

Radcliff brought his hand up. "Joey."

"Good to meet you, Joey."

Abraham stepped forward and shook hands all around. "Joey, Billy, you can call me Cole, but when we bag this, we go back to rank. I have the utmost confidence in both of you."

His subordinates beamed.

Maxwell smiled, then gave Abraham a thump on the back and said, "Okay, gather round, and let's go over this one last time."

4

08 September 2007

Lawrenceville, PA

"You gotta be fucking kidding me," Lance cussed.

When the sound of boots came clopping up the front steps of the cottage, Lance was sitting on the toilet. The painkillers had bunged him up.

He expected the door to blow off its hinges after being hit by a battering ram. Maybe a canister of tear gas would pop, filling the place with burning smoke. Then a cacophony of cops yelling, "Get down! You're under arrest!"

Instead, there were three hard knocks.

Bang! Bang! Bang!

Lance stood and pulled his track pants back up. He centered himself in the mirror, took in a deep breath, and looked himself over while whispering, "It's okay, stay calm, we don't know who it is."

He'd only taken half a Vicodin this time, and the pain in his shoulder was manageable. He washed his hands, checking himself for any seepage of blood. *Nothing. Good.*

"It's probably just a Jehovah's Witness or a lost..."

Bang! Bang! Bang!

"State police."

"I'll be right there!"

He flushed the toilet and exited the bathroom. When he went into his bedroom, he grabbed a hoodie to put over his t-shirt and took another look at himself in the dresser mirror. He inhaled, exhaled, inhaled, exhaled, and then whispered, "Stay calm."

Outside, Maxwell and Abraham stood on the porch, looking at each other after Abraham made the first knock. There were two cars in the carport, neither a Cavalier. There was stirring in the house, but no response. Maxwell reached inside his jacket and unsnapped his holster. Abraham reached down to his hip and did the same.

"Knock one more time," Maxwell whispered and motioned that he was going around back for a look.

Abraham nodded.

Maxwell stepped off the porch and walked briskly around the east side of the cottage; there were no windows on this side. He heard Abraham bang on the door a second time and announce, "State police."

When he reached the back, his heart was pounding coupled with an adrenaline shake he always got in times of high stress. There was a back entrance, but it was still closed. He surveyed the property. Shed, forty-five-gallon drum used as a burn barrel, and about five hundred feet of open property until the tree line.

From inside came, "I'll be right there."

More movement.

Maxwell placed his hand on his weapon, watching and waiting for the back door to open. Pulse pounding, eyes focused, and mind racing, his senses had become electric. He listened to the movement inside the cottage, trying to gauge the direction.

Wait for it!

Out front, the door opened, and Abraham stood face to face with a man in his mid to late twenties. He looked like an army recruit, hair cut to the skull, and he was dressed in track pants and a hoodie. The most striking detail was his eyes, gray blue, like a wolf. Below those piercing eyes, the skin on his cheeks was irritated by pimples.

"Yes?" the young man said.

"Good morning, are you Lance Belanger?" Abraham watched.

"Yes." Lance looked the big cop right in the eye. "What's going on?" *Maintain eye contact, don't look away. Stay calm. They're sizing you up.*

"I'm Lieutenant Cole Abraham, Lance."

Maxwell came back around then. "Can we come in and talk?"

Lance turned to face Maxwell, momentary surprise dawning on his face. He tried to push it away, but knew the FBI agent had seen it, so he said, "Where did you come from?"

Was that recognition? Maxwell wondered, and stared at the guy, using silence to create an uncomfortable edge as he climbed the porch steps.

"Lance, can we come in? We need to talk about Wellsboro."

Lance turned back to Abraham. "Wellsboro?"

"This should only take a little of your time," Maxwell said.

Chatty fucking Cathy!

Lance stepped back. "Please, come in."

Maxwell shot Abraham a glance.

"Thanks." Maxwell stepped in front of Abraham and passed Lance in the hall. It was deliberate; if something happened, Abraham would be able to draw his weapon faster. The doorway led into a large living area separated by an entryway. "Nice place."

"Thanks," Lance said.

To Maxwell, Belanger's demeanor was calm, but it also felt forced. "You here by yourself, Lance?"

"Yes," Lance said, and waved his arm toward the couch. "Would you like to sit down?"

"Sure," Abraham said.

"Then maybe you can tell me what this is about?"

"That's why we're here," Maxwell said.

They sat down.

5

"That's why we're here," they heard Maxwell say.

Leeman and Radcliff were listening on VHF tuned to the body bug on Cole Abraham's uniform. It looked like a standard handheld, but was tuned to a specific frequency they used for undercover work and broadcast directly on the VHF radio in the police cruiser. They were parked off the road a quarter mile from the cottage, listening and waiting for something to happen.

6

"Maybe you can tell me what this is about," Lance reiterated.

"Can you tell us your whereabouts on the first of September, mid to late afternoon?" Abraham pulled out a notepad.

Lance brought his hand up to his chin and said, "I've been here, but I couldn't tell you my comings and goings with any specificity."

Maxwell caught the tell and made eye contact with Abraham. The guy was lying. "Okay, well, how about to the best of your knowledge."

"You said Wellsboro?"

"Pardon?" Abraham gave Maxwell a nod.

"You said, 'We're here to talk about Wellsboro.'" Lance looked at Maxwell. "Who are you exactly?"

"So, you were in Wellsboro on the first of September?" Abraham said.

Maxwell stayed silent, watching.

"I might have been, I can't remember. You want to tell me what this is all about? Why I have a state cop and a..." He turned to Maxwell again. "Who are you?"

Maxwell could feel Lance's angst, but he had to give him credit. He was working overtime to maintain control, and he wasn't giving anything up. "Lance, my name is Special Agent David Maxwell, I work for the Federal Bureau of Investigation."

"Wow, I've never met an FBI agent before."

Liar, Maxwell thought.

"Okay, now I'm intrigued. Why do I have an FBI agent and a state cop interested in whether I was in Wellsboro on the first of September?" He looked from Maxwell to Abraham. "Should I call my lawyer?"

"Do you think you need a lawyer?" Maxwell asked.

"I don't know. You still haven't told me what's going on." Silence.

"Let's get back to Wellsboro," Abraham said.

Maxwell stayed quiet, letting Abraham take the lead. He continued to stare at Lance, dissecting every action. Looking for wandering eyes, fidgeting, anything that identified deception.

"Okay, if it will shine some light on why you're here." Lance turned back to Maxwell and locked eyes with him. "What happened in Wellsboro?"

Maxwell stared him down, and Lance turned back to Abraham.

"Were you in the Stop-n-Go grocery mart on the first of September?" Abraham was jotting down the questions and answers as they were asked.

"Maybe, was there a robbery there or something?"

Abraham feigned impatience. "This will go a lot faster if you just answer the questions. Were you in the Wellsboro Stop-n-Go on the first of September, mid to late afternoon?"

Lance looked defensive, but it was an act. He just didn't know if they were buying it or not. "I don't know if it was the first. About a week ago, I bought some things there. Probably."

Abraham jotted something down. "Was there an incident?"

"Incident? I'm not getting you. I bought some stuff."

Keep pushing, Cole, Maxwell thought.

"Okay, did anything happen in the Stop-n-Go?"

Lance smiled and then sighed. "Chatty Cathy." Then he laughed.

Both Maxwell and Abraham looked confused.

"Chatty Cathy?" Abraham wrote: *Individual offering information. Nervous.*

"That was what I called the cashier. Look, I'll cooperate anyway I can, but I feel like you guys are trying to box me into something here. How about you be a bit more forthcoming? Otherwise, I'm going to have to call my lawyer and explain the situation to him and see what he recommends."

Maxwell abruptly stood up. "Can I use your bathroom?"

"Huh?" Lance said.

"I need to take a leak. Do you mind?"

Lance sighed. "Down the hall to the right" and thought, *Go ahead, Agent Maxwell, you won't find anything incriminating.*

"Thanks," Maxwell said and walked out of the room.

Lance called after him, "Maybe when you're done we can get to the bottom of this?"

"Definitely," Maxwell shot back. He passed two rooms as he went, surveying them for anything suspicious. They were both neat and tidy. Suspiciously neat and tidy. He entered the bathroom and closed the door behind him.

"Nice little cottage," Abraham said.

"Thanks."

"You a hunter, Lance? This looks like a hunting cottage."

"My father was. I don't like killing animals."

"Where's your father now?"

"He died, both my parents were killed in a house fire in 2000."

"I'm sorry to hear that."

No, you're not, Lance thought. "Thank you."

"So, you inherited this place?"

"Yeah. I got a house up in Syracuse too."

Maxwell opened the medicine cabinet, spotted the painkillers and noted the name of them. The pills looked old. He leaned over the bathtub, looking for signs of blood, hair, anything that would indicate foul play.

He found nothing, everything was spotless, like the rest of the place. He lifted the toilet lid with his foot. Again, nothing. But he could feel it. This was their guy. Everything about this felt right, even Belanger's attempt to remain calm. He flushed the toilet, opened the door, and got ready for the second act.

7

"Lance, I'm going to tell you what's going on, and that way we can get out of here and let you get back to your life," Maxwell said.

"Good." Lance smiled. "Can I get you guys a drink or something?"

"No, I'm good," Maxwell said. Abraham declined as well.

"So, in your own words, tell us about the Stop-n-Go and..." Maxwell grinned. "Chatty Cathy?"

Lance appeared to relax, and then hesitated. "I thought you were going to tell me what's going on."

Maxwell continued with a friendly demeanor. "I'm going to get to that, but I want you to tell me what happened at the Stop-n-Go first." He leaned forward. "Here's the deal. Lieutenant Abrahams and I are conducting an investigation. Your name, along with a bunch of others, has come up. It's our job to interview everyone, no matter how remote. At this point, we are looking at knocking everyone off that list. But here's the thing. We don't want your statement biased in any way. So if you tell us what happened at the Stop-n-Go, we'll tell you what we're investigating."

Lance seemed to think about it. "Don't you have to tell me?"

Maxwell widened his grin. "No, we don't have to tell you anything. During an investigation, we ask the questions, we don't answer them. Personally, I just want to get this over with, both the lieutenant and I have about eight more people to talk to today. Quicker we get done here, the better. That's why I am going to tell you why we're here, but not until you can provide us with a small piece of information."

Lance thought about it for a second. "Okay."

"Excellent," Abraham said.

"Tell us about the situation at Stop-n-Go."

"I stopped in to get some food. I was in line behind two people, and the cashier was taking a long time. I guess I got sort of irritated. That's why I called her Chatty Cathy."

"You actually called her that?"

"No, I just thought it."

"Did you say anything?"

"No, not really. Maybe I sighed or made a dirty look or something. But I don't remember saying anything to them. Did they say I said something?"

Maxwell ignored the question. "Was something bugging you?"

"No. Actually, yes. I was in a hurry. I wanted to get up to Interstate Battery before it closed. The Impala outside needed a battery. This woman, she just wouldn't shut up."

"How?"

"Look, I was standing there with a pile of groceries in my arms, and the guy in front of me had, like, fifty cans of cat food. Meanwhile, the cashier, Chatty Cathy, is chatting up the customers. I guess I must have let out a sigh or something, but I caught their attention."

"Then what happened?"

"The guy with the cat food picks up all his stuff and tells me to go ahead of him and the other lady too. I said no, I think I even apologized, but they insisted. It wasn't that big a deal; I would have waited. Now they were all looking at me, and that pissed me off even more than waiting. I guess my true feelings must have been seen."

"What were your true feelings?"

"I was pissed off, in a hurry. Haven't you ever stood in line behind somebody in a line that was moving at a snail's pace?"

"Sure," Maxwell said. "So they moved you to the front of the line, and suddenly you're the center of attention. I get it completely." Maxwell smiled at Abraham, who nodded in agreement. "We've all been there."

"Yeah," Abraham said.

"Right, so maybe my feelings were being outwardly displayed, but I never said anything. I think I even apologized. Anyway, they stepped aside, and when I tried to decline, they insisted. I paid for my stuff, and I left," Lance explained.

"That's good. So did you make it?" Maxwell nodded.

"Make it?"

"To Interstate Battery."

"I did."

"You wouldn't happen to have a receipt for that battery, would you?" Abraham chimed in.

"Yeah, I do. It's in the pantry."

"This is good, Lieutenant. This will get him off the list for sure."

"Yeah, couldn't hurt."

Lance brightened. "Give me a second." He got up and went into the kitchen. Maxwell and Abraham shared a single glance. "You sure I can't get you guys something? I got some Pepsi in the fridge."

"I'll take a Pepsi," Maxwell said.

"Why not? Me too," Abraham agreed.

Cupboards opened and closed. Lance pulled something down and set it on the counter. Then there was the sound of a lid being peeled from a Tupperware container. Abraham got up and stood in the doorway behind Lance. He could see the clear container, it was full of documents. No gun or weapon. "Here it is," Lance said, and turned to see Abraham standing there watching him. "Shit, you scared me."

"Sorry, I was just going to ask if I could use your washroom."

In the living area, Maxwell felt his cell phone vibrate. He pulled it out and looked. The caller ID was blocked. He knew it was Bailey. He pressed the End Call button and shut the phone off. He'd call Bailey when the interview was done.

Lance returned to the living room carrying two Pepsi cans in one hand and a paper receipt. He set the cans on the coffee table and handed the receipt over. "Here it is, September first."

Maxwell looked at the receipt. "Good, when Lieutenant Abraham gets back, I think we'll be able to wrap this up after a few more questions."

"And fill me in?"

"Absolutely."

It was time for the third act.

8

Abraham sat down, cracked the Pepsi, and took a sip. Maxwell handed him the receipt. He looked at the date and time. "Well, this backs up your story for sure. Looks like you made it with about ten minutes to spare." He handed it back to Maxwell.

Lance grinned.

"Well, Lance. I want to thank you for being so honest with us." Maxwell stood up, and Abraham followed his lead. "I would say that about covers it. Abraham, we should get on down to Harrisburg."

"So that's it?" Lance looked confused.

"Yeah, your story makes sense," Abraham said.

"You said you'd tell me what was going on."

"Yeah, I did." Maxwell looked at Abraham. "I did say that, but there is one more thing I'd like to do, and then I promise I'll tell you what's going on."

Lance frowned. "And what would that be?"

"I'd like to take a walk around your property."

"Why?"

"It will rule out one last thing in our investigation."

Lance thought about it. He knew they were working him, but it was a mutual workover. He couldn't give two shits about their investigation, he already knew why they were here, but if he started talking lawyers or let them walk without at least playing along, they might come back. Dig a little deeper. "I'll tell you what. I'll give you a tour, but I want to know what this is all about. If you aren't forthcoming, you guys can head down to Harrisburg."

"Sounds fair to me," Maxwell said. "Abraham?"

"Me too, but let's make it quick." Abraham finished the Pepsi, and set the can on the table. Maxwell had never bothered to open his. Lance put on a pair of sneakers, and they went outside.

They walked around the west side of the cottage. Maxwell took a closer look at the two cars. A classic Chevrolet Impala and a dark green Oldsmobile Intrigue.

"Are these the only cars you own?" Maxwell asked.

"I have a Jeep, but it's at my place up in Syracuse."

The Intrigue was close to a Cavalier, but it was dark green instead of blue. Maxwell wondered if maybe the technicians were wrong about the car? Then he thought, *Maybe the witness in Wellsboro, Larry, was wrong. Perhaps he had mistaken a dark green Intrigue for a dark blue Cavalier.*

They walked around the side of the cottage to the back of the property. Maxwell looked at the burn barrel again. *Could Norris be in there?*

He walked toward it, mindful that Lance was behind him, confident Abraham had his back. When they got there, Maxwell looked in.

No remnants, no bone, only ash.

"Have you ever owned a Cavalier, Lance?" Maxwell said.

"No, do they even make those anymore?" Lance laughed.

Maxwell brought his eyes up to meet Lance. "I work for the behavioral science team in Quantico, Virginia."

Lance's face brightened as if he had an epiphany. "Shit, now I know why you're here."

"Why?"

"You're looking for those two guys."

Maxwell turned from Lance to Abraham, then back. "What two guys?"

"That Norris guy and the other one. The Highwayman. Shit, it's all over the news. Am I right?" Lance was grinning ear to ear.

Maxwell said nothing.

"How much of this land do you own?" Abraham interjected.

Lance turned away from Maxwell to Abraham. "Huh?"

"The property. How much of it is yours?"

"Three acres. Two and a half are in the forest."

"Let's walk back there, shall we?" Maxwell led, and they followed. As he walked, he spoke in an even discernable voice. "You're right, Lance. I'm am trying to track down two evil guys. The incident down in Wellsboro drew us to you, and I'm beginning to think that it's a wild goose chase."

He stopped to face him. "What I think is that our witnesses mistook your Oldsmobile for a Cavalier. I also think that you look an awful lot like the sketch. So here we are."

Lance grinned confidently. They really didn't know shit. "Was that sketch from Stop-n-Go, in Wellsboro?"

"No," Maxwell lied. "The sketch was from a witness in Frankfort, Virginia. We've been holding onto it. My boss decided to release it, and that spurred two calls from a tipster who identified you out of Syracuse."

"Syracuse. Who?"

"I can't tell you that."

Lance smiled. "Okay, but I'm cleared of it now?"

Maxwell looked at Abraham. "If it's all the same to you, I'd like to check out the rest of the property just so we can say we were thorough, then we can cross this one off."

"Works for me," Abraham said.

"Okay, Lance? Is that okay with you?"

"Sure."

9

Ten minutes later, they were back in the car and driving away. Lance waved from the porch and smiled. Abraham looked in the rearview mirror and said, "You think it's him?"

"Indubitably," Maxwell said.

"Look at you with the big words." Abraham got on the radio. "Billy, we're on our way out."

"Copy."

"You can pull out and meet us at the rendezvous."

"Copy. See you there."

"I gotta say, he was as cool as a cucumber. But in the end, he took the bait. I think if we started working him, he would've come apart." Abraham was laughing.

"Maybe," Maxwell said. "But we haven't got much, and I didn't want to push him into a lawyer."

"So now what?"

"I'm calling it in. We'll get warrants for everything he has. Cell phone records. Travel records. I want to know every place this Lance Belanger has been in the last seven years. Everything. This is our guy." Maxwell was sure of it.

"I think you're right, Max. I know it's a hunch, but I got a vibe from him. And he was working us over, or so he thought."

Maxwell turned his phone back on. "We gotta keep this under wraps. We don't want him running. I think his travel records alone will be enough to bring him down."

"Isn't that how they got Bundy?"

"Gas receipts."

"Yeah, but I think our friend here is a frequent flyer."

"Did you see his face when you said the sketch was from Frankfort?"

"Oh yeah."

Maxwell checked his messages. Three missed calls, all from a number with the caller ID blocked.

Bailey.

"I got a bunch of calls from my boss. I better check in."

"Sure." Abraham agreed. "We're only five minutes away; if you wait, I'll debrief Leeman and Radcliff, and that will give you a little privacy."

"Alright, that sounds good." Maxwell thought he might have to battle with Bailey over getting the warrants. They still didn't have much more than intuition. But Bailey hadn't seen the look on Lance Belanger's face or the tells. Maxwell was sure. He liked this guy for the Highwayman murders. He thought if he shook the tree hard enough all the pieces would fall into place.

Five minutes later, they were in the pull off, and Abraham left Maxwell to make his call. He dialed in, and Bailey answered. "Maxwell, where have you been?"

"Lawrenceville, the interview I told you about. We've got a suspect. His name is Lance Belanger."

"Go ahead."

"He lives in Lawrenceville, Pennsylvania, and he's rich. We interviewed him this afternoon, and he fits, sir. I think he's been flying around the country, finding victims, and flying out. We put the screws to him, and he got pretty jumpy, and he looks like the guy in the Identi-Kit sketch."

"We found the car," Bailey said.

"Where?"

"Colchester, New York. In the Catskills."

"That works, he probably dumped it and scooted back. I'm going to need warrants on this guy. Check his travel and phone records and..."

"Maxwell."

"I'm sure if we check his itinerary we can connect him."

"We found Norris' body as well."

"Shit, no way." Maxwell was ecstatic. "Jesus, that's great. We gotta get moving on these warrants, boss."

10

Abraham was standing with his troopers, and they were leaning over the hood of the marked car laughing when Maxwell came upon them. His face was milky white; he looked in a complete state of shock. Abraham had his cigarettes out and was getting ready to light up.

Abraham saw him first. "Max, what is it?"

"They found the Cavalier and Norris' body."

"That's good," Abraham said. "Where?"

"Colchester, New York." He reached over and plucked the cigarette from Abraham's fingers. He motioned for a light. "Not good."

Abraham lit his cigarette and took one for himself. "What do you mean not good?"

"They found Norris just south of Aberdeen, Maryland."

"Dead?"

"Starfished."

"Okay, but how long was he there?"

"I'm not sure, but it gets worse."

"Huh, why?"

Maxwell took a puff on the cigarette and said. "They found another victim outside of Stafford, Virginia. Same MO."

"Fuck."

"There's no way this guy did it. Not enough time. Highwayman is somewhere between Virginia and Florida. Sure as shit, he isn't Lance Belanger. I gotta get on a flight."

11

Lance received the text just after the unmarked car pulled out. He looked down at his phone, the text came from an unknown number, but he knew who it was from. He'd been expecting it.

The text read *Turn on the news*.

So he did.

On CNN, a helicopter hovered over a gravel road, filming the scene where they'd recovered the dark blue Cavalier. A banner below that scrolled **Fugitive Car Found In Catskills.**

A female commentator announced, "Police have recovered the car and two more bodies in the Highwayman murder case."

Then the scene flipped to a different location, this time a ground shot of multiple police cars gathered in a wooded area. Caption: **Body Found In Aberdeen, MD.**

The female anchor continued, "Unidentified sources inside the Maryland State Police have said that one of the victims is Norris Connelly."

Norris' photo popped up.

"Connelly was being sought for his involvement in the murders of four people, which included retired FBI Agent Lewis Ash. Ironically, Ash was a lead investigator on the Highwayman case until his retirement in 2006. It is alleged that Connelly and the unknown suspect dubbed The Highwayman abducted the FBI agent from his home in Roanoke, Virginia. His body would turn up outside an abandoned factory in Louisville, Kentucky."

Another shot, this one beside a highway, the banner reading **Murder Victim Found In Stafford, VA.**

"Police in Stafford have not confirmed the gender of this latest victim, but a source says that it is a victim of The Highwayman."

A male commentary broke in, "It appears they are no closer to catching a killer that has eluded them for over six years."

"We should warn our viewers that these are early reports and the connection to the case has not been substantiated."

"That's right, Jane, but there will be a joint press conference with the FBI and state officials from New York, Maryland, and Virginia. I am going to step out on a limb here and say that they will be confirming what our sources have already alleged."

Lance changed the channel.

FOX NEWS: **Major Break In Highway Case!**

He changed it again.

MSNBC: **Where Is Highwayman?**

"That's the question the FBI is asking itself. They've been concentrated in Louisville, Kentucky, but it appears that the killer is now somewhere on the East coast."

Lance smiled.

He flipped to the next channel.

Breaking News! Nationwide Manhunt Continues!

And the next.

ABC: **FBI Still Searching For Elusive Killer.**

Male commentator: "The FBI is feeling the pressure this afternoon, with the discovery of two more bodies, and it appears that one might just be that of Norris Connelly."

Female commentator: "I have to say, this reminds me of the hunt for Andrew Cunanan."

Lance began to laugh, flipping from one channel to the next. The Highwayman was on every channel, and they had no clue.

"No fucking clue," he said and laughed harder.

***

EPILOGUE

08 September 2007
Stafford, Virginia

The helicopter had come straight from Quantico. First circling the scene and touching down on the east side of US Route 1. Once on the ground, the right door opened, and two men exited, hunched over keeping their heads below the prop blast.

A special agent from the Virginia Bureau of Criminal Investigation went out to meet them. He was a lanky man, with a horseshoe of gray for a crown. His clothes hung on him. Behind him were state police vehicles, along with a white sprinter van. Emblazoned in blue decal were the words Virginia State Police and below that, Bureau of Criminal Investigation.

"I'm Special Agent Ron Hargrove, BCI. I work with the General Investigation Section for the Virginia State Police. To keep it short, I'm your liaison." He smiled and extended a hand.

"Good to meet you, I'm Special Agent in Charge Hugh Bailey, FBI. My main investigator is just getting in the air, so I'm here to grease the wheels." He took the man's hand and shook, then made an introduction. "This is Deputy Director Carswell."

They shook.

"Good day," Carswell said. "What have we got?"

"Female, approximate age thirty-five to forty-five," Hargrove said. "Probably killed two to three hours ago. The limbs and torso still have signs of rigor, but our crime scene and the local coroner gotta make the call. Looks like your boy. Head, arms, and legs all removed and repositioned."

"Starfished," Carswell said.

"Pardon?"

"That's what they've been calling it. Like a starfish, but cut into six pieces. You got anything else?" Carswell said.

"We found white fibers and what appears to be small globs of petroleum jelly at the scene. Samples have been collected by our crime scene people," Hargrove said.

"Yeah, looks like our guy," Bailey said.

They began walking.

"So who's the investigator you've got coming?" Hargrove asked. "And when will he be here?"

"He'll be landing in Washington and catching a puddle jumper. I think two to three hours," Bailey said. "His name is Special Agent Evan Ferguson."

Carswell stopped, looked at Bailey, and said to Hargrove, "Could you give us a minute, Agent Hargrove?"

"Sure, I'll wait for you up on the road."

"Thanks." Then he waited until the BCI agent was out of earshot. "Bailey, why isn't Maxwell on his way here?"

"I pulled him off, sir."

"I figured that. Now you want to explain why?"

"He dropped the ball in Pennsylvania."

"How exactly did he do that, Hugh?"

"I'd rather not say, sir." Bailey's face tightened.

"Bailey, I'm going to ask you one more time. Why?" Carswell's color was changing, heat blooming in his cheeks.

Then Bailey let loose. "Alright, if you must know. He broke the chain of command, leaked that composite sketch to the media. Because of that, the investigation got bogged down in Pennsylvania, and now we're looking at two more bodies."

"Bailey, I am only going to say this once. I want Maxwell back on this case," Carswell said, each word grating between his teeth.

"With all due respect, sir, I knew you would react this way. That is why I reassigned him, not only to avoid his career being hurt but to respect your friendship with him." Bailey had stiffened as well. "I have a report made up detailing the leak and the boondoggle in Pennsylvania. I have also mentioned the personal connection that he has with you. A connection which has become an obstacle to what is best for this investigation."

"Maxwell was right, you are a weasel."

Bailey frowned but held himself back. "I haven't filed the report, sir. All I want to do is reassign him. Please don't force my hand."

"You think you're pretty smart."

Bailey said nothing.

"You know what, Bailey? I've met guys like you before and I'm sure I'll meet a few more before they kick my ass to the curb."

Bailey looked over his shoulder. "The BCI is waiting, sir."

"I'm not fucking done yet."

"Okay, sir."

"Here's what's going to happen, Bailey. When we get back to Quantico, you're going to apply for stress leave."

"No, sir, I am not."

"Yes, you will. And let me tell what else you're going to do."

"No, sir, I..."

Carswell placed his hand on Bailey's shoulder. "Interrupt me again, and you'll be back on that helicopter and cleaning out your desk before the day is finished." Bailey stayed quiet. "You are going to apply for stress leave. But before you do this, you're going to write a formal letter of recommendation that Special Agent David Maxwell be promoted to take over your position as Special Agent in Charge. Then you're going to take a vacation, which I will approve."

"I will not."

"You will so."

"No, sir. I'll file a formal grievance."

"Arrogance, Bailey. That is what fucked you, because you are so arrogant you thought you could jam Maxwell up. But worse, you're stupid enough to think you could blackmail me into letting that happen. Except here's the thing. Maxwell was on to your game before you even had it figured out. He sent me a recording of your conversation. You know, the one where you told him to leak the composite. I have a copy in my desk, and then there's the original."

"I never told him to leak it."

"Your exact words were 'I'm not endorsing a release, nor am I suggesting it be leaked. But if it did, it might shake something loose.' True, you didn't come right out and say it, but it's clear what your intent was."

"Bullshit. I never told him to leak it."

"The political ass-covering won't save you. You know why? I have a formal report from Maxwell outlining his concerns about leaking the composite. In that document, he stated that he believed you were setting him up. He raised concerns about being replaced by Ferguson. He claimed that you impeded the investigation and were purposely trying to jam him up. That you refused available FBI resources. You wouldn't even give him a goddamned sketch artist. You know something, Bailey. You're a pathetic little piece of shit."

"You're just trying to save your pal."

"Maxwell contacted me, said that he felt he could no longer trust your leadership, and asked me to make a call. I authorized the leak after I cleared it with the director."

Bailey's cheeks were deep red.

"Now you gotta decide. You want to take leave and look at reassignment or get on that helicopter and clean out your desk? What's it gonna be?"

"This was my investigation, I..."

"This is Maxwell's investigation."

"You knew I replaced Maxwell?"

"Of course I knew. I'm the deputy director of the FBI. I knew what you were doing before we got on that chopper. So I'm going to ask you one last time. What's it gonna be?"

"I guess I don't have a choice?"

"You're right. I want your application for leave and the letter of recommendation for promotion before the day is out."

"Yes, sir."

Carswell gave the BCI agent a nod.

"Now go get on that bird and wait until I'm done here." Carswell left Bailey then, not looking back, and worked his way toward Special Agent Hargrove.

Bailey turned, shoulders hunched, broken.

Carswell didn't look back.

The hunt was still on.

The End

NOTES

"I was born with the devil in me. I could not help the fact that I was a murderer, no more than the poet can help the inspiration to sing."
– H.H. Holmes

AFTERWORD

Well, here we are. I sometimes wonder who reads the afterword in a book. Confession, I always do, especially if I enjoyed the story or if I was wondering why the story ended where it did. If you're here reading this after finishing my novel, first let me thank you for coming along on the journey. The questions now are: Why are you here reading this? Are you here because you wanted to learn more about me and my work. Or are you scratching your head because the killer got away?

If it is the latter, that will warrant some explanation.

Before I go any further, let me reference a Stephen King novel where I found myself in the exact same place you are right now. The book was called *The Waste Lands* and it was the third in the Dark Tower series that King wrote over the course of twenty-two years, resulting in seven novels. And that's not including an eighth book, *The Wind Through the Keyhole*, which he wrote after the completion of the series.

In *The Waste Lands*, King finished with a cliffhanger. Don't worry, I won't say what happened, I am not that cruel. But, like you, I found my way to the afterword in the hopes of an explanation as to why the story ended where it did. As I recall, King explained that the project he was undertaking was a massive effort and that he needed cooling off periods between Dark Tower novels. He also went on to say that the cliffhanger at the end of *The Waste Lands* was not intentional. It was just where the story ended in that book. He promised the constant reader (myself and millions of others) that he would be coming out with a new novel if he managed to live long enough. King did not disappoint, and as stated in the earlier paragraph, he finished the series.

Yeah, yeah, but what's the deal with the Highwayman? Why would you leave it there?

First, let me say that the Highwayman saga will be tied up in the next book. But I think it's fair to tell you how we ended up here in the first place.

So let's do that.

In 2015, I'd started a new novel with the working title **4**. Without giving away the story, I will say that Lance Belanger, aka Highwayman, played a central role in a string of spree murders in the Pittsburgh area. I was approximately eighty pages into this project when I happened to mention it to my then publisher, who suggested I write a novella to introduce it. I was sitting across from a gentleman named Philip Perron, in a pub in Portsmouth, NH.

Phil said, "You should write a throwaway."

"Throwaway?"

"Yeah, write a novella and give it away. So when your new book comes out, people will already be hooked."

Crazy as it sounds, I decided to take his advice and got down to it. Over the course of about six months, I wrote the novella Highwayman. It was 192 pages, and I never put it to print, because the story never felt right. The result of this endeavor into madness left me in a strange predicament. It was apparent that Highwayman was too small for the story and characters it contained. It just didn't work as a novella. An unhappy consequence of this reality was that my original novel, 4, also came to a grinding halt. I was struggling with what to do. I could abandon Highwayman and try to get back to work on 4, but the truth was Highwayman felt unfinished, and I was worried if I did that I might completely screw up the original book.

So I did what most writers do when they find themselves caught in a quagmire of literary siege. I put it down and went on to other projects. I published a couple of short story collections and did some freelance writing.

Eventually, my muse, bastard that he is, caught up with me and demanded, "This needs to be finished."

In the spring of 2017, I opened the Highwayman file and decided it was time to get back to work. First, I spent about six months in a state of intense research, reading up on everything from criminal profiling, crime scene examination, and true crime. I was living and breathing everything I could about serial killers and the people who hunted them. Admittedly, I have always had a fascination with the subject of serial murder. I believe the allure is rooted in my lifelong love of monsters. The serial killer is the most terrifying monster imaginable because they are not lore or mythos, but living entities that walk among us.

In modern literature, fictional serial killers like Dexter Morgan, Hannibal Lecter, or John Wayne Cleaver have muddied the waters, transformed from monsters into pop culture antiheroes. And while I think the authors who brought us these characters did a bang-up job, I had no intention of cloning their work.

I did not want Lance Belanger to be a likable character. That's not to say I didn't want people to relate to him on some level, but it had to be clear that this fellow is a horrible excuse for a human being. He is a psychopath, narcissistic to the core, and inside him, the monster waits to be unleashed and fed.

This story is the first half of a much larger tale. While it may not end wrapped up in a neat bow, it is most assuredly is not the end. You have not heard the last of the Highwayman case or its characters.

Lance has only just begun his quest.

I hope you will join me for the conclusion.

M.J. Preston
02/23/2019

ACKNOWLEDGMENTS

I've said this before. A novel of this size is a massive undertaking. Getting a project like this to print does not happen without the knowledge and input of several people. I would like to thank the following people for their help in getting this book to print.

Patti Holycross – Patti served as a beta reader, research assistant, and a general butt kicker. She was instrumental when it came to keeping my facts straight. Her help with this project has been immeasurable. I can't thank her enough. The fact that she volunteered to help me with this book speaks volumes about her character. She remains a constant reader, and I consider her a true friend.

Jake Anfinson – Jake was there as a beta reader in the early stages of Highwayman's development. What I call the dog days of the novella. Jake's honest critiques resulted in the metamorphosis from novella to novel.

Dan Hunter – A retired lawyer, Dan's insight and suggestions helped me navigate the murky waters of the American legal system.

Philip Perron – Who made the suggestion over a beer that I write this. Philip has always been a staunch supporter of my work and a good friend.

Kevin M. Sullivan – Research for this project included dozens of books, documentaries, and other source material on the subject of serial killers and the people who hunt them. While all of the source material was fascinating, one book was a standout. *The Bundy Murders: A Comprehensive History* by Kevin M. Sullivan provided a template for the madness of the Highwayman Killer.

THE HIGHWAYMAN PROJECT

In the infancy of this project, I asked the writers below if they would contribute a news article on a specific scenario in the book. Initially, I intended to lay out the novel in the same format as a true-crime novel with news clippings and photographs. In the end, a decision was made not to include the articles or photographs, but they are still available on a website dedicated to the HIGHWAYMAN novel.

I would like to acknowledge the following writers for their written contribution and enthusiasm about this project.

Gregory L. Norris – Writing as Horace Montillo for *Crime Scene Examiner*: "Where is the Highwayman?"

B.E. Scully – Writing as Roberta Barker for *Rogue Valley Register*: "Severed Arm Leads Motorist to Murder Victim"

Jo-Anne Russell – Writing as Terry Wolfe for *Mossyrock Citizen*: "Not Your Average Dog Bone"

Kristi Petersen Schoonover – Writing as H. Tierney for *Central Falls Witness*: "Central Falls Murder Victim Named"

Kyle Rader – Writing as R.S. Dower for *Westvale Herald*: "Authorities: Foul Play Now Suspected in Deadly House Fire"

Jake Anfinson – Writing as Abbey Shepard for *Painesville Daily Courier*: "Body Discovered in State Park"

These articles and more, including interviews and
other news items related to HIGHWAYMAN,
can be found on the internet at

http://mjpreston.net

*For More News About M.J. Preston,
Signup For Our Newsletter:*

http://wbp.bz/newsletter

Word-of-mouth is critical to an author's long-term success. If you appreciated this book please leave a review on the Amazon sales page:

http://wbp.bz/highwaymana

AVAILABLE FROM JAMES BYRON HUGGINS AND WILDBLUE PRESS!

DARK VISIONS by JAMES BYRON HUGGINS

http://wbp.bz/darkvisionsa

Read A Sample Next

ONE

Sitting upon a bough, the raven watched.

In the dying of the light the little boy swung slowly from the tree, his body broken, a noose around his neck. And at the edge of the forest a car burned and the raven watched as flame rose from the heat like hate rising from the heart of the sun.

The raven and the boy were together as the fire burned and burned and began to fade in the last of the day but still the raven did not move. It stayed upon the bough and did not leave the boy alone until the sun had descended and was gone.

The raven watched as the boy was claimed by the darkness of the night. It watched as the fire smoldered and the smoke vanished in the evening gray that overcame the day. It watched and it watched and it watched and it watched until something else had begun to burn in the dying of the light …

Fire rose in the raven's eyes.

* * *

Joe Mac felt the gray November cold more completely than he'd ever felt it before because he could no longer see the leaves fade from rust to gold or gaze upon the skeletal silhouettes of trees etched against the gray November sky.

Now he lived in the world of the blind, so feeling the cold was all that remained. The rest was darkness and he would inhabit this darkness until the day he died and they buried him in the dirt and this darkness.

The raven came as it always came; it descended with the sound of enormous wings to land with a thunderclap on the home Joe Mac had built for it.

Three years ago they met as Joe Mac was first learning to live in the world of the blind. The raven had come to him every day as he sat alone in the back of the barn, and Joe Mac named him "Poe" after the old poem. And every evening they would sit together in the back of the barn in Joe Mac's eternal night.

Poe did not rise or even seem to notice the familiar Mrs. Clemens as she approached, but then Poe rarely flew away when someone came close. Rather, he seemed to know the exact distance for danger and ignored anything else.

Mrs. Clemens brought Joe Mac his supper – an act Joe Mac reckoned to her uncommon human kindness – and spent a moment to inquire about his health. But Joe Mac sensed something different in Mrs. Clemens tonight. Her steps were halting and seemed to wander before she laid a hand on his shoulder.

Lifting his face, Joe Mac asked, "What is it, Mrs. Clemens?"

Mrs. Clemens shuffled, and Joe Mac felt the strength lessen in the hand; it was not much of a change, it was true, but a hand with little strength is even more revealing when what little strength it possesses is diminished ever more.

Joe Mac repeated more sternly, "What is it, Mrs. Clemens?"

"Oh," moaned Mrs. Clemens, "it's horrible, Mr. Joe Mac. Just horrible. Oh, god, I don't know how to tell you."

"Just say it."

She faltered, "It's about your grandson, Mr. Joe Mac. It's about Aaron. The poor thing disappeared from daycare today."

Joe Mac's left hand tightened on the arm of the chair. "How could they lose a four-year-old boy? Have they called the police?"

"Your poor daughter has called everyone! We're all scared to death something terrible has happened!"

With a shrill cry Poe erupted into the night sky as Joe Mac stood pulling his wool coat more tightly across his chest; he snapped his cane to length. "Why didn't someone tell me about this earlier?" he demanded.

"They've been too busy searching for him, Mr. Joe Mac! They've looked everywhere! And you can't even ..."

She let the sentence die.

"Take me to my daughter," said Joe Mac. "And compose yourself, Mrs. Clemens. We don't know that anything terrible has happened. Compose yourself! Stay calm. And take me to my daughter.”

TWO

“Here’s the case file on that little kid.”

Jodi Strong raised her eyes as the file was laid upon her desk. The veteran New York City detective, Thomas Grimes, who delivered the file pulled up a chair and leaned back, folding hands on his chest.

“What do you want with this thing, Jodi?” Grimes asked and didn’t attempt to conceal either his curiosity or confusion. “There’s already a million cops on this, and we got twenty cases of our own to work.”

“I took the original call last week when I was in uniform,” said Jodi. “I interviewed the daycare workers, the mother, the father. And then they found the little kid but he was already dead. Just like the others.”

Grimes spoke in a weary monotone, “Jodi, it was your case when you were in uniform. It was your case when you took the missing person report. But you got promoted to detective three days ago, and it ain’t your case no more. It belongs to the task force and you ain’t on the task force, neither. So what are you doing?”

Jodi shook her head, “Grimes, I know it’s always a mistake to get personally involved in a case but –”

“Then don’t.”

“But that scene at the house really shook me up,” Jodi continued. “I saw the little boy’s room. I saw his picture. I felt like I knew him. And then he ends up … like he ended up.” She slapped the file. “I’m tired of this psycho!”

Grimes sighed, "Jodi, the FBI has a thousand people on this. We've got about a million. One more cop ain't gonna make no difference in this. And we need you *here*."

Jodi made a slight sound as she sucked breath through her teeth. Then she said, "He's made a mistake, Grimes. They're just not finding it. Nobody's perfect."

"Well, this psycho is pretty close to perfect because right now the task force guys tell me they don't have a clue. One of 'em told me they're no closer to catching him now than they were four years ago."

Jodi opened the file and leaned back; "Aaron Roberts. Four years old. Abducted from the playground of his daycare. His body was found one hour after sunset —"

"Same as the rest of 'em."

Jodi continued reading as Grimes stood and leaned over her desk.

"Jodi," he began in a patient tone, "listen to me; I'm glad you made detective. I think you're a natural. But you're wasting your time. Whatever mistake this guy made ain't gonna be in no file. There's no fibers, no hairs, no prints, no DNA. There's no witnesses, no video, no tracks." He pointed toward the door. "This guy has killed twenty-four people, and he could walk through that door right now and confess to everything we've got and we wouldn't be able to pin him to a single thing. He doesn't take anything. He doesn't leave anything. He has no motive. He has no face. He has no name. *He's a ghost*."

"Excuse me."

Jodi lifted her face to see an exceeding large man standing on the far side of her desk at the same moment she realized he was blind.

The man was slightly less than six feet but built like a brick. His body seemed one uniform size from his linebacker shoulders down through his barrel chest to his waist and weightlifter legs. His head was a square granite block set on a short neck. His white hair was standard military high-and-tight. His arms were heavy and the hand holding the cane was thick with strong-looking fingers although he held the shaft with a fisherman's touch.

Jodi was instantly curious why the man's presence gave her a palpitation of alarm. There was certainly nothing obviously threatening about him. And yet an aura of doom seemed to cloak him even more than the knee-length undertaker coat or the impenetrable black glasses; it occurred to Jodi that his appearance could not have been more unsettling if he'd been wearing a black funeral veil over his face. In all he reminded Jodi of a Texas tombstone she'd once seen that read, *"As you are, I once was. As I am, you will be…"*

Jodi whispered, "Good god …"

Grimes turned, gaped, and grabbed one of the man's blacksmith arms. "Joe Mac Blake! I haven't seen you in years, Joe! How ya been, man?"

"You're lookin' at it," said Joe Mac. "They still got you in robbery, Grimes?"

"Same 'ol same." Grimes theatrically lifted a hand toward Jodi as she rolled her eyes; *he's blind, you dolt.* "Jodi, this is ex-homicide detective Joe Mac Blake. Joe is a legend! Joe, this is Detective Jodi Strong. She's the newest member of the team." A laugh. "Well, this is a blast from the past, buddy. What are you doing downtown, man?"

Joe Mac lightly tapped the desk with his cane. "Got a seat for me?"

"Sure." Grimes pulled up a rolling chair. "Sit down."

Joe Mac felt, found the chair, and sat. He turned his face toward Jodi, "Nice to meet you, Jodi. Grimes is a good man. He'll help you get the lay of the land around here, but it won't take you too long." He paused. "Can one of you tell me who's handling the Aaron Roberts case? He was the little boy that got killed last week."

"Officially that case belongs to the task force," said Jodi. "He's another victim of a serial killer we've been trying to catch for a long time."

"The Hangman?"

Jodi stared, then, "We've been ordered from on-high not to use that phrase, but, yeah, it was 'The Hangman.'" She glanced at the file. "But as it happens, Joe, I've got a copy of the file right here."

Joe Mac lifted his face. "Have you had a chance to look at it?"

"No. I just got it. What can I do for you, Joe?"

"Aaron was my grandson." Joe Mac's face was stone. "I know I can't contribute to the forensics, but if you have any personal questions about Aaron, maybe I could help you out a little bit."

Jodi stared. "I'm sorry for your loss, Joe."

"Appreciate it."

After expelling a long breath Jodi said, "Look, Joe, they've got a task force briefing in about twenty minutes. Why don't you come with me? The FBI will be there along with Captain Brightbarton. He's in charge."

"I don't have a badge anymore."

"You're with me. You'll be okay."

Joe Mac rose, his hand moving his cane.

"Let's go."

http://wbp.bz/darkvisionsa

**NOW AVAILABLE FROM RICHARD
GODWIN AND WILDBLUE PRESS!**

SAVAGE HIGHWAY by RICHARD GODWIN

http://wbp.bz/shreviews

Read A Sample Next

1.

Midnight.

Beyond the stained window the hissing scar of the highway was deserted. Patty was aching with hunger. The diner was empty apart from the guy in the corner. He'd been eyeing her all night.

'I don't suppose you have a light?' he said, walking over.

'Sure,' Patty said, flicking her Zippo, then snuffing out the brief flame. 'Spare a smoke?'

'Oh *yeah*.'

The waitress bristled past, all swish of starched uniform and the click of over-chewed gum. She looked at them out of the corner of her eye, a slight curl of her lip.

'They call me Jim,' he said. 'You coming?'

Patty followed him outside into the mix of ice cold and diesel fumes. After the initial silence, they started the smokers' chat. Weather, journeys, directions, bitching about this and that, and then he said it. Just like that. No interlude, no buildup. As if he was ordering a burger.

'Last night I killed a man.' He took a deep drag and blew it skywards then turned and looking her right in the eyes. 'A guy got smart. He was nobody, really. I shot him. Twice.'

'That right?'

Silence. And just two burning cigarette ends in the cold and the smog. A truck whizzed by.

'Why you telling me this?' she said.

'Cause there's one thing I always feel like doing after I kill someone.'

'No shit?'

'You look good to me with your dark brown eyes and your long hair. Got a good figure on you. Good ass, too. You're a real brunette bombshell.'

'I ain't gonna sleep with you.'

'I ain't asking you to sleep with me, honey. How old are you anyway?'

'Twenty-six.'

'That right? There's a bad dude out there, in case you ain't heard. He's been chopping women up. Much badder'n old Jim. I don't kill ladies, just fuck 'em.'

'I can look after myself.'

'Heard one woman got her throat opened up. Out here, alone, just her thumb in the air and only her poontang to pay. They call him the maniac trucker, although I hear this guy drives a pickup.'

'Thanks for the smoke,' she said, walking back in.

Inside, the waitress stared at her from behind the counter, hands on her hips. Just another anonymous small-town judge. Patty watched as she went out back. She felt weak as Jim walked in, laughing, almost dancing across the diner to where she sat.

'Come on, we can do it in the john,' he said.

'What makes you think you can buy me?'

'I know desperation when I see it.'

The smell of pizza drifted across the air.

'How much you got?'

'I knew you were a pickup. I reckon you're worth a hundred.'

'Hundred and fifty.'

'Done.'

He peeled a stack of tens out of his wallet and laid them in her palm.

'I'll see you in the john,' she said, taking her worn canvas bag from the seat next to her.

After a few minutes Jim made his way there.

She was standing at the back, past the urinals, outside the only clean cubicle. The place stank of urine. Patty stared at the piss on the floor as Jim walked in and put a broom against the door.

'Well, hallelujah baby,' he said, rubbing his hands together.

'Come on,' she said, walking into the cubicle, pulling down her jeans.

'You're as sweet as cherry pie, ain't you?'

'Put this on,' she said, pulling a condom out of her faded denim jacket.

'That's like playing the piano with gloves on.'

'Well, Beethoven, it's either that or no pussy.'

'You really want me to put that thing on?'

She crossed her arms and waited for him to do it.

'Give me a little help here,' Jim said, unzipping his fly.

She touched him and thought of food, a bed for the night as Jim tore the packet open with his teeth and pulled the condom out.

'Happy now?' he said.

She leaned back against the wall and saw endless miles of road as his skin made contact. He shoved his right hand inside her blouse and groped her breasts. His skin was callused and felt like sandpaper on her nipples. She thought she heard someone trying the door as he entered her.

'You're safe with me, but you sure picked a bad place to stop,' he said. 'If I was you I'd get out of here, this place will eat you alive.'

She looked over Jim's shoulder at a fly crawling across the graffiti. Someone had scrawled 'Animals' on the chipped and tarnished paint. She looked into his eyes and watched them empty of desire. She felt the cold wall against her buttocks as he stopped.

He winked and ran his finger across her cheek.

'Told you I ain't the maniac trucker.'

After he left she heard a pickup drive off as she readjusted her clothes and checked herself in the mirror.

Then the door swung open and the waitress walked in.

'I knew it,' she said. 'I saw him leave, I'm calling the police.'

'Why you such a bitch?'

'You just made a big mistake, you hooker.'

'You don't get to call me no hooker. You're just a fucking waitress.'

'You don't belong here.'

'Belong where? This is nowhere.'

'We have regular customers who like things a certain way. You don't muscle in on territory that ain't yours. I'm giving you two minutes to git.'

The diner was filling up when Patty went back outside. The waitress was smiling at a trucker in faded Wranglers and blue suede cowboy boots who was leaning on the counter.

'What can I get you Pete?' the waitress said to him.

'Oh, just a coffee.'

Patty headed outside and stood among the women who were gathering to trade sex. They wore hot pants and halter tops, some of them sheer blouses. She looked at her clothes. Her blouse was missing a button, and her bra showed through the gap.

'Hey, how about it?' a large man with a thick matted beard said.

'I don't think so.'

Patty wandered off as she heard the women talk among themselves.

A black Chevrolet drove past her and pulled into the truck stop. A tall lean man in a red coat got out and walked over to the women. He stood there with his hands in his pockets, said something to a small dark prostitute in a black skirt, nodded, and then entered the diner. He waved at the waitress.

'Evenin' Theodore,' she said. 'We have some fresh pizza.'

'Sounds good, I'll just use your restroom.'

The waitress continued chatting to Pete. She didn't pay any attention to the prostitute in the black skirt who wandered in, the waitress merely glanced at her, then touched up her lipstick using a makeup mirror that she pulled from her purse. The woman went to join Theodore in the cubicle Patty had recently vacated. She was in her early twenties but had the used look of a life that held no pleasure except the diminishing high she got each night as she shot up.

Theodore didn't look at her but waited as she pulled up her skirt, slipped down her G-string, and fumbled with his fly. He lifted her halter top. His small black eyes gazed at her breasts. She leaned against the door and Theodore entered her. She didn't look at his face as he penetrated her. Theodore began to sweat as he increased his rhythm, and the smell of grease broke from his pores. When he stopped he ran his hand through his thick black hair and stared up at the ceiling, then pulled out and zipped up. He counted out the cash and waited until she left.

He was washing his hands at the cracked sink thinking about the meat loaf the diner served when the door opened. Then someone reached over his shoulder and ran a straight razor across his neck. Theodore never got to see his killer. He was holding his hands to the wound as the door closed. He staggered across the room and collapsed by the urinals. As he lay there drowning in his own blood, it looked like his red coat was melting into the urine.

http://wbp.bz/shreviews

AVAILABLE NOW FROM CRAIG HOLT AND WILDBLUE PRESS

HARD DOG TO KILL by CRAIG HOLT

Winner of the 2018 Independent Publisher Book Awards Gold Medal for Suspense/Thriller!

Stan Mullens is an American mercenary in the Congo who sees himself as a good guy with a bad job. Stan's self-assigned mission to protect his long time brother-in-arms, Frank, takes a serious hit when their boss sends them on an unsupported mission into the jungle to track and kill Tonde Chiora, a former company employee accused of stealing vital company mining technology.

As their mission takes them deep into the violent heart of the Congo, Stan soon discovers that his victim hasn't done anything to warrant being murdered. And as he struggles to survive the jungle, his enemies, and Frank's random acts of violent stupidity, he finds himself increasingly drawn in by the innocence and optimism of the man he is supposed to kill.

With his enemies closing in and his friendship with Frank falling apart, Stan has to make a dangerous choice between his old loyalties and his new friends. Maybe hardest of all, he has to make peace with the realization that despite what he's told himself all these years, he is not one of the good guys.

http://wbp.bz/hdtka

www.ingramcontent.com/pod-product-compliance
Lightning Source LLC
Chambersburg PA
CBHW050956180726
48291CB00006B/1848